THE FACE
OF THE
ASSASSIN

THE FACE
OF THE
ASSASSIN

DAVID LINDSEY

WARNER BOOKS

NEW YORK   BOSTON

Grateful acknowledgment is made to quote from "Poor Edward," written by Kathleen Brennan and Tom Waits. Copyright © 2002 Jamal Music (ASCAP). All rights reserved. Used by permission.

Warner Books

Time Warner Book Group
1271 Avenue of the Americas, New York, NY 10020
Visit our Web site at www.twbookmark.com.

Printed in the United States of America

First Printing: April 2004
10   9   8   7   6   5   4   3   2   1

Library of Congress Cataloging-in-Publication Data

Lindsey, David L.
    The face of the assassin / David Lindsey.
        p. cm.
    ISBN 0-446-52929-X
    1. Americans—Mexico—Fiction.   2. Mexico City (Mexico)—Fiction.   3. Undercover operations—Fiction.   4. Brothers—Death—Fiction.   5. Police artists—Fiction. 6. Criminals—Fiction.   7. Twins—Fiction.   I. Title.

    PS3562.I51193F33 2004
    813'.54—dc22

                                                                            2003026333

To Joyce:

The face changes
with the passing years;
the heart remains constant.

I have wandered in a face for hours,
Passing through dark fires.

Robert Bly
The Light Around the Body

Acknowledgments

Mil gracias to my friends in Mexico City:

To Rogelio Villarreal, who knows, but seldom tells, the secrets that the secret keepers keep;

To Costanza Viale, "Tanchy," who opened doors in the city for me that would never have been opened without her help;

To Marcela Fuentes-Berain, fellow writer, who shared her insights with me, as well as her morning coffee and cigarettes;

And to Tim Wiener of the *New York Times,* for a glimpse of a correspondent's perspective on a culture of puzzles.

And a thousand thanks, too, to my friends in Austin:

To Karen T. Taylor, forensic artist and portrait sculptor, who introduced me to the face within the face, and who awakened in me an awareness of the mysteries in the eye of the beholder;

To Mike Waugh, who taught me more than he knows about gates and doorways, and of the Janus faces of intelligence.

And, as always, my greatest thanks to my friends in New York:

To all the people at Warner Books including Colin Fox, who patiently helped me through the fog of writing; Harvey-Jane Kowal, the Queen of Careful Scrutiny; and Carol Edwards, who copyedited the typescript;

To Lisa Erbach-Vance of the Aaron Priest Literary Agency, who admirably performs the difficult job of reading the tea leaves of a writer's mind;

And to Aaron Priest, for whom, after all these years and books, my gratitude flows readily and freely.

THE FACE
OF THE
ASSASSIN

Chapter 1

Mexico City
Lincoln Park

"Something's going on."

These were the first words out of Mingo's mouth, and he could hardly wait to say them. Even in the shadows of the park, the other man could feel his anxiety.

"What's the matter?" The other man's voice was calm, softened by a Texas accent. In his late thirties, he was a decade older than Mingo and far more seasoned. Even so, he was caught off guard by the younger man's agitation.

"Khalil's been gone three days. Don't know where. When he came back two days ago, the first thing he did was meet with a guy I'd never seen before. This guy's staying in a rented room in Tacubaya, not far from Khalil. I've seen them huddling together in a *pastelería*."

"What's he look like?"

"Uh, balding, maybe early forties, not athletic, kind of

puffy-looking. Office type. Very serious. Never relaxed. Then this moring, same *pastelería,* they met with Ahmad."

"The three of them?"

"Yeah."

This was contrary to their own strict rules of operational discipline. Mingo was right to report it.

"Okay."

"Afterward, everybody was tense, edgy. Things looked different. Something big has happened."

They had met where the broad sidewalk bisected the long, narrow park across the middle of its length, between the statues of Lincoln on one side and Martin Luther King, Jr., on the other. It was just after dusk in the rainy season, and the sidewalks of the park were still glistening from the evening shower that came every summer day at this hour to cool the air and tamp the city's suffocating smog.

The younger man had fallen in behind his slightly older companion as they began walking, ignoring each other as they turned onto the sidewalk that ran along the perimeter of the park. They headed toward the clock tower at the western end of the park. The man in front hadn't slowed down so that the other one could come up abreast of him until they had reached the point where Calle Lafontaine intersected the park to their right.

"What else?" the Texan asked. What the younger man had to say was interesting, something to factor into the overall picture, something to keep in mind. But it wasn't news. They were supposed to meet face-to-face only if there was news—and news meant something that significantly affected the operation.

"I think I spotted your man."

The Texan didn't even break the rhythm of his casual pace. Eagerness was a mistake. Always.

"Who is that, exactly?"

"My boys watching your place last night, they picked up a guy in Parque México. He stayed there an hour and a half. He was watching your place. He was using night-vision binoculars. Thomas went down there with his tele-photo night lens and got a shot of the guy. Just one shot. It sure as hell looks like Baida to me."

Mingo handed an envelope to the Texan. "Check it out for yourself," he said.

This was it. The point of all the months of hard work. The point of so much patience and effort and planning and risk.

"Do you have any other information about him being here?" the Texan asked, putting the envelope into his pocket and forcing a calm tone into his voice.

"He's never showed up anywhere else, if that's what you mean."

"This was last night?"

"Yeah. Nine-thirty to eleven o'clock."

"They try to follow him?"

"No."

Good. Good. Mingo was worth the money. He did exactly what he was supposed to do, and he didn't do a bit more. He had been trained well. Follow instructions precisely. Even when you can do more, don't. That way, everyone knew exactly where you stood and where the operation stood.

"You think this is him?" the Texan asked.

"Yeah, I do."

Though the park was in the middle of tranquil streets,

the city's traffic rumbled in the surrounding gloom. In fact, the Paseo de la Reforma, the city's main boulevard, was only blocks away. But besides that, 22 million people simply made a lot of noise.

They rounded the corner and crossed the end of the park under the clock tower. He was surprised that Baida had been watching his place. He would have thought they would have spotted him at Ahmad's first. That would have made more sense. But then, making sense would make too much sense. If any of this had made sense, he wouldn't be doing what he was doing. And he wouldn't spend so much time in fear's claustrophobic little rooms, in the dark, air-starved cubicles of his own imagination.

"You've got nothing else?" the Texan asked. "Just this ID?"

"Yes, *just* this ID."

He caught Mingo's emphasis. "No, you've done a fine thing, Mingo."

"Good, then."

"Check your pay drop the day after tomorrow."

"*Bueno.*"

"The next time he shows up," the Texan said, "push it just a little further. Be careful. There's nobody better. He'll spot your boys the second one of them loses concentration. If they glance at a woman . . . just that quick, we're screwed. Of course, the pay goes up, too."

"And so does the risk."

"Listen, you're getting paid a hell of a lot more than I am."

"But when you're through," Mingo said, "you can go home to Texas. You've got U.S. government benefits waiting for you."

Right now, all of that seemed half a world and a thousand lies away. It seemed remote, and that remoteness had begun to eat at him in the last couple of years.

"Yeah," the Texan said. "Those benefits."

He looked over Mingo's shoulders at the two figures moving toward them from the other end of the park. A couple, huddled together, breathing each other's breath. Lovers. He did not think or fear that they were anything other than what they appeared to be, but they reminded him that it was time to be moving on.

"Keep in touch," he said.

Mingo was used to the abrupt departures, and he nodded good-bye. The Texan was already walking away.

Chapter 2

Four hours later, the Texan was alone. He was in another part of the vast and sprawling city, a world away from the upscale park in Polanco. Here, the treeless maze of ancient streets was narrow and twisting and filthy, and being a solitary gringo here at night was suicidal.

He was in Tepito, near the heart of the city, in a barrio that had existed for over five centuries and had often made its living off of things that the rest of the city had thrown away. Tepiteños married Tepiteños and had done so for centuries. They were as clannish as Gypsies, and to them, all the rest of the world was made up of outsiders.

During the day, the stalls of illegal street vendors practically blocked access to legitimate stores here. The places on the sidewalk for these squatter stalls were "bought" from Korean thugs who, despite the neighborhood's closed culture, had viciously usurped much of the control of Tepito's institutionalized banditry. Mexico was now third, behind only Russia and China, in the commerce of pirated goods, selling fake labels on everything from condoms to caviar, and anything plastic. Tepito was the beating heart of this illicit trade.

He had taken a taxi, but at a certain point the driver had refused to go any farther into Tepito. The Texan had climbed out of the car and started walking deeper into the labyrinth.

Every once in a while, he stepped into the recess of a doorway that smelled of urine and ancient stone. He listened. He was sweating, despite the fact that Mexico City sat in a valley at an altitude of 7,340 feet and was surrounded by mountains nearly twice that high. The nights were always cool. He stepped out of the doorway and continued walking.

Samarra was a street of silences. Off the beaten track, even during the day, it was alleylike and foul-smelling, the wafts of sewage mixing with the odor of frying onions and dust. The flat faces of the buildings were stark and unadorned. Occasionally as he moved through the ocher-tinged shadows, the fluorescent glint of a television seeped through the crack of a shutter or flickered off the ceiling of a second-floor room with an open window. Now and then, he caught snatches of voices dripping with pathos—a telenovella—or the surging canned laughter of a sitcom. But mostly, he heard only his own footsteps, muted as they crunched on the grit of the old stones. His shoe fell on something soft, followed a moment later by the pungent odor of animal feces.

It wouldn't be long now.

Suddenly, a few yards in front of him, a door opened and a figure stepped out on a spill of dull light. He raised an arm horizontally, directing the Texan inside. Though he had never before met them in Tepito, he knew the routine. He turned and went in.

The empty room was shrouded in a hazy, feeble light from the bare bulb hanging from the ceiling. He raised his arms while the Korean patted him down. The guard wore a misshapen suit and street shoes, a cutoff M16 slung over his shoulder.

He followed the man through a darkened room and then out into a courtyard bathed in the same jaundiced light as the street outside. The limp silhouettes of banana trees were scattered about the compound, and other rooms, some dark, others with dull lights, surrounded them. A second Korean guard fell in behind him, and a shorthaired dog appeared from the smudgy corners of the enclosure and snuffled at his legs and nudged his hand with its damp nose, the only compassionate creature that the Texan was likely to encounter during the entire long night. They crossed to an outside stairwell and started up.

On the second floor, they doubled back and approached another lighted doorway, where yet another guard waited outside. They went in, interrupting three men huddled in deep conversation around a small wooden table. None of them was Korean or American—or Mexican.

"Judas," said the man who had been sitting with his back to the door and was now turning to look at the Texan. His name was Ahmad, and when he stood to shake hands, there was no characteristic smile, and his eyes regarded the Texan with a pained solemnity. Something was up.

"Khalil," the Texan said, nodding at a man his own age who was sitting directly across the table from Ahmad.

8

Khalil hadn't shaved in several days and looked as if he had missed a lot of sleep. He was surly and didn't offer his hand.

The third man at the table was a stranger to the Texan and sat opposite an empty fourth chair. The Texan stared at him cockily, suggesting by his pointed gaze that a name was expected. It was all a game, and it mattered very much how you played it.

But the man didn't look at him, and apparently he was not going to be introduced. He was hollow-cheeked, with an olive complexion gone pasty, bald, and had thin shoulders, which made his head look too big for his body. In the deep crease at the upper right of his mouth was a dark mole the size of a raisin. Without making eye contact, he leaned forward and sipped from a teacup in front of him, holding the cup by its rim, not its handle.

"Please," Ahmad said, "join us." He offered the fourth chair at the table.

The Texan sat down and was aware of the two Koreans remaining in the room, although they stood out of sight behind him. The three men at the table were drinking the familiar strong, sweet tea, but none was offered to the Texan. A significant sign, one that caused another wave of perspiration to rush to the surface of his skin.

Silence followed. Now Khalil averted his eyes, too, but Ahmad continued looking at him, his expression grave.

"Bad news, Judas," Ahmad said, and it was painful to hear the genuine note of sadness in his voice. The two of them had learned to like each other, and actually had grown close in a perverse way. Friendship as rape—it was another talent the Texan had perfected, another admirable

9

human trait that he had corrupted in the service of a questionably higher calling.

Khalil looked up now, too, and he and Ahmad stared at him in silence. The third man continued to look down.

"It's over, my friend," Ahmad said. "We know."

He hadn't seen it coming. Something else, maybe. There were always fears. But this . . . he hadn't seen this coming.

From somewhere, he summoned the strength not to panic and bolt for the door. He frowned, gave them a dumb, puzzled look. But before he could stop himself, he swallowed. Goddamn. It was as good as a confession. He felt something against his leg and glanced down. The dog had followed them up the stairs and was standing there looking at him. Waiting, it seemed, just like the rest of them.

The unidentified man, his eyes still averted, coughed a little and cleared his throat, pulling up a wad of phlegm, which he worked with his tongue.

Oh shit. The Texan's heart stopped. It didn't beat at all. It just hovered in his chest, not even touching the surrounding tissue. The light in the room dimmed. . . . No, no, not this. He did not want to faint.

"What is this?" he managed to say, but the intended tone of bravado was not convincing.

The stranger's head shot up, and he sprang to his feet and spat with a force that shook his body. The crap from his throat flew across the table and slapped against the corner of the Texan's mouth.

Before he could react, someone grabbed his arms from behind and wrenched them backward, snapping one of his elbows. He screamed out, hardly aware that someone was taping his wrists together as someone else taped his ankles to each of the chair's front legs. His head was clamped between two hands sheathed in rubber gloves.

The bald man slammed his hands down on the table, exploding the cups of tea. Lurching forward over the broken cups, his face rigid with violence, his hands planted in the syrupy mess that was running off the edges of the table, he shrieked, "*Jasus! Jasus!*"

The Texan heard a door behind him open and close and then footsteps approached. Somebody set down something with a thud. A man stepped around in front of him, holding two insulated electrical cables with bare ends. He wore a mismatched jogging suit, which was unzipped to his hairy stomach.

When the wires touched either side of the Texan's neck, it was as if a bomb had gone off in his throat. He thought his head had been blown off his body. But that was only an illusion. The sensation that he was involuntarily pissing his pants was not.

The stranger who had spat on him yawed back his head, mouth wide open, wide as a baboon's maw, his eyes glittering, the veins in his neck engorged, standing out like great plum-colored worms.

They were all standing. Suddenly, Ahmad's arms flew out wide, as if he were conducting an orchestra with brio, and the spray of his brains fled the blast from Khalil's outstretched arm. No more Ahmad.

The wires again, rammed precisely into his ears.
Silence.

The stranger was straddling him, his face contorted like a Francis Bacon portrait, his mouth twisted grotesquely up the right side of his head, one eye pig-size and wandering, the other protuberant and goggling.

The Texan felt the man inside his mouth, and for a split second he thought the whole man was in there, because he couldn't see him, but he could feel him walking around.

Then the stranger held something in front of the Texan's face, jabbing at it insanely with his knife for him to see, then slapping his face with it, again and again.

But the Texan was already drowning, and he found it difficult to care too much about what the man was doing. It was hard to drown in your own blood, even so much of it. He found that drowning wasn't a progressive event, as he might have imagined. Rather, it was a lurching sort of thing: Choking on the surge of blood, he faded; then he coughed, spewing a geyser of blood, and was instantly back in the brutal clarity of the moment.

He tried to go ahead and die, but he was disappointed to realize that he couldn't force it. He went through the whole cycle again. Then he smelled the feces, which were undoubtedly his own, and he was surprised to feel a sad, profound embarrassment.

Then, just when he began to die after all, and he knew for certain that he was dying, he saw the man with the contorted features toss to the dog the thing that he had been flourishing and stabbing in his wild rant. The poor cadaverous creature pounced on it in an instant, and with hunched shoulders and great gorging efforts of his outstretched neck, he wolfed it down.

It was only then that the Texan realized that the man had cut out his tongue.

Chapter 3

Austin, Texas

"I've got a client coming in about half an hour," Bern said, leaning over and blowing eraser crumbs off the sketch he was finishing. He was making a last-minute alteration to the composite drawing of a man accused of raping a University of Texas student.

The victim had been brought to him the night before, and in sporadic, sharp observations she had described the face that had now emerged from under his pencil. Early that morning, the detective had called and asked for a variation in detail.

Alice was sitting on her stool, an arm's reach away, a sketch pad on her lap, watching over his shoulder. When he stopped drawing, she immediately returned to her own creation for the morning, a conga line of Kewpie doll stick figures, each with a single curl of hair standing upright on its head, all marching toward a cliff.

Alice Lau was seventeen.

Paul Bern sipped coffee from his black mug and looked at her. She was oblivious now, absorbed in her drawing. Wearing designer-faded hip-hugging jeans that revealed her navel, and a cutoff T-shirt that exposed her midriff, she was sitting with one leg crossed over the other at the knee, waggling her bare foot in the universal teenager's fidget. She was spreading a piece of gum with her tongue and lips, as if she were about to blow a bubble, but the bubble never materialized. Her straight black hair was pulled back in a long braid that was draped over the front of one shoulder.

She was the only child of Bern's closest friends, Dana and Philip Lau. He and Philip had been undergraduates together at Rice, and though their careers had taken them to different parts of the world, over the years they and their wives had regularly managed to spend a few days of vacation together every couple of years. When Philip became a tenured professor of political science at the University of Texas, he and Dana started lobbying Paul and Tess to move to Austin. Eventually, they were persuaded, and it had been a wonderful decision in every way . . . until just about a year ago.

They were listening to Tom Waits's CD *Alice,* an appropriate choice for many reasons, all completely lost on the girl on the stool. She couldn't understand anything Waits was singing. She couldn't understand anything Bern was saying, for that matter, but he always talked to her as if she understood everything. And, mysteriously, it seemed that she often did.

He stood and looked down at his drawing, one hand in his pocket, the other holding the mug of coffee. The guy's eyes were wide-set, his nose was broad and slightly upturned, and his maxilla was distinctly sunken, emphasizing his prominent front teeth. Unfortunately for him, it wasn't a flattering combination, and it stuck very clearly in the victim's mind. She also remembered that his hair was worn in a mullet, a feature that only added to the stupidity of his appearance.

"This is as far as I'm going to take it," he said. "Don't want to push it."

Alice looked up while he was talking and glanced at the drawing, too.

"It's no way through the legs so," she said, "but if there's a really wrong, then who would fly on it?"

"I don't know," he said. "They only asked for one variation, and I've given them three. I don't want to start putting ideas in her head."

Alice shrugged and smiled and then went back to the Kewpie dolls.

He looked at his watch. No time to start anything else. Tom Waits was singing about Poor Edward—"On the back of his head/He had another Face/Was it a woman's face/Or a young girl?"—and Alice's foot was waggling, but not in time with the music. Bern knew she appreciated music and understood the beat and rhythm of it, if not the words.

Over a period of months, he had experimented with her and had found that she responded to particular musical moods. Sometimes she was upset if he put on Miles Davis, and she wouldn't settle down until he switched to Yo-Yo Ma's Bach. Other times, it was the other way around: Not Bach; let's have *Tosca*'s tangos.

But she wasn't often so definite about it. Usually, anything he liked, she liked. She was pretty simpatico that way. The way Tess had been. Jesus. Alice didn't often remind him of Tess anymore. Not often. Still, sometimes . . . But he didn't let it derail him now like it used to.

He had gotten used to having Alice around. It was a little awkward at first, and he had worried that it was awkward for Alice, too. But it didn't take him long to get to know the new Alice, and he realized that his concern was unnecessary. For her, the situation was not so complex. Not in the same way it was for him anyway.

When the doorbell rang, Alice looked up at him, waiting for his reaction.

"That's my client," he said, starting back across the room.

He passed the drawing tables, easels, and workbenches cluttered with the tools of his craft—cans of paintbrushes, partially used tubes of oil paints, sketchbooks, sticks of charcoal and pastel chalks. There were cabinets of materials and supplies, books on shelves, and a complete skeleton dangling from a chrome stand. He went up the six steps, which were nearly the width of the room itself.

"Don't go anywhere," he called back.

Alice said something in response, the tone and cadence of which sounded reasonable, though the syntax of the words made no sense whatsoever.

"Okay," he said as he opened the door. "Be right back."

He saw the woman through the heavy grillwork of the iron gate as he approached her across the interior courtyard. She was standing in the lacy morning shade of a mesquite tree, holding a cardboard carton about the size of a small hatbox in her hands.

He quickly took her in: a simple sleeveless summer dress of lemon yellow, straight, just above the knees. She had a berry-brown suntan. Five eight or nine. Early thirties. Dark blunt-cut hair worn just shorter than shoulder length, but long enough for her to pull it back out of her way and fix it with a practical rubber band. At this moment, she had the sides of it tucked behind her ears. She was trim and fit, not in the sense of an athlete, but more like someone who enjoyed the outdoors, maybe hiked a lot.

"Becca Haber," she said, peeping at him through the grille as he approached. "Sorry I'm late."

"It's all right. Everybody gets lost out here," he said, sliding back the bolt on the gate to let her in. "I'm used to it."

Bern lived in one of the countless bends of the Colorado River, which had been dammed up more than half a dozen times as it passed through the hills of central Texas. The dams formed a chain of wooded lakes northwest of Austin, with the lower two lakes coming right into the city where Bern had built his semisecluded house.

He and the woman crossed the courtyard under a canopy of wisteria, which spanned the open space, draping across it from the high stone walls of the surrounding house. He had been watering plants earlier, and the odors of dampened soil and stones still filled the warm morning air.

"You got into town last night?" Bern asked. The woman was walking just a step behind him as they entered a barrel-vaulted corridor of brick and stone slurried over with white plaster.

"Yes, more or less," she said.

Okay. The light from the other end of the tunnel spun toward them, as if anticipating their arrival, but they turned into an open doorway halfway around the tunnel's arc and stepped into Bern's studio.

The woman paused on the landing and took in the large airy room that lay below the short flight of steps. Built piecemeal over a period of years, much of the work having been done by Bern himself, the studio was an assimilation of concrete, angled glass walls, and limestone boulders, with a high, sloping ceiling supported by steel beams. The glass wall on the far side of the room was slightly cantilevered over the lake, which was twenty feet below the floor of the studio.

He saw Becca's eyes come to rest on Alice, who, knowing the routine, had moved her stool over to the sitting area near the glass wall, awaiting their arrival.

Becca said nothing as they crossed the room to the massive slab of mesquite that served as a coffee table. There were several armchairs and a sofa.

"This is Alice," Bern said.

Alice smiled. Becca Haber nodded soberly.

Bern offered her a place on the sofa, but she chose one of the armchairs instead. She sat down with her sandaled feet close together on the concrete floor, holding the box on top of her thighs. She glanced at Alice.

"This is, uh, this is very personal," she said softly to Bern.

He nodded. "I know, but it's okay. She's—she can't understand you."

Becca Haber kept her eyes on Bern. "She's deaf?"

"No—"

"Oh. Chinese."

"Chinese, yes, but her family's been in the United States for more generations than mine. She can't understand you because she has brain damage. A waterskiing accident about a year ago."

"What do you mean, 'she can't understand'?"

"It's complicated," he said. "Brain injuries, they're quirky things. There's a cognitive disconnect of some sort."

"'Cognitive disconnect'?"

Bern had hoped she would just accept that and they could go on. But he could see what he always saw in people who were told about Alice's condition: puzzlement and a ton of questions.

"Basically, she can't recognize or understand the meaning of words," he said. Over the past year, he'd developed a long and a short version of this explanation. She was going to get the short one.

"Even though she doesn't understand the meaning of the words you're speaking, she's verbally fluent. I mean, she'll hold a conversation with you. She'll pause to let you have your turn at the appropriate time; then she'll take her turn. She even punctuates her sentences correctly—for the most part. But it just doesn't compute. It makes no sense whatsoever. The strangest part is, she *thinks* she understands the conversation. So I just go along with it."

Becca glanced again at Alice, who was staring back at her with a birdlike curiosity, insensitive to the indelicacy of her frank gaze.

"Who, uh, who is she?"

"She's the daughter of old friends. Actually, I'm her godfather." He pulled around another chair and sat on the other side of the coffee table from her. "It calms her to watch me draw, and we've discovered that it has a kind of therapeutic effect on her. So Alice's mother brings her by here a couple of times a week to watch me work. It frees her up for a few hours to do some shopping, run errands."

"She doesn't bother you?"

"Nope. We just talk, listen to music."

"But she doesn't make any sense?"

"Nope."

Alice was still looking at Becca Haber with a penetrating concentration, waggling her foot, working her gum. It was as if the woman were a newly discovered object and Alice was trying to figure out her meaning and usefulness. It wasn't exactly a calming thing for Becca Haber, who already seemed to be a little tightly wound.

"Let's see what you've got," Bern said.

Chapter 4

Glancing tentatively one more time at Alice, Haber leaned forward, carefully placed the box on the mesquite slab in front of her, and opened it, revealing the underside of a human skull cradled in a nest of shredded paper. Inserting her thumb into the foramen magnum on the underside of the skull, she lifted it out of the box. With her other hand, she took out the skull's detached mandible, its horseshoe-shaped lower jaw.

With an odd expertise, she put the mandible just behind her suntanned bare knee, its two sides straddling her thigh like a beret, the teeth pointing away from her. Then she turned the skull upright, facing Bern, and held it on her thighs.

"It's in good shape," she offered, as if this were an audition. She looked down at the top of the skull.

He had already noticed that. It was in excellent shape. Rare. It looked as if it had been harvested from a hospital for academic purposes. Usually by the time he saw them, they had been through a lot of abuse, buried and etched by soil acids or worms, or left out in the open for months or years, teeth missing, gnawed by animals, bleached by the stresses of exposure. But this one was perfect in all respects, except for the separated mandible. It was pristine, all the teeth firmly in place.

Becca Haber had called early that morning and introduced herself. She said that she was from Atlanta and that she had just come into Austin. She told him she had a skull and that she hoped he would agree to reconstruct its face.

He'd asked her if she had been referred to him by someone at a law-enforcement agency. She'd said this was a personal situation. She had read an article about him in Atlanta a few years ago.

How did she happen to have the skull? he'd asked.

There had been a pause at the other end of the line.

"I'd rather explain that to you when I get there," she'd said. Her voice had a southern lilt, but that hadn't disguised the underlying hint of tension.

Now here she sat, holding a skull that looked eerily fresh. He didn't reach for it, though he wanted to. Instead, he sat back in his chair and crossed his arms.

"Why don't you start by telling me how you happen to have this," he suggested.

"Sure," she said, nodding. "I understand." She squared her shoulders. "I bought it from a street kid in Mexico City."

But she didn't go on. At first, Bern thought she was reconsidering what she was about to say, but as he looked at her face, he realized that she was looking at him without seeing him. Something seemed to be happening. He waited.

As a forensic artist, he was used to talking with clients who were upset. The people who were brought to him were victims of rape or attempted murder or kidnapping or mutilation, or had been witnesses to such things. Re-creating in one's mind the faces of the people who have done such things is often an excruciating experience, and sometimes the mind rebels at being asked to recall the horrors it has recorded. Memory is a fragile and mercurial thing, and responds most reliably, he'd found, to tender treatment. He glanced away, giving her time to gain control of her emotions.

Becca Haber looked up.

"I'm positive . . ." she said, looking down at the skull in her lap, "almost positive, that this is my husband."

The corners of her mouth pulled down involuntarily as she fought her emotions.

Out of his peripheral vision, Bern saw Alice's foot suddenly stop waggling. He glanced at her. She had stopped kneading her gum and it rested like a little pink pellet exactly in the center of her slightly parted lips. She was staring at Becca with slack-jawed fascination, as if she were watching the woman metamorphose into something alien right there in the stream of sunshine.

Becca Haber launched into a story that sounded like a million other stories. She had met her husband a couple of years earlier and had married him after knowing him only a few months. He was an artist. They'd had about half a year of glorious marriage, followed by a half year of hell, before they'd agreed to separate and see if things wouldn't cool down.

He moved to Mexico City, where he had lived several years before. They sent each other E-mail messages every day; she flew down a couple of times for long weekends. Then, about four months ago, he'd stopped sending her E-mail. After a couple of weeks, she went down there. She found his house in perfect condition, but he was gone.

She stayed a few weeks, asking around about him, but his few friends said they hadn't heard from him, either. The police couldn't even stir up a modest curiosity about her panicked concern, implying these things happened all the time and that eventually he would come back when he got tired of the other woman.

Then one day when she answered the phone at his house, a man told her that her husband was dead and that he had proof, but she would have to pay for it. After a long negotiation, she found herself on a dark street somewhere in that vast city. A kid handed her a paper sack, and she handed him the money. She thought she was buying photographs of his bullet-riddled body. Instead, she was horrified to find the skull.

Becca Haber stopped here to gather her composure, but before Bern could speak, Alice, who had been squirming with increasing agitation, blurted, "Can you think of what if you should, Paul?" With an expression of disbelief, she asked, "Can you see through a flowing window on the outside of another thought that you believe?" She was incredulous. She turned her wide eyes on Becca. "I don't think in a hundred wonders of it!"

Oh shit.

Alice scowled at Bern and screwed her mouth into a problematic pucker, as if she couldn't believe what she was hearing.

"Jesus." Becca was taken aback.

Bern was surprised by Alice's reaction, too, but not for the same reasons as Becca Haber.

"Just a second," he said to Becca, and he got up and

went over to Alice and squatted down in front of her. Her sketch pad was in her lap, and she was still holding her pencil, though she had lost interest in the Kewpie dolls.

"Now listen, Alice," he said softly, putting his hand on hers to get her attention. "It's okay; it doesn't matter. It doesn't matter. Okay? It's all right."

"What doesn't matter?" Becca Haber asked suspiciously.

"It doesn't matter what I say to her," Bern said, not turning away from Alice as he spoke to Becca. "She can't understand me. I've got to make her understand the meaning of my words by the way I'm behaving, by my expressions."

What he wanted Alice to understand was that what the woman was saying was okay with him. What Alice had to do was to control her agitation. She couldn't disrupt the conversation.

It took some time. Alice kept wanting to look at Becca, moving her head from side to side to look around him as he tried to make eye contact with her to get her attention. It was as if Becca Haber had become the most outrageous thing Alice had ever seen.

He reassured her again, telling her that it was okay, that it didn't matter.

Alice pulled her head back in dramatically mimed skepticism at his reassurances.

"You're in ropes if that's on this very side," she said, flinging an incredulous look at Haber.

Bern took Alice's oval face in his hands and gently guided her attention to the sketch pad in her lap. He began drawing a face, all the while telling her it didn't matter, that it was all right.

Gradually, the face he was drawing took on an expression that was not immediately understandable, one of conflicting emotions, of mixed signals. As Alice noticed this and began to focus on the problem of figuring out this emotional puzzle, she began to calm down.

This went on for ten minutes or more, though it felt longer to Bern, who was acutely aware of Becca Haber's close observation from behind. Finally after several jerky sighs, Alice became absorbed in trying to decipher the expression on the face that Bern had drawn.

After a few more minutes, he stood and returned to the coffee table.

"Look, I'm sorry," he said, deliberately taking a different chair at the coffee table now. "I know it's hard enough for you to talk about this without that kind of distraction. It must seem strange to you, I know. Sorry."

"No, it's okay," Becca said, glancing warily at Alice. "Is she going to be all right? What was the matter?"

"Yeah, she'll be fine. Who knows what the deal was," he said.

Now Bern had a clear view of both Becca's face and Alice's. Becca took a moment to decide where to start over; then she leaned forward and put the skull on the table, facing Bern, and took the mandible off her knee and laid it beside the skull.

"You know, there's probably a better way to do this," Bern said. "If you need positive proof of identity, you'd be better off getting a DNA test."

"Can't," she said, her hands now gripping the short lemon hem of her dress to keep it from working up.

"They can do it with bone now," he said. "Mitochondrial DNA—"

"I've already been through all that," she said. "He was an orphan. Abandoned. Parents unknown. Siblings, forget it. We don't have any children. No medical records. No dental records."

"He never went to the doctor or the dentist?"

"Not while I knew him." She nodded at the skull. "There's dental work there. Not much, just a little. But he never went to the dentist while I knew him."

"What about before then?"

"I don't know anything about him before then, except what I've already told you."

Alice stifled a groan and rolled her eyes at Bern.

Chapter 5

The awkward little drama of Alice's adolescent histrionics had the unintended effect of convincing Becca Haber that Alice really was beyond understanding what Becca was saying. But, in fact, that wasn't precisely true.

The truth was more complex, as almost everything was when it came to dealing with Alice's disability. The accident had deprived her of the ability to understand the meaning of words, either written or spoken. But even stranger than this was what Alice had gained as a result of her loss.

Human speech is automatically accompanied by an elaborate, and often unconscious, repertoire of facial expressions, voice inflections, tonal shifts, and gestures. These sometimes delicate and subtle expressions are called "feeling tone," and they play a key role in our understanding of the meanings of spoken words because they give them an emotional context beyond the simple meaning of the words themselves. As we converse with others, we usually process these feeling tones unconsciously, hardly even aware of what we are doing.

People with brain injuries like Alice's, however, being deprived of the ability to understand the literal meaning of words, compensate for this disadvantage by carefully observing the speaker's feeling tone. They develop, to an uncanny degree, the ability to understand the intent of the spoken words without being able to understand the actual words themselves.

This complex sensitivity enters into an even stranger process when spoken words are used to disguise truth, to deliberately deceive. When people lie, they try to camouflage their deception by miming genuine feeling-tone characteristics.

However, not even the most accomplished liar can re-create genuine feeling tone. False feeling tone is always off-key. But most of us are distracted from noticing these off-key signs of lying because we are more intent on parsing the meaning of the words that the speaker is choosing.

People who suffer from receptive aphasia, like Alice, are almost supernaturally sensitive to the unconscious quiver of a facial muscle, to a strained nuance in a syllable, to a manipulated vocal modulation, or self-conscious intonation. They know intuitively that there is an emotional truth in feeling tone that transcends the speaker's merely verbal expression, and they focus on the distortion of this truth as if it were a sour note in a solo.

It is this uncanny ability to sense when someone is lying that has prompted doctors and scientists to refer to people with this particular form of aphasia as "human lie detectors." It was this sensitivity to the subliminal tones of deception that Alice was reacting to with such anxiety.

Bern knew what was happening.

Becca Haber didn't acknowledge Alice's audible moan,

but she heard it, and from the disconcerted look on her face, Bern thought that she understood its derisive tone, as well.

"Look," she said, "do you mind if I smoke?" And she bent down to her purse on the floor and took out a pack of cigarettes before Bern could respond. She quickly lighted one, and then stood, her eyes still avoiding Alice, and walked over to the glass wall, where she looked out at the late-morning light on the surface of the lake. She stood there, her back to Bern, the smoke billowing in front of her as white and dense as spun sugar in the summer glare.

She was nervous, and he thought there was more to it than the awkwardness of Alice's undisguised skepticism. He stood and threw a look of admonishment at Alice, who rolled her eyes again, this time in silence, and then he joined Becca at the glass wall.

"Let me ask you a question," he said. "Why didn't you just take this to the police to start with? Why come to me?"

"Because I want to know first . . . if this is, or isn't, him," she said without turning to him, her face inches from the glass. "If it isn't . . . well, then, I was just screwed out of my money. If it is, then I want to check into my legal rights, from an international perspective. I want to know what my options are—what I can expect to encounter— when I walk in there and tell the police that some kid in Mexico City sold me my husband's skull in a paper sack."

"Why not go to the lawyer right now?" Bern suggested. "That seems reasonable. Then you'd know what you're up against no matter what happens."

She turned to him.

"That's not the way I see it," she said. She drew on the cigarette, her eyes on him. "There are just too many unanswered questions the way it is." She turned her head aside, lifted her chin, and blew the smoke into the room. "I don't have anything. Nothing. Just that he's gone and this kid sold me this . . ." She nodded toward the skull. "And if it's not . . . him, then I don't have anything. Just a missing husband, which is nothing but a conversation, right?"

"Yeah, I guess that's right."

"Well, it's not a conversation I want to have," she said.

That sounded reasonable. What could he say? The lies could be insignificant, embarrassing things, private things that were legitimately none of his business. The circumstances weren't the normal kind that he was used to dealing with. Usually, these requests came from state or federal law-enforcement agencies or some other institution.

"How'd you get it across the border?" he asked, hoping he sounded curious rather than suspicious.

"Yeah, well, I paid someone to smuggle it across," she said. "I knew it wasn't going to go through customs without a hassle, some kind of long rigmarole."

"And you just happen to know people who do that sort of thing."

She smiled for the first time. "I was in Mexico City. All things are possible there. Things like that anyway."

"How do you know it's the same skull?"

"I made teeth impressions in modeling clay, top and bottom. I told them I wouldn't pay the rest of the money on the other side unless the impressions matched. They did."

"Oh! For in the single sort of thing!" Alice blurted.

Again, Becca resolutely ignored her, but when Bern glanced Alice's way, he saw her head was tilted dramatically to the side, and her eyes were rolled heavenward,

31

as though she were enduring the most unbelievable silliness.

"I'd have to consult an anthropologist," he said. "I'll have—"

"I've already done that," Haber said. "I knew from the article that you'd need to know the race and sex of the skull before you could work on it. And besides, I needed to know if I'd been sold some . . . thing out of a graveyard in one of the *colonias*. I took the skull to Dr. Graciela de Aceves, an anthropologist with the Autonomous University of Mexico. She thought it was an American Caucasoid, based on data presented in Rhine and Moore's findings. She said to mention those names to you, that they'd mean something to you."

They did. And he knew of Dr. de Aceves's work, too. She was a well-respected medical anthropologist.

"I have a letter from her," Becca added, "if you want to see it."

Bern was surprised. If he had been in Becca Haber's shoes, Dr. de Aceves would have been the one person in all of Mexico that he would have gone to. The fact that she didn't go to one of the scores of less qualified professionals scattered throughout the country meant that Ms. Haber knew a thing or two about doing things the right way.

She was studying him, trying to read what he was thinking. She was six feet away, her arms folded as she leaned one shoulder against the glass wall. The truth was, he wasn't exactly overwhelmed with work right now, and she had offered over the telephone earlier to double his fee if he would drop everything and get right on it. That was enticing. He saw no reason why he shouldn't go ahead with the project.

Of course, there were Alice's dramatics, but again he re-minded himself that if Alice was detecting falsehoods in Haber's story, it didn't necessarily have to mean that they were in the category of mortal sins. Maybe Haber was hav-ing an affair with her husband's best friend and didn't want to bring that into the equation. Maybe her husband had been having an affair with her sister, and she understand-ably wanted to leave that out of it, too. Maybe she wasn't even married to the guy. Maybe . . . hell, maybe anything.

"Okay," he said. "I'll do it."

"Great," she said, but her face didn't register great. Maybe there was a little relief, but if that's what it was, there wasn't a whole lot of emotion in it. It wasn't as if she was happy to finally be headed toward a situation that might bring her closure. It was more like she had gotten a business negotiation settled.

"You'll have to leave it," he said.

"Yeah, okay. How . . . long?"

"Let me spend some time with it. I'll give you a call to-morrow."

She gave him her name and a telephone number at a residential hotel downtown on the lake.

That was it. She didn't want to hang around to ask him questions. She didn't want him to explain anything about his process, about what he would do first. She didn't ask, as private individuals often did, if she could watch him work. Becca Haber had done what she wanted to do, and she wanted out of there.

He could hardly blame her. Alice's behavior had been a little over the top.

Becca stepped over to the coffee table, put out her cig-arette in an ashtray, and picked up her purse. With Alice staring rudely at her, she headed for the door without looking around.

At the courtyard gate, he told her he'd call her the next day, then watched as she walked to her car and drove away.

When he got back to the studio, Alice had opened one of the tall, narrow windows along a side wall and was dumping out the cigarette that Becca Haber had left in the ashtray.

"If there was a tune flight into the sails," she said saucily, "it was a long way from the side of her hair."

She returned the empty ashtray to the table.

"Good going," Bern said sarcastically. "You were terrific, Alice. What the hell got into you anyway?"

She shrugged, went back to her stool, and started drawing. He stood with his hands in his pockets and looked at the skull on the table.

"Well, I'm going to do it anyway," he said.

"Over without a care," she said with deliberate indifference, not looking up from the sketchbook. "Anyway, the brushes won't feel like lady flowers."

Bern looked at her. Sometimes he wondered about the two of them. Talking to her was like talking to yourself, because it really didn't go anywhere. But somehow it seemed to make sense a lot of the time anyway. If Alice didn't know that they weren't communicating, then who the hell was he to worry about it? They seemed to do all right whatever was happening.

"She really got under your skin, didn't she?" he said, walking over to the coffee table. "I've never seen you quite like that before." He sat on the sofa in front of the skull and studied it.

"It could be anything," he said after a little while. "Who knows how many people tell you lies during the course of a day." He reached out and picked up the mandible. "Little lies. Big lies. And we don't even know it. And I wonder how much difference it would make if we did know?"

The teeth were set solidly in the bone. This guy wasn't that old. Could've been his age. He picked up the skull and carefully fitted the mandible's condyle into its temporal socket. He looked at it from the side and then turned it so that it faced him.

"I wonder how many lies these jaws have spoken," he said. "Maybe that's what got the poor devil killed."

Alice closed her sketchbook with a loud slap, and Bern checked his watch. She was always right on the second. Alice got down from her stool and together they walked outside and through the courtyard to wait under the mesquite tree for her mother.

Chapter 6

When Bern returned to the studio after walking Alice to her mother's car, he picked up the letter from Dr. de Aceves that Haber had left on the coffee table. It was brief, clinical, to the point. Beyond what Haber had already told him about Dr. de Aceves's conclusions, she also estimated that the skull was that of a man in his late thirties or early forties. Bern was indeed going to be reconstructing the face of a man approximately his own age.

He sat down at his computer and created a file for "John Doe (Haber?)." After recording the requisite data for a new file, he turned around in his chair and looked across the room at the skull, which was still sitting on the coffee table. Since the thing was in such good condition, he decided that he would do a two-dimensional reconstruction of the face as well as a three-dimensional one. The drawing wouldn't take that much longer, and it would give him a quick idea of where he was going.

He looked at his watch, which confirmed what his stomach was already telling him. He backed out of the computer program and hurried up the steps. He turned right into the white corridor and followed the arc around to the kitchen. Glancing out through the dining room, which overlooked the terrace and the lake beyond, he saw a Jet Ski cut a lateral white wake across the water just below the house. In the distance, a trio of sailboats tacked in the meridian heat like single-winged butterflies lofting on the breeze.

Grabbing the car keys from a red clay bowl on the countertop, he went through the doorway and descended a shallow flight of curving stairs to the garage. He got into the old Triumph TR3, a black relic from his London years in the seventies, and cranked it up. The driveway ascended from the garage in a long, rising curve that was cut into the hillside and emerged from the tunnel of overhanging cedars onto Camino Cabo.

It was a seven-minute drive to the Far Point Grill. He sat at a favorite small table in a window alcove and watched the comings and goings in the marina below while he ate a platter of grilled shrimp drizzled with lime juice.

He thought about Becca Haber. She had a hell of a story, and if the remnant sitting on his coffee table turned out to be her husband, her story was only beginning. That is, if her story was true. Some of it had to be true, he supposed, but how much? Maybe it didn't matter. She had a skull, and whatever its story, it deserved to have its face back, to be freed from the limbo of anonymity.

He had always had a kind of quixotic zeal for his work. The world was awash in anonymous skulls scattered across continents by wars, pogroms, massacres, slaughters, and murder. Somehow he felt he had a genuine mission to turn the wasteland of trivialized death into individual moments of significance, face by face by face. It was a small thing in the grander scheme of things, he knew.

On the other hand, it was no small thing at all to give an identity, a history, and a kind of redemption to what had been only a lost and empty bone before he touched it.

He finished the last shrimp, took one more sip of iced tea, and dug into his pocket for a ten and a five, which he left on the table. That covered the meal and a generous tip. He waved at Katie, who was behind the bar, and she smiled, blew him a kiss, and he was gone. The routine didn't vary much, two or three times a week.

Back at the studio, he put on three CDs, Miles Davis's *Kind of Blue,* Ellington and Strayhorn's *Jazz 'Round Midnight,* and a Dexter Gordon collection. With the first strains of Davis's horn, he set to work.

One of the worktables was already set up for these preliminary procedures. He put the skull on a cork ring and proceeded to glue the mandible to the cranium, using a specialized glue that dried quickly. While the glue was setting, he began cutting the tissue-depth markers, using the cylindrical refills for machine erasers. He had the depths memorized for the twenty-one various points on the skull of an American Caucasoid, and by the time these were cut, numbered on one end, and lined up on the bench, the skull was ready to go.

The adjustable skull stand was already mounted on one end of the workbench, and now Bern slipped the armature into the base of the skull and secured it. He put the armature on its own base, which was bolted to the bench, and firmly mounted the skull.

With this done, he began gluing the different lengths of numbered eraser pieces to the skull at specified points, each marking the approximate flesh depth according to long-used anthropological specifications. It was a delicate procedure, but experience had taught him to adjust the placement of the markers slightly this way or that, at variance with the traditional marking sites, depending on the particular peculiarities of each skull.

After the markers were in place, Bern carefully leveled the skull. He loaded the camera that was fixed on a stand at the other end of the bench—its distance and angle predetermined to avoid perspective distortion—and adjusted the lighting by using reflectors. Then he proceeded to photograph lateral and frontal views of the skull.

Turning up the CD player, he went into the darkroom to develop the film. Joe Thomas's trumpet was slipping into "Black Butterfly" by the time he came out. While the prints were drying, he set up his two drawing boards side by side, one for the frontal view, one for the lateral. The mounted skull with its markers in place was still in front of him.

The afternoon shadows lengthened out into the lake as he sketched on the two transparent vellum sheets that covered the frontal and lateral photographs of the skull with its tissue markers. Moving back and forth between the two views, he worked steadily and quickly, his years of experience guiding his judgments when judgments had to be made. He emphasized those features that were most dominant in the skull's structure, and left intentional ambiguities where no bony architecture was available to guide him. Eyelids and eyebrows were two areas where he often drew the frontal view with each eye having different characteristics, leaving a final judgment until he had more information and was actually in the process of reconstructing the skull.

By dusk, he had most of it done, and two views of a generic version of John Doe sat on his drawing board. But Bern was uncomfortable with them. Something didn't seem right, though he had no way of knowing what it was. He looked at the two drawings in one of the three mirrors that he moved around the benches when he was sculpting or drawing in order to see what he was doing from a slightly different perspective. But in this case, it really wasn't much help at all. There was still something about the drawings that left him dissatisfied. In fact, he was oddly uncomfortable with them.

But he had worked long enough.

He turned out the lights, and blue flooded the studio as he walked over to the large glass wall and stood looking out over the lake. Across the water, lights were coming on all along the shoreline, and the hills above them were momentarily purple before nightfall. He pushed on a section of the wall, which swung open on a center-post hinge, and stepped outside. He could smell the water and the cedars on the hills. A waft of cedar-wood smoke came by and was gone, and the sound of a launch way off in a distant cove grumbled across the water.

He didn't much think of the skiing accident anymore, but after having mentioned it to Becca Haber, it was on his mind again. A year was not enough time for any of the details to have melted away. Every hour of that day was still vivid, too easy to recall.

It had been late August, and Alice and a couple of her girlfriends had talked Dana and Tess into taking them skiing one last time before the summer vacation was over.

Neither he nor Philip had been able to go. The sky was bright and blistering as they pulled the Laus' boat out of its slip at Oyster Landing in midafternoon and headed up the long green avenue of Lake Austin.

The lake was calm, a perfect ski day, and there was a lot of activity on the water. The third girl had just gotten up on her skis when four college-age guys came up behind them in a spanking new powerboat. They had passed them a couple of times, going in the opposite direction, but the kids had noticed one another and some light flirting was going on. Then the guys were behind them, cutting back and forth in the wake of the third girl's skis.

Before anyone had time to realize that it was about to get out of hand, the powerboat throttled wildly and roared past the girl on skis and then up beside Dana, who was driving. The guys were waving beer bottles and shouting, when suddenly their boat swerved recklessly and slammed into the side of the Laus' boat.

Tess and Alice were sitting on the side that the power-boat rammed. Tess was thrown headfirst into the other boat's hull, and Alice was pitched into its stern. Both boats came to a dead rest in the water, the powerboat piercing the other boat's hull. Tess and Alice were both unconscious in the water.

Tess died on the way to the hospital. Alice was in a coma for three months. When she finally recovered, she was an enigma to the world.

In the aftermath of the funeral, Bern had thought he would sell the house. He had thought he would grow to hate the lake and all the things associated with it that he and Tess had loved so much. Those things, like the sunsets over the water, the night swims, the stars in the still waters that doubled the great expanse of the night sky, had become their things, like a song became your song because the two of you fell in love with it together.

He stayed on, waiting for the dissonance that shared things took on when the one you had shared them with was gone. He waited, sorry for it in advance of its coming.

But Tess's death didn't affect his life the way he had imagined it would. The familiar things they had shared, the house they both had worked so hard to build over the years, the lake, with its sounds and light and smells, that was so much a part of them both—all of that didn't go hollow for him. They didn't haunt him. Instead, he loved them all the more because they reminded him of her, and rather than making him lonely, they gave him comfort.

Even Alice had been a comfort to him. Her survival did not remind him of his own loss. Instead, it only reminded him that everything changes, that nothing is guaranteed, that there are degrees of loss, and of hope, too. It wasn't a trade-off, Tess's life for Alice's. It didn't have to be either one of them.

It just was what it was. There was no fate involved; there was no grand dark scheme. It simply happened, like the changing breeze, like that waft of smoke he had smelled just once and then was gone and would not come again.

Chapter 7

Washington, D.C.

Richard Gordon walked down the long hall on the third and top floor of a motel on one of the commercial thoroughfares in Fairfax, Virginia. The place was generic in spades, like a blank piece of paper, or the surface of the moon. But you knew people had been there. The management had tried to cover up that fact by soaking the blue-green carpet in untold gallons of antiseptic air freshener, the spoor of their compliance with governmental health regulations.

He stopped at the door with the right number on it and knocked. The bare walls of the corridor converged in the fluorescent distance in both directions. These motel room rendezvous grew increasingly depressing with the passing years. They typified the whole shabby business he and his colleagues toiled in, as if mocking the high ideals that had launched their careers but which, over the years, they often lost sight of and sometimes even forgot entirely.

When the door opened, he walked into a room lighted only by the cool bluish halogen illumination from the streetlamp on an overpass just outside the window.

"Richard," a strangled voice said. "Good, good," and Lex Kevern walked away from the door, leaving Gordon to close it himself, the back of Kevern's bearish shoulders presenting a bulky silhouette.

They didn't shake hands, even though they hadn't seen each other in nearly a year. Despite the fact that they didn't much like each other they were working together on an operation with a "Sequestered" classification. This was a new and rarefied sensitive compartmented information designation that indicated that the operation was clandestine, rather than covert. That is, apart from it being known to a handful of men, a few in the CIA's Directorate of Operations, and a few in the National Security Council, the operation did not exist.

Gordon looked around. No one else was there. The light sifted through open venetian blinds in horizontal bars, revealing furnishings that were wholesale warehouse decor, 1975. The air was stale and heavy, suggestive of rampant flatulence. A small suitcase lay open on the bed, its contents rifled, as if something had been roughly pulled from underneath the carefully packed contents.

Kevern picked up something off an end table and fell heavily into an armchair against the wall, under the window of blue light.

"It's been awhile," Gordon said. "Montevideo."

"Yeah, yeah, Montevideo," Kevern grunted. With the light coming in from above him, he was more shadow than man. He stretched out his beefy arm, and the television screen flickered. He was already watching it.

Gordon looked at Kevern's profile in the pale, grainy light from the television. His body was thicker with age, but still in operational condition. The military haircut was gone, but his hair was still neat, trimmed. He was wearing street clothes, not the jeans and muscle-revealing T-shirt of former years, but there was no mistaking the condition of the body underneath the clothes. Lex had been in intelligence and special operations a long time. It would never wear off.

"So what is it?" Gordon asked, taking a vinyl-covered chair. There was a sofa, but he didn't want to sit on the damn thing. He imagined the fibers caked with the effluvium of an endless parade of transient lodgers with piggish habits.

Kevern had called him on their secure line from Mexico City early that morning and said he wanted a meeting and that he would be there that evening. No explanation. But Gordon didn't need one. For the last six weeks, the small cadre of people involved in Operation Heavy Rain had all been obsessed with only one thing. Kevern had to be bringing something of extreme importance.

"Got it a month ago," Kevern said, not answering the question.

"It what?"

"You'd better watch it."

The CD began playing.

Surveillance camera: Three men sitting at a table. The camera is situated high and behind a balding man whose face is not visible, the image slightly distorted by the wide-angle lens. The two men whose faces are visible seem to be of Middle Eastern descent. Voices outside. A Korean comes into view from the right side, carrying an automatic weapon and followed by an Anglo and another Korean.

Gordon froze but said nothing. He eased to the front of his chair, forearms on his knees as he leaned toward the television screen.

There is an awkward exchange among three of the men; then suddenly the bald man jumps to his feet, upsetting the cups and saucers on the small table, and spits at the Anglo as one of the Koreans grabs the Anglo's arms from behind and wrenches them behind his back with an audible snap as the Anglo screams in pain. His hands are tied behind him and his legs are taped to the chair legs. "Jasus! Jasus!" the bald man screams as he leans across the table.

"Spy! Spy!" Kevern translated in a low, raspy voice.

Someone appears in a jogging suit and jabs electrical wires into either side of the Anglo's neck, convulsing his body. Suddenly, the other two men jump up, something is shouted, one man's arm flies up, and he fires a gun at the man across the table from him, blowing out the back of his head. Once again, the electrical wires are applied to the Anglo, and he is again convulsed. Then the bald man produces a knife, and while someone holds the stunned Anglo's head, he quickly cuts out his tongue.

"Oh shit!" Gordon blurted.

The bald man hits the Anglo repeatedly in the face with his own tongue, then tosses the tongue to a dog, who immediately eats it.

"Oh! Oh! Jesus!" Gordon fell back in his chair.

The Anglo slowly chokes to death on his own blood while everyone watches. The bald man says something inaudible. Someone else speaks. When it finally looks as if the Anglo is dead, the bald man suddenly plunges his knife into the Anglo's chest and leaves it there as everyone walks out of the room. The video runs for a few minutes, recording nothing but the silence and the still bodies of the two dead men. Then the screen goes blank.

Kevern flicked off the CD player.

Gordon's face was burning. They had reluctantly accepted the probability that Jude Lerner was dead, but this was a brutal way to have it confirmed. He stood and went over to the CD player, took out the disk, and then returned to his chair.

"Where the hell did this come from, Lex? What's going on here?"

"Agencia Federal de Investigaciónes," Kevern said. "They'd been watching these Lebanese for the better part of a month. Didn't even know what they had. I was down there running traps. Anything new? Anything off-the-wall? Any interesting hits? Agent said, '*Pues, tenemos éste.*' I said, 'Lemme see.'" Kevern gestured toward the television. "This is what the little shit showed me."

Gordon just shook his head. Good God Almighty.

Kevern rolled his head to the side, grunting softly. God only knew what inspired such a pantomime, or what it was supposed to convey to people.

"Mexico's got half a million Lebanese," Gordon said. "Why were they watching these guys?"

"Drugs, my man said."

"Just drugs?"

"S'what he said."

"They didn't know about their ties to Hezbollah?"

"I don't think they did."

"So who did they think the gringo was?"

Kevern shrugged. "Some guy trying to make a buck.

47

They were puzzled by the 'Spy! Spy!' thing. They had run it by the DEA, which couldn't ID the gringo."

Lebanese had begun immigrating to Mexico during the nineteenth century, and today they were a culturally significant force there, representing some of the country's wealthiest and most influential citizens. As an ethnic subgroup, they were thoroughly integrated into the Mexican social fabric. They were as invisible as the Irish are in the United States, and they presented the same problems to the intelligence community in Mexico as the Irish would in the United States if the IRA suddenly decided it was their moral and religious obligation to kill as many Americans as possible by any means possible. Although 99.9 percent of the Irish would find the idea abhorrent, that .1 percent who sympathized would be a hell of a problem for Homeland Security. It was the same with the Lebanese in Mexico. Those affiliated with Hezbollah were finding it easy to hide in plain sight. Racial profiling sure as hell wasn't an issue.

Gordon said nothing. His officer was dead, and a crack Mexican intelligence team trained by the DEA and the French National Police had a digital recording of it. The problem was that Heavy Rain was operating under the radar of all foreign intelligence agencies, including that of the Mexican government. Even more serious than that, it wasn't even known to the U.S. embassy or the CIA's own station chief in Mexico City. This was too damned close for comfort.

"Has Mejía seen this?"

Kevern shook his head.

Well, it was all over, finally. But there was one bleak question. He looked at Kevern. "How did Khalil and Ahmad get onto Jude?"

"Don't have a clue."

"The bald guy?"

"Not a clue. Look, this came out of nowhere. You can see by the video that Jude didn't have a clue when he walked in there, either. He was too good for that. If he'd smelled something, he'd never have shown up in Tepito."

"When did you say you got this?" Gordon asked.

" 'Bout a month ago," Kevern said without a hint of apology.

Jude had been missing six weeks.

Gordon was trembling. The CD had been damned gruesome, but anger had more to do with the way he was feeling.

"You've had it a month," Gordon said, and the two men stared at each other. "You'd better have a fucking good explanation," Gordon said.

"Two thousand miles of Mexican border, Gordy," Kevern rasped. He always sounded like he had a raw throat. "Five thousand five hundred miles of Canadian border. Two million railcars and eleven million trucks come into the country every year. Eight thousand ships make fifty-one thousand port calls every year. Five hundred million people come into our airports and seaports every year, over eight million of them illegal immigrants." He paused for emphasis. "That's my explanation.

"It took Jude nearly seven months to get in there, gain their confidence, meet Baida, gain his confidence—marginally," Kevern went on. "Best guy we had, and it took damn near a year to put him in place. Hellacious effort. We don't want to lose track of these people, Gordy. You know what's coming out of the Triple Border area. Those guys are on the move; they're scattering—to São Paulo, to Isla de Margarita in Venezuela, to Panama, to Iquique in Chile. Shit. And from those places, they'll scatter again. The cyst is festering and pus is seeping out. We don't have much time."

"What the hell are you talking about?" Gordon said. "This was always a long shot—and it almost worked. But it was a one-off operation. Jude *was* the operation." He held up the CD. "And you just showed me the end of it."

Kevern sat very still, and Gordon saw the look in his eye, a too-still look, which put Gordon on instant alert. The son of a bitch had already done something extreme. And he had taken a month to set it up and do it.

"Get to the goddamned point, Lex."

"Ghazi Baida's about to get a little jolt of enlightenment," Kevern said, grunting under his breath. "He's about to find out that Jude's not dead after all."

Chapter 8

Lex Kevern was still holding the remote control for the CD player. After the television screen had gone dark, the room had returned to its cool blue glow.

But now Richard Gordon wanted to see Kevern's face clearly. He was sitting next to a table lamp, and he reached up and turned it on. Instantly, the weak incandescent bulb threw a sallow cast over everything. Kevern's suntan turned dark and leathery.

Heavy Rain, like many clandestine operations, was straightforward in its concept but complex in its execution. The objective was to put someone very near the inner circle of Ghazi Baida, a much-feared Hezbollah terrorist who U.S. intelligence was now placing in and out of South America's Triple Border region. This territory, a dense jungle no-man's-land where the Iguaçú and Paraná rivers meet at the converging borders of Brazil, Argentina, and Paraguay, had become a lawless sanctuary for international criminals and terrorists. It was feared that Baida had targeted the United States and was laying the groundwork in the Triple Border region for operations that would be launched from bases in Panama, Venezuela, and Mexico.

A CIA operations officer, Jude Lerner, was put into play, posing as an artist from Texas and using the alias Jude Teller. He became a fixture in Mexico City's large arts community. He began to hang out at a lap-dancing club in the Zona Rosa that was frequented by Ahmad Rahal, one of two principals in a cell that had been tied to Baida. Over time, the two men became friends, and eventually Jude let Rahal in on his little sideline: trafficking in stolen pre-Columbian artifacts.

Gordon's people in Washington had backstopped an entire smuggling operation set up by Kevern's people over a period of six months. They had created routes, contacts, covers, informants, buyers, everything needed to support a smuggling network that stretched from the jungles of Guatemala's Petén, where Jude bought artifacts from Mayan Indians who raided archaeological sites, to Houston, the destination of the merchandise and its distribution point.

When Ahmad expressed an eager curiosity about Jude's operation, Jude invited him along on a couple of trips, and Ahmad got a firsthand look at Jude's entire system. Shortly after the second trip, Ahmad introduced Jude to the cell's leader, Khalil Saleh. After another month of wary association, Khalil was also shown the smuggling route, and very soon afterward, it was mentioned to Jude that they were looking for a safe conduit into Texas for certain items. Would Jude be interested? The Texan was always interested in making a tax-free dollar.

Eventually, Khalil took Jude to Paraguay's Ciudad del Este, located in the Triple Border region, and introduced him to Baida. Suddenly, security backstop flutters were rippling all the way back to the second level of Jude's layered legend. Baida was looking into him in a serious way. When that didn't throw up any flags, Baida called Jude back to Paraguay. At the third meeting, Baida agreed to move some contraband in a trial run through Jude's underground system.

But when Jude returned to Mexico City from his last trip to Ciudad del Este, he disappeared. Now here was confirmation of what had happened to him, but for some reason, Kevern had withheld this information from Langley for four weeks. Now Gordon was waiting for an explanation.

After his last enigmatic statement, Kevern was silent. He leaned forward, resting one elbow on the arm of his chair. Gordon could hear him softly grunting under his breath, a big animal, forced to make nice in an environment that constrained and frustrated him. But he was calm. When Kevern was getting close to something he wanted, he became very placid. Achieving proximity to his prey was like putting him on ice. His metabolism dropped to the level of a scorpion's.

Finally, Kevern nodded. "Turn off that light," he said. "You need to see something else."

Again the screen came alive in a fluorescent haze of static. The images were indistinct at first, and this time the dateline indicated a period twenty-four hours after the first recording.

The opening images are murky and then a door is flung open to a lighted room—the same room as in the first recording, but this time the camera is being held by someone coming into the room. Khalil, the bald man, and the

*two Koreans wheel around in stunned surprise. The cam-
era hurtles into the room behind the intruders, who are
clad in black balaclavas. They begin firing their automatic
weapons immediately, and then receive a few bursts of fire
from two of Khalil's men, who rush into the room through
another door. The intruders spray the room with more
automatic-weapons fire, and everyone in the room is down
in less than fifteen seconds. The black-hooded intruders
then methodically go to each of the victims and finish them
off with short bursts at point-blank range.*

*The bald man, still dying, is recorded up close, black-
gloved hands lifting his head off the floor and holding his
face straight so that he can be identified. The dead Khalil
is also recorded up close for identification, as are each of
the three Koreans and the two other men. Three times, a
shirt is lifted and pants are pulled down to record tattoos
or scars to corroborate the ID.*

*Someone gathers up piles of money on the table around
which the men had been gathered, as well as a dozen kilo
packages of drugs stacked beside the money. Then the
handheld camera records the removal of the ceiling-high
surveillance camera that had been secretly mounted in the
corner by the* Agencia Federal de Investigaciónes, *and
which had captured the previous recording. One last pan
of the silenced room, and the images end.*

Kevern snicked off the CD player and the television.

Gordon sat in stunned silence. The entire cell they had
spent nearly a year to penetrate was gone in less than five
minutes.

He suspected he knew what he had just seen, but he
stopped himself from saying so. He had to hear this out.
He had to wait and take it as it came, and he had to read

very closely between the lines. He wanted Kevern to explain every step of this, everything, especially the stuff Gordon thought he had already figured out.

He reached up and flipped on the lamp again. This time, he wanted to see everything Kevern's face had to offer, though it seldom offered much.

Kevern, grunting, sat up in his chair and leaned forward a little.

"Unlike his Muslim buds, Baida's never been squirmy about the ethics of drug trafficking to finance his operations." He nodded toward the television. "That's what Khalil was doing here. Hezbollah's accelerating its initiatives in South America. Those crumbling economies down there are like fertilizer to organized crime, and Hezbollah's sucking into that.

"My guess is that Baida's turning some of the people from those criminal organizations into surrogate soldiers. They've got the infrastructure he needs for transborder operations. They've got no national or religious loyalties. They're greedy, so their services go to the highest bidder, and with the drug money, Baida can bid high. They're ideal terrorist mercenaries."

Kevern paused. Gordon could hear him breathing, as if his lungs and throat were laboring under the compression of secrecy.

"This is our situation: Until Jude, we'd never been able to make any headway getting inside one of Baida's damn cells because of his obsession with three things: compartmentalization, decentralized organization, and fractured communication." He paused for emphasis. "And those are exactly the things we're going to use to bury him."

Gordon wasn't sure where this was going, but he was

getting an edgy feeling that they were headed toward one of Kevern's more creative enterprises. Kevern was famous in special operations for designing and executing impossible schemes that paid off beyond anyone's wildest expectations. He had engineered some legendary operations. At the same time, when one of these things went awry, someone higher up always had his head handed to him on a platter for having authorized the scheme. But somehow, Kevern always survived.

The reality was that managers and administrators could always be replaced. They came and went with inevitable regularity, like the changing seasons. But a creative operations officer who was also meticulous was a rare commodity, and every intelligence agency had to have a few men like Kevern, men who didn't mind playing the role of Satan in the complex moral drama of clandestine operations.

"We'd already documented everyone in the cell," Kevern said. "Even the Korean guards they'd hired to provide them with protection and freedom of movement in Tepito."

Kevern tossed a glance at the television, as if reminding Gordon of what he'd just seen.

"Those were Mondragón's men who made the raid and shot the video. We got the whole fuckin' cell, roots and all."

Gordon couldn't get his breath. Good God. Even in this new terrorist-harried environment that allowed more lenient uses of lethal force, it was a dumbfounding act of preemption for an American officer to arrange the slaughter of cell members who weren't even remotely important enough to be on the Directorate of Operation's high-value target list, along with a roomful of men who were nothing more than hired local gang members. And all of this done without any directive from the DO. It was a totally independent act.

Kevern must have seen the look on Gordon's face.

"Just a second, Gordy. Listen to me here."

Kevern was the only person on earth who called him Gordy. It was a shrewd mixture of good ol' boy camaraderie and subtle derision, the difference at any given moment depending on Kevern's nuanced manner.

"Now listen, okay?" Kevern repeated. "By killing these assholes and taking the money and the drugs, we made it look like one of Baida's drug deals had gone sour. That's what Baida heard from the security guy he sent up to Mexico City to find out why he wasn't hearing anything from Khalil's cell.

"Postmortem: Baida writes that cell off to the cost of doing business. As far as he's concerned, it's a total wash. And, because there's no communication between Baida's cells, each one locked down, totally independent except for communication to and from Baida himself, Baida never learned that Jude was a spy. Khalil sure as hell didn't report it to him. He was trying to cover it up. So as far as Baida's concerned, Jude's still clean.

"But Baida's worried: Where's Jude? He hasn't heard anything from Jude. Not a damn thing. Baida made four calls to Jude's dedicated cell number in the five or six days following the Tepito massacre. He wants him. He wants Jude's underground route north. The story on the street is mixed. Some say Jude was killed in the raid. Some say—a rumor we started ourselves—no, he's laying low until he figures out what the hell happened that night. Baida's investigator takes this mixed report back to him in the Triple Border."

Kevern stopped and looked at Gordon like a challenging professor looks at his brightest student, waiting for him to see the answer ahead of the rest of the class.

"I don't get it, Lex."

Kevern smiled. "That's the brilliant thing about this, Gordy. Neither will Baida."

Kevern got to his feet and went to the battered suitcase lying on the bed. He lifted a pile of clothes and pulled out a folder, then went back and tossed it into Gordon's lap.

Gordon saw the red border on the folder and the solid red pyramid next to the name tab. It was the coding emblem for a new category of CIA operations officer, one that was closely held by the CIA's security system. Jude Lerner was one of the few officers whose 201 file bore the red pyramid and who also had a separate red-stripe file with a "Sequestered" limited-access classification.

But Gordon still didn't see what was coming, and Kevern could see it on his face.

"You know what's in his file, don't you?" Kevern asked.

"I know my people, Lex."

Kevern returned to his chair and fell into it with a grunt. He watched Gordon as he opened the folder and numbly began paging through it. It didn't take him long. Kevern had red-flagged the relevant document and had paper-clipped a sheet of handwritten notes to it. Gordon didn't even have to read the notes.

He looked up at Kevern, who wore a deadpan expression.

"You're out of your skull," Gordon said.

"Nice choice of words," Kevern grunted.

"What the fuck have you done?" Gordon asked.

"I want two things from you," Kevern said. "I want you to hold with the story that Baida's cell went down in a drug hit." His eyes were leveled on Gordon. "And I want you to get me clearance for the Bern operation. I'm already way down the road on this one, and we're just about ready to jump. I want you to make it okay."

Chapter 9

By seven o'clock the next morning, Bern was sweating heavily. Wearing only shorts and tennis shoes, he climbed over the rocks on the shoreline below the house, lugging heavy stones into a growing pile where he was preparing the foundation for a concrete quay at the water's edge. He had been toiling on the project every morning for two months, getting up at dawn to work for a couple of hours before showering and having breakfast.

By eight o'clock, he was at his drawing board, laying down the first contour lines of a sketch of what Becca Haber hoped would prove to be a picture of her husband's face. A little after ten o'clock, Alice and her mother arrived.

"Hey, Paul," Dana said from the head of the stairs in the studio as the two of them came in.

"Morning!" Alice said brightly, leaving her mother and taking the stairs two at a time as she breezed past Bern on her way to the glass wall overlooking the lake. She stepped outside and leaned her elbows on the railing of the deck to watch a couple of sailboats just emerging from around the point as they left the marina.

Bern met Dana at the bottom of the steps and kissed her on the cheek.

"Wow, you smell good," he said.

"New stuff." She smiled.

"It gets my thumbs up," he said. "Cup of coffee?"

"No thanks. I just wanted to say hello. The last couple of times I've dropped Alice off, I've just waved from the car. We haven't talked all week. You doing okay?"

"Sure, fine. Listen, yesterday when you picked up Alice, did she seem a little out of sorts?"

"Yeah, I noticed that. But gosh, Paul, you know, I've gotten so that I take most of the surprises from her in my stride. The abnormal has become normal around our house." She smiled ruefully, looking at Alice outside on the deck. Then she shifted her attention back to Bern. "Why, something happen?"

He told her about Alice's exasperation with Becca Haber, and they both laughed about it.

Dana Lau was a handsome woman, the only Chinese news anchor in the South when she met Philip in Atlanta. Bern and Tess got to know her while she and Philip were still dating, and it was the beginning of a friendship that never looked back. When Alice came, it was like having their own daughter, and it even seemed to bring them all closer together.

As Alice reached middle school, she and her friends began having slumber parties at Bern's house. Tess would take them to movies, grill burgers in the evenings on the terrace, and cook popcorn for their all-night gigglefests. They swam and played around on the little sailboat that

Bern bought for them and kept in the cove. Tess adored the girls and always got a kick out of watching them stumbling through adolescence. And they all loved Aunt Tess.

After a few more minutes of visiting, Dana called bye to Alice and left, and Bern walked back to his drawing board, where Alice had already pulled up her stool and was looking at the two views of the face that had emerged from the paper in the past two hours. She was intent.

"It's a single, very purple mix," Alice said with some concern in her voice. She looked at Bern, frowning. "Why walk under a seen sky?"

"What's the matter?" he asked. He was standing in front of the drawing, while Alice sat on the stool beside him. She smelled of morning freshness and a douse of perfume.

"You're taking a lot more than a pencil would make," she said slowly, and maybe with a tinge of agitation.

Bern looked at her. She had laid her sketch pad on a nearby table edge and had put her hands between her legs on the seat of the stool, her arms locked straight as she leaned toward the sketch. She seemed to be trying to see something she couldn't quite make out, the way she had studied the drawing with the contradictory facial expressions that he had made for her the previous day. Then he saw her look at the drawing in a couple of the mirrors, as she had learned to do from him, and he saw a distinctive change in her eyes and brow.

"Something wrong with it?" he asked again. Unlike her reaction to the picture yesterday, when her puzzlement at what she saw had resulted in a calming fascination, the sketch on the drawing board had the opposite effect.

She hesitated, cocking her head another way. "In every

certain way," she said carefully, "it would be crazy if you put a face on it."

The drawing was finished, although it lacked detail. It was a mistake to overrender a drawing at this point of the reconstruction process. Some things were better worked out on the actual skull. But the proportional arrangement of the different features was in place, which, for identification purposes, was the key thing. Though some individual features may be rendered entirely wrong, the face will still be recognizable if the relationship between the features, and the proportions of some of them, is accurate. It is the correct relationship of the aggregate elements of a face that is the essential ingredient in the process of recognition.

As Bern watched Alice, she slowly shrugged one shoulder defensively and unconsciously turned her head away slightly, though she was reluctant to stop looking.

"It's a black song with eyes behind," she said. "Not even the music, not even if you cry." She began shaking her head no, a little at first and then a lot, and finally she pulled her gaze away from the drawing and looked hard at Bern, her expression one of deep-seated disappointment.

"I'm not want from this. Ever. No."

She solemnly got down off the stool, picked up her sketchbook, and headed for the sofa. Bern was completely surprised at her reaction, and puzzled.

"Okay," he said, watching her as she sat on the sofa and opened her sketch pad. "You want to watch me do the clay work, then?"

She liked the clay modeling even more than the drawing because he didn't do it as often, and she hadn't seen as much of it. She knew he was already working on the skull, because she had seen it set up on the next bench, the eyeballs and first strips of clay already in place around the tissue-depth markers. But she wasn't going to have anything to do with it. She didn't even respond. She had put her bare feet on the edge of the coffee table and was drawing in her sketchbook, which was resting against her slanted thighs.

Even more puzzled now, Bern sat on the stool to look at the drawings from her vantage point. He studied the face, trying to see it afresh. He was comfortable with the accuracy of the proportions. What the hell had she seen here that had been so disturbing? After a few minutes, he gave up and set to work on the skull.

At noon, he stopped, and they drove to the Far Point Grill in the old Triumph, Alice looking like a carefree kid in her sunglasses and with her Côte d'Azur smile. They did this every couple of weeks when Dana volunteered at the battered-women's shelter at Seton Hospital, as she was doing today. Alice liked watching the sailboats come and leave the marina, and the fact that she had almost been killed in a boating accident never seemed to bother her.

Katie had known Alice before the accident, too, and out of sheer compassion had quickly learned the give-and-take of Alice's nonsensical conversation. It was easier for some people than for others. There were those who still found it disturbing to have this attractive girl speaking to them in an Alice in Wonderland syntax. It required a little creativity and willingness to laugh at yourself.

They were back at the studio in a little over an hour. Alice deliberately avoided the workbench where he had been reconstructing the face on Haber's skull, returning to the sofa instead. Bern put on a Bach CD because Alice seemed in a Yo-Yo Ma mood, and within twenty minutes, he saw her put her sketch pad on the mesquite-slab table and curl up at one end of the sofa. She was soon asleep.

He had trouble with the sculpture almost as soon as the contours of the face began to emerge from the clay applications. From the very beginning, he found himself making a mistake that was common to beginning forensic sculptors—that is, projecting his own features onto the clay model. He went back to his measurements again and again to double-check tissue measurements, bone projections, and spacing, figures that he had determined only hours before or already knew by heart.

It was particularly frustrating because he was rebuilding and reshaping on a skull that was in perfect condition. The guesswork was as minimal as it was ever going to get. Which left his judgment to consider. He wasn't arrogant, but he did have a lot of confidence in his ability to read a skull, and in his artistic skills.

But something was wrong. This thing didn't feel right at all. Each adjustment he made simply resulted in a variation on a theme. Nothing substantive actually changed in the reconstructed face, because the substantive indicators remained the same no matter how many times he measured the skull or checked the tissue charts. He was just shoving around clay.

When Alice woke an hour later, she wanted to go swimming. She went to the lower bedroom, which opened onto the terrace, and changed into her swimsuit. When she came upstairs again, Bern quit working and sat on the deck outside the studio with a glass of iced tea and watched her swim back and forth in the cove below. Once in a while, he'd glance into the room and look at the head he had sculpted sitting on the workbench. The thing was beginning to get on his nerves. He had the vague feeling that there was something about it that was familiar somehow.

Alice messed around in the water, swimming, floating on a rubber raft, letting the breeze move her around in the sunny water. When she finally climbed out of the lake about an hour later, she sat on the deck with him and ate an ice-cream bar. She was just finishing it when Dana called to say that she was leaving the shelter early and would be there in half an hour.

After Alice had dressed and dried her hair, Bern thought he would try to get her to look at the reconstructed face again, now that it was finished. He tried to coax her over to the workbench, but she wouldn't go, wouldn't even look that way. He even tried humoring her, playfully putting his hands on her shoulders and guiding her toward the bench. But she wouldn't be humored, either, and she pulled away from him, throwing him a painful look, mumbling something he couldn't hear. She returned to the sofa, where she remained absorbed in a kind of distant sadness until her mother arrived.

After they had gone, Bern poured a gin and tonic, added a big chunk of lime, and went back to the reconstructed face. He sat down at the workbench and studied what he had done. Should he photograph the head now, and then go back and put a smile on the face? Since the teeth are the only part of a person's skull that is seen by others while the person is living, sometimes showing them can be crucial to identification.

He decided against it, but he couldn't resist doing a little more detailing, articulating the individual hairs in the eyebrows, and using the tips of the bristles of a toothbrush to lightly texture the area of the face where a beard would grow. By the time the gin was gone, he felt like he had taken it about as far as he should.

It was a little after 8:00 P.M. when he finally ate dinner on the terrace outside the dining room, a light meal of warmed-up quiche and a fresh green salad. The summer days were long and it was still more than an hour before dark, though the shadows from the house and studio now stretched far out into the water and the light on the hills across the lake was taking on the amber tones of the dying sun.

He had had a couple more gin and tonics since the first one, and now he made another as he finished putting the dishes in the dishwasher. He was feeling the drinks as he crossed from the terrace to the deck outside the studio. On the lake, the last of the sailboats were heading for the marina, which was just out of sight around the bluffs to the south, and the lake was growing still and glassy in the cove where Alice had been swimming.

As he pushed on the panel in the glass wall and stepped into the studio, the light of the reflected sunset was flooding everything inside in a honey haze. He was no more than a few steps into the room when he stopped and saw his own reflection in two of the three mirrors around the workbench.

It was odd that his image was perfectly framed in that one brief moment. Odder still was that he had caught his own reflection in a frozen moment, as in a snapshot. Profile. Frontal. His features softened in the muted honey light. It was a weird moment: The world stopped; his reflection gave no sense of movement or of life. It was as if he were looking at a wax image of himself.

Then with a sudden dizziness that he did not attribute

to the gin, he realized that he was looking at the reconstructed sculpture that he had finished only hours before.

In an instant, he understood what Alice had seen in the drawing that disturbed her, why she had furiously refused to look at the sculpted head. With very careful calculation and with all of his experience and talent brought to bear on the task, he had meticulously reconstructed the skull that Becca Haber had brought him, only to discover that when the skull belonged to a living person, that person had lived with his face.

The glass slipped out of his hand.

Chapter 10

The glass hit the concrete floor with a sharp smack-and-shatter. Bern didn't even notice. Shards of glass crunched under his shoes as he moved past the coffee table toward the reconstructed skull as if mesmerized, his eyes fixed on the face he had made but hadn't seen. At least he hadn't seen the face within the face. He had been intimate with its technical construction but not with its spirit. It was Alice who had seen the spirit of the thing.

Focused on the sculpture, to the exclusion of all other sensory awareness, Bern went to the workbench and turned on the lights. He sat down on a stool in front of the face and looked at it, his eyes moving over the details of its features as if they were the fingers of a sightless man. Good God. It was as if he had had some kind of myopia when he was building the face, some kind of break in visual-cognitive synapse, much like Alice's disconnect from words that she had heard all of her life but could no longer comprehend.

But now, suddenly, he had been startled from a daze.

He remembered that from the very beginning he had fought the tendency to reproduce his own features on the skull. What the hell was this? What was going on here?

He moved the stool over beside the face. After readjusting two of the mirrors, he sat down beside the reconstruction and put his own face inches away from it, side by side. He looked in the mirrors.

A warm flush spread over him. It wasn't exact, but the accuracy of the proportional relationships was unmistakable. It was easy to see why he had tended to put his own exact features on this skull. Everything indicated that he should have. It was all there. He had indeed understood what he was looking at when he had been sketching the naked skull and then reclothing it with clay flesh. The bony architecture had told him that his own face had every right to be there.

He could hardly pull himself away from the mirrors, where the reverse angle emphasized the similarities between his own face and the reconstructed face even more. Jesus Holy Christ. What was he supposed to think?

Suddenly, he got up from the stool and hurried up the steps and out of the studio. A few years earlier, maybe four years ago, he had been working on a pergola that stretched along one side of the terrace. He'd been working alone, as usual, and needed an extra pair of hands to hold a raw cedar four-by-four while he drilled a hole at one end of it for a bolt. Tess had been helping him, but she had run into town to the hardware store. Rather than waiting for her, he contrived a complex balancing act for the beam. It slipped, and he fell from the top of the pergola and the beam fell on top of him as he landed. It broke his jaw.

Now he was in the bedroom, going through boxes

stored in one of the closets. Somewhere in here he had the X-ray films of the lower part of his head.

When he found them, he hurried back to the studio, turned on the light table, and grabbed the photographs he had made of the skull. At the time he broke his jaw, he had insisted, despite the pain, that the X rays be done life-size and with particular care to avoid distortion. As a forensic artist, he couldn't resist the opportunity to have an accurate record of his own skull. Now he realized that it might have been the most fortuitous thing he had ever done.

In actual fact, using photographic negatives for comparison was rarely practical. For the comparisons to be helpful, you had to have two perfectly photographed skulls, without any of the perspective distortions that were usually present in photographs. In Bern's experience, that had never happened before. Until now.

With his heart hammering, he laid his own negatives over the skull's negatives that he had done earlier and began aligning the lower part of the eye sockets, noting the precise angles of the orbital edges, the shapes of the frontal sinuses, and going from point to point down the skull. The teeth provided the startling finale.

The skulls matched.

Bern's legs went rubbery, and he sat down hard on the stool, unaware of what he was doing. Stunned, he stared at the glow of the light table, which seemed to take on a creepy pale aura. He didn't even know how to think about this. What in the hell was his frame of reference here? The possibilities? The implications? This was beyond strange. *Way beyond strange.*

He swallowed. He stood shakily. Bracing his arms, palms down, on the light table, he looked at the two overlaid skulls. But he saw only one. Oh Jesus. He flipped off the light.

He thought of Alice's preternatural reaction to the sketch. He thought of Becca Haber. His thoughts went directly to her quick departure after he had committed to reconstructing the skull. That wasn't right. Thinking back now, that was suspicious. Shit, she was suspicious.

He went to his desk and found the piece of paper on which she had written the phone number of the hotel where she was staying. He dialed the number and asked for her room.

"Yes, sir," the night clerk said.

Silence.

The night clerk came back on. "How do you spell that name, sir?"

He spelled it.

"Sir . . ."

Bern felt it coming.

"We don't show anyone by that name as a guest with us."

He put down the phone. There was no use in checking anywhere else. He looked at the piece of paper. She had written it herself. If he had written it . . . maybe . . . but he hadn't. Immediately, he cast his thoughts back over former cases. What was going on here? Did this have something to do with one of his former cases? Was somebody doing something here, coming back at him for something they thought he'd done? Someone who felt like they were wrongly convicted because of one of his drawings or reconstructions? Is that what this was?

He sat down at his computer and flipped it on. He went to his index and started with *A*. One at a time, he called up each case and thought about it, re-created it in his mind, re-membered it, brought it back to life. Who were the odd-balls? Who were the bitter convictions? Who were the angry ones?

Fifteen years flew through his head. Names, stories, and faces came to mind that he hadn't thought about in years. The files were reminders of a sad and murky world, of ruined lives, of unthinkable deeds, of men and women who had spent their last living moments in some madman's private hell. But there were happy endings, too; a child found, a lost relative relocated, an unsolved crime finally puzzled together to give closure to a tortured family.

After a little more than an hour, he had no ideas what-soever. There was nothing here that even hinted at the creepy coincidence that was sitting on the light table a few feet away.

Without a cue, he remembered the gin and tonic he had dropped, and the broken glass. He got up and went to the broom closet, got a roll of paper towels, a dustpan, and a hand broom, then crossed the room to clean up the mess.

While he searched around for the scattered glass, he re-played Becca Haber's performance, which is the way he now thought of her interview. Okay, so what was the pur-pose of her visit? To get him to do the job. Why?

He threw the glass into a trash can with a loud crash, and then began mopping up the gin that had splashed nearly to the edge of the sofa. He could see the slivers of glass glinting in the paper towel, and was careful to get all of it, thinking of Alice, who liked to walk around bare-footed.

When the mess was finally cleaned up, he put every-thing away and turned off all the lights except a lamp near the sofa. Then he went outside and stood on the deck and looked out at the lake.

For a moment, he tried to be aware of everything around him. A motorboat moving away from the marina and into the darkness headed up the lake. From a home on a point of land to his left came the faint, comforting sound of music traveling across the surface of the water. It was a summer sound, and it brought to mind youth and love and possibilities. From the woods nearby, a little screech owl sent its strange warbling concerns out over the water.

Suddenly, it hit him like a slap to the side of the head. Everything . . . everything paled into insignificance in the light of one shocking and incomprehensible reality: The skull on the workbench inside the studio was identical to the one that contained his own brain . . . and the entire existence of what he had always understood to be the one and only Paul Bern.

Chapter 11

It was just after 3:30 when Bern's racing mind slipped over the edge into dreams, and he was able to get a few hours of sleep. He didn't wake up until 8:15.

Before he even got out of bed, he rolled over and picked up the telephone and called the hotel again. He knew there would be a different desk clerk on duty by now. Again he asked for Becca Haber, and again he got the same "no one here by that name" response.

Incredible. But he had already decided what he needed to do next. He sat on the edge of the bed and dialed another number.

"Texas Department of Public Safety."

He asked for Ines Cortinas.

"Crime Lab. This's Ines."

"Ines, Paul Bern."

"Hey, Paul," she replied, "it's been a while. I'll bet you want something."

"A quick question."

"Shoot."

"You can do DNA testing using a bone from a skull, right?"

"Yeah. Well, mitochondrial DNA, not nuclear."

"What's the difference?"

"Mitochondrial is less specific. It's passed on only through the female line, and we can't distinguish between individuals. If we hit a match, we'd know the skull belonged to the descendants of a certain female line, but we wouldn't be able to ID the skull itself or even tell if it was male or female. We'd just know it was a member of a particular female lineage."

That wouldn't do Bern any good.

"You have a skull?" she asked.

"I know someone who does."

"Is it old?"

"I doubt if the thing's a year old."

"No kidding? Well, has it got teeth, then?"

"Yeah, all of them."

"There you go. We can do a regular nuclear DNA test using the teeth. We can extract the pulp from the inside of the tooth, and then we're on the way. No need to go the mitochondrial route."

"Any particular tooth the best?"

"A molar. They have more pulp to harvest. And, of course, no fillings. Preferably no work at all on the tooth we test."

"What about time? How long would it take?"

"Sounds like a rush."

"Yeah."

"We could do a nuclear short tandem repeat test in . . . maybe a day. Two days."

Bern thanked her and was off the line in a few minutes.

While he showered, he worked it out. He didn't know what the hell was going on here, but he did know that he didn't want people he worked with regularly to be aware of it, whatever it was. The DPS crime lab was out.

He made coffee, hurriedly ate a couple of pieces of toast, and then returned to the studio, where he photographed the reconstruction from every angle he could manage. Then he disassembled the lower jaw and located two molars that were without fillings. He removed them and put them in a small Ziploc bag. Checking his watch, he picked up the phone and called Southwest Airlines and booked a flight to Houston. Then he dialed another number in Houston and had a short conversation before hanging up and heading for Austin-Bergstrom International.

Two hours later, he arrived at Hobby Airport in Houston. He took a cab to the GTS labs in the Texas Medical Center complex and filled out the necessary paperwork for having a DNA string run on the two molars. He paid extra for a rush to get the results the next day. From there, he went to another private genetic-testing lab just off North Loop West. There, he filled out the paperwork to have a genetic string run on himself, again paying extra to have the results by the next day.

From there, it was short cab ride to Willow Lane in the upscale Meadow Wood section west of the Galleria. On a street nearly covered over with old water oaks, he had the taxi drop him off at a two-story Georgian home, its dun-colored walls carefully adorned with precisely trimmed fig ivy.

While he was still walking up the sidewalk, the front door opened and Gina stood in the doorway, smiling at him.

"You handsome devil," she said, opening her arms to hug him. She was the prettiest seventy-four-year-old woman he would ever see. Her smile was as beguiling now as it had been thirty years ago, when he fallen in love with her as a small boy, and her hair just as blond, as well.

Aunt Gina had cut an elegant swath through Houston's society set, marrying three men of significant wealth and influence, the departure of each leaving her appreciably better off financially than the previous one. The first, her real love, had died in a car crash in Mexico. The other two marriages were unconscious searches for something as happy as the first, and both ended in divorce. From then on, she dated profusely, while understanding the wisdom of remaining a single woman.

They had lunch together in her bright dining room, which overlooked her beloved rose garden, catching up on news of each other. Then following dessert and a lull in the conversation, she leveled her bright eyes at him across the table and her smile softened.

"What brings you here, Paul?" she asked. "You seem to have something on your mind."

He nodded and swallowed the last bite of his cream tart, the last half of a strawberry.

"I want to talk about my parents," he said. "My bio-logical parents."

She tilted her head to the side and her face took on a look of endearment. "Oh, dear boy, it's taken you such a long time."

"Well, it never seemed important before. Sally and Ted raised me, loved me, nurtured me. They were my parents, and I thought they deserved my loyalty."

"So you've just kept your wondering to yourself?"

"They didn't offer to tell me. I took my cue from that."

She laughed gently. "You were always so obedient, Paul. You should've kicked your heels up once in a while. Well, they had different attitudes about adoption in those days, and God knows your mother wasn't the adventuresome sort. She wasn't about to buck conventions. Ted, either, as far as that goes. They were dear people, though, and they did what they thought was best for you."

"I knew that. I just didn't want them to feel as if all that they had done for me wasn't enough."

"But now you want to know."

"They've been dead a dozen years now," he said, and let it go at that.

Gina smiled again. That was the way it was with her. She had learned a long time ago that life went down better with a smile, and she had always had a ready one. He tried to smile, too, but he found it hard to hide the weight of what was waiting for him on his workbench back in Austin.

She nodded, understanding. Then she looked out through the tall windows to the sunny garden. Her thoughts drifted, and he wondered if he would ever know what she was thinking at this moment. Gina's buoyant attitude about life made it possible for her to survive her disappointments with aplomb. But it did not mean that she didn't feel the ache all the same.

She sighed and looked at him again.

"I'm afraid you're going to be frustrated," she warned him. "There's just so very little to know."

"There are ways to research things these days," he said. "Things we've never had before."

"They're not going to help you," she said. She paused,

then shook her head slightly, ruefully. "You were abandoned at a hospital in Atlanta," she said. "Your biological mother, God bless her little heart, just walked into that old Lanier Memorial Hospital and left you in a little chair in the maternity ward. The ward nurse got a call saying you were there." She smiled wanly and shook her head. "That's all there was to it, Paul. It just doesn't go any further than that."

He didn't know what he was supposed to think about that. He didn't feel anything in particular.

"And we tried to pursue it," she added. "Your mother and I. When you were about four, we went to Atlanta and tried to find out if there was anything more. We saw the official Lanier report about that night. Just a little ol' piece of paper saying what had happened. Six lines. No more. You were handed over to child protective services, or whatever the people in Georgia called it back in those days. Your mother and daddy adopted you when you were only six days old. And that was all there was to it. When you were just a little over two years old, they moved back to Texas."

"You checked it out?" He found it hard to believe that there was no way to go any further with it.

"We tried. We tried very hard. You know your mother. She just thought if she could find your biological mother, she could do something good for the poor thing. She, Sally, was so thankful to have you. She stayed in touch with that agency—child protective services, whatever—for years to see if any woman ever inquired about that night. But nobody ever did."

Bern was surprised again. He had always assumed that if he ever wanted to know who his real parents were, he would be able to find out. It was a shock to discover that

that door had closed for good. In fact, it had never even been open in the first place.

"I suppose," Gina said, "that in a very real way, you really were born to Sally and Ted. I mean, you practically had no history at all before they took you in."

Bern just sat there. It wasn't what he'd been expecting.

He took a final sip of coffee to cover his surprise and disappointment. He said nothing, and in the silence he could hear the heavy old grandfather's clock that Gina had shipped back from Heidelberg on her first honeymoon ticking in the living room.

She saw that this abrupt end to his search had caught him off guard, and he knew that she realized that he had probably imagined a far more compelling history for himself.

"I guess you didn't expect this," she said softly.

"No, I didn't," he said.

"I wish I had something for you," she replied. She reached across and laid her hand on his, her right hand, which was never without the beautiful Colombian emerald ring that matched her eyes. "If I'd known you were coming to ask me that question," she added, "I would've made up a most wonderful lie for you, dear boy, something that would have made you happy."

Chapter 12

After visiting for another hour or so, Bern left Gina's in a taxi, leading her to believe that he was headed to the airport to fly back to Austin. She would have insisted he stay with her if she had known he was going to be in Houston overnight, but he wanted to be alone. He went to a pharmacy, where he bought a toothbrush and toothpaste, a plastic razor, and shaving cream. Then he checked into a hotel overlooking the West Loop Freeway.

He stood at the window, watching the traffic going north and south in the blistering heat of the summer afternoon, and thought about his situation. He was caught up in something very weird here. He had no doubts now that the genetic testing was going to confirm that the skull was indeed that of his twin brother. That was a huge leap of logic, he knew, but something told him it was inevitable.

He remembered Becca Haber saying that her husband (was he really?) had been an "orphan. Abandoned. Parents unknown." Now Bern had discovered that his own origins were exactly the same. He could not believe that this was a coincidence.

What about Becca herself? How much of her lie was a lie? What part of it was truth? The thing that concerned him about all of this was that someone was orchestrating it—if not Becca, then someone else. If someone wanted him to know that he had a twin brother who was now dead, why would they do it this way? What was this approach going to achieve that couldn't also have been achieved by simply coming to him and telling him?

According to Gina's story, Bern must have been separated from his brother at birth, because the hospital documents made no reference to another child. Or perhaps there had been two children left at the hospital, but someone there—or at child protective services—decided to split up the two boys and falsified the documents. Maybe they'd thought it would be easier to put the boys up for adoption as singles rather than as a pair. Was that sort of thing done? It seemed improbable, although conceivable.

Or had his biological mother separated the brothers at birth? And the reasons why she might have done such a thing could be endless.

Picking up the ballpoint pen and notepad from the hotel desk, he sat and jotted down these questions and others, then looked at them, as if staring at them would bring some clarity to the bizarre problems that they presented.

Did someone want him to investigate his brother's death? Had he been murdered? Who would have known about the twins? Someone at the hospital. Someone at child protective services. His biological mother? Or his father? Again, why wouldn't whoever was behind all this just come to him and reveal the truth and ask for his help? It seemed unnecessarily perverse to do it the way it was being done.

Or maybe none of these questions came even remotely close to what was happening. Maybe he had been swept into an unimaginable situation, as bizarre and unbelievable to him as Alice's aphasia had been to Becca Haber when he had tried to explain it to her. He could imagine now how she must have felt.

He stood up from the desk and went down the hall to get a bucket of ice. From the minibar, he took a miniature bottle of gin and some tonic and made a drink. No lime. He really wished he had a lime. He stared out the windows again. The freeway was packed now as the rush-hour traffic began to build up.

Picking up the telephone, he called home and listened to his voice mail. Several messages, though none from Becca Haber. But there was a curious one. A man's voice. He said only, "Important that you call me," then gave a number. No name. Houston area code.

Bern was beginning to lose patience with apparent coincidences. He took another drink of gin, picked up the telephone again, and dialed the number.

"Hello."

"Who is this?" Bern asked.

There was a momentary pause and then the man said, "Hello, Paul. How odd that you are in Houston."

"Who is this?" Bern repeated.

"Vicente Mondragón," the man said. "I knew your brother."

It was a strange moment. Though Bern had convinced himself that the skull that he had reconstructed in Austin was indeed that of his brother, to hear this idea—never before even imagined by him—confirmed so casually by a stranger was disorienting.

"I'm sorry," Mondragón said. "I know you must be horribly confused by what is happening to you. I would like to explain some of it to you, if I may. Can you meet with me this evening?"

Bern felt a flurry of emotions, some of which he couldn't explain. On the one hand, he was eager to talk to this man, but on the other, he was furious at being jerked around like this, and, rightly or wrongly, he immediately blamed this Mondragón for it. Also he was, irrationally, angry at the sound of Mondragón's voice, which was mellow and sophisticated. But there was also something else about it, too, a hint of a speech impediment. That, and an air of the imperious.

"Where? When?"

"I'll have someone pick you up at eight-thirty."

"Just give me an address. I'll be there."

"I'm afraid I'll have to insist," Mondragón said.

Chapter 13

Washington, D.C.

It was already dark as Gordon pulled into the parking lot of a low-dollar motel on Jefferson Davis Highway near Reagan International. He locked his car and went inside, where he found Kevern in the stale gloom of the cocktail lounge. He had commandeered a relatively quiet corner, despite the creepy piped-in music. Gordon quickly ordered a scotch and soda and Kevern tapped the tabletop for another one of whatever he was having. Gordon just wanted to get it over with.

"When's your flight?" he asked.

Kevern looked at his thick wrist.

"Coupla hours." He was wearing a white guayabera, and his hairy, muscular forearms rested on the table.

"Okay," Gordon said. "You've got your clearance for your jump start. The Bern deal's a go. But I'm telling you, they broke into a collective sweat before they checked off on it. Lots of discussion, some of it heated. Lots of agonizing."

Kevern nodded.

Gordon stared at him in the silly, moony light of the lounge. Expressway atmo. Jesus.

Kevern asked, "So . . . how'd you handle Mondragón's Tepito thing?"

Gordon didn't flinch. "I didn't."

Kevern was a sphinx, but Gordon knew that he understood the implications of two of Gordon's decisions. One, he'd given Kevern the break he wanted. The drug hit in Tepito was the official story and would remain the official story. If the Heavy Rain group had learned the truth, they would have pulled the plug on the operation. Two, the only way Gordon was able to push through the Bern operation was by not telling the group that Kevern had already initiated it six weeks earlier.

Gordon had covered for Kevern twice and had lied to the group twice by omission. Kevern owed him. But there was a flip side.

"Now, give me the downside," Kevern said.

Gordon didn't even offer a preface.

"If either the Tepito slaughter or your six-week jump on the Bern operation ever come to light," Gordon said, "I'll deny I knew anything about it. I'll swear to that in court. I'll swear to that before a special intelligence panel. I'll sign documents to that effect. You stepped out into the void all alone on this one, Lex, and whatever happens to you as a result, you'll have to deal with all by yourself."

Kevern's expression was a mixture of sobriety and sour amusement.

"Well, I appreciate it, Gordy," Kevern said. The irony of his remark wasn't lost on Gordon. "That's one of the benefits of being up here in Washington, isn't it?"

Gordon waited for the explanation that he knew Kevern wanted to lay out for him.

"I mean," Kevern said, "you think this little scheme just might work after all, don't you? Fuckin' twisty, you think. Twisty and, by God, maybe a real possibility. And if it does work, well, then all the talk up here is, 'Goddamn, old Gordy, he's an ace. You want a clandestine op to go sweet, get Gordy. Hell, let's promote him.'

"On the other hand, if this thing goes south, well, nobody can blame you. Your man got killed, for Christ's sake. And then you had the nuts to get innovative to try to save the thing. Hell, heroic effort. Slap on the back."

Kevern wasn't smiling. Gordon wasn't going to respond. He'd learned a long time ago about the interpretive possibilities of silence. He took a drink of the scotch.

Kevern, still not smiling, took a drink of whatever he was having.

Gordon could taste the lingering essence of scotch at the back of his sinuses.

"I've got to tell you, though," Gordon said. "You have to rein in Mondragón. The group's more indulgent these days about the contractors we deal with, but I'd say that Mondragón pushes the limit of their indulgence."

Kevern strung out a long grunt under his breath, as if he were straining at something.

"And I'm really going to worry about the limit of their indulgence," he said.

"Listen to me." Gordon lowered his voice and leaned forward. "These people sit on the NSC, for Christ's sake. You do something stupid, you bring them blowback, and they'll hang you out to dry so fast, your nuts will shrivel up like they were freeze-dried."

Kevern's thick neck seemed to swell even thicker when he was holding in his temper.

"Cobalt-sixty," he grunted slowly. "Cesium-one-thirty-seven. Plutonium. And that's just the little stuff. But I doubt if Baida's even bothering to put anything together at that level. We've been through this . . . shit"—he shook his head—"how many times? Intel points to something bigger. We think he's been at it—what, nearly two years? That points to a significant scheme, something complex. Complex means big.

"I'd piss off a whole army of NSCs to get Paul Bern next to Ghazi Baida, because the alternative is just too fucking freaky. And if Mondragón can help me do that, I don't much care who he shits on in the process, and I care even less about some Washington fatties' limits of indulgence."

This was precisely the kind of situation that drove Gordon mad. The intelligence about Ghazi Baida was grim and scary, like the rumors of a beast lumbering through the night in your direction. If you don't act on the rumor and it turns out to be a reality, then you're screwed and people will die in numbers so large that it will change the way historians will write about the century.

But if you do act, you do so with the full knowledge that the only way to stop the beast coming after you is to send your own beast out into the night to meet him. And your beast has to be fed and nurtured and indulged and treated in the same way you'd treat a friend or someone you respected. You have to collude with him, and abet. You have to get close enough to him to feel his warmth and smell his breath. And you have to do all of that knowing full well that he isn't any different from or any better than the beast you are sending him out to meet. Except that your beast doesn't want to eat you, and the other one does.

"Look," Gordon said, "all I'm saying is that you've got a reputation, Lex. Reputations have a way of gaining weight. When you get too heavy for those guys to carry, when it's just not worth the effort to them anymore, they'll cut you loose." He paused. "Just don't let Mondragón take it too far. There are limits."

"Not for Ghazi Baida," Kevern said evenly.

Gordon said nothing more. They'd been in this circle too many times to count, each taking his respective side and pushing it as far as he could. It made for constant tension. Maybe some people would call it balance, neither side giving anything to the other, but both of them keeping the other from indulging in extremes. It was exhausting, unrelenting, never ending.

He shifted his weight, and the subject.

"Tell me something," Gordon said. "Just for my own curiosity: How in the hell did you get Jude's skull?"

"One of the Koreans," Kevern said. "Before he got killed in the drug raid, we had the opportunity to put him through a little questioning. Turns out he'd dumped the bodies himself. Him and his buds. He took us out to a garbage dump in Nezahualcóyotl."

Kevern hesitated a beat, just enough for you to notice something if you were perceptive, but he kept it tough.

"There he was"—he shrugged—"all crumpled up under an old truck radiator and some other shit. The feral dogs had been at him. And the possums and cats. He was kind of scattered around. We got what we could. At first, we didn't believe the damn slope, didn't think it was him. And then we found his head. Rats had cleaned it slick, but they hadn't chewed on it. It was weird. Clean as a lab specimen. I knew the key dental markers, so . . .

"We shot the slope right there and left him where Jude had been. Kind of a swap. Made the rats happy."

"Shit," Gordon said. He took another drink. "And the woman who took the skull to Bern?"

"Paid and gone."

Gordon was going over all of it in his head again. Hell, he hadn't stopped going over it from the moment he first heard the plan from Kevern. When he presented it to the group the first time, they were dumbfounded; then the more they thought about it, the more it began to seem like a crazy kind of possibility to them. Especially in light of the potential horrors of the alternatives.

One of the deciding factors in favor of letting Kevern go ahead with it had been his successes in the past. He had that much of a reputation. He also had another kind of reputation. These were the things the group had weighed, and in the end, they went with the devil they knew, as wild as he was, because the devil they didn't know was just too appalling to imagine.

"And the idea . . . of doing it this way?" Gordon asked. "Sending him his brother's skull—"

"I told you," Kevern said. "The idea was to get the guy emotionally invested before we approached him. He's a forensic artist, Gordy. We wanted him to puzzle it out, rev up his curiosity. We wanted him motivated and steaming under his own momentum before we approached him."

"I know, I know, I remember that, but what if it just scares the hell out of him instead?"

Kevern shook his head. "No. Won't happen. We think he's too much like his brother. What if you'd done that to

Jude? You have any doubt about what would've happened?"

"But let's just ask ourselves this: What if he isn't convinced?" Gordon said.

Kevern leveled his eyes at Gordon. "Mondragón will convince him."

And that was exactly what Gordon had warned Kevern about. Jesus H. Christ, putting a psycho in charge of psy ops. Gordon looked across the table and held his tongue. With a sense of resignation, he decided to let Kevern go with it. In twenty-four hours, forty-eight at the most, they would know. He would let it go that far.

"Okay, fine," he said. "What about Jude's partner? Mejía's going to have to prep Bern, right? I'm guessing this is creating a little stress."

"Mejía's got guts. That's why we went through the big ordeal in the beginning, remember? These were two of the best people that ever went through training at the Farm. There're damn few like them. Mejía will do what's got to be done, and what's got to be done comes from me. Mejía's on board."

Where did these people come from? Gordon had monitored the five-month training ordeal that these two officers had gone through in preparation for Heavy Rain. At the time, it had seemed over-the-top, and Gordon had chalked that up to the overzealous, gung ho types at the Farm. That was their deal; he left it up to them.

But now it seemed that the extreme psychological preparations had been right on target. He didn't want to think what was waiting for Mejía and Bern as they tried to salvage the operation in the wake of Jude Lerner's death.

"One last thing, Lex." Gordon lifted his scotch and

finished it off. He put down the empty glass and then slowly shoved it across the table until it touched Kevern's beefy hand, and left it there.

"By wiping out Khalil's cell, you may have kept Baida from finding out that Jude was a spy, but it seems to me you've also created a big problem for yourself. How the hell are you going to find out who exposed Jude in the first place?"

He thought he saw a beat of hesitation in Kevern's eyes, but then maybe he only imagined it. Maybe he had wanted to see it just so he'd know that the guy had something left in him that could still be scared.

"We're working on that," Kevern said.

Chapter 14

The windows of the large Mercedes were dark-tinted, so Bern couldn't see where they were going. The driver, efficient, polite, and clearly also a bodyguard, explained that it was for Mr. Mondragón's security, and he even apologized for it, as if it were an impolite inconvenience for Bern.

As best as Bern could tell, they drove roughly in the direction of the posh River Oaks section of West Houston, and after about ten to fifteen minutes stopped at what seemed to be a security gate, and then went down a slope into what must have been an underground garage. They descended several floors, then entered an elevator and ascended thirty-four floors, where the elevator doors opened into a private entry hall. Mondragón had the whole floor, wherever they were.

The lighting was subtle here, and the furnishings were uncluttered, sleek, and elegant, with a predominant color scheme that seemed to favor dun and deep chocolate. A young Mexican woman who wore a simple black cocktail dress and was just as sleek as the decor ushered Bern into a living room situated on the corner of the building. Houston spilled out before him, glittering into the distant darkness.

The woman offered to get him something to drink, but Bern declined. She said Mr. Mondragón would be with him in a moment, and then she left.

Bern's attention was at first pulled to the dazzling view of the city laid out against the night as if for an exhibition, the lights shimmering in a single iridescent color spectrum of white and aquamarine and powder blue and beryl. But very quickly, his eyes caught sight of something more fascinating. Scattered about in the twilit room were a dozen or so clear acrylic cubes sitting on glistening black pedestals about chest-high. The cubes were slightly more illuminated than the rest of the room, so that they seemed to hover and float in the dusk. Displayed in each cube was a human face.

More fascinated than startled, Bern moved toward the first face and leaned in close to the acrylic case. The face, which appeared to be that of a man in his mid-twenties and of Chinese descent, stood on a pedestal of its own inside the box. The face was complete up to the hairline, including the ears, but the back half of the head was replaced by a smooth, black, and slightly concave surface upon which the face was mounted. It looked rather like the theatrical masks of Comedy and Tragedy.

But the reality of detail was extraordinary, and the face was the most lifelike creation Bern had ever seen. He could even see the pores in the flesh, and moisture in the caruncula lacrimalis, the pinkish tissue in the corners of the eyes. This was striking and gave Bern an uneasy feeling. The reality was . . . shocking. How in the hell could the artist have done this?

He moved to another face. A young woman, a Mayan Indian, he thought. A stunning creation. The subtle colors and texture of the tissue as it changed from one part of the face to the other, from cheek to lip to eyelid, were exceptional. .

He moved to a third, a blond woman, of German descent perhaps. The same subtle changes in flesh tissue were far superior to any sculpture he had ever seen.

"A marvelous thing, isn't it?" a voice behind him said, and Bern turned, to find a tall, thin man standing in a web of shadows about twenty feet away. His face was hidden, but Bern recognized the sophisticated voice and its odd impediment. Mondragón was dressed in a dark, elegantly cut suit. He wore a crisp white shirt that luminesced in the low, warm light of the room. His silk tie was a deep amethyst color.

"Yes," Bern said. "Someone has an extraordinary talent."

"Indeed." Mondragón paused. And then as he took another step toward Bern, he said, "Mr. Bern, I should have prepared you. As I move into the light, you will see that unlike these unfortunate people you see here"—he indicated the display cases with a gentle sweep of his arm—"who have a face but no body"—he took another step, which slowly brought him out of the shadows—"I suffer just the opposite misfortune . . . of having a body but no face."

Mondragón stepped into the pool of light between them, and Bern almost staggered. Nearly all of the epidermis had been removed from Mondragón's face, as well as much of the muscle tissue and cartilage. The place where

THE FACE OF THE ASSASSIN

his face had been was a nearly flat, raw, glistening plane. His eyes seemed to bulge from their sockets, an illusion due to the absence of eyelids and surrounding tissue. His nose was gone and the triangular nasal aperture that remained was covered with a translucent film that allowed a visual hint of the nasal spine. His cheeks were missing and much of the jaw tissue. His lips remained, but the cartilage where his chin had been was gone, so that the sharp lines of the jawbone immediately presented the framework of the skull.

He was standing directly under one of the hidden lights, and Bern could not make himself turn his gaze away from the truly hideous sight.

In comparison to his stripped-away face, Mondragón's lips appeared abnormally protuberant, though this, too, was an illusion, resulting from the absence of so much facial tissue. The reality was that Mondragón had no features except eyeballs and lips. Without these, Bern would not have known that this raw, glistening mass that he was looking at was the remains of a man's face.

"Get a good look, Mr. Bern. Accept your curiosity for what it is and satisfy yourself. I have accepted the fact that I am a spectacle, and the sooner you accept it, too, the sooner we can talk about far more important things."

Mondragón moved closer to Bern, who resisted an impulse to step back. Mondragón raised his hand and spritzed his face with a small mister he carried in his palm. The beads of moisture glittered momentarily in the shaft of light before dissipating.

"You can hardly see it," Mondragón said, "but my . . . facade"—his tone shifted to sarcastic irony—"is covered by a sheer, transparent membrane. A marvel of modern medicine. It's an antiseptic barrier. But it breathes and requires moisture. The spray also contains a necessarily potent analgesic."

He turned his head slightly, allowing Bern to get a look at him from a different angle. His naked eyes seemed to be operated by remote control. The facial flaying ran just below his hairline, in front of each ear, and dipped down just in front of his throat.

Bern could see that his lips had been carved around and isolated from the rest of the mess in a very precise way. A bit of the philtrum remained in the upper lip, as well as a bit of the mentolabial furrow in the lower. But the surrounding flesh had been peeled away up to the corners of the mouth, causing it to seem to float, almost unattached, just above the surrounding raw tissue. Obviously, Mondragón had suffered extensive nerve and muscle damage in this area, and he must have gone through a great deal of therapy to be able to speak with only this small degree of impediment.

"I am only weeks away from beginning a lifetime of surgeries and skin grafts," Mondragón's mouth said. He turned his walleyed stare toward Bern again. "I'll never have anything that you could call a proper face, but I will have a . . . sheath of sorts, to dampen the repulsion that others feel at seeing . . . this."

Bern didn't know what to say. He wasn't repulsed, but his fascination did make him self-conscious. Still, he stared. In some places, the excising had been deep, gouging into the subcutaneous tissue and well into the muscle itself. Without skin or features, it was impossible to convey an expression.

"Do you have any questions about . . . this?" Mondragón asked. He behaved almost as if he were in an anatomy class and the body in question had nothing to do with him at all. Except it did, which made his detachment seem abnormally cold, and his pretense that his flayed face was something they could get past in just a few moments of intense observation seemed, in itself, pathological.

Bern said nothing.

"Then we're through with the anatomy lesson?" Mondragón stared at him and spritzed his face again. "Good. This way, then."

Chapter 15

He turned and Bern followed him to a corner of the twilight near the windows that overlooked the city. In the near distance, downtown, one of the city's several satellite clusters of skyscrapers rose in the night sky. They went down one step to a grouping of armchairs and sofas that went right up to the glass wall. Mondragón sat in an armchair, his head and feet in shadow, a band of soft light falling obliquely across the middle of his elegantly attired body. Bern chose a chair at an angle to Mondragón.

From the surrounding shadows, the young woman appeared and set a drink on a short black acrylic pedestal at Mondragón's elbow. She bent down, her lovely face disappearing into the shadow with Mondragón's wraith. Bern heard the hissing of sibilants as she whispered. It was an odd tableau, two beautifully attired bodies, their heads lost in lightless, silent communion.

Then the young woman straightened up and walked out of the room.

"It's ironic," Mondragón said, "that you are a forensic artist . . . considering." He paused, then gestured toward the area behind Bern where the clear acrylic display boxes held their fine sculptures. "What do you think of my exhibition?"

"Beautiful," Bern said. "Extraordinarily well done."

"These are my favorites," Mondragón said. "I have others, nearly fifty altogether."

"Who sculpted them?"

"God." A soft aspirated laugh came from the shadow. "Those are real faces," Mondragón said.

Real faces. Bern couldn't help glancing toward the darkened space where the softly illuminated display cases floated in the murk. As he recalled the stippled texture of the skin and the delicate vermilion borders of the lips, a sense of the bizarre crept into the room.

"Plastination," Mondragón said. "Plastination."

"Gunther von Hagens?" Bern asked.

"Exactly." Mondragón was pleased that Bern knew who the man was. "He invented the process, replacing the water and fat in a specimen with a variety of polymers that render the tissue permanently preserved in a state of near reality. The process is rather complex. Von Hagens did not prepare these particular ones. They were done by someone with a more artistic sensitivity, a familiarity with aesthetics. She improved on the more crude medical specimens that are usually associated with von Hagens's work."

Though Bern was nearly as intimate with cadavers as a pathologist or a mortician, this display of faces struck him as ghoulish. Perhaps it was the motivation for the display, rather than the actual display itself, that was slightly creepy.

"It's remarkable," Mondragón said, "how thought-lessly we take our faces for granted."

He paused a moment, a break signaling a change of subject.

"I don't know who has involved you in this," Mondragón began. "I don't know who was responsible for sending you your brother's skull."

"How did you know about it, then?"

"Your brother was near the center of a complex intelligence operation," Mondragón said. "Among the people who orbit around such an enterprise as this, everyone knows everything. And no one knows much. This isn't a contradiction. It is, unfortunately, the reality of much of the intelligence world these days. This is why I know what has happened to you, but I don't know who did it. Or why."

"*Intelligence* operation? What do you mean?"

"Jude was an operations officer in the CIA," Mondragón said. "A special kind of operations officer."

Bern was taken aback. This was a hell of a revelation. Suddenly, he was skeptical.

"And how do you happen to know all this?"

"I'm an asset to the U.S. intelligence community in . . . several enterprises."

Bern didn't know what to say. So why was he here? What was going on here? Before he could speak, Mondragón did.

"Tell me," Mondragón said, "what do you intend to do about this?"

"Do about it?"

"Yes. Before you heard from me, where were you going to go with your knowledge, which will be confirmed by the DNA results tomorrow?"

Bern noted the positive use of the future tense, and he answered him honestly. "I don't know."

"I have a proposition, then," Mondragón said. "Let me help you find out who did this."

"Why?"

Mondragón hesitated. "Because I have suspicions, and if I'm right, then I have business with this person."

This sounded ominous, and Bern was getting the uneasy feeling that he should have declined the invitation to this meeting.

"I don't know that I care who did it."

"That's difficult for me to believe," Mondragón said, a hint of displeasure in his voice.

Mondragón studied him. It was a little disturbing to see so much of the man's eyeballs. With no eyelids, he couldn't blink, and Bern realized that the spritzing was also intended to supply moisture to his eyes.

"Your brother was involved in a part of that agency that didn't even exist a year ago," Mondragón said, reaching for his tall cocktail glass and bringing it to his lips. His eyeballs swiveled downward as he drank. Very deliberately, he set the glass on the short pedestal, and his eyeballs jerked back to Bern.

"He used to be a case officer in South America, but in the recent reorganization of things, some people with special talents were shifted to new . . . clandestine operations. Have you ever heard of the Triple Border region of South America?"

"I've heard of it."

"It's that area where the borders of Argentina, Brazil, and Paraguay come together. Jungle. Everything there is untamed—the animals, the vegetation, the people. Two cities have sprung up out of the jungle there, one on either side of the wide Paraná River: Ciudad del Este in Paraguay, and Foz do Iguaçú in Brazil. Ciudad del Este has been around for thirty years and has always been a retreat for smugglers and murderers and anyone seeking the comfort of a society of outcasts.

"The area has prospered as a refuge for international terrorists and criminals. Today, commerce is flourishing there: There are over two hundred thousand people, shopping malls, apartment buildings. Everything. And everything is lawless. Chaos lives there, and she is thriving."

Mondragón stopped and spritzed his face, and again the mist dazzled momentarily in the angle of the dim lights, then disappeared.

"The underworld there—if one can distinguish such a thing in such a place—is run by Asians and Middle Eastern criminals. There are tens of thousands of Muslims there, among them Hezbollah terrorists. But they are not alone. This lawless place is the refuge of Hamas, as well, and the Aryan Nations. And the IRA. And Colombian rebels. This place is the lair of the scourge of the earth. They fester there, breed there, give birth there."

Mondragón picked up his glass again, drank, and put it back. There was a moment when his head came into the dim light, and the horror of his butchered face was shocking in the surrounding elegance. His eyes and lips were startlingly out of place in the featureless mass of moist, decorticated flesh.

"U.S. intelligence has known about this cesspool for a decade, but it wasn't a primary concern. Just something they kept their eyes on. Now, of course, it seems more important to them. The Hezbollah element there being the most important of all.

"Your brother was involved in an operation that was trying to locate a Hezbollah operative named Ghazi Baida. Baida is a terrorist strategist, and increasingly reliable intelligence has placed him in various cities throughout Latin America in the last ten months: Buenos Aires, Montevideo, Rio de Janeiro, Asunción, and . . . Ciudad del Este.

"The U.S. intelligence community was very alarmed about these reports, and they initiated an intense search for Baida. Your brother was at the heart of an operation to locate him. His work placed him in enormously risky situations. Six weeks ago, he disappeared."

"Six weeks? Only six weeks?"

"Yes. That surprises you?"

"A little. I was told—"

"By this woman who brought the skull?"

"Yes . . . that he'd disappeared four months ago."

"No," Mondragón said curtly. "It was only six weeks ago."

All of this was coming fast. Bern's curiosity was taking him further than he had imagined it would. Common sense should have kicked in long ago. It would have said: Go to your lawyer and tell him someone has brought you your twin brother's skull in a box, a brother you never knew you had. Then ask him what in the hell you should do now.

Mondragón leaned forward slightly in his chair, nearly enough to expose his face. He seemed to want to speak carefully.

"Mr. Bern," he said, "your brother was . . . important in his secret world. It is a small world, one in which decisions are made and things are done that have ramifications in times and places far removed from him. The people he worked for knew more about him than he knew about himself. That is not uncommon in his profession. That is the way his world handles its business. He knew that, and he accepted it."

The implication was that Bern would be wise to do the same.

"Look," Bern said. "All this is a good story, but I don't know who in the hell you really are. I don't know if you're telling me the truth about . . . my brother, about his being an intelligence officer, about the CIA . . . about anything. I don't even know if I should be sitting here talking to you. This doesn't exactly feel right to me."

" 'Feel right'?" Mondragón's tone was laden with disdain. "I see. Well, Mr. Bern, tell me, what would you require to make you comfortable with talking to me and believing what I have to say?"

"What would I require?" That was a good question, and it was like calling a raise in a poker game. Did Bern even want to stay in? He guessed so. Instead of walking away from this, here he was talking to a man without a face and allowing himself to be drawn, almost moment by moment, deeper and deeper into what any fool could see was a dangerously murky business.

And yet, even as it was happening, he wondered if his willingness to continue with this had something to do with his newly discovered second self. Did the same elements in Jude's DNA that had made him seek a life in this foggy world of espionage that Mondragón was describing now provide Bern the wherewithal to follow him . . . a little way, at least? It was a gravitational pull that was difficult to resist.

"I know a guy in the Houston Police Department's Intelligence Division," Bern heard himself say. "If he told me I was in good company, I'd believe him."

"What is his name?" Mondragón asked.

"Mitchell Cooper."

Mondragón nodded. "I'm going to leave you for a little while and make a phone call. When I return, we can continue to talk."

He rose to his feet and walked away into the shadows, and almost immediately the young woman appeared again. This time, she actually seemed to see Bern and smiled.

"I understand you may want something to drink," she said.

She was right about that. "Tanqueray and tonic," he said. "And a good slice of lime, if you have it."

She nodded and left. Bern took a deep breath. This thing did not reach a point of correction. It just kept going and going further out into the unknown, breaking all bonds of gravity as it went. What was going to bring him back?

The woman returned with his drink, and he sat alone, waiting, drinking. The gin was welcome. Several times, he turned and looked back toward the floating faces. Jesus. He stared at the city glittering in the darkness behind the chair where Mondragón had been sitting. This was an evening he wasn't likely to forget very soon.

He had almost finished his drink when the woman

reappeared and approached him, handing him a cell phone.

"Mr. Cooper," she said.

Bern took the phone, clearing his throat. "Mitchell?"

"Yeah, Paul. You okay?"

"I'm fine, sure. I appreciate the call."

"Well, look, I, uh, I guess you know what this is all about. I just got a call from a friend of mine, who's going to have to remain nameless. He, uh, he's CIA, Paul. Maybe you actually know more here than I do."

He paused, inviting a response, but Bern didn't seize the opportunity. Cooper went on.

"Anyway, I guess the point is that I've known this man a lot of years, in intelligence work, and he's . . . reliable. I trust him. I understand you need to know that. I'd trust him with whatever I had to. He told me that you're talking to a guy—wouldn't give me his name—and my man says he's to be trusted, too. You can believe him, okay?"

"Yeah, okay, then."

"Now listen," Cooper added. "That being said, I don't know what's going on there, but . . . well, those people, these are curious times. Lots of hocus-pocus going on in the intelligence world right now. Just be careful. Whatever. Anyway, I want you to know that all I'm vouching for is that I trust this guy who called me. I, personally, am not vouching for whoever you're talking to. I mean, I can't do that, obviously." He hesitated. "You get what I'm saying here?"

"I do. Sure. I appreciate it."

"Yeah. Okay. I guess that's it, then. . . . You sure you're okay? You sound kind of funny."

"No, I'm fine, Mitchell. I appreciate the help. Sorry that we had to bother you."

"Well, okay. No problem from this end. I hope it's what you wanted to hear."

That was it. Bern handed the cell phone back to the woman, who had been waiting, and she went away.

Chapter 16

Mondragón appeared immediately after the woman's departure and returned to his dark leather chair, resuming his position in the partial shadows. An inch or so of the white cuffs of his shirtsleeves glowed in the low light as they rested on the arms of the chair. Bern could just make out the whites of Mondragón's lidless eyeballs through the slanting shadow.

"That was impressive," Bern admitted.

"Do you feel better now?"

"I feel better. I can't say I feel comfortable."

This elicited no response from Mondragón. They sat in silence a moment, and then Mondragón said, "You will find this interesting, Mr. Bern. Your brother was also an artist. It was his profession as well as his cover. He had what I think you would call classical training. He studied in London. I don't remember where exactly. He was a very good draughtsman. His nudes were elegant, more than mere academic exercises. They were . . . human. But he excelled at portraiture. His portraits were exceptionally fine,

I think. He got behind the eyes of his subjects, into their minds. I think it was his ability to see . . . underneath a face that enabled him to excel as an intelligence officer."

An unfamiliar feeling surged through Bern, sending a pungent taste into his mouth. Jesus. Strangers in everything but the moment of birth, he and Jude had gravitated to an artistic medium that focused on the face, a human attribute that was famous for its infinite variety, except in rare cases such as his own.

"You are, you know, remarkably like him," Mondragón went on. "Aside from the obvious, there are things about you that are eerily evocative of your brother. Sometimes it's . . . just a gesture, the way you turn your head, or . . ."

Mondragón's voice trailed off, and Bern was surprised to feel a sudden deep sorrow. It was a baffling but undeniable moment of yearning for something that could never be. If only he could have talked with Jude. The questions he would have asked flooded his thoughts, swelling and multiplying into an explosion of curiosity. And regret, regret that this extraordinary experience of having had a brother, of having been a twin, was completely beyond his reach by the time that he realized that it had even been a part of his life in the first place.

Bern had always had the reputation of being something of a loner, and now this vague sense of isolation that he had lived with, and which he had simply accepted as being his own peculiar kind of individuality, was cast in an entirely different light. There was no way that he could have known that somehow, in some tragic and inexplicable way, he had been robbed, almost from the beginning, of his second self.

"Mr. Bern." Mondragón's voice had a sterner tone now, which caught Bern's attention. "Paul," he said then, seeking to redefine their relationship. Then he paused to spritz his face and eyes. When the sparkling mist settled out of the slanting light, Bern felt a change in the tension in the room.

"As you must surely see by now," Mondragón continued, "you are in a unique position. All the more so when you consider your situation from the point of view of your brother and his role in the unfolding events in Mexico. And more to the point, what was left undone when he was killed."

Mondragón paused and slowly, calmly clasped his hands together in his lap. It seemed a gesture at once careful and preparatory.

"Whether he was present or not, we don't know," Mondragón said, "but we are sure that Ghazi Baida was responsible for Jude's death."

He raised a hand; the mist flew through the light.

"I will tell you something, Paul, a critical truth about hunting men. War has a thousand faces. Behind the public face of war, behind the florid rhetoric of politicians who whip up the public will to move armies and navies in pursuit of other men, the truth is that a man like Ghazi Baida is eventually brought to ground because another man possesses a relentless desire to see him brought to ground. It has always come down to the fearful, sweaty efforts of one man against another man. It has always been, and always will be, personal."

He paused, and when he spoke again, his voice carried forcefully from the shadow and the faceless head, driven by more than breath and discipline.

"Surely you see where this is going," he said. "We need your help, the kind of help that only you can give us. We want to use your face to find Ghazi Baida. All you have to do is cooperate with our people, who will guide you. You will not be asked to be a soldier or an assassin. You will not be asked to perform heroic and fearsome feats. Just lend us Jude's face and body. Help us finish what he began."

Bern couldn't believe what he was hearing. The dismay must have showed on his face. Mondragón expanded.

"We need to convince Baida that Jude is still alive," Mondragón said. "Jude needs to be seen. He and Baida had established a relationship. Jude had accomplished an astonishing thing, convincing Baida to reveal himself to him. But more than that, he had convinced Baida to trust him—at a certain level, of course, not unreservedly, not wholly, but at least enough to engage in an enterprise with him. We need to keep that connection alive."

"That's impossible," Bern said. "It's . . . it wouldn't work for ten minutes."

"It would."

"It couldn't."

"Why?"

"How could it, for Christ's sake?"

"Several answers. One: the sheer improbability of it. Who would believe, at first blush, that a man who looks like Jude, talks like Jude, acts like Jude, has the same artistic talents as Jude—and, God, even has the same DNA as Jude—who would believe that he would not *be* Jude? The absurdity of such a thing provides us with our greatest advantage."

"At first blush?"

"Yes! That's the second answer: You will not be in a sit-

113

uation in which you will have to portray Jude in the sense that you will have to live as Jude, interact with others as Jude. No, we simply want you to present the physical Jude to observers. You need to be seen as Jude, and little more. It is not necessary that you be Jude for an extended length of time."

"What's the objective? Exactly."

"For now, just reestablish contact with him. Help us buy time."

"You're right about one thing," Bern said, feeling more agitation than he was showing. "It's an absurd idea."

"No," Mondragón insisted. "It isn't."

But Bern didn't want to have anything to do with this. Why hadn't an official officer of the CIA come to him to make this plea? Why this roundabout way of getting word to him that Mondragón was legitimate? He didn't care whose asset Mondragón was; he knew that the further you got from the official business of anything, the closer you got to the kinds of things that never saw the light of day. He didn't want to have anything to do with that kind of darkness.

He looked at the elegantly dressed Mondragón, this man decapitated by a shadow, and he saw the epitome of menace. This was the other side of the looking glass, but instead of encountering the Queen's nonsense, he was looking at the devil's creep show.

"There's got to be a better way," Bern said.

"No. This is the best way. It's . . . an unbelievable opportunity. Jude had an identical twin! And the CIA had the good sense to keep it a secret from the very moment they discovered it. Even from Jude himself."

Bern mentally lunged at this revealing slip.

"He didn't know?"

Mondragón tried to cover his hesitation by responding in a slow, calmer voice. "That's what it says in the piece of the file they gave me. He didn't know."

" 'Piece' of the file."

"This is the CIA, Paul. 'Need to know' is a mantra with these people. Everyone accepts it."

"How the hell did he not know?"

Silence. This time, Bern sensed the stark eyeballs staring back at him from the impenetrable shadow. He felt another change in the energy in this room of faces, and he didn't like what he felt.

"Look," Bern said, and he sat forward in his armchair, "this isn't for me. You're going to have to find another way to do your business."

"You need to reconsider, Paul."

"No, I don't. I'm not Jude. Nobody's paying me to do this shit."

"Oh, if money is a factor—"

"No. It's not. I wouldn't do it for any amount of money. I appreciate the fact that this guy's a terrorist and needs to be stopped, but you're talking about something that requires special training, special skills. And I don't have either of those."

"Your face," Mondragón said. "Your DNA. These are the things that no other man on earth can bring to us. How much more specialized could you be?"

Bern was shaking his head. "This is CIA business, for Christ's sake. This is way past dicey. This feels suicidal, and I don't want any part of it."

He stood.

"Just a minute, Paul," Mondragón said with chilling

equanimity. The young woman appeared, handed a folder to him, then waited. "I have another file," he said.

Bern hesitated.

"Sit down," Mondragón said politely. "Please."

Bern remained standing.

Mondragón opened the file folder. "This pertains to Dana and Philip Lau," Mondragón said. "And their daughter, Alice."

Bern must have been expected to respond at that moment, because Mondragón paused, as if waiting for a reply. But Bern was struck speechless. He was afraid. He didn't know why yet, but he knew instinctively that he should be. He sat down.

"Here's the way it will work," Mondragón said. "During Alice's visits to you, she often swims. She changes clothes in the lower bedroom of your home, the one nearest to the terrace door that leads down to the cove. Alice is a healthy young girl with a vivid imagination. She . . . fantasizes and sometimes she . . . caresses and . . . gratifies herself in that bedroom when she changes clothes. The pictures we have are very clear . . . and explicit."

Bern was paralyzed. Mondragón went on.

"Over the years, Jude had occasional disciplinary problems. A couple of years ago, he had a mistress. As insurance for us, she was able to collect a quantity of semen for our safekeeping. That semen, of course, shares your identical DNA.

"You will remember that a few weeks ago, Alice misplaced a swimsuit. Her mother was frustrated, but she has lost them before. They bought another. Never gave it another thought."

Bern's ears were ringing, his mind frozen.

"These are the components that comprise the story of the end of your life, Paul," Mondragón said, and then he fell silent, letting it soak in.

Bern reeled, his mind flickered, and his thoughts lurched into the past, into the imagined future, into a nightmare.

"Something like this," Mondragón went on, "has no satisfactory resolution. It isn't possible. Statutory rape, and the death of a disturbed girl's innocence. Devastated parents. The betrayal and destruction of a long and close friendship. The end of your anonymity and reputation. Our people are very good, and the evidence would be incontrovertible.

"But even if, somehow by some miracle, you were able to escape the facts," Mondragón elaborated, "the media coverage and the imagination of the public would condemn you. Maybe his lawyers got him off, they would say, but we know that he did something terrible to that poor girl." Mondragón sat perfectly still. "The birth of suspicion, Paul, leaves an indelible stain. Nothing cleans it."

Silence.

Mondragón held out the folder. "Would you like to see the pictures of Alice?"

The young woman took the folder from Mondragón and handed it to Bern, then disappeared.

Bern had to look. At least he had to identify Alice. He would be an idiot if he simply took Mondragón's word for something like this.

With unsteady hands, he slid the photos out of the envelope and looked. They were of Alice, of course.

They were stills from a video recording. Video. The sons of bitches.

He couldn't look at more than a couple of them, and then he dropped the envelope and the pictures on the floor beside his chair.

"Jesus Christ," he said, and he leaned forward, his elbows on his knees, and buried his face in his hands. Mondragón cruelly remained silent, and Bern felt as if he had fallen into hell.

Finally, Mondragón spoke.

"But, as they say, it doesn't have to end like this. Those photographs never have to be seen by anyone. What I'm asking you to do, after all, is not an impossibility. Think about it. If these pictures were ever to get out, what wouldn't you give to have the chance to make this choice all over again? Pretending to be your brother would seem like a godsend, and a small price to pay to make it all go away."

Chapter 17

Bern sat on the edge of his bed in his underwear and stared out the window of his darkened hotel room. It was 2:40 in the morning, and the traffic on West Loop South was sparse. The night sky was hazy with moisture, and the lights that stretched eastward toward downtown receded into the misty distance. He was nowhere near sleep.

His thoughts cycled over and over and over variations of the same three concerns: his fear of the exposure of the photographs (the storm of emotions that this would unleash for the Laus was almost unbearable to consider), his anger and frustration at being extorted without any recourse, and his inability to imagine or prepare for what he was going to have to do to for Mondragón.

He wasn't a total innocent. He had heard and read about the contractors that U.S. intelligence used all over the world with increasing regularity. He knew nothing of their legal standing, but he knew enough to understand that they were proxies for a reason. Somehow they managed to squeeze between the threads of the legal fabric to do things for the CIA that the CIA didn't want to get caught doing themselves.

He had no doubt that an end-run effort around Mondragón's extortion would trigger the anonymous release of the photographs, and then he could kiss his old life goodbye. Essentially, he had no choice.

And he grieved for Alice. Just knowing that those pictures were out there somewhere and that someone could look at them as much as they wanted made him ache for her. She would be so ashamed. And Dana and Phil. Goddamn Mondragón.

It was a spooky feeling, too, that someone had been in his house and installed digital video-surveillance cameras in the lower bedroom, and he hadn't even had a clue. This was scary stuff.

Midmorning the next day, Bern picked up a printout of his own DNA string at the private laboratory off North Loop West. From there, he went to the GTS labs in the Texas Medical Center, where the skull's DNA was being sorted out. After last night, the result of the DNA reading had even more importance for him than it had before.

He sat in a small sterile room with a humming fluorescent light while a molecular geneticist with a pallid complexion and round eyeglasses of pinkish plastic examined and compared the two strings. Bern noticed that the pocket of the doctor's crisp white lab coat was still starched closed.

"Monozygotic twins. Yeah." The doctor looked up. "Identical. Yeah."

The flight back to Austin occupied a time zone all its own, and the fifteen-mile drive from the airport to his house on the lake was completely lost to him.

As soon as he got back to the house, he parked the TR3 in the garage and went up and checked his messages in the kitchen. He took a flashlight out of the drawer under the telephone and went down the steps to the guest bedroom that opened out onto the terrace. He stood in the middle of the room and looked at the wall opposite the French doors. The garage was on the other side of the wall. That was the likeliest spot. Near the ceiling.

He dragged a chair over to the wall and stood on it. Starting at the left corner of the room, near the ceiling, he shined the flashlight flat against the wall and carefully followed every inch. And then there it was. A little smooth spot about the size of his thumbnail. Color was the same, but the texture was too smooth. Drywall texturing was hard to duplicate in a patch.

With his arms, he measured the distance from the intersecting wall to his left, and then he went upstairs and then down again to the garage. He climbed up on the workbench that was built against the bedroom wall and measured from the front of the garage. And there it was. The bastards hadn't even bothered to patch the hole in the garage. A hole the size of the diameter of his thumb, and next to it a shelf with cans of paint pushed to one side, where they had set something.

He looked out the garage door to the rock wall and the lake beyond. It wouldn't have been that hard at all. Easy, in fact. Shit.

Back in the kitchen, he opened a bottle of Shiner beer and made a ham sandwich. He went outside to the terrace and sat at the table under the arbor while he ate. He gazed at the lake sparkling in the summer light and thought about what he was going to have to do.

After he finished, he put the dishes into the dishwasher and walked over to the studio. As he stepped inside and breathed in the familiar odors, his eyes fell on the partially dismantled skull of his brother.

His brother.

Would this ever seem real to him? Monozygotic. Who in the hell had their mother been? What in God's name had happened to her that scattered them in those critical days of their infancy?

He walked over to the workbench. The weird suspicion that had gripped him last time he saw this skull—that he had some mysterious connection to it—had now been replaced with a scientific certainty. Now there a total reorientation regarding himself and this incredible relic, and he could hardly bring himself to touch it.

But more than that, he didn't want it to wear his by-the-numbers reconstruction when he knew that it should have his own face. And then an astounding thought hit him: If fate had been otherwise, if he had had the opportunity six weeks ago to reach out and touch this same human bone, he would have touched the living face of his identical twin.

It was approaching dusk by the time Bern finished thoroughly cleaning off the clay face and reattaching the jaw to the skull. Now he retrieved an old ebony box that he had bought in Paris when he was a student studying anatomy. The box smelled richly of oil paints and seemed an appropriate resting place for Jude's skull.

He dragged some old green velvet scraps out of a storage cabinet and cut a piece to fit in the bottom of the box. Then he set the skull inside and loosely wadded more velvet around it for protection. He put the box on a bookshelf among his art books.

He deliberately had avoided drinking while he was doing all of this, because he was thinking about what he was going to do, and he wanted to be lucid. But now he poured a gin and tonic from the cabinet in the studio, tossed in some ice and a fat wedge of lime, and took his cell phone to the sofa. He turned out all the lights so he could watch the clean arrival of night and dialed the sterile number Vicente Mondragón had given him.

The phone rang several times, and Bern tried to imagine why it wasn't answered right away. What did a man like Mondragón do at dusk, without a face?

"Hello, Paul," Mondragón said.

"Okay," Bern said, "I'll do it."

"Good," Mondragón said quickly, although without seeming eager. "Then you can leave immediately?"

"No. I've got to make arrangements for someone to look after the house. Maybe by tomorrow afternoon. I'll try to book a flight."

"Not necessary. I'll fly you down. It's important that you arrive at Jude's place at night. We don't want anyone to see you for several days, until you've had some time to be briefed."

"How does that happen?"

"We have someone who knew Jude very well. That person will have everything you will need to be briefed. Be ready by seven o'clock in the evening. Someone will pick you up and take you to a charter plane. It's a two-hour flight. In Mexico City, someone will meet you and take you to Jude's place in Condesa."

"I hope to hell this is something I can handle."

"We are well aware that you are not a professional, Paul. We'll do everything we can to make this work for you. Everyone is working toward the same goal."

"You want this guy to think Jude's still alive," Bern said. "You've got to know that this kind of thing can't be taken too far."

"Yes, we do know that. But we are going to take it as far as we can."

And without another word, Mondragón ended the call.

Chapter 18

Mexico City

The Dessault Falcon settled down through the clouds and floated into the light field of Mexico City's dusk. From this distance, the ancient city's lights were a dull coppery glow, a hue that added to the mystery of the six-hundred-year-old metropolis.

Bern sat forward in the cabin, ignored by two men who had entered at the last moment, walked past him without acknowledging him, and sat together at the back of the small aircraft. As the Falcon banked and descended toward Toluca, forty-two miles west of Mexico City—private and charter jets were not allowed at Benito Juarez International—the grid of Mexico City's avenues and boulevards emerged out of the light shimmer as the city became three-dimensional.

The Falcon whispered onto the tarmac at Toluca and came to rest at the dark end of a runway far from the terminals. Bern glanced back at the two men, who were now silent and staring straight at him without expression. He left the aircraft and descended the steps to a waiting Mercedes, where a door was being held open for him by a young Mexican man with a snappy suit and a ready smile.

"Mr. Bern?" he asked.

"Yes."

"Welcome to Mexico."

The young man sat on the passenger side as the driver maneuvered into the traffic, heading to Mexico City. There was no conversation during the hour's drive, but occasionally the young man spoke softly into a cell phone when it blinked at him, or when he placed a call by punching a single number.

Once they were in Mexico City, Bern gazed out his window at the famous city of contrasts. The summer-evening rains had left the streets washed and glistening, but the grime remained in the shadows, and this was a city of shadows. Beauty was a queen here, but a dying queen. This city of the twenty-first century owed much of its undeniable charm to the nearly seven hundred years of its past. The allurements and the enchantments remained, but they were dressed in melancholy.

Condesa was the gentrified neighborhood of Mexico's elite when it flourished during the 1920s and 1930s. It was rich in fine examples of Art Deco architecture. During the latter half of the twentieth century, it had fallen on hard times, but it was now something of a cause célèbre with young artists, writers, and foreigners who had moved into the area and had begun a serious movement to save the exquisite architecture. Now the neighborhood was booming with sidewalk cafés and hip new restaurants springing up everywhere.

The heart of Condesa was the lush and beautiful Parque México, which had been built on the site of a nineteenth-century racetrack. The park was oval and was surrounded by two concentric oval avenues, the innermost of which was Avenida México, into which the Mercedes now turned. The car cruised slowly under the jacarandas that were planted on the outermost ring of the park and formed a canopy over the encircling sidewalk and street.

After they had gone nearly half the distance of the park's length, the driver pulled to the curb on the park side of the street. He cut the motor.

The young man who had held the door open for him now turned and put his arm on the back of his seat and looked over it at Bern.

"He lived right here"—he jerked his head toward the building across the narrow street—"the one with the leaded-glass doors."

Bern looked out the car window at the building's entryway, where a slightly amber light came through the frosted-glass panels, throwing the Deco design of the leading into clean relief. The building was narrow, three stories, its Deco facade different from its neighbors on either side.

"Second and third floors. There's no one there now," the young man said, speaking softly. He reached over the seat and handed Bern a ring with two keys on it. "Hang on to them. They are a special kind, and it'll be hell to replace them if you lose them. The fat one is for the outside door. The other is for the front door of the apartment."

"So I go in there. Then what?"

"Someone will contact you. Don't answer the door. Not yet. People will see the lights and think that he's returned."

"They'll wonder why I'm not answering."

He shrugged. "Let them wonder."

"That's it?"

"This is all we're supposed to do, bring you here, give you the key, tell you not to answer the door, tell you someone will contact you."

Bern nodded. "Okay. Thanks."

He opened the back door of the car and got out. Avenida México was little more than a narrow lane. He crossed it in a few steps, and when his feet hit the sidewalk on the other side, he heard the Mercedes start up. He didn't look back as he heard it pull into the street and drive away.

An awning made of wrought iron and inset with square glass blocks hung over the front doors, the frames of which were made of a deep amber wood. Bern put the key in the lock and went into a small entry with a tessellated floor of black-and-white tiles. There was another frosted-glass door in front of him, and to his left the stone stairs ascended sharply in a turn to the second floor.

He started up the stairs, his shoes scraping softly on the stones. For some reason, he counted them, but when he reached the top, he didn't even remember how many there had been. The landing was small, illuminated by the soft glow from a globed light over the door. A window looked out on Parque México. There was a portrait, a pencil drawing, on the wall next to the doorbell. It depicted a young man whose hairstyle and clothes seemed to place him in the 1930s. No signature.

Bern put the second key in the door, unlocked it, and pushed the door open. He stood there a moment, looking into the darkness. The anxiety he felt had nothing to do with fear. It was the anticipation of walking into a paradox, the life and world of a stranger he knew intimately. Already he could smell the rooms in the darkness in front of him, and they reminded him of the apartments in Paris that he had lived in, the odors of old wood and paints and canvas and cigarettes . . . and, yes, of the faint presence of women.

He fumbled along the wall and found the light switch. He was in a small entry hall, which had glass panels above the wood wainscoting. There was mail scattered all over the floor. But not enough to be six weeks' worth. Someone had been picking it up every few days, he guessed.

He closed the door behind him, stepped over the mail, and went into the front room. Comfortable furniture, the walls covered with framed pictures—drawings, oil paintings, pastels, along with some black-and-white photographs. He went straight to the artworks. They seemed to be of every age and era, but a few contemporary ones bore the signature of Jude Teller. Eagerly, he looked closely at these. Jude had been good, as Mondragón had said. His classical training was indeed evident in the portraits, and even in the few nudes. His eye was fresh, and his style was sure and confident.

Art magazines were scattered about the room, and a few small sculptures stood here and there. One bust. Bern went over to it. Bronze. This, too, bore Jude's signature, a woman's head, as well as her neck and the tops of her breasts. As he bent down and studied the work closely, he was surprised by the admiration, and maybe even a twinge of envy, that he felt. Jude had been very good indeed, and Bern doubted if he could have accomplished the quality of animation that this bust exhibited. Jesus.

He turned away and scanned the rest of the room.

Every wall bore some kind of artwork. The room was also divided by wainscoting with glass above. On one side, a stairwell ascended, turning to the right. A short, wide corridor led past a dining room, a bathroom across the hall, and then to a large kitchen that looked out over an inner courtyard on the ground floor.

Bern returned to the front room and went up the stairs, turning on lights as he went. The stairs opened into a spacious third-floor studio scattered about with the paraphernalia of an artist's craft and smelling of wood and resins and oil paints. A row of windows looked out over the treetops of Parque México.

There was a bedroom off the far side of the studio; it was a long one, with windows on the street end that had the same view of the park as the windows in the studio. The other end of the room opened onto a rooftop terrace. This was Jude's bedroom. His clothes were in the closets. Bern checked the sizes in the suits and the shirts. Same as his. The styles and colors would suit his own tastes exactly, and they could easily have been found in his own closet.

He went to the bathroom and stood at the sink. Jude's razor was there on the marble countertop in a green glass bowl, just the right shape for it. There was a tall, cylindrical black-and-gold tin of talcum powder. An amber bottle of cologne. Bern picked it up and swept it under his nose. It was the saddest fragrance he could imagine.

The place was instantly saturated with familiarity, as if he were in his own home after his own death, longing to be alive again, and sad beyond expression to have left so much behind.

Suddenly, he thought he heard the door downstairs.

Startled, he held his breath and touched the sink to ground himself, to steady a slight dizziness.

"Jude?" A woman's voice. "Hey," she called, "when did you get in?"

He heard the door close and her footsteps crossing the wooden floors of the rooms. She started up the stairs.

Chapter 19

Bern froze, looking at himself in the mirror as he listened to her footsteps ascending the stairs and growing nearer. What the hell should he do? Her footsteps hit the landing in the studio.

"Jude? Why did you just step right over your mail?"

He heard her starting across the studio, having seen the light on in the bedroom, he supposed. Turning away from the sink, he hurried out of the bathroom and across the bedroom, reaching the door to the studio while she was still a few feet away.

"Hey," she said, breaking into a huge smile as he stepped out of the bedroom. She came up to him and kissed him with unexpected gentleness and then embraced him tightly, nuzzling his neck.

He put his arms around her, her shape new and strange to him. He was tense, half-expecting her to recoil at any moment, realizing he wasn't Jude. But she didn't.

"It's been too long," she whispered, her face still against his neck. He could smell her hair, and he felt the softness of her breasts against him. He recognized her face from the bronze bust, and from two of the nude studies among the drawings downstairs.

There was a moment's hesitation before she pulled away and looked at him quizzically, her arms still around him, her face just inches from his.

"Are you okay?"

She was Mexican, in her early thirties. Her shoulder-length black hair was thick, parted casually in the center, and framed a noticeably asymmetrical face. Her eyes were large and black, the pigment of the surrounding flesh subtly shaded. Her lips were full and evenly proportioned, with a distinctive philtrum in the upper one that was immediately appealing. There was a very slight upturn at the outside corners of her mouth that did not suggest a smile.

All of this he captured in the brief moment that she had her arms around him, her face so close to his that his first instinct was to bend and kiss her.

"Just tired," he managed to say, again expecting to see in her eyes a startled reaction to the sound of his voice. But there was none.

"Well, let's have a drink," she said, letting her arms slide down along the sides of his body, as though she couldn't get enough of touching him. "Let's catch up on what's been happening." Her voice was in the lower registers, not husky, but mellow.

She walked across the studio. She was high-hipped and wore a knee-length charcoal skirt and a white blouse.

"I was at Claudio's all afternoon," she said wearily as she opened a wooden cabinet near the windows and took out a green bottle of gin. Next to it was a small refrigerator, from which she took ice and then dropped a few cubes into each glass as she closed the door with her hip.

"How was your trip?" she asked, sloshing some gin into each glass. She opened a small paper bag that she must have brought with her and took out a lime, which she sliced. She squeezed the two wedges simultaneously, one with each hand, into the glasses.

She turned around and held out a glass for him, shaking her dark hair out of her face. They looked at each other.

"What," she said, "is something the matter?"

This felt impossible to him, but he managed to make himself go over to her and take the glass. Who the hell was this? Did she live with Jude? He hadn't thought to check for women's clothes in Jude's bedroom. Why hadn't Mondragón at least mentioned that Jude was living with someone?

He had to say something, for God's sake.

"And what were you doing at Claudio's?" he asked. He was so self-conscious that he thought his voice had changed. He was afraid he would start sweating.

She gave him a strange look. "What was I doing?"

Shit.

Silence. He sipped the gin. What the hell was he going to do? Where was the person who was supposed to be here to prevent this sort of thing from happening until he'd been briefed?

She was studying him.

"The usual," she said, sipping her gin and looking at him over the rim of the glass, her dark eyes full of suspicion now, alert with caution.

"Tell me about it," he said, moving to the windows to look out, hoping to cover his discomfort.

Silence. The park was dark except for the glint of lamps visible here and there through the dense canopies of the trees. He could see the tall silhouettes of palms against the city light. Still she hadn't spoken. He turned around.

She had put down her glass and was pulling out the tail of her blouse, began unbuttoning it, saying nothing as she started toward him.

Bern couldn't think fast enough.

She slipped off the blouse and, without looking, lay it with gentle unconcern over the corner of a tilted drawing board as she went by, her arm reaching across her bare stomach as she began unbuttoning her skirt. Just as she was about to push it down over her hips, he stopped her.

"Wait a second," he said softly, but she was already over to him, close enough for him to have leaned down and kissed the soft tops of her breasts.

She stopped.

"Look," he said, "I . . ."

But her face was already changing even as they were looking at each other. The anticipation in her eyes grew cold, and her hazy expression of seduction faded into a weary look of impatience.

She turned and stepped over to the drawing board and picked up her blouse, but she didn't put it on immediately. Instead, she went back her glass of gin and took a drink, holding the blouse down at her side as she swallowed the first sip, looking at him, and then took another.

Bern scrambled for a way to finish his sentence, but nothing came to him.

"You didn't handle that well at all," she said. The coy mistress was gone, and an irritable woman had replaced her. "When you came to the bedroom door, you were visibly confused, right from the very first moment. You held me awkwardly. You were speechless. Jude, whatever his other faults, was never speechless."

Bern was flustered.

She put the glass down again, ran the fingers of one hand through her thick hair, and sighed heavily. Then she slipped on the blouse but didn't button it.

"Just for the record," she said, "I told them this was the worst idea I'd ever heard in my life. I tried to stop it."

Bern had whiplash. He was relieved, and in the same instant, he was pissed, really furious.

"Who the hell are you?" he asked.

"Susana Mejía. I was working this thing with Jude. I'm supposed to make you . . . passable."

"By making me feel stupid."

"That's how it's going to feel," she said. "Even after you've had hours and hours of briefing. Every moment of being Jude, you're going to feel exactly the way you felt just now. You're inexperienced, and no matter how much you've been briefed, you're still going to feel stupid, and anxious. You're always going to be afraid that the very next thing someone says will expose you."

They stared at each other. She was smoldering, not at all happy with what she had been assigned to do. She sipped her gin, eyes on him, studying him. She began to shake her head slowly.

"God," she said, "you really *were* identical twins."

"That's the only reason I'm here," he said.

"That's the reason they wanted you here. But what's the reason *you* are here?"

He was evasive. "It's not complicated," he said, feeling that it was so complicated, he wasn't sure he would ever sort it out. "Four days ago, I thought I was an only child. Then a woman brought me a skull in a box. Two days later, I found out that the skull was that of my identical twin." He hesitated a beat. "Now I don't know, but I'm guessing that's probably more reason than you have for being here."

Susana Mejía sipped her gin and turned to look out the windows at the park. Neither of them said anything for a moment, and then she looked down at her glass, thinking. When she turned back to him, the tension she was working under showed in her face and in her posture.

"I've read your file," she said. "You're an intelligent man, so I'm betting you're smarter than to have walked into this on your own."

"I sure as hell didn't volunteer," he said. About the smart part, he wasn't so sure anymore.

She stepped out of her shoes and rubbed one stockinged foot on top of the other as if her feet were aching. She ran the fingers of one hand into the thick hair above her forehead and held it there, thinking.

"Look," she said finally, "neither of us wants to be doing this. Me, because I think the risks are astronomical. You, I don't know, maybe you just think you can't do it. But whatever our reasons are, they don't cancel out the reality that this is a damned important thing, and regardless of what our reservations are, it's got to be done. And regardless of what our reservations are, we're going to do it."

This time, Susana drank her gin as if it were a glass of water, three big gulps and then it was gone. She paused, looking at him.

"Right?"

"Yeah," he said. "That's right."

"I'm going to be blunt with you," she went on; "there's

no time for games between us. You don't know this yet, but you can trust me. You need to grab hold of that fact as quickly as you can. It'll save you a lot of anxiety. You can trust me. I want to get this job done, but I don't want to lose your life doing it. And, more important to me, I don't want to lose my life, either."

She rattled the ice in her glass.

"How much do you know?" she asked.

He told her what Mondragón had told him.

"Shit," she said, looking away. "Shit." Silence ensued while she seemed to try to control herself, though he guessed she really wanted to throw the glass of ice across the room.

"Look," she said, turning to him, "essentially, Jude and I were on our own. In fact, until Jude was killed, we hadn't met face-to-face with anyone connected to this operation in over a year. Communication was constant, encrypted, and always to Lex Kevern." She stopped. "You don't know Kevern."

He shook his head. "No."

She nodded. "Okay. Quick overview: This operation originated somewhere in the rarefied air of Washington's national security and intelligence circles. It's a clandestine operation, rather than a covert operation. In a covert operation, the objective, the act that's performed, might become known, but the country responsible for that act remains unknown. In a clandestine operation, the act itself remains unknown. It never happened. A guy named Richard Gordon was brought in to put it together. Gordon's an old CIA hand, a good guy. But he's Langley. He called in Lex Kevern to be the case officer. Kevern's also an old hand, but in-country. Does dirty work. Deals with the contract people. Runs agents. Takes risks.

"Gordon picked me and Jude to be the operations officers, the people who actually do the work. We'd met before, but we'd never worked together. But at separate times, we'd both worked with Gordon in other Latin American postings, and he trusted us. Jude had special qualifications. He knew Ghazi Baida inside out. And he went to the same university as Baida: the University of Texas."

She sighed heavily.

"Where did he grow up?" Bern asked. "Jude, I mean."

She looked at him, and he could see that she had some inkling what this must be like for him, that he must be in near shock.

"Austin."

Jesus Christ. Of all the places he could have chosen to live, he had ended up in Jude's hometown. But by the time he got there, Jude was gone for good.

"His parents still live there?"

"Only his mother," she said. "His father, a doctor, died a few years ago."

Susana turned and walked across the room and stood in the doorway of Jude's bedroom, looking in, her body turned three-quarters away from Bern. From that angle, he couldn't really see the expression on her face, but her posture said a lot. Even the baggy shirttail hanging over her skirt didn't hide the shape of the woman in Jude's drawings.

"The truth was," she said, her back still to him, "Jude was more likable when he was pretending to be someone else than he was when he wasn't." She turned around.

"When he was Jude Lerner, he was very, very complicated. Lerner seemed to require a certain kind of complexity in order to operate, a complexity that Jude carried around with him like a sack of rocks.

"But when he was Jude Teller—Teller was his cover name—he was so busy funneling his psychology and energy into being that other man—and it was a hell of a job—that he was actually . . . endearing. Jude was very graceful in deceit. It suited him perfectly."

Bern was suddenly alert. Now she was sounding like a woman instead of an intelligence officer. But she didn't allow herself to go too far with that. The discipline was intact. She shook her head wearily.

"Come on," she said. "I need to show you something."

Chapter 20

He followed her into the bedroom and then into the bathroom. She gathered her skirt and got down on her knees in front of the sink.

"Come on. Get down here," she said.

Bern dropped to his knees and watched as she got down on her elbows and moved under the sink. He did the same. She pointed to the four-inch-high baseboard on the wall.

"These two nail heads here," she said. "Press them simultaneously with one hand while you lift here with the other."

A two-foot section of the baseboard folded up on hidden hinges, revealing a compartment and two handles. She pulled on one of the handles and a metal tray slid out revealing four CDs lying flat and layered back at angles so that the front edges of all four CDs were visible. She retrieved two CDs and then pushed in the drawer and closed the hinged baseboard.

"Every time you take something out," she said as they

backed out from under the sink, "close it. Otherwise, you may forget you left it open, or be interrupted and have no time to run in here and do it."

They went into the bedroom, where she opened a night-stand and took out a laptop and crawled onto the bed with it. She opened it and powered up.

"Always use the computer in here in the bedroom. Anyone coming to see you will have to cross the whole studio from the landing, and that'll buy you time to ditch what you're doing."

She tapped in the security code, and while she was waiting for it to clear, she continued explaining.

"The CDs are a complete library of everything pertaining to the case. One of the things you'll read about is how Jude worked his way into the cell run by a guy named Khalil Saleh. Jude used being an artist as a cover, along with a second life as a smuggler of pre-Columbian artifacts. That's how he finally got to meet Ghazi Baida.

"It was arranged for Jude to fly to Ciudad del Este, Paraguay, in the Triple Border region, to meet an unnamed man who was interested in his smuggling operation. We knew from other intelligence that this was probably a feeler from Baida's people.

"On the first trip, Jude was left alone in a bar full of noisy parrots near the Paraná River waterfront. Soon, a man of Middle Eastern descent appeared and introduced himself as Mazen Sabella. He said that he represented the man Jude had come to meet, but before that meeting could take place, Mazen needed to ask Jude a few questions.

"They talked for nearly two hours, entirely in Spanish." She stopped. "You don't speak Spanish."

"Not much. No, hardly any."

She didn't waste her time being exasperated by that.

"The man was polite, but thorough. He explored Jude's life through a series of questions that seemed more like a casual conversation between friends than a vetting. By the time the guy left, he had very skillfully extracted a bundle of leads he'd use in the inevitable background check. But no one claiming to be Baida ever showed at the bar."

Susana kept one eye on the screen and slapped in a few more codes on the keyboard.

"A month later, another meeting was set up. Again Jude flew down. Another bar on the waterfront. Again Sabella arrived. Again they spoke in Spanish, and the major point of the discussion this time was the structure and operation of Jude's smuggling route. The guy posed a series of hypothetical situations involving unexpected events, asking how Jude would handle them. It seemed that every possible scenario was played out. Then Sabella excused himself, saying that his boss would appear within the half hour. But Baida never came. Finally, Jude left the bar and flew home.

"Two weeks later, Jude was summoned again. Jude sent word back that everyone in Ciudad del Este could go fuck themselves, especially Sabella, who had been lying to him, *and* the guy who never showed up. Ahmad said, No, no, no, this time it was guaranteed he would meet Baida. The meeting place was the lobby of a small and smelly hotel in the oldest part of the city. Jude said the place reeked of raw sewage, had a jungle of potted palms in its rancid lobby, hosted the largest amber roaches in Latin America, and employed the most beautiful whores on the globe."

Susana made this last remark with as much gravity as

she had the rest of it. There was no attempt to make light of it.

"This time, a guy he'd never seen before walked into the lobby," Susana said. "He went over to Jude with a smile on his face and said in impeccable English, 'I hear you've grown impatient with us. That's understandable.' He extended his hand and said, 'I'm Ghazi Baida.'"

"Wait a minute," Bern said. "Why didn't Jude recognize him from your files? You've got to have pictures, don't you?"

"Yeah, we do. But they're at least a decade old."

"It's not that hard to age them."

"Right, and we'd done that. But we weren't sure it was doing us any good. We had pretty good intelligence that Baida had cosmetic surgery about four years ago in Zurich, but we'd never been able to confirm it. So we weren't sure who the hell we were looking for."

"And this was your confirmation."

"That's right. And the alterations were significant."

"And then Jude made drawings."

"Very detailed ones." After a couple more taps on the keys, she turned the laptop around for him to see the screen. "Ghazi Baida," she said.

Jude had done four frontal drawings of Baida in four different styles, smoothly blended, smooth controlled, sketchy controlled, and sketchy hatching. Below each picture were active toggles that would take you to variations in each of the styles: profiles, three-quarter views, smiling, with beard, with glasses, with mustache, thin, heavy, and several combinations of these variations. Bern toggled through the variations.

"These are very good," he said. "Very good."

Susana pulled one of the pillows from under the bed-spread, jammed it against the wall, and sat back against it, one leg drawn up, the other stretched out on the bed.

"Only three people have seen these drawings," she said. "You make the fourth."

He didn't say anything, but he kept staring at the sketches. He looked at the way Jude had handled his materials, how he had switched pencils, used the long side of the lead, used the point, laid on some chalk here and there. Very subtly, he had given Baida a kindly appearance. Is that what he had seen?

"What about their conversations?" he asked.

"After each trip, Jude sat down at the computer and typed out a detailed account of the meetings."

"I want to read them."

"You have to read them," she said. "Everything's on the CDs—operation reports, Baida's dossier, information on the Triple Border area, pictures and brief bios of everybody significant. There are also some drawings that Jude made of Mazen Sabella. The whole thing was put together for you. It's a lot to read, and the sooner you do it, the better."

She slid her other leg up and rested her elbows on her upright knees as she pushed her fingers into her hair again. It was an interesting habitual gesture, a physical reflection of a psychological state. She looked as if she were pushing herself, as if she had drained her energy right to the bottom and every hour that went by was costing her double.

She sat that way in silence for a few moments, and then she sighed and looked up at him.

"I just can't do this any longer. I've got to get some sleep."

Without another word, she rolled off the other side of the bed, went to a wardrobe against the wall, and took out a gown. Then she headed to the bathroom and closed the door.

Bern got a chair from the studio and took it over to the windows that looked out onto Avenida México and the park. He sat down with the laptop and began scrolling through the index of CDs. Night air moved tentatively through the window.

When Susana came out of the bathroom, she was wearing a simple chocolate brown silk gown. Her hair was combed out, and when she came around the end of the bed, he could see that she had washed her face.

"Let me show you how to lock up," she said.

They went downstairs, where she showed him how to set the locks. He turned out the lights and followed her upstairs, watching her hips, seeing now and then the cleavage of her buttocks beneath the swaying nightgown.

He turned out the bedroom lights as they came through the door.

"You don't have to do that," she said. "The way I feel, I could sleep inside a lightbulb."

"I don't need it for the laptop," he said.

He returned to the chair and the city glow coming in through the windows. Susana sat in the near dark on the edge of the bed, just a few feet away. He tried to concentrate on the screen, but he was aware that she was sitting there looking at him. After a few moments, she asked, "What did they do . . . to make you do this?"

He wasn't sure he should tell her. He seemed to have been dropped into a world where the shapes of your friends and enemies could change even as you looked at them, where one could easily become the other, depending upon a criteria that was completely outside his understanding.

But he found himself in desperate need of a friend right now, and the tone of her voice alone seemed genuine and inviting, and he wanted to believe, as she had said he should, that he could trust her.

He closed the laptop to get the cold glare out of his face, and the shadows closed around them. He could just make out her figure on the edge of the bed, her back straight, her hands in her lap, unthreatening, almost absent of bravery.

He told her about the conversations with Mondragón and then with Mitchell Cooper. He told her of Mondragón's proposal, of his refusal to be any part of it, and then of Mondragón's extortion. He went on and told her of Alice and her family, of Tess's death and Alice's disability, and of their close relationship. He told her that he would do just about anything not to destroy his connection with that family.

When he was through, she said nothing. He waited for her to speak, to ask another question, to commiserate in some way, however perfunctorily, but she said not a word. He felt the air move through the window and pass over him.

"Tomorrow, you need to start wearing Jude's clothes," she said.

Jesus. He hadn't fully appreciated how strange this was going to be. He imagined it would be like looking at himself in a mirror with his reflection out of focus, two overlapping selves.

She was studying him. "You sit the same way he did,"

she said. "Exactly. It's very strange. You cross your legs the way he did. Your hands look like his, too, and you use them the way he did." She was speaking softly, almost meditatively. "And the way you use your voice. And show impatience."

He could see her on the bed, her figure a little lighter than darkness.

"The way you look at me," she went on, "my face first, absorbing it completely. You tend to look at my mouth more than my eyes when I talk. He did that."

She suddenly stopped, as if catching herself.

"Sleep here," she said. "I don't want to wake up and not know where you are."

She was quiet a moment, and he felt that he should say something, but nothing seemed quite right to him. And then the moment passed, and she stood. He could only barely see her, and at moments he wasn't sure he could see her at all. He heard her turn back the covers, and then the barely audible rustle of her gown coming off slipped through the darkness to him like a fugitive memory. The sounds of her body moving between the covers made him ache with memories of Tess.

He opened the laptop again and made himself concentrate on the screen. It wasn't hard, because he began with Jude's biography file. The information was riveting, and he read until his eyes felt like they had been rubbed with sandpaper. Susana was breathing the heavy sleep of exhaustion as he returned the CD to its hiding place and plugged in the laptop to recharge.

He went back to the windows and looked down into the black trees of the park. He recalled the nude drawings that Jude had made of her. He hadn't slept next to a woman since Tess's death, and even though Tess had been dead for almost a year now, he couldn't shake the odd feeling of guilt simply at the thought of crawling into bed with Susana. But it was going to be good just having her there beside him, sharing the silence and the darkness . . . the way it used to be.

He lost track of time by the windows. He heard sounds in the park across the narrow street. Once, he thought he heard footsteps on the sidewalk underneath the trees over there. Hours passed, it seemed—he deliberately didn't look at his watch—before he was too tired to stand there any longer. He went around to the other side of the bed, pulled off his clothes, laid them over a chair, and carefully crawled under the covers.

His hand was on the cell phone after the second ring, but he was still asleep when he picked it up.

"Yeah."

"Judas," the voice said. "It's Mingo."

But before Bern could respond, someone grabbed the cell phone. Foggy-headed, he struggled to open his eyes. The room was highlighted in a blue dusk. Confused, he couldn't move.

"*Sí,*" he heard a woman say.

She was on one elbow, leaning against him. "*¿Quién es éste?*" Pause as she listened. "*No, se enfermo.*" Pause. "*¿Quién es éste?*" Pause as she listened. "*Dos o tres dias.*" Pause to listen. "*Sí. Sí. Bueno.*"

She stayed on her elbow and punched off the phone. He could see her profile against the light from the window.

"Did he say anything to you?" she asked.

Bern was awake now. The guy had said something. . . .

"It's . . . I think he said, 'It's Mingo.'"

"Mingo?"

"Yeah. Yeah, he . . . that was it."

"Mingo," she said.

"Yeah."

She was quiet, looking at him, though her face was in shadow, the light coming in from behind her.

"Don't answer the phone," she whispered hoarsely.

She kept the phone and put it on the table on her side of the bed. She lay down again.

He turned on his side to look at her. She was lying on her back, the sheet folded down to her rib cage, the surface of her bare breasts dusted in a pale powder blue light. She was staring into the darkness above her, and he could see a glint in the moisture that glazed her eyes.

They lay that way for a long time, and her eyes were still open when he lost consciousness.

Chapter 21

The twin towers known as Residencial del Bosque faced Avenida Ruben Dario and the sixteen-hundred-acre Bosque de Chapultepec (the Woods of Chapultepec), a sprawling park in the heart of Mexico City. Once the site of the palace of the Aztec poet-king Nezahualcóyotl, Chapultepec was now the home of Los Pinos, the palatial residence of the Mexican president.

Designed by the U.S. architectural firm of Cesar Pelli & Associates, the postmodern towers were the most expensive residential structures in the city. Constructed of alternating bands of dark glass and terracotta tile and brick, they were home to some of Latin America's richest men, and it was rumored that many of them had acquired their fortunes by dubious means and maintained them by the same.

The walled compound had the requisite gated security service, but the real protection was in the hands of the men in dark suits and sunglasses who lingered in the shade of the trees along the boulevard and the surrounding wooded streets. With their automatic weapons casually slung underneath the open lapels of their shiny suits, they smoked with passive faces. Like blind serpents at the mouth of a den, they sensed danger without having to see it.

Even at night, Vicente Mondragón could see the lights of the presidential palace from his twenty-ninth-floor suite near the top of the second tower. He always felt different in Mexico, even after being there for only a few hours. In Mexico he was more alert, more aware of the depths of the water he swam in.

He had arrived in the late afternoon, before Paul Bern had even left Austin. Like the president, he had choppered to the helipad at the Residencial del Bosque from his private airstrip on the southwestern edge of Santa Fe. Now he was standing at the display case of one of his plastinized faces, which were exhibited in the same manner as those in Houston, floating in pools of soft light, scattered across the breadth of the shadowy room.

Lex Kevern, looking uncomfortable but stubborn, sat in the typical gloomy twilight of the Mondragón residence, his thick body filling one of Mondragón's lush leather armchairs.

"You hang on to those videotapes of that girl," Kevern said. "If those things get out to some damned underground porn circuit, I'll kill you myself."

There was a whisking sound as Mondragón spritzed the raw front of his head, the mist dazzling and falling through the pale light from the display case.

"He didn't even fight it," Mondragón said. "When he saw those pictures, it was all over."

"Yeah, okay," Kevern said.

"Does that worry you?"

"You mean because he didn't kick up a fuss? If he's like Jude, he wouldn't. You had him by the dick—no use wasting his energy. But my guess is he won't forget what you've done to him. If I were you, I'd be ready to do the right thing with those pictures when this is all over."

"Why wouldn't I?"

"I don't know, Vicente. Why wouldn't you?"

Mondragón leaned in closer to the face. This one happened to be a Spaniard, a poor but beautiful young woman from Tarifa who had died of a blood disease. She sold her face for the price of the remaining mortgage on her mother's grim little cottage facing the Strait of Gibraltar. The old woman had sat at a window there, looking toward Tangier, mooning over her youthful years in Morocco. Mondragón remembered most of the stories connected to the faces, and this one especially, because it was so pitiful. This girl could have been a film star, or at least a damned good mistress.

He straightened up and went over and stood near Kevern in a dark pocket of the room

"I keep waiting for the other shoe to drop," he said.

"Yeah?"

"Mejía. If somebody found out about Jude, what about her?"

"Well, we've been over that, haven't we, Vicente?" Kevern's scratchy voice sounded strained. "What's the matter? You forgetting how to think like a Mexican? Look, she's deeper than Jude. He was out there, pushing it. She was doing what Mexicans think women ought to do, taking her clothes off. How many men in this goddamned country have a piece of ass on the side? And how many of these women do you suspect of being clandestine CIA operatives? Hell, she's playing a role that makes her as common as a damned street vendor. She's not going to be at the top of anybody's list."

He paused and then added, "She and Jude were as good as a damn team could get. She's played this as smart as I've ever seen it played. And it's hard to say which one of them had the biggest balls."

"Okay, fine. But she didn't like this idea with Bern," Mondragón said. "Can you be sure she's going to stay with it?"

He watched Kevern, knowing the question would irritate him, and knowing that Kevern didn't like it when he stood in the darkness. He would much rather see Mondragón's goggling eyes and his isolated lips stuck onto the hamburger that used to be his face than for Mondragón to stand hidden in the dark. Mondragón wasn't quite sure why this bothered Kevern so much, but once he discovered that it did, he did it as often as he could.

"You know what, Vicente? You wouldn't understand," Kevern said. "A guy like you."

Kevern was sitting forward in the leather chair, his hefty shoulders as wide as a bull's, his forearms on his knees, the thick fingers of his big hands interlaced. Mondragón could see Kevern staring at the shadow where his head was hidden, and he sensed Kevern's aggravation.

"This is unfinished business for her now," Kevern explained. "She's feeling stuff like loyalty and determination . . . and a sense of doing the right thing. She knows damn well the risk to her and Paul Bern in a cock-up scheme like this, but she's gonna put that out of her head. And you know why she's gonna put that out of her head? Because she's disciplined. And she's loyal. And because she lies awake at night wondering what in the fuck Ghazi Baida's going to do if he gets his hands on a safe, reliable underground connection into the States. She cares about shit like that."

Mondragón waited without responding. In that brief monologue, Kevern had exposed more of himself than he had ever done in the eight years of their association. It was a telltale sign of the pressure he was feeling. Kevern had never let it show before, and this brief outburst—by Kevern's standards—was all that he was going to let show now. He fell silent.

Mondragón waited a few beats before he said, "And what do you do now?"

"Wait," Kevern rasped.

"What do you think the odds are that Baida knows who was behind the Tepito killings?"

"Nil."

"Maybe he suspects something."

"Sure he does. People like that are suspicious. Guys like him, they never bend down to get a drink of water."

Mondragón wasn't going to ask him what that meant. Kevern was full of those kind of Americanisms, mixed in with operational lingo. He used to be worse, but Mondragón had told him to stop it.

Kevern grunted in his chair and shrugged his beefy shoulders.

"It was a drug hit," Kevern said, jutting his chin forward and stretching his thick neck as if his tie was too tight. Only he wasn't wearing a tie. "I do know that's the story that his man took back to him. I haven't heard rumors that it was anything but a narco hit, and the street is pretty reliable about that sort of thing. If something else had been out there, something with more credence, it would've come around to me."

Mondragón turned away, walked to the glass wall, and looked out over Mexico City. He could see Kevern in the reflection of the dark glass. He spritzed his face.

"I think it's been too long," he said, his voice bouncing off the glass. "He suspects something. If you lose an entire cell, you think somebody was inside. It's been six weeks." He shifted the focus of his eyes and picked up his own eyeballs gawking back at him. His lips floated alone, unattached.

"He lives in a spooky world," Kevern grunted. "He has his people, runs his traps like the rest of us. Like I said, he sent his guy up here. People disappear in his world all the time. Can't know everything. You live that life, you live with uncertainty. You acclimate."

"Jude had already had three meetings with Baida when Khalil killed him. How was he going to deal with Jude's sudden disappearance? Or Ahmad's?"

"Probably lay it off on somebody in Jude's smuggling world," Kevern said. "That's what I'd have done. Guy like that disappears, what can you say about it? Shit, the odds caught up with him. Besides, Khalil was more afraid of Baida's wrath if he'd found out they'd introduced him to a spy. Baida doesn't tolerate that kind of sloppy work from anybody, especially cell leaders. That's why Khalil killed Ahmad. Hell, they weren't even supposed to be meeting together in one place. Khalil was running a sloppy cluster."

Mondragón saw Kevern jut out his chin and neck again. The man was full of quirks. What did it feel like, being pumped up like that, having your muscles swollen because of steroids? He must always feel as if he's wearing a second skin, another layer of flesh weighted down with muscles.

Mondragón was still facing into the glass, his focus readjusted to pick up Kevern's reflection again.

Kevern grunted under his breath, as if in preamble to speaking, like he first had to haul the words up from his gut. But he said nothing.

Mondragón watched him. Kevern had handsome eyes. Good shape to his eyebrows. Mondragón wouldn't mind having something like that when he got his new face. There was a fullness above his eyelid that almost obscured it, and it gave him a look of strength. At least it read that way to Mondragón. Strength. And it made him look as if he kept his own counsel. Which Kevern surely did. Even in this conversation, Mondragón had had to pull things out of him. The man was just made that way. It was maddening.

Chapter 22

The next morning, Bern was shaken awake by Susana, who was leaning over him, a towel wrapped around her, another draped over her wet head.

"Wake up," she said.

When he opened his eyes, she resumed fluffing the towel through her hair. It took him a second to remember where he was, and then he rolled over and raised himself on one elbow.

"Listen," she said, "we've got to go somewhere. You need to get up."

He wasn't sure about the tone of her voice, and for a second it seemed urgent. His heart lurched. But then she bent over and let her hair fall over her head as she continued to dry it, and it seemed he'd misread her. She wasn't frantic. Bern could smell the shampoo. She straightened up quickly, flinging her hair back.

"I've made some coffee in the kitchen," she said. "While you're showering, I'm going to run a quick errand.

I'll be back in less than an hour, and I'll bring some pastries with me. You grab a bite and then we'll go."

"Go where?"

"I'll explain it to you on the way."

"So who was that on the phone last night?" he asked.

"I'm not sure." She picked up a comb from the foot of the bed and started combing her damp hair, tilting her head to the side.

"I thought I wasn't supposed to go out," he said, "until you've had time to bring me up to speed."

"Did you read last night?"

"Yeah, until late."

"Then I guess you're picking up speed."

She turned around and headed for the bathroom. "I'll be out of there in five minutes."

Bern got out of bed and slipped on his pants. There was a chest of drawers near Jude's closet, and he looked inside. Underwear, T-shirts, socks. This was going to be strange.

He looked around the room. On one side of the door that led out to the studio was a wardrobe, which he hadn't even noticed before. He heard the hair dryer going in the bathroom, so he went to the wardrobe and opened it. Susana's clothes. Or some woman's clothes at least. He lifted one of the blouses and smelled it. Susana's perfume. A smaller chest on the other side contained her lingerie.

He went back to the closet and stared at the clothes. Would he find things in the pockets, an old theater ticket, a receipt for some small purchase? The hair dryer stopped. He didn't want Susana to find him staring blankly into Jude's closet, so he went back to the door that led to the studio and looked out. It felt familiar. Being there one night couldn't have done it. There was more to it than that.

"Okay," she said, coming out of the bathroom, "it's all yours."

Her thick hair was fluffy from drying, and she was rubbing lotion on her arms. Bern guessed she would now go around to her side of the bed, the side near the window, and sit on the edge of the bed and rub lotion on her legs.

She went past him and around the end of the bed. She sat down and began putting lotion on her legs, leaning over, her bare back to him.

It was just that easy. He could fall back into the routine in less than a day. The thought of it left a hollow place in his stomach. He headed for the shower and closed the bathroom door behind him.

He stood at the sink a long time, the towel wrapped around his waist, his hair still wet, looking at the shelves in the medicine cabinet. He looked at the tube of toothpaste, neatly rolled from the bottom. A tin of bandages. Over-the-counter antihistamines. Razor heads. Antiseptic throat spray. Advil. Midol. A packet of emery boards. Dental floss. Deodorant.

He closed the door. The jar of shaving cream was on the marble countertop. Bern used shaving cream, too. Most people didn't, but millions did, he guessed. There was no need to believe there was any special significance in that. He opened it and caught the scent of almonds. His own cream was almond-scented, too. But then, he figured, millions of men must use that also.

Looking into the jar, he saw where Jude had run his fingers through the cream and scooped it out. Good God. Slowly, he put his own fingers into the same grooves of the cream and carefully pulled them through the same shallow flutes created by Jude's fingers. He looked at the cream on his fingers and then looked into the jar. The striations of Jude's fingertips were gone. Paul had taken the first steps of replacing him. He began to lather his face.

The next forty minutes or so were a nearly hallucinatory experience as he slowly crawled into the minutiae of his brother's life. He deliberately did not replace the razor head, wanting a tactile intimacy with Jude, though he didn't stop to reason why. After shaving, he used Jude's lotion on his face, then put Jude's talcum under his arms.

In the bedroom, he opened the chest of drawers and took out a pair of Jude's shorts and put them on. He put on a T-shirt. As if in a trance, he went to the closet and chose a pair of trousers, selected a belt from a rack of them on the closet door, picked out a freshly laundered shirt. The shoes. Jesus Christ, he had forgotten about the shoes. He chose a pair, then got a pair of socks and put them on. Everything fit. Everything suited him.

He looked at himself in the full-length mirror on Susana's wardrobe, and it was only at that moment that it hit him how important it was for him to become Jude as deeply and as completely as humanly possible. None of this was going to work, not even for a moment, if he didn't.

It was something that should have hit him like a lightning bolt from the very instant that it was proposed to him by Mondragón back in Houston, but it hadn't. He thought he had understood, but he hadn't. Not really. Not until this intimate intercourse with the details of Jude's small moments, not until he saw himself in Jude's clothes and slept in the same bed with the same woman that Jude must have slept with, not until this very moment in front of Jude's mirror, looking into Jude's face, did the full impact of the reality of his situation actually hit him. His life depended upon the resurrection of the face in the mirror. If he wanted to live, Jude had to be reborn, whole and believable.

He was standing at the studio windows when he heard the front door open and close. A few minutes later, Susana's quick footsteps crossed the living room and stopped at the bottom of the stairs.

"Jude," she yelled.

Caught off guard, he felt a wash of panic, and then he immediately caught himself.

"Yeah," he called back.

"I'm bringing up the pastries. You want some coffee?"

"I just got a fresh cup," he said, and heard her start up the stairs.

He turned away from the windows and was halfway across the studio when she came around the top of the landing and saw him. Her quick pace halted abruptly, as if someone had yelled at her, and then she came toward him slowly. She was holding the white sack of pastries, and the look on her face was a conflation of surprise and an effort to conceal it. Her eyes were all over him, absorbing the sight of him.

When she got to him, she reached up without hesitation and put her hand softly along the side of his face, looking at him as if she were remembering him, not seeing him, and then she dropped her hand and put it flat against his chest, feeling him breathe.

Suddenly, she took her hand away and went around him and put the pastries on the coffee table in front of the sofa a few feet away.

"We need to get moving," she said, her back to him as

she shrugged off her shoulder bag and began looking into it for something. "You'd better grab a bite. It's going to take us about an hour to get there."

They descended to the street and stepped out into the quiet morning on Avenida México. Bern could hear the roar of the city only a few blocks away in any direction, but the park was an island of tranquility, the loudest distraction coming from the songs of birds in the high canopies of the trees.

Susana took her secure cell phone out of her purse and made a call, which resulted in a series of exchanges and another call. Then they walked up Teotihuacán to Avenida Amsterdam, where they caught a cab and headed south on Avenida Insurgentes.

"This is a good surveillance-detection route," she said, turning halfway around in the seat and looking back over her shoulder through the rear window. "The traffic's always terrible, so anyone following us will have to take some risks. Sooner or later, they'll have to run a light, squeeze through an intersection, cut across traffic, something that'll give them away."

The next half hour was spent running the surveillance-detection route. Instead of going into Coyoacán as she had told the driver, at the last minute she sent him into San Angel, up into the hilly and narrow *callejones*. She made phone calls to two friends whose homes shared a common garden wall in the rear, though the front of their properties opened onto different *callejones*. Using these private gardens, they switched taxis and headed back downtown on Insurgentes again.

Soon they were in Roma Norte, where many of the limestone buildings from the late nineteenth century still survived, their gray stones streaked with charcoal tears from a century of pollution. They got out of the taxi on a small cross street and walked until they arrived at a leafy little park called Plaza Rio de Janeiro.

Susana stopped and made another phone call while keeping her eyes on an old neoclassical building through the trees. When a man stepped out of the foyer of the building and lighted a cigarette, they crossed into the park and angled toward the opposite corner, passing a replica of Michelangelo's *David* rising above the mists of an encircling fountain in the center of the park. On the other side, they crossed the street, walked past the man with the cigarette, who ignored them, and entered the building. Ascending an old marble staircase, they circled the landing and walked into one of the three doorways around the stairwell.

Two women, a strawberry blonde and a Mexican, looked up from laptop computers that were sitting on folding tables. They were obviously expecting Susana and Bern, but their eyes went to Bern, and he could see the marvel in them. Cell phones lay around on the tables, along with grease-stained take-out sacks, empty plastic water bottles, and take-out coffee cups. Both women were wearing sidearms.

"Yeah," the blonde said. She stood, looking at Susana, and then with no further greeting, she snapped her head to the side and said, "He's in there."

"Come on," Susana said to Bern, and they crossed the room, which had no other furniture in it besides the two tables and chairs, and opened the door into a second room.

Chapter 23

A big man with hefty shoulders and a thick neck looked up from where he was squatting on the floor over a banker's box full of manila file folders.

"Susana," he said as he stood, his expression softening as he stepped over to her. They hugged a little awkwardly, and Bern remembered that she had told him that it had been over a year since either she or Jude had seen anyone from the operation in person.

Immediately, the man's eyes turned to Bern, and he extended his hand and said, "Paul, Lex Kevern."

They shook hands as Kevern's eyes took him in, assessing, Bern felt, how well his prime bait was going to play with Ghazi Baida.

"We got here okay?" Susana asked.

"Yeah, we didn't pick up anyone on you." His eyes went back to Bern. "I appreciate this. It's got to be rough on you."

"Yeah, well, it's happening pretty fast," Bern said.

"You're in good hands," Kevern said. "You'll be all right. She'll get you where you need to be."

"Let's get right to business," said Susana, cutting in.

Despite having said she would, she hadn't told Bern where they were going or why. Kevern, Bern gathered from his behavior, didn't know what this was about, either. It seemed to Bern that Susana was pushing something here.

"You wanted the meeting," Kevern said. "Go ahead."

Susana began pacing. Kevern, glancing at Bern, crossed his arms and sat on the edge of his desk, waiting for her to get on with it. With one hand flat against the small of her back, her head down, Susana made a couple of passes in front of Kevern's desk, between him and Bern, who stood near the open window overlooking the street. Then she stopped abruptly.

"Lex, I need to know what you're not telling me here," she said.

He gave her a puzzled look.

"Somebody's already spotted Bern," she said. She told him about the telephone call at 3:30 that morning.

"Mingo?" Kevern asked.

"Yeah." Susana was watching Kevern closely, but it seemed to Bern that his face conveyed nothing.

"When they call on that phone," she elaborated, "I should know who they are, Lex. That was Jude's secure phone. And this guy knew Paul was there." She paused. "Something else is going on here. The people who have that number think Jude was killed six weeks ago in the drug raid. But that number has rung eight times since that night, as you know. Four of those times, we think, were Baida. Just checking. Four other times, it was traced back to another encrypted phone."

"This guy?"

"Yeah, same phone. And I think you know who it is."

Kevern stared at her a moment. Bern watched them. He couldn't see much on Kevern's face, but he could see that Susana saw something, and she didn't much like what she saw.

"Lex, goddamn you," she said, "what in the hell are you doing to me?"

Kevern stood up and raised his beefy hands, palms out to her.

"Now wait a second. Listen to this before you explode. Then if you think it's not right, be my guest."

Susana was seething.

Kevern looked at Bern. "This is classified. Could you just give us—"

"No," Susana snapped. "This is the way it's going to be, Lex."

Kevern's face registered something this time that even Bern could see: a flare of anger that he instantly suppressed, stopped cold.

"In the next couple of days," Susana said to Kevern, "I'm going to be telling him everything I know. Everything. No secrets. We're a team. You wanted it; you got it. I'm not going to be put in a position of having to decide what I'll hold back from him and what I won't. He needs to know everything I can get into his head in order to stay alive. This is hard enough without adding another layer of secrecy."

Kevern's eyes were fixed on her again. It seemed that Susana was telling Kevern that she was going to pull out all the stops and throw operations protocol out the window in favor of a survival regimen. Her attitude seemed to be, Thank you very much for pushing us off the cliff, but now that you have, we're going to be in charge of the falling.

And the landing. If Kevern and Washington didn't like it, they could shove it.

"Fair enough," Kevern said, but it seemed that the words were hard for him to get out.

"Here's what I think's going on," Kevern began, "but I can't be sure. I've gone over and over it. Just about the time your training for this was coming to a close at the Farm, Jude pulled me aside, wanted to talk, outside. We met at a bar, and he pitched his deal."

Susana's face went stiff. Bern suspected that Kevern had just delivered a successful thrust in their little duel of nerves.

"Jude didn't think the smuggling story would sell without some kind of credible intelligence operation of his own in place. The way he saw it, a guy in his position couldn't operate a top-notch smuggling op without some kind of security rig. He wanted permission—and the financing—to put together his own smuggling intel deal."

Kevern wiped a hand over his face and snorted. He stared at the floor and grunted, then crossed his arms again.

"We went over the pros and cons," he said, looking up. "He'd given it a lot of thought and had an answer for everything. He was afraid that if Baida's people probed too deep when they were checking him out, they might catch him running counterintelligence measures. If they did, he could easily claim it was for the smuggling operation. Jude figured Baida would be satisfied with that explanation. It made sense.

"And even if Baida was still suspicious, it would make it a hell of a lot harder for his people to dig up a secondary explanation. In a sense, Jude had come up with another form of backstopping. It was a lightning rod that would ground any suspicion of his actions firmly into the smuggling operation. It was smart."

Kevern paused and sat down on his desk again. He looked tired. It had been a long run for all of them and now, instead of arriving at a resolution to all their hard work, they were beginning a second round.

"Jude had one caveat," Kevern went on. "He didn't want to tell you what he was doing. He reasoned, and he was right I think, that there was no need to add to the balancing act you were already handling. If your cover didn't involve you in his smuggling operation, then why should you be burdened with having to keep track of the operation's intelligence concerns? That would simply add to the stress on you."

He paused, raising an eyebrow, and looked up at her as if he were trying to read her real thoughts.

"That's the whole big secret," Kevern said. "That's all there is to it." He hesitated. "Incidentally, Gordon doesn't know about that little operation, either. Just me. And by God, I put it out of my mind."

In the silence that followed, Bern saw the hurt in Susana's face. Or maybe he only imagined it. He knew the importance of trust between partners, especially partners who had learned to submit to the free fall of espionage, where the assumption was that the other partner was securing the lifeline that would prevent the plunge from being fatal. That kind of trust came with an emotional price, especially between partners who might have shared more than the secrets of state.

Now she was learning that Jude had kept this secret from her the whole time. And she had never even suspected it. That was deception, and in the context of their world, it was akin to adultery.

"Okay?" Kevern asked.

Susana nodded. "It would've been a weak point in the continuity." She nodded. "He was right to want to do it that way."

There was a flurry of conversation in the outer office, and both of them paused, listening, until it quieted down.

"Okay," she said, clearing her throat. "Give me something, anything. We've got to deal with this guy."

Kevern shook his head. "I told you. That day in the bar was the last time we talked about it. I always assumed he'd done it, but that was Jude's thing. For me, it didn't even exist. I didn't know anything about it then, and I don't want to know anything about it now." He gave her a significant look. "Jude was on his own with this one. Even for the downside—if it came to that. And if you use this guy, it'll be the same for you."

"You would've given him permission to dig his own grave if he'd wanted to, wouldn't you?"

"You going to give me a lecture on letting him stick his neck out?" Kevern asked. "Come on, Ana. That's why all three of us got pulled into this one. We all know the story. It's an old story." He glanced at Bern again, then back at Susana. "They want Ghazi Baida. Whatever it takes."

Susana looked at Bern. "It's like announcing a job opening for people who like adventure," she explained. "When the applications come in, you throw them all out except for those few who are addicted to Russian roulette. Then you send them into a Chinese gambling den to find a guy who's selling a revolver with only one shell in it. Odds are, your agents will eventually find your man for you, but you're not really surprised when you lose a few of your people in the process. You figure that into your overhead in advance."

Kevern looked hard at her. Bern thought he was trying to see inside her head to see if she was changing on him.

She turned to Kevern. "You don't know if this guy knows about Baida?"

Kevern shook his head. "But I'm guessing that he does."

Silence.

Susana walked over near Bern and looked down onto the street. It was a quiet, densely populated residential area, and looking between the branches of the trees, he could see a couple of maids sloshing soapy water onto the sidewalk and sweeping it off into the street.

"Jude liked to juggle," Susana said, watching the maids take a few moments to chat, looking up and down the street to see what life could show them. "He liked having a lot of limes in the air at once, having complete control of a complex situation." She nodded. "Yeah, I'm guessing Mingo knows about Baida, too."

She turned around. "Okay," she said. "We've got a lot to do. How's Gordon?"

"Good," Kevern said. "He's good."

Susana nodded. "Okay."

So much for the tight family thing.

"We're going to bury ourselves in background," she said. "We'll be in touch when we get a grip on the best way to handle it."

"Good," Kevern said. "I've got a cell upgrade for you." He stood from edge of his desk again, went to a table jumbled with electronic gear, and picked up a cell phone and its charger. He went over and gave them to her.

"Give me your other one," he said.

Susana went to her purse, retrieved the other cell phone, and gave it to him.

"Okay," Kevern said, "this one has everything built into it. We'll know where you are every moment. We want updates as often as you can send them or need to send them. Punch oh six oh and start talking. It's as secure as an electronic signal is capable of being. We monitor it live around the clock. We'll respond immediately. Everything else is the same."

"Okay. Fine."

"I guess you'd better assume that Baida could get wind of this within hours. Maybe already knows. If this guy Mingo knows that Jude's alive, we've got to assume everyone knows. Just be ready to handle that."

"We'll push as fast as we can," she said.

She put the cell phone and the charger in her purse, and they left.

Chapter 24

They took a taxi to Paseo de la Reforma, where they got another taxi to a *pastelería* on the fashionable Avenida Masaryk in Polanco. Susana had said nothing during the ride, gazing out her window in thought. At the *pastelería*, they ordered coffee and found a small table in a corner. Susana began talking immediately.

"What I did was way out of line," she said, referring to their trip to see Kevern. "They'd just moved the operations to a new location, and I risked exposing it by doing that. Kevern was furious."

Her face was weary, serious.

"But I had to do two things. I needed to find out what the Mingo business was all about. I wasn't expecting what Lex told me, but then I didn't know what to expect, so I guess I'm no worse for wear. And I wanted you two to meet."

"I wouldn't have met him if you hadn't done that?"

"Probably not. If he could've kept his distance from you, he would've done it. Lex and Jude were a mutual-respect society. They weren't friends. Neither of them had friends. They had informants, sources, targets, agents, superiors, subordinates, mistresses, but no friends. But Kevern took Jude's death hard. Especially because of what he had to do. Or thought he had to do."

She told him about Jude's death, about the Agencia Federal de Investigaciónes' surveillance images, what had happened to the remaining members of the cell, how they had found Jude's body, Kevern's plan to use Bern as a stand-in, the device of using Jude's skull to lure Bern into cooperation, and how he had initiated the plan before getting clearance from the group, the small circle of men who had initiated the operation in the first place.

All of this was told to him in a quiet, calm fashion, and the enormity of the words were diminished by her controlled demeanor, so that the remarkable implications of what she was telling him followed her recitation by some moments. Still, when she was finished, Bern was floored by the audacity of Kevern's actions. And it put into startling perspective the boldness of what he'd gotten himself into. Feeling like a man knocked off his feet by a sudden blow to the head, he was still trying to collect his thoughts. She was quiet for a moment, waiting for his reaction.

"One question," he said. "Will Mondragón use those pictures if I don't do this? These people will let him do that to her?"

"No, they can't do that," she said. "But then, they can't let Ghazi Baida do what he wants to do, either. They make a choice. They make a chain."

"A chain."

"They create a chain between themselves and you. Each additional link is farther away from them, and because each link is its own independent entity, the less real control they can legitimately claim over it. And the less responsibility they feel. The more links they have, the more deniability they have."

"But the fact is," Bern said, "when Washington yanks its end of the chain, the other end rattles."

She didn't say anything. He studied her. "And so you're telling me this . . . why?"

"It's a personal thing with me," she said. "I told you before, and I told Kevern, we're joined at the hip on this one. We've got to commit to each other, and you've got to have as much of the picture as I can give you to be able to do that. It's a matter of survival."

Yeah, Bern thought, and he'd just gotten through seeing how difficult it was for even Susana to have the whole picture. He remembered the surprised look on her face when she found out about Jude and Mingo.

Jesus. He was nearly a basket case of scrambled emotions. He was scared. He was recklessly curious about what he would discover about Jude's life. And he was horrified that those pictures of Alice would surface somewhere, and that Dana and Phil would never, ever, no matter what, be able to look at him the same way again.

Hell, there was no way to turn back the clock. Yeah, he was committed, the same way he was committed to the coming of night, to the passage of time, to the surety of death.

In the afternoon, Bern went on reading the files. He moved the laptop to the sofa in the studio and kept plowing through the pages and pages of data. When he had questions, Susana explored every detail with him. They were both determined that Bern would grab as much information as possible in the short time they had.

They plunged into Ghazi Baida's life.

"Maybe the main thing about Baida," Susana said, "is that he's not your typical Hezbollah terrorist. For one thing, he's not an angry young man. He was born in 1954 in Beirut, the only child of a couple whose backgrounds seem to begin with the birth of their son. We don't know anything at all about where they were from or who their families were. The father was a textile merchant, and when Ghazi was eight, his father moved the family to Mexico City, where there was already a large Lebanese community. Ghazi attended private American schools here and became fluent in English and Spanish.

"When it came time for him to go to university, he enrolled at the University of Texas at Austin. He had a hell of a time there, went nuts over the freewheeling life of a well-to-do university student. He totally bought into the American collegiate idea. Ball games, parties. Even a spell in a fraternity. Women. He was good-looking, and charming. In short, he had a blast."

Susana went on to outline his graduation, his unhappy return to Mexico, his falling-out with his father after a year in the family business, his rebellious move back to Beirut while the country was in the throes of a civil war. Then he seemed to have fallen into a black hole. For the next decade, information about him was scarce, except for a few key facts: The war politicized him, as did his love affair with Rima Hani, a young Lebanese woman who was educated at the Sorbonne and was also from a wealthy Beirut family. In April of 1981, the two married.

In September of 1982, Lebanese Christian Phalange

units swept into the Palestinian refugee camps of Sabra and Shatilla and massacred some eight hundred civilians. Israeli forces who were responsible for the camps' safety stood by and let it happen. Rima, who was working as a medical volunteer in the camps, was killed in the massacre.

"When Ghazi surfaced again," Susana said, "he was Hezbollah's most skilled operational designer." She nodded at the laptop. "You've got them there, the list of horrors that bear his trademark—bombings, kidnappings, assassinations throughout the Middle East and Latin America.

"But after 2002, Baida dropped off the intelligence radar screens again. Rumors placed him in Latin America. And rumors were all they had, until Jude spoke to him in Ciudad del Este a little more than two months ago."

They spent the rest of the day and into the night studying Jude's smuggling route from Guatemala to Houston. Names. Names. Names. Places. Places. Places. Code words. Contacts. Whom he paid for what. What he paid to whom. Names. Places.

The next morning, they began with Jude's notes on his meetings with Mazen Sabella and Ghazi Baida. Names. Places. Jude's impressions. Susana told him little bits of details that Jude had shared with her during their long conversations, feelings and hunches, the sorts of things that didn't make their way into his official reports. Not facts, just feelings, the way Jude felt at the third meeting in Ciudad del Este when the stranger walked into the ratty hotel and introduced himself as Ghazi Baida. What Jude thought of Baida's facial surgery, how it had dramatically changed his appearance, and how Jude imagined that it must have affected his personality as well.

By late in the afternoon of the second day, Bern was beginning to get a good feel for the way his brother had been trying to ferret out the pieces of the puzzle. The sun was coming through the studio windows at an acute angle, just clearing the trees and the cityscape. The sharp contrast of light and shadow would not last long. In a few minutes, the sun's rays would hit the densest layer of the city's notorious smog shroud. The light would soften, and then the clouds would move in, gathering for the summer afternoon's rain showers.

Bern stood stiffly from where he had been grounded for hours on the sofa. His muscles needed stretching; his body yearned for a swim in the cove. But his mind was electrically charged, and his new knowledge was generating an intense energy, which made him as antsy as a cat.

He walked over to the windows, where the sun was streaming in, and looked out over Parque México. The windows were open, and he could feel the cool, soft late-afternoon breeze that carried the burble of pigeons and, occasionally, the lilt of children's voices from the park. He leaned on the windowsill and marveled at the strange and alien feeling of the moment. He might as well have been in Bangkok or Samarkand.

"Jude used to stand that way," Susana said. "Just like that. Right there in that window."

When he turned around, she was standing, too, looking at him with an expression of haunted memory.

"I've got to have a drink," she said. "I've waited long enough."

"I'll get it," Bern said. He went over to the ebony cabinet and made the drink just as she had shown him how to do that first night. He made one for himself, too, then took Susana's over and handed it to her.

"If you're right about Mingo," he said, sipping his drink, which he held in one hand, the other hand in a pocket, "then it seems to me—"

Jude's cell phone rang, startling both of them. Susana put down her drink before she picked up the phone.

"Yes."

Hesitation at the other end.

Bern went over to her, and she tilted the phone so he could hear.

"Why are you answering this phone, *señora?*"

"Who is this?"

"I need to speak to Jude."

"You don't understand," she said. "I have to know who this is."

Pause. "Tell him it's Mingo."

"Look," she said, "he's sick; tomorrow would be better."

"Give the phone to him," Mingo said. "Even if he is sick. This is very important."

"I have to have—"

Suddenly, Bern grabbed the phone from her. She gasped, stunned.

"Mingo." His instincts told him to keep his voice calm. Very calm. "This is Jude."

He cut his eyes at Susana. She was looking at him as if he had shot her.

"Judas? Jesus, man, we thought you were dead. I can't believe it. Where the hell have you been?"

"Who thought I was dead?"

"Everybody, man. Are you okay?"

"I'm okay," Bern said.

There was silence on the other end. Bern imagined the

other man's face, his eyes narrowing, straining to see what was in store for him as he stared into the diminishing light of suspicion.

Mingo said, "We thought the *narcos* got you."

"I was lucky."

"No shit."

"You said you had something important to tell me."

Pause. "This phone, it's still good?"

"Yeah, it's clean."

"It's about Baida, Judas. I need to talk to you."

"Okay, good—"

"The same place, then?"

"No. Can't do that anymore. Look, give me fifteen minutes, then call me back."

"*Bueno.*"

Chapter 25

When he punched off the phone and turned around, Susana was gaping at him, breathing hard, her eyes still wide in disbelief.

"What in the *fuck* was that? What are you—"

"He said he needed to talk to me about Baida. That was his urgent message."

"Shit." She stared at him. "What in God's name do you think you're doing? You think you're ready for this? Is that it? Is that what this is? Listen, you wouldn't be up to this if you'd spent a goddamned decade getting ready. That"— she was so pissed that her voice had changed—"kind of stunt"—she pointed at the telephone—"will get you killed so fast that they'll be shipping *your* head back to the States for someone to . . . to . . . reconstruct!"

"Look," he said, "I should've . . . I just didn't—"

"You didn't! You didn't! Hell no you didn't! You didn't tell me what you were going to do. You probably didn't know what you were going to do. You didn't give it any thought. You didn't know enough about anything to *do* anything!"

The intensity of her emotion had literally changed some of the features of her face.

And for a moment, Bern almost believed her rant was justified. For a second, his conviction wavered, and the instantaneous clarity of the idea that had driven him to grab the phone almost slipped away from him. Almost, but it didn't. It was still there, clear and sure, and he knew, as surely as he had known anything during the last four days, that he had done the right thing.

He forced himself to be calm, to keep his voice level. He wanted what he was about to say to be measured and clear.

"Listen to me," he said. "We've got fifteen minutes for you to figure out how, and where, you want me to meet this guy."

"We don't even know what he looks like!" she snapped.

He pointed at her, the phone still in his hand.

"You said something just then that's probably true. If I had a decade, I couldn't get ready for this thing. Hell, you were probably right, too, when we first spoke and you said that you thought this was the craziest idea you'd ever heard. Okay, so why the hell are you so insistent on being rational about this?"

"Rational?"

"Yeah. What were you doing stalling my meeting with Mingo for another day? Did you think we could get ready—ready by your standards—by tomorrow? Hell no. The fact is, you didn't know what the hell you were doing, either, did you? All you knew was that you didn't think I was ready. You were buying time, but you didn't really know what for, did you?"

She said nothing, too angry to respond. He wasn't even sure she was hearing him. She stood there in front of him, rigid, still unable to believe what he'd just done.

"Here's the truth about what we're doing," he said. "Logic isn't going to get us where we want to go. The odds of this thing being even remotely successful aren't going to improve because you're able to buy me another twelve hours to cram for the test."

He stopped, calmed himself. He wanted to be methodical, though he wasn't really feeling methodical. But he did feel right about what he was doing. He felt sure of himself. He only hoped he wasn't being delusional.

"What do we want?" he asked. "We want Baida to believe that I'm Jude. For a day? Two days? A week? Two weeks? And you haven't even told me why. When were you going to get around to that, Susana? Why were you holding back? Is this some of that 'need to know' shit? Well, who in God's name would need to know more than me?"

She didn't answer. He didn't know if she couldn't or just wouldn't. Right now, he didn't understand anything that he saw in her face.

"Look, this would've been hard enough to do if I had known Jude," he went on. "Hard to do, even, if I'd known his friends. The only thing we have going here is that I look like him as much as any human being possibly could. That"—he hesitated, not knowing if this would sound embarrassingly absurd to her—"and the fact that we share the same DNA. Maybe . . . Mondragón was more on target to emphasize the advantages I do have than we are moaning about the disadvantage we can't overcome. Maybe I do have instincts that'll serve your purposes. Maybe, as you've said, I just naturally act like him without even knowing it, do things that he would do, small things. Things that sometimes are more telling than the things we carefully plan. Things that will say more to Mingo . . . or Baida . . . than all the imitation truth that we could accomplish in a month of dress rehearsals."

She swallowed. He saw it, and he saw her listening now, saw her finding a thread in what he was saying that she could hang on to.

"That's what we're going to have to rely on," he said. "That's the best we've got. I've read all the files now. Only once, I know. And I don't have a photographic memory. But we've been over and over and over the two most important elements that'll make me convincing to Baida: knowing the details of the smuggling scheme and knowing the details of Jude's conversations with Sabella and Baida. It's been little more than a crash course . . . but that's all we've got."

She stared at him in silence, and then she said, "You son of a bitch."

Then she reverted to an already-familiar gesture: She ran the fingers of one hand over her brow and into her thick hair and held them there, eyes fixed.

"But you don't know Baida's bio well enough, not like Jude did. And you haven't studied it the way you sh—"

"Susana! Listen, Jude the smuggler doesn't know Baida's bio, either. What I don't know about the details of his life will be no disadvantage to me in convincing him that I'm Jude."

She turned and walked away, head down.

Bern felt the buzz of his accelerating free fall.

Susana suddenly turned and went across to one of the workbenches, where they had laid out maps of Mexico

City for him to study as she told him of Jude's movements, his galleries, homes of friends, favorite restaurants.

"Come here," she said, and she was already bending over the maps as he joined her. She spread one of the maps flat with both hands.

"We're here, okay?" she said, jabbing the map. She slid one finger across the streets to her upper right. "This is Zona Rosa, a kind of tacky collection of streets chockablock with restaurants and clubs and bars. Used to be an elegant district, but it's tending to go to seed with lap dancing and prostitution now. But the tourists still come, plodding around, begging to be ripped off.

"It's crowded there, which is good, and it's close to Kevern's group. They can cover it. Jude used to meet Ahmad at a club there." She leaned closer to the map. "Here, near Génova and Hamburgo, there's a place called Club Cuica. It's a samba club. Very popular. The street in front is a pedestrian walkway, with planters and flowers and palms along its center, like a promenade. The place is usually crowded with people out strolling."

She straightened up and sat on a stool at the table.

"Meet him in front of the club. Don't go inside. There's a life-size bronze statue of a nude samba dancer in the median right in front of the club. Have him wait by that thing. It has the advantage of being hidden from the other side of the esplanade, so anyone who wants to watch him will have to do it from the same side. That'll give Lex's people an advantage."

"Mingo's going to wonder why the hell I'm doing this."

She looked at him, her eyes hard.

"And what are you going to tell him?"

Okay. Fair enough. He hesitated only a moment.

"I won't have to tell him anything. He won't be wondering, will he? He'll know I'll be trying to pick up surveillance."

"But that's his expertise," she said. "Don't you think he can get there clean without you having to double-check him?"

"I won't give a shit what he thinks. I'm the one who nearly got killed. I'll do what I think I have to do."

She looked at him. She nodded. "Okay." She looked at her watch. "Let's put it at eight o'clock. That'll give us another couple of hours."

Before he could agree, Jude's cell phone rang. Bern was still holding it in his hand. He looked at her.

"You might as well go ahead," she said.

Bern punched the button and put it to his ear.

Chapter 26

For the two hours that remained before Bern had to leave, they continued to concentrate on the lengthy reports that Jude had provided on his meetings with Sabella and Baida in Ciudad del Este.

As dusk fell, the evening rains came in on rumbles of thunder. There was no wind, and the rain fell straight down and hard, slapping the thick canopy of trees in the park as if it were popping on canvas awnings, a monsoon sound that distracted them from their desperate concentration. They stopped talking and stared out the open windows as the last of the purple light deepened into night, and the mesmerizing sounds of the rain-splashed streets evoked in each of them closely guarded memories.

Finally, Susana broke the silence.

"There's no reason to think you'll be in any danger," she said. She had been pacing back and forth in front of the sofa as they talked, but she had stopped now to stare out at the rain. Bern was still sitting in one of the armchairs, where he had been flicking through pages on the laptop, reading from the CDs of Jude's reports.

"We know nothing about the guy," she went on, "which makes people like us nervous, though there's no real indication that we should be. Obviously, he's been helpful to Jude, had access to the encrypted cell number. No one else had that."

Bern looked at his watch. He backed out of the program and then popped the CD out of the laptop. He put it in a clear plastic envelope, stood, and handed it to Susana.

"I'll do the best I can," he said. "I'll try not to screw it up."

Susana didn't react to the last remark.

"Lex's people will be trying to pick up surveillance," she went on, "so you need to stay right there at the statue the whole time. You get inside a club or near a street musician, it'll play hell with our audio pickup. If this guy wants to leave, don't. And remember, you're going to want to do everything differently now. If he wants to talk in Spanish, say no. You don't have to explain. If he wants to continue anything 'the way we've always done—'"

"Then I say no. I want to change it. And I don't explain anything."

"Exactly," she said. "The implication is that you've got your reasons, and they're none of his business. Jude pulled that kind of shit on people all the time, and my guess is that this guy is already very familiar with it. That gives you a lot of room to maneuver."

Bern nodded. He was surprised at the absence of butterflies. As the two hours had dwindled, he had become increasingly focused, and with that had come an odd kind of serenity. He noticed it. Didn't understand it. But he didn't dwell on it, either, gratefully accepting it for what it was. He was okay. He could do this. There was so much to lose that there was no realistic way that he could shoulder the weight of it. That realization was liberating.

He told the taxi driver to drop him at the corner of Florencia, and he began walking toward Génova along Londres. The rains had passed and the streets and sidewalks glistened in the city's lights. He couldn't just jump out of a taxi and go right into it. He wanted to feel the pavement first, move along the sidewalks, walk through the smells and sounds. He hadn't even been out of Jude's apartment in twenty-four hours, and it was beginning to feel as though he was orbiting the city rather than living in it.

As soon as he passed Amberes, the crowds picked up and the feeling of impending carnival increased with every doorway he passed. The district's wise guys smoked and lounged along the sidewalks, which were crowded with young clubgoers and hangers-on. A solitary woman with the lifeless expression of someone who saw it all every evening watched him pass by as she smoked a cigarette and held the leash of a mongrel who was shitting at the base of a solitary ficus growing in a circle of bare dirt.

At Génova, the evening was in full swing. The street had long ago been closed to automobile traffic, and an island of garden plantings and palms ran down its center. Both sides were lined with outdoor cafés and restaurants, clubs, bars, hotels, and art galleries and antique shops. The crowd was roughly divided among three groups: those curious folk who came here to taste the spicier side of the city's nightlife, those who wanted to sell them something, and those who wanted to prey on them. Like all streets of this kind in major cities the world over, none of the motives ever changed.

As Bern moved through the crowd headed in the direction of Paseo de la Reforma, he was aware of being the watcher and of being watched. He wanted to glimpse the statue of the naked samba dancer before Mingo had the chance to see him. He wanted at least that much of an advantage.

He heard the carnival beat of Club Cuica well before he saw its sign, and he moved closer to the rail of a sidewalk café to get a better angle on the palmy median of the esplanade. Finally, through sporadic gaps in the bobbing heads of the pedestrians, he glimpsed the bronze dancer raised on a stone pedestal a couple of feet high. Cautiously, he moved ahead, then stopped outside the door of an art gallery where two shoe-shine boys had squatted down on their boxes, taking a break from the crowd. They watched the stream of nightlife with bleary disinterest while they ate red Popsicles that dripped on the stones between their feet.

Then Bern saw him, hanging close to the statue, a well-dressed young man, perhaps in his late twenties. His hair was carefully barbered, and he had the comfortable good looks of a sophisticated *capitalino,* a man who understood the mysteries of the city where he had lived all of his life. Seemingly unconcerned about having to wait, he leaned a shoulder against the hard thigh of the nude statue and watched the women coming and going through the doors of Club Cuica. Bern liked him immediately.

Without hesitating further, Bern cut through the crowd and approached the young man. He instantly saw the recognition in the young man's eyes.

"Hey, Judas," Mingo said, straightening up as they

shook hands. He threw a look around with a half shrug. "This is a strange way to do it, huh?"

"A little," Bern said. He could see Mingo looking at him closely.

"What's the deal?" Mingo asked. "What happened to you?"

"I was hurt a little," Bern said. "I've been recuperating."

Mingo's eyes opened in surprise. "No shit? They shot you?"

"Look," Bern said, "what's the story here?"

"Yeah, okay, you want to go somewhere so we can talk?"

"Got to do it right here."

Mingo's eyes flickered, and Bern could see him trying to figure out the logic of it, why Jude would want that. But then he nodded, accepting it. He glanced around and hunched his shoulders a little in an unconscious gesture of confidentiality, then moved closer to Bern.

He was wearing an expensive suit without a tie. He had a very precise coal black mustache, which complemented his handsome features. Just behind his head, one of the naked breasts of the luscious samba dancer shone brightly, its dark patina worn away to a clean brassy shine by the nightly caresses of randy young men.

Mingo raised his eyebrows with a knowing look. He shifted his weight and leaned in closer. Close enough for Bern to catch a whiff of cologne.

"I did what you said to do," Mingo rasped. "*Tuvimos cuidado*, Judas. Ver-ry careful, okay?"

Bern nodded.

"It took us a while," Mingo went on, "but my *capitali-*

nas, they are very clever girls, very light, like moths. They went where you said to go; they did the things you said to do. And, of course, they were very inventive, too."

The shoe-shine boys appeared in front of them and one said something in Spanish to Mingo, who nodded casually and kept talking as he ruffled the kid's hair affectionately and put an already-polished shoe up on one of the little wooden stands. Bern shook his head at the other boy.

"I have found a woman who has the thing you want," Mingo said. He waited for a response from Bern.

Bern's heart fluttered. "Oh?"

Mingo reacted subtly. Something in Bern's reaction. Mingo had expected something different? Something more?

"And?" Bern asked.

Mingo carefully handed him a piece of paper. Taking his cue from Mingo's caution, Bern surreptitiously unfolded it, read what was there, and then looked at Mingo. He needed to react. Mingo was anticipating something, as if the information was momentous.

But Bern wasn't quick enough. Mingo's eyes scrambled quickly over Bern's face, sensing that something wasn't right. The shoe-shine boy tapped his foot, and Mingo looked down, adjusting his foot on the stand.

The second boy very casually went around his kneeling partner, working on Mingo's shoe, and stared at the statue behind Mingo. The boy on his knees opened the side of his box to take out a tin of polish as the second boy reached up and took Mingo's arm.

Mingo looked around to see who it was just as the kneeling boy came up with a glistening chrome pistol the size of the boy's head. Holding the huge gun with both small hands, he heaved it up, his arms straight out, pointed it at Mingo, and fired. The recoil was so powerful that the boy's thin little arms flew up over his head, almost out of control, and the sound of the report was as deafening as a cannon blast.

Bern watched, frozen, as the little boy with the gun then brought the pistol down again and jammed it into Mingo's stomach while the second boy, holding his arm, kept the stunned young man from lunging away. The second and third shots were loud, but muffled, and drove Mingo into the naked embrace of the samba dancer. The fourth, fifth, and sixth shots, all buried in the depths of Mingo's torso, blew blood and viscera twenty feet away.

It all happened before Bern could even draw a breath of astonishment.

Women screamed and people scattered from the samba dancer. The music in Club Cuica pounded away, but in an instant, there was no one there to hear it. The two shoeshine boys ran as if they had thrown a ball and broken a window, leaving behind the bloody chrome gun at the dancer's bare feet.

Mingo had been thrown back into the palmettos by the force of the rapid blasts, and only his well-shined shoes and expensive trousers protruded from the bed of ivy.

Then Bern ran, too. He was the last to run, and he headed for the darkest streets in Mexico City.

Chapter 27

Kevern's tech had patched Susana into their audio surveillance, and she listened on her new cell phone as she sat on the edge of the sofa in Jude's studio. When the first shot was fired, she sprang to her feet. She pressed the cell phone to her ear, unconsciously raising her free hand in defensive shock as she listened to the sporadic distribution of subsequent shots, flinching with each one, not knowing who was on the receiving end of the blasts.

Then silence.

She didn't even think. She grabbed her shoulder bag and flew down the stairs, through the apartment, down the building's stairwell, out onto Avenida México, and into the park. Dialing furiously, she sought the darkest part of the park, then stopped in the middle of one of the wide paths to listen.

The rings were too long. Endless. Each one a toll announcing Bern's death. She couldn't believe it. God.

"Yes! Yes!" His voice was frantic.

"You okay?"

"Yeah, yeah, I'm okay." He was still running. She could hear him huffing. "God, it was kids, just kids, just a couple of kids."

She could hear the wild dismay in his voice.

"Listen to me," she said, every nerve in her body focused on a plan. "Are you alone?"

"Yeah—" He was still running.

"Listen to me: The place I told you about where Jude used to sketch the dancers—don't say the name—do you remember it?"

Don't say the name? Oh Jesus. Remember. Remember. The pages in Jude's file flew through his mind, swirling like litter scattered in a storm.

"Yeah! I got it. Yes."

"Get a taxi. Go there. Okay? You have that?"

"Yeah, good. I . . . I've got it."

"Now, get rid of the phone!" Susana snapped. "Throw it away right now. Drop it. Now! Go, get away from it!"

She ran through the dark edges of the park. When she got to Avenida Sonora, she flagged a taxi.

He threw the damn cell phone against a building, shattering it, unable to get rid of it fast enough, and kept running. He ran for another block without thinking, just getting farther away from the shooting, from the phone, from the images in his head. Finally, he had to stop to catch his breath. He fell back against a building, bent over, and grabbed great desperate gulps of Mexico City's thin, resinous air.

In the darkness his mind cast up images of the shooting. He saw the shoe-shine boy's little hunched shoulders as he burrowed the muzzle of the huge handgun into

Mingo's stomach, each blast digging deeper into him. He saw Mingo's astonished face: shock, pain, realization, dismay, horror. Every explosion from the hands of the child assassin reflecting in his face as he spun deeper and deeper into his vanishing mortality.

Horrible.

He began running again, but it couldn't have been more than just another block before he had to stop once more. Jesus. The altitude. Where was he? Shit. He was hopelessly disoriented by his mad dash into nowhere. Though he couldn't have gone all that far, the streets were narrow and murky, the doorways were hollows descending to unknown horrors, and the few people he encountered under the trees hurried past without looking, wanting nothing to do with a marked man, wanting nothing to do, even, with the night air that moved around him.

To his left, across the street and near the middle of the next tree-lined block, he saw light spilling onto the sidewalk from a doorway, a few people milling in the glow inside. He forced himself to walk slowly, to control his breath, not wanting to approach them gasping for air.

It was a small hotel, its lobby door thrown open to the cool night. Pausing in the low wattage of the foyer, he saw a young woman standing behind an old curved registration desk, an older woman mopping the terrazzo floor, and a young man with no apparent purpose other than to talk to the young woman. They turned their eyes on him.

He asked the girl if she would call a *sitio* for a taxi. It was dangerous to flag a taxi off the street, especially the little green Volkswagen cabs. These innocuous-looking little vehicles had a brutal history of collusion with armed robbers and kidnappers, and not a few people had lost their lives after stepping inside one of them.

The girl did as he asked, and he thanked her, moving out of the spill of light to wait alone at the curb. Immediately, he heard sirens. He looked back at the small foyer and saw that all three pale faces were turned to him. But their expressions were unreadable. It was a learned trait in a city of secrets. No one knew anything. And no one, *no one,* was curious.

The night shadows are impatient in Mexico City. They stick close to you when you turn off a major street, crowd you as you walk, and overtake you by the time you've gone only a few yards. So Bern stood surrounded by them, his back flat against a stone wall a few feet from where the taxi had left him.

He was in a neighborhood on the edge of Colonia Roma, not all that far from Condesa—a fact that made Susana's choice wildly reckless to him. Across the street and a little farther down, Beso Azul—the Blue Kiss—stood on the corner under a old jacaranda that fractured the light falling onto the sidewalk from a nearby streetlamp. The club's entrance was on the angle of the corner, and through the dappled haze in front of its opened doors, a languorous music floated out into the darkness.

Should he go inside, then? Wasn't that implied? He didn't know what the hell was implied. The words stood alone, stubbornly without implication. "Go there" was all she had said.

It seemed rash to leave the shadows. Jesus Christ. To show his face anywhere seemed insanity. Suddenly, he was aware of his legs trembling. She had said, "You don't know this yet, but you can trust me. You need to grab hold of that fact as quickly as you can."

He stepped out of the shadows and crossed the street.

Once inside, his eyes began to adjust to the gloom. He saw immediately that the Beso Azul was not *de moda,* was not *de ambiente.* This was not the gathering place of the chic young crowds that frequented the stylish and trendy clubs in Condesa and Polanco. There were no cell phones here, no sunglasses, no pounding electronic storm.

Though the decor was an unintentional faded memory of the Art Deco era of the late 1920s, the crowd was, in fact, a mixture of the middle-aged and young. Here, in a blue haze, the dancers embraced closely, exuding a poignant sexual melancholy as they glided about the dance floor in the fluid slow-quick-quick, slow-quick-quick rhythm of the graceful Cuban *danzón,* a sweet and romantic music played by a cello, a couple of violins, an old piano, and a flute.

"Aaaah, Judas." The purring woman's voice caught him by surprise. He turned to see her as she was passing by with her partner, a woman his own age, the bare tops of her breasts swollen by her partner's tight embrace. Turning her head to follow him with her eyes as she danced, she smiled, her white teeth iridescent. Her swarthy partner jerked his head in a serious greeting without speaking, and they slowly danced away.

He was on the edge of the dance floor moving among the tables along its perimeter, moving to nowhere.

"Judaaaas." A middle-aged man smiled and lifted his chin at Bern from a tiny table, cigarette smoke streaming from his nostrils, his woman leaning on him, smiling at Bern, too.

Jesus Christ. He thought he spoke to them; he thought he smiled at them; he thought he seemed at ease.

Someone hissed through the *danzón,* and he turned and saw a woman smiling from a table farther away. Another man nodded his head soberly in greeting.

This was surreal. Enveloped in a smoky sapphire glow, surrounded by the languid music and dancers who seemed to belong to another era, Bern began to feel a weird disconnect from the heart-hammering velocity of his flight. The tacky Club Cuica, the blast of the child's gun, the blown blood and viscera—all of it seemed to recede, as if it had never been anything but a memory anyway, as if it were being absorbed, even obliterated, by this reanimation of a scene from an old movie.

Inexplicably, he even began to feel as if he were remembering this place, the Blue Kiss in Roma, as if he were returning to an old retreat, returning to these strangers, old friends forgotten. He felt that he understood these people, that he knew why they came here, seeking one another's company in this melancholy place with its sweet, heartbreaking music. Instinctively, he knew exactly why Jude had come here to sketch the somber faces of these lovelorn men and the coy smiles of their women.

Gently, she took his arm from behind, and when he turned, she was as close to him as the embracing dancers, as close as when she had kissed him the very first moment that they met. She pulled his face to her, not for a kiss this time, but to whisper. His lips were at her neck, in the shallow of her collarbone, and he smelled her skin. And he smelled fear.

Chapter 28

Kevern's small team of four, including himself, was well versed in electronics, but for the more complex ops they depended on Mondragón's techs, who were all ex-Mexican military or intelligence officers. But there hadn't been time for them to put together video surveillance, though they did have a good audio feed.

Mondragón's security goons were there, blending in with the crowd, though they were there only as observers this time and had no real responsibilities beyond providing more eyes and ears. Everyone half-expected Baida to have people there also, if he was indeed looking for an opportunity to contact Bern, and Kevern hoped someone would be able to pick up on some of his people. A good percentage of the crowd on Calle Génova belonged to a surveillance entity of one kind or another.

At the sound of the first shot, Kevern's team bailed out of their car, which was double parked near the French embassy on Calle Niza. But by the time they had all hit the pavement, the last shot was being fired, and by the time they had reached the corner of Calle Hamburgo, they slammed into a tide of screaming Zonistas fleeing in the opposite direction.

When they finally fought their way upstream, the samba dancer was dancing alone, though some people in the crowd were already slowing down and turning around to glance back from a safer distance. Kevern dived into the palmettos, getting bloody up to his elbows as he deftly retrieved Mingo's wallet.

Then they were gone, leaving the Policia Judicial to discover the body for themselves and to sort it all out on their own, which they weren't going to be able to do.

Moments later, after they had returned to the car, Kevern discovered that Susana wasn't answering either her surveillance cell or her regular encrypted cell. But the tracking equipment had picked up her encrypted call to Bern's phone.

Kevern's officers immediately began homing in on the GPS signals from the two phones. Bern's was stationary.

Kevern began going through the possibilities of why Bern's signal wasn't moving as their car eased through the streets, sneaking away from the chaos in the Zona Rosa. He had been killed. Or he had been kidnapped and his phone discarded. Whatever Susana's reasons were for not answering, he just had to trust her.

He hunched over in his seat and concentrated on listening to the playback of Bern's conversation with Mingo, listening to it again and again. *"They went where you said to go; they did the things you said to do."* Kevern replayed it once more and then looked at the agent sitting across from him in the backseat. *"I have found a woman who has the thing you want."*

"What the hell's he saying?" Kevern grunted.

Jack Petersen said nothing. He had worked undercover in Latin America for thirteen years. Buenos Aires, Iguaçú Falls, Bogotá, São Paulo. He had last worked with Kevern in Colombia. He put his head down and listened, shaking his head.

"Shit," Kevern said. He fast-forwarded to Bern's response. *"Oh?"* Again. *"Oh?"* Again. *"Oh?"* Then: *"And?"* Again. *"And?"*

Then the recording fell silent, except for the samba music that was being picked up in the background. Samba music. Samba music.

Then the first blast. Screams. And then the other blasts following rapidly.

Kevern didn't replay the shots.

They followed the GPS signal from Bern's cell phone, approaching carefully, reading the traffic on the sidewalks. As they neared the signal on the dark street, pedestrians disappeared altogether. Finally, a dozen blocks from the Zona Rosa, they found Bern's cell phone scattered all over the sidewalk.

Using his cell phone, Petersen finally reached Quito Lopez, Mondragón's main ops guy, but Lopez said it all happened so fast, they didn't even get a chance to cover the crowd. The truth was, nobody was expecting a hit, not in a meeting between partners, and the shooting caught everyone off guard. "By the way," Quito said, "Mingo passed something to Bern, a piece of paper. Bern read it and put it in his pocket."

Kevern stood on the dark sidewalk, listening to Petersen's report and putting Susana's actions through his mental analysis mill. The car sat idling in the street, its rear doors open. Lupe Nervo, one of Kevern's two female team members, had gotten out to gather up the pieces of the cell phone, and now she was fiddling with them as if she could put the phone back together again. As if it mattered.

"Son of a bitch," Kevern grunted.

Petersen was lighting a cigarette. "This guy was still looking into something, even though he thought Jude was dead? I think he confirmed something Jude had suspected. Probably what was written on the piece of paper."

"That's what it sounds like." Kevern was pissed. He wasn't sure what was going on here.

"It'd be a mistake to assume too much here," Petersen said, mostly talking to himself as he worked it out. "The hit doesn't necessarily have anything to do with what Mingo was telling Bern. Could've been totally unrelated."

A light breeze moved down the narrow street, bringing heavy moisture. The early-evening rains had not moved out entirely, as was their habit, and a fog was beginning to settle in. Kevern could feel it on his face and could see it gathering around the few streetlamps that stretched far down the diminishing street.

"Lex," said Mattie Sellers, the second female team member, who was sitting in the car with her door open, watching the signal from Susana's phone on her GPS monitor, "she's not far away. Southern edge of Colonia Roma."

Lupe had gotten back into the car to get out of the mist, which was growing heavier.

Petersen hunched his shoulders, turned up the collar of his shirt, dropped his cigarette butt—he never smoked a whole one anymore—and put his foot on it.

"I trust her," Kevern said, as if Petersen had asked him if he did. He was still staring into the distance. "She'll do what has to be done." He didn't move his eyes off the street, which seemed to be receding into the soup of dark and mist. "Let's get back into the car and see where she's going."

Vicente Mondragón was finding it hard to breathe. Sometimes the membrane covering his nasal cavities was affected by the peculiar atmosphere in Mexico City. The high altitude made the air very dry, even in the rainy season, and then the pollution added to the ineffectiveness of the membrane's porosity. Sometimes the whole raw front of his head, where his face used to be, ached, despite the analgesic spray. To help dampen the pain, he continuously consumed a farrago of mixed drinks.

The events in front of the samba dancer had been narrated to him by Quito Lopez, who was reporting from his position on the dark roof of Club Cuica, where Quito's technicians were broadcasting to Kevern a live feed of the conversation that they were picking up with a parabolic microphone. He was waiting for the phone call he knew he would be getting soon from Kevern. Quito had seen Kevern retrieve Mingo's wallet, and soon Kevern would want Mondragón's men to find out where he lived and to strip the place for information.

This had been a good contract for Mondragón. Lex Kevern always paid well, gave Mondragón and his men a lot of leeway, and still believed that the law of spoils was a justified concept. As long as the operation was done well, Mondragón was welcome to pick up the debris that inevitably followed in its wake.

But the downside of working with the Americans was having to put up with their arrogance. Their superiority in everything was so automatically taken for granted that they fell into it as naturally as shitting. They thought that the people they hired knew only the things that the Americans told them, that the hirelings had no real creative abilities of their own. It was hard for those who came from a powerful country to believe that they could be outsmarted, that they could be manipulated just as easily as they manipulated others. Although it would seem that in the age of terrorism, and in an age when the Colombian drug cartels, with whom the American's had been "at war" for decades, were still earning more annual revenue than McDonald's, Kellogg's, and Microsoft *combined*, the Americans might get the hint that they were not always the smartest people in the world.

But the truth was, there couldn't be enough downsides in this operation to dampen his enthusiasm for finding Ghazi Baida. Sometimes maniacal fate handed you a gift, and Kevern calling Mondragón for this operation was one of those times, as rare and sweet as an angel's breath. Mondragón had inhaled the opportunity with a vicious enthusiasm. Kevern did not know it, and Mondragón would not tell him, but hunting Ghazi Baida had been Mondragón's obsession for nearly three years. Kevern had only provided Mondragón with a kind of legitimacy, and a face, to do the very thing that kept his heart beating.

When the telephone rang, he picked it up.

"I got the guy's wallet," Kevern said, "and I've given it to Quito. Name's Domingo Huerta. Ever hear of him?"

"No."

"Well, I need as much as I can get on him, and I need it as fast as I can get it."

"Sure," Mondragón said. "Did Quito tell you about the pass?"

"Yeah."

"So where is Bern now?"

"Don't know. Susana had him ditch his cell phone, which was smart. She's picking him up. I'm waiting to hear. I'll tell you one thing: We weren't the only ones putting up wires on that street tonight. Whoever did this had some investments to protect. We need to know if this guy was killed because of something else he was into, or whether it had to do with Jude. Let's find out what the hell's going on here."

That was it. Kevern broke the connection. Mondragón dialed his encrypted phone and told Quito that he was to check with him first about whatever they found at Mingo's.

Outside his windows the fog that was moving in was melting the city's lights, creating a coppery glow, which was quickly enveloping the entire valley of lights.

Mondragón fought depression. Having no face was a living hell. He turned his back to the windows and looked into the half-light of his room of floating faces, everything bathed in rose-gold luster.

God, God, God, how he wanted a face.

The Náhuatl poets—the Mexica philosophers—believed that the human face was the most intimate manifestation of the intrinsic nature of each individual. It was the physical representation of the spiritual self. The personality. Without a face, a man vanished. He was nothing.

I cause sorrow to your face, to your heart.

If he had a thousand lives to live, he would forfeit them all in exchange for just one with a face.

*A lover of darkness and corners . . . he takes
things . . . a sorcerer, destroyer of faces, he causes
others to lose their faces.*

If he had a thousand lives to live, he would hunt Ghazi
Baida in all of them and destroy him over and over without ceasing.

He stared with his never-closing eyes at the floating
faces in the clear boxes. Even detached from their bodies,
even separate from their selves, they were more than he
was. Here was a man. Here was a woman. You see their
faces, you see their lives. Here is the woman who is no
more, gone to paradise. Here is the man who is no more,
gone to hell.

But he, Vicente Mondragón, was evanescent. He would
be forgotten. He was *desaparecido*—disappeared—his self
raided and stolen from him, his existence removed from
him in strips of flesh, in strands of muscle, in shards of cartilage.

Mondragón drew close to one of the faces in its clear
acrylic cube and put his raw head close to it, closer to it
than he could have done if he had had a nose. His lips
breathed a wavering ghost on the acrylic. His eyeballs, no
lids, no lashes, nearly touched the cube. It was a woman's
face, one of his favorites, for she was Asian, and he had
grown to love the clean lines of the Asian race. This
woman, Chinese.

As he stared at her, his vision caressing her graceful
contours as intimately as if he had been touching her with
his fingers, Mondragón began to weep, keening softly so
that his servants wouldn't hear.

Chapter 29

Someone in the crowd took his arm even as Susana was still talking, and he turned around and saw a man his own age staring at him, still holding his arm.

"Please, you need to come with us, Judas," he said. He raised his eyebrow coaxingly, and his expression was not threatening.

Bern turned to Susana, who was looking at him, too, and saw a man holding her arm, as well. Everyone exchanged looks, and then the man leaned close to Bern's ear and said, "Mazen Sabella."

Bern caught Susana's eye again and she nodded, or he thought she nodded, and then without anyone saying anything else, the four of them began moving slowly through the crowd.

Pushing through a clutch of people standing at the edge of the dance floor and against the wall adjacent to the orchestra, the man holding Susana's arm opened a door and they stepped into a narrow, musty hallway stacked with cases of empty liquor bottles and worn-out brooms and mops. At that moment, another door opened just ahead of them, blocking their way, and a woman stepped out of the rest room with her hands under the raised skirt of her dress as she finished adjusting her underwear. Surprised, she dropped her skirt, gave them a quick sheepish smile, and then with a "So what?" flick of her head, she squeezed past them in the tiny hallway.

"Did you say Mazen Sabella?" Bern asked, to let Susana know where they were going.

"Yes," the man said curtly.

They turned a corner and were at the back door of the club. The man with Susana opened the door, but then he let go of her arm and held his own arm out, blocking her.

"Alone," the man with Bern said.

"Hey, wait a second." Bern shook his head.

"I'm sorry," the man said. "You must be alone."

In a tense moment, everyone assessed the situation. Then the second man held both hands up in a placating gesture.

"It's better for her if she doesn't come," he said.

"It's okay." Susana reached out and touched Bern's chest with the flat of her hand, as if to convey the sincerity of her words. "It's okay. You heard what I said?"

He nodded. "Yeah."

"You remember it?"

"Yeah?"

"No problem, then, okay?"

He was adjusting, reading between the lines of every gesture, imagining the communication in every tick of her expression.

She looked at the man with Bern. "I'll see him later, right?"

"Yeah, sure, no problem."

"It's okay, then," she said to Bern, and she backed away slowly. They waited until she turned around and disappeared around the corner, heading back the way they had come.

He sat alone in the backseat of the car, a Lincoln, like the many *sitios* in the city. There was no effort to conceal their route, and his grim first thought was that he wouldn't be coming back, so it didn't matter. But he pushed it aside. Maybe Sabella was only going to be at this location for this one meeting. Or maybe at some point along the way, he would be blindfolded, maybe switched to another vehicle.

For a while, he stared out the windows, letting the image of Susana walking away play across his mind. God, how final that seemed now. At that moment, he was very close to accepting the fact that he simply couldn't do this. Very close. The fact was, he just didn't have the kind of guts that this was going to take. The best he could do was just fake it. Hell, he could fake it; he could do that. Play an audacious con game, a grand charade. At least until something unraveled that he couldn't control.

They entered the dark wood of Chapultepec Park, the headlights of the cars searching through the mist and fog that enshrouded the dense forest of giant *ahuehuetes*. The traffic was heavy, and people waited for transit connections along the broad sidewalks flanking the boulevard.

Staying on Paseo de la Reforma, they continued into the elegant neighborhood of Lomas de Chapultepec, moving higher into the hills, until the streets grew smaller and became serpentine. This was Bosques de las Lomas, a rarefied part of the city, where business magnates and wealthy politicians with dubious connections lived. It was also where most of the foreign ambassadors in the city had their homes.

They entered a section of ascending turns, the narrow street doubling back on itself again and again. Even on such a foggy night, he could make out the phenomenon for which this area was famous. Here the hills were so steep and close upon one another that girded pillars of concrete rose three, four, five stories up the hillsides in order to support plush gardens for the expensive homes that perched on the ridges. Trees and sprawling gardens, tennis courts and swimming pools—all were suspended above the city on superstructures massive enough to support whole buildings.

The mist grew heavier and the car took a sharp turn into a steep incline, passing through two wrought-iron gates. They turned yet again, the car's tires spinning in jerks on a pavement slick with the moist breath of fog. The headlights picked up a sheer cliff very close on the right, covered with hanging vines. On the other side, the hillside fell away and the coppery night sky of the city spread out across the valley far below.

They stopped in the circular courtyard of a two-story Spanish Colonial home. A window here and there glowed with amber light, but the exterior of the home was visible only because of the coppery glow from the valley.

As he got out of the car, Bern saw the dark silhouettes of palmettos against the building's facade, and now, too, the armed guards were visible, milling about the courtyard. Looking through a porte cochere that led into a second walled courtyard, he could see other cars and men carrying armloads of boxes out of the house and putting them into the cars.

He was escorted through the front door and into an un-
furnished entry hall where voices echoed off the stucco
walls and marble floors, making it impossible to tell the direction they were coming from.

They ascended a wide staircase, his two escorts having
to move to one side as three men started down with armloads of laptops. Armed guards appeared in the empty
entry below, speaking occasionally into wire mikes dangling from earpieces. Bern noticed that the painted plaster
walls were peeling.

Turning into a barrel-vaulted hallway, they followed it
to double wooden doors on the left, which swung open just
as they approached. They entered a long room that looked
as if it might have been a grand *sala* at one time. Here, too,
men were busily working, breaking down electronic equipment and loading it into boxes that were then being carted
away. French doors opened off the opposite long wall, revealing a terrace.

He was quickly marched through the room and out
onto the terrace, where a waiting bodyguard motioned to
Bern, who followed him to a trellis-covered alcove. Three
men were sitting in patio chairs in the gloamy light, and as
Bern approached, one of them stood and walked out of the
arbor, heading in the opposite direction.

"Judas." One of the remaining figures stood, came
around the table, and extended his hand, his face now visible out of the arbor's shadow. Bern recognized Mazen
Sabella from Jude's sketches. "*Bienvenidas,*" Sabella said.
He was unremarkable in either size or height, maybe thin-
ner than Jude's drawing had led him to expect. He wore a
dress shirt, sleeves rolled nearly to the elbow. He needed a
shave.

Bern shook his hand, but his eyes immediately sought the other man, who was still sitting at the table.

"Judas," the other man said, and he stood also, but remained where he was. "It's good to see you again."

Though he didn't step out of the arbor, Ghazi Baida's face was visible in the reflected copper glow from the valley, and Bern looked into the face of Jude's portraits. He look into the face of a murderer, an assassin, a terrorist. He looked into the face of the man that the CIA very much wanted to kill.

"Hello," Bern said. What the hell else should he say? He reached over the table and they shook hands.

Baida was a nice-looking man. The light was poor, but it was good enough for Bern to see that Baida needed a shave, too, that his white dress shirt was badly wrinkled, the cuffs rolled back from his forearms with rough indifference, the front unbuttoned nearly to midchest.

After hours of concentrating on Jude's portraits and studies of this man, the real thing was fascinating. Even in the coppery light, he could see how fine a job Jude had done. Still, the flesh-and-blood face of Ghazi Baida was more complicated, his features more interesting, than Jude had been able to portray. He was at once more rugged and more refined than Bern had expected.

"Please sit down with us," Baida said. There was a loud crash as something fell somewhere in the echoing rooms of the house. "We'll be gone from here shortly," Baida said, referring to the noise. "We have to make the most of our time."

Baida paused, but Bern had nothing to say. Jude would have had something to say, he knew, never having been at a loss for words. Baida considered him a moment from across the table. Games. He sat in his chair with a relaxed authority, unperturbed.

"I've been trying to make contact with you," Baida said. "But that hasn't been easy to do . . . at least not if we wanted to avoid being discovered. In the panic that followed the shooting, we lost you. But we also had someone watching Susana. When she ran out of your apartment on Avenida México, we guessed that if we stayed with her, we would have a good chance of finding you."

Bern heard car doors slamming down in the courtyard, engines starting, tires rolling over gravel, and then engines accelerating as the vehicles hit the paved drive and started down the hill. The place was emptying rapidly, but Baida didn't seem to be in a hurry. He was completely unruffled and sat in his chair as if he had the entire night to talk, as if he knew just the moment when he needed to move to avoid whatever misfortune it was that all the others were hurrying away from.

Chapter 30

In the silence, Bern rehearsed his role as Jude. He had just come out of hiding. He had met with his intelligence man, who had discovered that he was still alive, and then someone had shot him. A couple of kids. What would Jude have been thinking? What would Mingo's death have told him? What would Jude have seen in all of this? Would he have been thinking of anything except what he could do to save his skin?

Balda sat slumped in his chair, his right elbow on the arm of the chair while his face rested in the fingers of his hand, two fingers folded across the right side of his mouth, two fingers vertically bracing his temple. Bern noticed a black military-style watch on his left wrist. As he stared at Bern, watching him closely—did he sense something, suspect that this wasn't Jude sitting in front of him?—Baida gave off a sense of animal masculinity, which was probably one of the first things anyone would notice about him.

"Tell me," Baida said finally, straightening up in his

chair, "why you were at that place in Tepito the night of the shooting."

"Khalil called me and told me to meet him there. Didn't say why. I nearly stumbled right into it."

"And how did you manage to avoid that?"

"Dumb luck."

"Did you see what happened?"

"No."

"You heard the shooting."

"Yeah, and I ran. Ran like hell."

"Do you know what happened?"

"I heard . . . on the street, like everybody else."

Baida nodded pensively. "And why have you been hiding all this time?"

"I didn't have anything to do with what happened in Tepito that night. I just wanted to make damn sure that the word on the street had that straight before I showed my face again."

There were raised voices in the courtyard below, and then someone was running somewhere on the second floor. Baida seemed oblivious of this, and his eyes remained fixed, boring into Bern. He appeared to have something on his mind, maybe a decision to make, and Bern could only assume it had something to do with Jude. He tried to follow the logic of it, follow it the way he thought that Jude would have, play it the way he thought Jude would have played it.

"What was Domingo Huerta doing for you?" The question came from Sabella, who had been sitting quietly, watching Bern. He had sipped once from a white demitasse cup. Coffee, Bern guessed.

"You know what he does," Bern said. "I went over that with you when we talked in Ciudad del Este."

"And you weren't in communication with him . . . while you were *waiting* during these past weeks?"

"I think you know damn well we haven't been in touch." Bern focused on Sabella. "You've been all over him, I'd guess."

"Who else does he work for?"

"He doesn't tell me."

"He works only for you."

"No. I can't afford that."

"Who else, then?"

Bern glanced at Baida, who remained quiet, watching him, then back to Sabella.

"What the hell's going on here? What's the matter?"

"After you disappeared," Sabella said, "Domingo began looking around in places where he shouldn't have been looking."

"Shouldn't have been?"

"What was he talking about tonight when he said that he had done what you had said for him to do? That he had found a woman who 'has the thing you want'?"

Bern felt a warm flush envelope him. This was insanely beyond him. He wouldn't be able to sustain this.

"I have a client looking for a certain kind of pre-Columbian figurine. I had heard of a woman here who might have such a thing. That's what I thought he was referring to."

"What is the woman's name?"

"No, I can't do that. I don't mention your name to other people. I don't mention her name to other people. That's how I do it. That's the way I stay in business. People know they can trust that."

"Where does she live?"

Bern shook his head. "No."

Sabella didn't respond. Both men sat in the coppery half-light and looked at him. They didn't glance at each other or communicate in any way that Bern could detect, and yet it seemed to him that they were both weighing his response on the same scale, using the same criteria for finding him worthy . . . or not.

The slip of paper in his pocket burned into his groin like an ember.

"Are you sure that's what he was referring to?" Baida asked.

"I said I thought that's what he was referring to. I didn't have any reason to believe otherwise. He didn't live long enough for me to be sure."

They said nothing, watching him in silence. Bern was scared. Suddenly, what little bravery he had been able to screw together was slipping away. This is a smuggling deal, he reminded himself. A smuggling deal. Just a smuggling deal. Terrorism is not on the table.

"Look," he said. "If this isn't what you want anymore, then fine. I'm not exactly comfortable being on the edge of your fucked-up drug deals, either. Just remember, your people came to me. It wasn't the other way around. I'm not pushing my way into your business here. I can walk away. Easy."

Bern could hear more running.

He waited for Baida's reaction, but the other man sat there like a sphinx, a handsome sphinx, a sphinx with blood on its breath, with dead souls hanging around its neck like a necklace strung with withered lives. Bern thought of the paragraphs Jude had written about him, a kind of free verse about a man who was entirely likable, a man unworthy of his own personality.

"How long has it been since you were in Austin?" Baida asked.

Bern was staggered by the question. Jesus Christ. He suddenly felt nauseated. He knew. Baida knew. Bern was not going to walk out of here alive. And then just as suddenly, he remembered: Austin was Jude's home, too, and Baida's city of fondest memories, his halcyon university days, before the world turned cruel for him.

Jude had written that Baida loved to reminisce about it, about little things he remembered, a lane, a hilltop view (was it still the same?), a bar (was it still there?), a coffee shop, a bookstore. Details. The minutiae of memory, the small things that one missed and longed for, which grew larger and larger as time pushed them further and further away.

"Three months, maybe," Bern said.

"April," Baida said, his voice actually softening. "That's a good time." Another pause, then he said, "I had a friend whose family owned a home on the lake. Lake Austin."

Bern felt faint. What was this? Did he know after all, then? Was Baida toying with him?

"I used to go to this guy's house all the time. Beautiful place. Idyllic, really. We swam off the dock and watched the people skiing up and down the lake. Those wooded cliffs. They're still there, aren't they?"

"Still there."

"This guy's name was—what was it—Holbrooke. You know any Holbrookes?"

"No."

Baida nodded, as if understanding that it would have been a fluke. He kept his eyes on Bern, but Bern had the feeling that Baida was reading his mind, that every time he elicited a response from Bern, the red needle on his bullshit detector registered a "This is not Jude" response.

Alice popped into Bern's mind. She would be laughing her head off at his counterfeit performance. She would be making fun of him, mocking him in her Wonderland language and striking eye-rolling poses that made no bones about what she thought of his dismal imitation of a man he'd never met.

Baida fell silent. Maybe he was thinking of April in Austin, or the lake, or the wooded cliffs, or the Holbrookes. He thought about it so long that Bern began to wonder what the hell was going on.

"We want you to get a package to Houston for us."

This time, it was Sabella who spoke. Baida continued looking at Bern. Was that it, then? Had he passed some kind of test? Had Baida mysteriously communicated to Sabella his decision that Bern was clean enough to work with them after all? What the hell was going on here?

Bern knew only one thing: His job was to reestablish contact with Baida, using Jude's bogus smuggling route as a lure. This was the first sign in this whole damn nightmare that maybe he was going to have the chance to actually do that. He just wanted to get it over with. He just wanted the hell out of this situation.

"How big's the package?" Bern asked.

"About a cubic meter," Sabella said. "Maybe twenty kilos."

"When?"

"Soon."

THE FACE OF THE ASSASSIN

"Soon meaning?"

"Maybe tomorrow."

"Where do my people pick it up? Guatemala?"

"No. It's here," Sabella said. "Mexico City."

Bern gave it some more thought. "I'll have to check with my people, set things up, make some arrangements."

"There's not a lot of flexibility here," Baida interjected. "Practically none."

Bern got the picture.

Sabella looked at his watch. "As soon as you have final plans," he said, "let us know. If we don't hear from you by ten o'clock tomorrow morning, we'll be forced to do it some other way."

"Fine. How do I get in touch with you?"

"Call the American British Cowdray Hospital," Sabella said, "any hour, at exactly a quarter before or a quarter past the hour. Ask for the pharmacy. Ask for Flor. When she asks, tell her you are Luis. She will tell you what to do."

As if on cue, they could hear people entering the *sala*, the loud voices echoing in the vast empty room. They fell silent as someone rapidly crossed the room and then came out onto the terrace and approached them.

"Take him wherever he wants to go," Sabella said in English to the man who waited at the edge of the arbor. Then the three of them stood, and Bern saw that Ghazi Baida was not a big man, but he was powerfully built. Baida casually put his hands in his pockets.

"Ten o'clock tomorrow," Sabella said.

"Yeah," Bern said, and that was that.

*   *   *

Bern sat in silence, alone in the backseat of the car. Most of the architectural monotony in Mexico City was created in the latter half of the twentieth century, when the millions who flooded into the metropolis from the impoverished countryside strangled its lakebed plains and its foothills and ravines with a metastasizing blight of squatters' shanties. Fleeing the destitution of their small villages, where even industrious Death could hardly stir the energy to take them, they sought hope among strangers and created a new kind of misery for the masses.

The car entered one of these vast spiritless *colonias* of two-story cinder-block buildings, where every structure had started to deteriorate the moment its crude construction began. The streets were narrow, straight, endless, and full of potholes, and the few low-wattage streetlights that worked glowed sullenly. Despite the fog and closed windows, the car filled with the odor of dust. The whole surreal scene was a physical representation of Bern's mental state: stark and alien and menacing.

The driver pulled to the curb and cut the engine. He rolled down his window, and they waited. Bern looked at his watch. Five minutes passed. Ten. He rolled down his window also. Twenty. Twenty-five. The driver's cell phone rang. He opened it and listened.

"*Bueno,*" he said. He snapped the phone closed, started the car, and then drove away.

Chapter 31

The driver dropped him off at one of the Sanborn's stores on the Paseo de la Reforma, just around the corner from the Four Seasons Hotel. He walked around to the hotel, went into the men's room, and washed his face with cold water. When he came back out, he went to one of the *sitios,* which could always be found outside hotels.

For the next half hour, he went through a series of cab switches, using major hotels as his changing points because they provided ample opportunity for him to exit the hotel unseen. Finally, he gained a little confidence in his execution of a highly difficult technique, and he made his last stop. He got out of the *sitio* and started walking into the darker streets.

Now he was standing under a laurel tree in front of a *pastelería* that was still open. About fifty yards away, this quiet, small street merged with a larger one that was brighter and much busier. He was on Calle Pasado.

He turned to look across the street. Cars were parked on either side of the lane, and about four cars down, almost obscured behind the laurel trees, was a small hotel in a narrow building several stories high. The pale blue neon sign that hung unobtrusively over the sidewalk could just be glimpsed through the trees: Hotel Palomari, the words Susana had whispered to him in the Beso Azul. Bern crossed the street and entered the hotel.

The elderly man who sat behind a reception desk of heavy dark wood topped with green marble seemed startled to see him walk into his tiny foyer. The name Palomari was set in blue tile in the center of the white tile floor. The desk clerk, whose complexion seemed to have been deprived of sunlight for several decades, had heavy swags of flesh under his watery eyes, and a too-black pencil-thin mustache sliced across his long upper lip. While Bern signed an alias in the ancient registration book, the clerk wriggled subtly with pleasure, flicking nervous smiles at him. From somewhere Bern caught a disconcerting whiff of gardenia.

He had asked for room 202, which was on the second floor, up a winding narrow staircase that groaned miserably as he ascended. The Palomari was only three rooms wide, and his was the center one in the short hallway. But he didn't go to his room. Instead, he stopped in the gloomy hallway and tapped softly on room 201.

Silence. Nothing. Maybe it was only a few seconds—he didn't know, as time had become a wildly elastic thing in the past few hours—but however long it was, it was time enough for his mind to seize upon every disastrous possibility: He had heard the name wrong. Something had happened. It was a trap. She was dead.

Susana opened the door.

"God," he said, and she stepped back to let him in.

She had not turned on the lights in the room, but she had thrown open the two panels of the room's window, which let in the faint glimmer of the hotel sign below, and the glow from the *pastelería* across the street. It was a ghostly light, but bright enough.

Susana said nothing as she turned and walked over to the window. They looked at each other. A sluggish breeze stirred the gauzy curtains on either side of the window, just once, like a desultory breath.

He glanced around: a bed, one nightstand and one chair on either side of the bed, an old armoire with a mirrored front sitting against the wall across from the foot of the bed. The door to the bathroom was open, and an old-fashioned white porcelain bidet stood alone, framed in the doorway.

Susana's reticence was strange, but he was so wrapped up in himself, in his fear, his confusion, his relief at seeing her, that he didn't realize how unusual the moment really was, nor, again, how long it had lasted. It could've been only seconds.

"Paul," she said—the first time she had called him by his name, he realized—"are you all right?"

Maybe he was the one behaving strangely, not her. Yes, that must be it.

"Yeah," he said. No, he wasn't, but what would it matter if he had said otherwise?

There was a second, only that, or maybe two, when he thought that if he walked over and embraced her, as he wanted desperately to do, that she would understand, that, in fact, she wanted him to do it. He was as sure of that as he had been of anything since all of this had begun. And then, instantly, he was hit by the reality of how absurd that would be to her, how utterly unexpected and inappropriate . . . and out of control.

"God," he said again. He felt weak suddenly. He went over to the bed and sat down. "Damn," he said.

"Did you talk to him?" she asked. A perfectly logical question, it cut through the instability of his emotional fantasies.

Bern pulled off his suit coat—Jude's suit coat—and tossed it over the chair on his side of the bed.

"Yeah, I did. And no, I don't think he had a clue that he wasn't talking to Jude."

"Incredible," she said.

He told her everything that had happened, all that had been done and said from the moment he left her at the Beso Azul to the time he knocked on her door at the Palomari. Susana remained silent. She didn't interrupt him to ask questions or to ask him to expand on a particular point, or to ask for clarification.

At first, she stayed by the window, but then she began pacing, arms folded. Finally, she returned to the window again and looked down at the street, her profile cast against the glow. When he finally finished, she turned toward him again.

"Holy Christ," she said. She remained still, her forearms crossed low above her waist in the way women do. She was studying him, the faint light from behind her allowing her to get a good look at his face. "Look, I want you to know that I think you've done a magnificent job. But I'll be honest with you: I didn't think you'd be able to pull this off. I'm sorry, but I didn't. And especially after the shooting—"

She stopped herself for no apparent reason.

"No, I didn't think I'd be able to do it, either. It doesn't matter. Let's just get on with it."

"Okay," she said. Uncrossing her arms, she went over and sat on the foot of the bed. "Okay, now listen. You need to tell me quickly what happened before the shooting. I heard everything that was said, but I want to know everything that was happening. Was Mingo buying you being Jude? How was he reacting?"

Bern turned, one leg resting on the bed, the other on the floor. It took him a moment to get his mind around something that now seemed so long ago.

In the half-light of the aging hotel room, its furnishings giving off the odors of decades of transient living, its walls embracing the secrets of countless biographies, he told Susana everything he could remember—and he concentrated in order to remember every detail—while she sat on the bed and listened.

He was unnerved by how much detail he could recall, how vividly he could relive the shock and fear and panic. Not only did he recall the facts in detail but he also experienced every emotion that had accompanied those facts. To call it a debriefing hardly did justice to the experience.

When he finished, she waited a little before she asked her first question. She waited long enough for him to be aware of the sounds of the street rising to the window, long enough for him to be aware that it had begun to rain, softly, quietly.

"It seemed to me," she said, "that near the end, just before he was shot, something happened. Mingo said that he had found a woman that had the thing Jude wanted. You said, 'Oh?' And there was a bit of a pause and then you said, 'And?' And there was more silence . . . and then the shots."

Bern went back to that moment, recalling the seconds before the little boy stood up with the pistol.

"Oh shit," he said, and he leaned back against the headboard and rammed his hand down into his pocket. He felt the piece of paper and pulled it out.

"This," he said, "he gave me this."

Before he could even react, she snatched the piece of paper from his hand and was turning on the lamp on her nightstand. She stooped over the paper, her head up under the light.

"It's a woman's name," she said, reaching up and turning off the lamp, plunging the room into the pale glow again. "Estele de León Pheres. Her maiden name is Lebanese. I guess it's the woman he was talking about."

She stood, half-turned away from him, and stopped, staring out the window to the street. Looking through the limp curtains, Bern could see the pale light glittering off the rain.

Every silence like this was excruciating for him now. He never lost his awareness of time's flight, of it sweeping through the dark hours, hurling him toward his next encounter with Ghazi Baida.

"Look," he said. "Baida's waiting for me to get back to him."

"I know that," she almost snapped. She returned to the window, then moved back a little and leaned a hip and shoulder against the wall. All Bern could see of her now was her face in the icy light. She was staring down to the *pastelería* across the street.

"I'm going to call Kevern again," she said, turning to him. "They got Mingo's ID, and he's sent Mondragón's people to search his place. I need to give him this name, too, turn Mondragón's people loose on it."

"So what's the deal with Mondragón?" Bern asked. "He's Kevern's pit bull, is that it?"

"Essentially, yeah, but he's a hell of a lot more than that. Vicente used to be a major force, a section chief, in CISEN, the Center for Investigations and National Security. At the time, it was Mexico's superintelligence agency, the FBI and the CIA all rolled into one. Only thing is, it was totally a tool of the PRI, the political party that had been the sole power in Mexico for over seventy years. That is, until Vicente Fox was elected president. CISEN collected dossiers on the PRI's political enemies, on powerful corporate executives, the wealthy and influential in Mexico. Bugged everybody. Spied on everybody. Had more stuff on individual citizens than the old East German Stassi.

"When Fox came into office, he made a big deal out of 'reforming' CISEN, and one of the ways he did that was to kick out some of the agency's most notorious figures. Mondragón was one of them. But nothing ever changes much in Mexico. CISEN is still a PRI tool. Mondragón still has contacts inside. He's Kevern's back door to their vast files. And he even uses some of their tech people. Off the record, of course. They moonlight for him."

She turned her face to watch the rain, her profile floating like a ghostly mask in the pale light.

"He'll find her," Susana said. "And he'll find her tonight."

"You seem to be a little sobered by that," Bern observed.

"We're in a hurry here. Mondragón's people . . . they'll find out what she knows. We just have to concentrate on what we're going to do with the information. How they get it—you don't let yourself think about that."

Chapter 32

The battered panel truck clattered off the Periferico on the far northern edge of the city and made its way into a grid of featureless straight streets that stretched out across the plain of the former lakebed of the Valley of Mexico. This part of the city had missed most of the rain showers that had hammered the heart of the city earlier in the night, and the panel truck threw up a spume of gritty dust that drifted lazily over the cinder-block houses that clung to the ancient lakebed like crustaceans.

Soon the hovels gave way to a vast hinterland of warehouses interspersed with an occasional street of more dark cinder-block houses. Some of the warehouse compounds were brightly lighted by the coppery glow from perimeter lights on high poles within an encirclement of high chain-link fences. There were guards and guard dogs. Some of the warehouses had loading docks that were still operating, but most of the district was quiet and deserted.

The van kept going until the sharp, clean lines of the brighter modern warehouses gave way to the warehouses of another era, out of date, deteriorating, derelict, and abandoned. These buildings were less well kept, less well lighted, or entirely dark.

The men in the van had been sending and receiving burst communications, so the van's approach was well noted, and its secure status was well documented. It had been running a surveillance-detection route for the past half hour.

Then the van slowed, turning into a side street that burrowed into a sector of densely packed buildings. Soon it turned again, moving into an alley and going past four long rusting warehouses before it pulled to the side, overgrown weeds scraping noisily against the undercarriage of the truck before it came to a stop and the driver cut its lights.

Three men with automatic weapons slung over their shoulders bailed out of the rear of the van and immediately spread out. Then the door on the passenger side of the van opened slowly and Mazen Sabella stepped out. While his bodyguards spoke into their headsets, Sabella walked to the edge of the nearest building, unzipped his pants, and pissed against the rusty metal siding.

He smelled the staleness of his surroundings. Dereliction had an odor all its own, like none other in the world. He was intimate with that odor, having smelled it in a dozen countries, and aboard rusting, creaking ships in the Mediterranean, the Persian Gulf, the Caribbean, and the Gulf of Mexico. He had smelled it on the breath of women in all those ports, and on the clothes of their children. He had even smelled it on the moonlight, when there was a moon, and when there wasn't, he had smelled it on the dust of the stars.

He shook himself off and zipped his pants. One of his

guards had walked 150 feet ahead, where a warehouse door opened and two armed men stepped outside to greet the bodyguard. Sabella came along the rutted alley with his other guards and approached the men waiting for him.

The darkness outside receded as they went through the door into the warehouse. The vast open space was dark except for an isolated lighted area about fifty yards away and roughly in the center of the gloomy cavern. This spot was lighted by hooded lamps that hung down from trusses hidden high up in the dark recesses of the warehouse.

Half a dozen men were busy carrying personal items in duffel bags, cardboard boxes, and a few suitcases, emptying tents that sat in the shadows beyond the lighted work area. The isolated pocket of activity in the vast space of the warehouses reminded Sabella of coming upon a busy guerrilla base in a hidden desert wadi. But the bustle of activity here had to do with breaking camp. The bivouac had served its purpose, and now the mission was moving into another phase.

As Sabella and his armed guards arrived, three men broke away from the others and came out to meet them. Empty buckets were turned upside down and a few plastic chairs were brought over to form a small gathering place, and Sabella sat down with the three men.

"Okay," Sabella said, addressing a short, stocky man with prematurely thinning hair and a black mustache, "Ghazi says that this is the final check. It's the last time we meet. Where is the product?"

The man jerked his head toward one of the dark corners of the room as he lighted a cigarette. "Over there," he said. "El Samy will take it away within the half hour."

"How many did you finally get?"

"A case. Twelve cans with labels exactly like the real ones. They're boxed and sealed."

"Perfect," Sabella said, studying the man in front of him. The flesh around the man's eyes was dark, marked by months of too little sleep, the pressure of managing a clandestine operation, too many cigarettes.

"And our friends," Sabella asked, "where are they now?"

"I paid them off with the money you sent, and all of them are on their way. I have a man with each of them to make sure they are out of Mexico by this time tomorrow." He gave a long pull on his cigarette, squinting through the smoke at Sabella. "And what about the six guys?"

"They're across now. All of them. The last one had arrived last night. No problems. Everything's fine."

Sabella turned his eyes to another man, a small, wiry man with a beaked nose and watery eyes that protruded slightly. "What about your information?"

The man nodded. "Every mentor has his instructions for the timing and sequence. The prime contact has the code for Ghazi's 'go' signal. When he receives that, the rest will follow in rapid sequence."

"*Bueno.*" Sabella nodded. "Good job." His gaze fell on a third man. "Alfredo?"

"We've been alternating through the same three crossings for six weeks now. The bribes are in, and all of them have been completely reliable. The product never travels with drugs, so there is no chance of an accidental discovery."

Alfredo was waving a rolled *harina* tortilla as he talked. There was nothing in it. He paused and took a big bite of the diminishing snack, which he held in the stubby dark fingers of one hand. He was sitting on a plastic bucket, his heavy legs spread. Not finished chewing, he went on, talking around the food.

"In Chihuahua our cans will be slipped into a shipment of the real product from the *maquiladora*," he mumbled. "When they reach the warehouse in El Paso, our case will be divided into three groups of four, and our cans will be mixed in with cases of the real thing. Each group will be transported by a wholesale distributor, remaining in plain sight all the way. Eventually each can will reach a different city where it will be picked up by the mentors who will hold them until they receive the signal from Baida."

During the conversation, the language had been a garble of Spanish, English, and Arabic. Sometimes one of the men would throw in a couple of words of French. The bustle behind them had begun to die down. The personal effects of the men who had lived here for just over a month had been carried out to cars in the cool of night, and a few men stood around, looking here and there at what was left, as if making sure they hadn't forgotten something.

"Any problems with the money?" Sabella asked. "Only one more payment, right?"

Alfredo nodded, almost unconcerned. His job was to handle all of the negotiations with the Mexican narcos, whose routes they were paying to use. He was used to lies and violence and pressure. Nature had provided him with a high threshold for excitement. Only imminent death changed his heart rate.

"What about the machine?" the first man asked, looking across the lighted area to the assembly line of supply tanks, transfer pumps, pressure fillers, a heat exchanger, exhaust system, and hot-water supply, all connected by a network of pipes lying on the concrete floor and suspended by wires and cables from the high trusses.

"Everything goes," Sabella said.

Still looking at the equipment, the man shook his head at the shame of it. The expensive equipment had cost them a fortune, and a hell of a lot of trouble to acquire. And they had gotten only twelve "items" with it. Still, he knew it was worth it. It just seemed a waste to get rid of it this way.

"They'll be able to reconstruct it," the second man said. "They'll know what it is."

"They could," Sabella said, "if they knew what was here. But nobody is looking for anything. And there's all the other stuff stored in here. It will just be a warehouse of stuff. Who will give a shit? Just bulldoze it away." He glanced at the equipment. "Besides, it will all be too late then. It really won't matter what they reconstruct. They'll already know what we had to have to do it."

They all pondered that a moment as Alfredo jammed the last of his tortilla into his mouth.

Sabella looked at each of them. "Anything else?"

They shrugged and shook their heads.

"Ghazi sends his congratulations and sincere gratitude to each of you," Sabella said. "Everyone has been paid?"

Nods all around.

Out of habit and without even arranging it, the men drifted away from the warehouse one at a time over the next half hour. A few more loads of personal items disappeared as well, and soon everyone was gone except Sabella and his driver and bodyguards.

Each of them retreated into the dark reaches of the warehouse and returned with five-gallon plastic containers of diesel fuel. They kept retrieving containers until twenty of them stood around. They did not want an explosion, but they needed a fire that would be very destructive. Because diesel fuel burned hot, this would be guaranteed. They began emptying the fuel over everything under the wash of lights, working quickly to prevent fumes from accumulating and building to an explosive density.

The fire was burning along a trail headed into the warehouse as they got into the van and sped out of the maze of old buildings. Despite their plans, there was a concussive *whump!* an almost lazy, muffled explosion, as the warehouse was engulfed in flames. They felt the shudder of the concussion even inside the van, which was now many streets away.

As the van rattled back into the heart of the city, Sabella gazed out of the window, the sporadic bursts of secure communication playing softly in the background. His thoughts turned to what he had to do next.

Jude had been a puzzle to him from the beginning, when he first met him in Ciudad del Este. At first, Sabella had been sure that Jude was somehow connected to U.S. intelligence. He had come within a hair of having him killed, along with that impetuous idiot Ahmad, who had brought Jude into the picture. But something had made him hold off.

Sabella had watched Jude carefully on a video feed from the lobby of the shabby waterfront hotel. Jude had handled being dragged through the maze of his initial vetting with an accepting equanimity. It seemed that he knew what was happening, and he endured it the way a donkey endures a hailstorm, with wincing patience, with resignation and the understanding that it wouldn't last forever. If he was nervous at being put through the scrubbing process, he didn't let it show.

But when he had had enough, when he thought they'd taken it too far, he told them to fuck off. And he meant it. He had made the judgment that whatever good they might be for each other, it wasn't worth the price of admission. But then when Baida finally arrived, Jude held no grudges and quickly got down to business. That was when the conversations got interesting, and Sabella grew to like the Texan, who kept his own smuggling operation very close to the vest.

And then there was the discovery of commonalities. Sabella remembered having to drag these bits of information out of him when he interviewed him in Ciudad del Este. Jude grudgingly revealed his background, and the behavior that gave Sabella some relief from his suspicions. Often a mole would too readily reveal mutual interests with his target, trying too hard to establish a common ground in an effort to make the target identify with him and feel comfortable.

Not Jude. His world was his world, and he wanted to keep it that way. If Sabella didn't ask, Jude didn't tell, and even when he did, he didn't tell very much. Jude never volunteered anything. He was more interested in how he could make money moving anything they wanted him to move. Anything but drugs, that is. No drugs. Which was okay with Sabella, who already had that covered anyway.

So eventually they had gotten around to their pasts, and Sabella finally managed to get Jude to reveal that he had attended the University of Texas, too. One thing led to another, and as time passed, Sabella found himself liking the guy. Which was a mistake. You could trust people (up to a point, of course, never absolutely), you could rely on them and give them responsibility, but you could never allow yourself to like them.

And maybe that was the only problem with Jude, and nothing more than that. Sabella just liked the guy, and that in itself set off the infinitesimal tremors of suspicion. Maybe, after all these years, it had come down to that: Circumstances were more meaningful than the people who populated them. Situation overrode character and personality. The extraordinary efforts that Sabella had to employ simply to stay alive had become what it meant to be alive. He had become the process to the extent that he was now little more than the process.

But now he had to move on to the next phase of his plan. And Jude was either exactly the right man to make it work for him or exactly the wrong man. It was time to find out which of the two he was.

Chapter 33

From her place at the edge of the light, Susana called Kevern on her encrypted cell phone. Bern gathered from her side of the conversation that they were in a safe house, and that Kevern was as stunned as they were that Bern's impersonation had actually worked. Susana also passed on the name of Estele de León Pheres, and then she explained the situation with Baida and said he was waiting for a response from Bern. There was some conversation about that, during which Susana said very little.

Bern watched her profile as she listened; she was shifting her weight, her movement nearly imperceptible at the edge of the shadow. He sensed that she was weighing her options. She must do that a thousand times a day, he thought, weighing the consequences of speaking or not speaking, of revealing or not revealing, of finessing a phrase this way or that. It was a life of calculation, of factoring in, of making choices.

It was, he guessed, a life of never really knowing if you had done the right thing or not, because the ramifications of having made a different choice were too complex to play out to a logical end. He wasn't even sure there were any logical ends in the life she lived.

Finally, the conversation ended, and she snapped the phone closed.

"Okay," she said, "Mondragón's boys are at Mingo's place now. Kevern's going to pass on the information about Estele de León.

"In the meantime, we need to come up with a plan for you to meet with Baida again, something to drag this out a little. There's a possibility that Quito's people will come up with something useful from Mingo's girls. Or if they find Estele de León in time, maybe she'll come up with some information that will help us in arranging this next meeting. If they do, that could change things. But for right now, we have to play this as if those possibilities don't exist. Kevern and his team are going to put their heads together, and then we'll get back in touch and see what we've got."

The rain continued off and on.

"Every hour, a quarter past the hour," Susana said, confirming Baida's instructions.

"Yeah," Bern said. All he could think of was that this was impossible. How were the two of them going to contrive a convincing plan? And what in the hell was he going to do when the meeting actually took place? Like so much else about this madness, it seemed to be over-the-top. He couldn't believe that people actually did these sorts of things, and that whether they lived or died depended upon success or failure in these endeavors.

The rainy night was breathless now, and the curtains hung as limp as old promises.

Bern turned on the bed and bent over and pulled off his

shoes and socks. Then he shed his shirt, draping it over his suit coat on the chair.

Susana didn't say anything. In the dusky light, he couldn't see the finer points of her features—the little wrinkle between her eyebrows that showed she was worried or thoughtful, the pull at the corner of her mouth that foretold a change of mind. She was staring toward the window again.

With a sigh, she turned to the window, unbuttoned her dress all the way down to her stomach, and then fanned the sides for air. After a little while, she turned and came back to the bed and sat down, leaning against the headboard like Bern. She seemed oddly reluctant to begin the planning.

"What happened to Mondragón's face?" Bern asked.

"Somebody took it off for him," she said. "No one knows the real story. There are only outrageous rumors, everything from *brujo* curses to a sexual fantasy gone wrong. I don't think anyone really knows. No one's talking anyway."

"When did it happen?"

"A couple of years ago. Maybe a little more."

"Here in Mexico City?"

"Who knows." Susana pulled her legs up, her feet flat on the bed, the skirt of her dress pooling into her lap. She rammed the fingers of both hands into the front of her thick hair and held them there as she leaned forward, her elbows resting on her knees. She stared into the mirror on the armoire.

Bern couldn't tell if she was staring at herself or at him, but in the blue haze he could see the white crotch of her panties between her raised thighs.

"It was Jude," she said, "who was supposed to kill Ghazi Baida."

There it was, baldly stated. What Bern had suspected all along, but had never been told, was now laid out in front of him like a corpse on a slab. No more euphemism of silence. No more implication. There it was, without apology.

For the past few days, Bern had been unable to escape the slightly out-of-focus feeling that he was constantly accompanied by a doppelgänger. Jude was always there—in front of him, behind him, looking over his shoulder. Everyone he met spoke to him from within a context occupied by his double. Bern was constantly at a loss, struggling to read the hidden meanings, the implications, and the nuances in their remarks. But now, the doppelgänger—his brother—acquired an altogether different dimension.

"Jesus Christ," he said, "Jude was . . . he—" He stopped himself. He wanted to get it straight. "He'd done this before?" he asked.

Now Bern was sure that she was looking at him in the gloomy reflection of the old speckled mirror, using it as an intermediary, as if it would make the truth less shocking, or maybe make it somehow more comprehensible.

"Yes," she said simply.

"That was . . . that was what he did?"

"He had done it before," she said; "that's all I know."

"He told you that?"

"Yes."

Bern was stunned, and he knew that she could sense that, even in the gloomy obscurity of the rainy light. He knew that she was well aware that suddenly he was nearly overcome with questions.

Still staring at him from between the wrists of her hands planted in her hair, she said, "Look, I know you've got to be . . . just . . . boiling over with questions, but we don't have the time to do that right now." She took her hands out of her hair and wrapped her arms around her knees. "I want you to understand the situation here, the situation Jude was in. It'll help you understand what we're up against. Just . . . just bear with me here. I promise you we'll talk about it all you want later. I'll tell you everything I know. But not now."

Bern couldn't bring himself to say a word. He nodded. It was all he could do.

"Okay," she said.

He heard her take a little breath before going on.

"But this job, Baida, it couldn't be, you know, a targeted killing," she said. "No bomb, no booby trap, no missile from a chopper. It couldn't be seen to be a political assassination. Remember the clandestine aspect to this. Jude had to make it look like a drug hit. Plant a false ID on him. Better yet, just make him disappear. Baida lived in secrecy; he would die in secrecy. As if it never happened. Jude knew it wasn't going to be an easy thing to do."

Bern tried to concentrate on the logistics of it. He tried to ignore what was really making him light-headed—the genetic factor: What were the implications here for him?

"He couldn't do it down in Ciudad del Este," she went on, still using the mirror as an intermediary. "It would've been suicidal. Baida was well protected down there. By this time we had pretty good intelligence that he was moving into Mexico, and we thought it would be easier to do here, where our resources were better.

"And then Jude was killed. The assassination was

shifted to Mondragón, and you were recruited to set up Baida."

She hesitated, then said, "Before we get on with this, I want you to know something else." Hesitation again. "Your first meeting with Baida tonight—we didn't know what he might've learned during that month or so after the killings in Tepito. There was no way we could know. Jude was our man inside. There was no other access. If Baida had . . . somehow learned the truth, that Jude had in fact been killed in Tepito . . . they would've killed you tonight."

She was as still as the curtains.

"That's the part that Mondragón—that none of us told you. There was always that little bit of possibility—well, that's not right, because we didn't know, had no idea, what the degree of possibility was—that you wouldn't make it back from your first meeting with Baida."

Bern looked at her dark eyes in the mirror, and suddenly Susana was transformed into an absolute stranger. In an instant, her nearness to him on the bed was turned into a proximity filled with danger, as if he were lying next to a woman who had walked in off the street. Her manner, her glance, even her pauses and silences emanated a sense that, with her, anything could happen. The next moment with her could bring anything from the ordinary to the fantastic, and all were equally likely. She simply did not distinguish between these vastly different contexts. He had no idea who she was. He knew nothing about her, could not imagine what her life had been like a moment before she walked into the room.

"Remember," she asked, "how upset I was about . . . finding out that Jude had been working with Mingo behind my back?" Her voice took on a reflective tone. "You could tell, I know, that that hurt me."

She hesitated. When she went on, she spoke more slowly, and more softly, as if she was afraid to touch the subject.

"The thing about working with a single partner undercover . . . it's more complex than you might imagine. It's a cliché, I know, but we were close in a special way. No one can ever understand just how that is unless they experience it for themselves. And precious few people qualify for that."

The sound of the rain lent a sense of consecration to the moment. She had lowered her head a little, her chin nearly resting on top of her knees. Her eyes glinted in the mirror, fixed on him from beneath her parted dark hair.

"What Jude and I needed from each other . . . and gave to each other during this last year, was as special in its own way as any personal sacrifice could ever be. We learned to turn loose of all the lifelines that people cling to, and we submitted to a kind of . . . free fall. Against all of our instincts, we . . . committed to the idea that the other person would always be waiting at the end of our fall. We were faithful unto death."

She cleared her throat, still looking at Bern.

"But that kind of trust doesn't come without a price. It changes you, a piece of you, forever."

The rain came hard now, no breeze, just straight down, slapping the leaves of the laurel trees below the window, thundering in the street.

He heard her clear her throat again.

"I needed you to know this," she said. "I told you that you could trust me, and then . . ."

Her voice trailed off. Uncharacteristically, she couldn't bring herself to come right out and say it.

"I wouldn't have done that to Jude," she said. "Ever. I couldn't have. And I shouldn't have done it to you, either."

She was very still, and Bern felt as if he were being lifted off the bed by the sound of the pounding rain.

"I'm . . . I'm telling you this," she said, abandoning their reflections in the mirror and turning to look directly at him, "because . . . this is only going to get rougher. I want you to know . . . that I'll give you the same kind of loyalty that I gave to Jude. I'm willing to go against my instincts . . . to be waiting at the end of the free fall."

She was still looking at him, close enough for him to reach out and touch her face. He didn't know what to say. She had just told him that she had been willing to risk letting him be killed to see if he could pass as Jude. And then almost within the same breath she had pledged a loyalty to him that superseded her loyalty to the ideas that had enabled her to betray him. The first revelation had been shocking; the second one seemed reckless in its promise.

As suddenly as it had begun, the downpour stopped. Silence. And then dripping, like far-off whispers, a world of whispers.

"What in God's name do you expect me to say to something like that?" he asked. Oddly, he wasn't furious; he was simply at a loss for framing a response. Despite himself, he believed her. He believed the betrayal, and he believed the pledge of loyalty. It was the staggering simultaneity of them that confused him, and made her seem wildly unstable.

She let go of her knees, leaned away from him, and got off the bed. She stood a moment with her back to him, and then she sat down in the chair near the nightstand, her legs apart, her hands sunk into the skirt gathered between her thighs, the front of her dress still unbuttoned. She was looking toward the window, her profile powder blue in the wet light.

The city had vanished, and the universe was nothing but a dripping darkness as far as the mind could imagine.

Chapter 34

Sleep was impossible, so Mondragón had reverted to what was becoming a way of life for him—cruising the city's streets in the dead hours of the night. As he stared through darkened windows, his thoughts often drifted into the familiar doldrums of self-pity, and at other times they were sucked into the superheated whirlwind of his loathing. Regardless, it all led to the same theme of his constant meditation: his hatred for Ghazi Baida. It was an ulcerated wound, one that was never allowed to heal.

He was halfway across the city when he got the call from Quito that they had picked up one of Domingo's girls, and immediately he instructed his driver to head toward the *colonias* near Benito Juarez International. Then on the way, he got the second call about Estele de León Pheres, a name that gave him great hope the moment he heard it. He knew that name, and he knew the possibilities it implied.

Mondragón spritzed his head. He sipped straight scotch from a glass. Tonight, his raw skin was throbbing.

Stress. That's what it was. For some insane reason, stress made it worse.

The front of his head was on fire. He spritzed it again. He wanted to close his eyes and wait for the cooling effect of the analgesic. But he couldn't. He sat there in the half-light of the sedan, his eyes goggling at everything, seeing, seeing, seeing, taking in everything. His eyeballs fanned around like searchlights that couldn't be extinguished.

He took another shot of scotch. He was on the edge here. A few more sips and he wouldn't be able to think straight. He would be in that zone, that strata of exquisite self-deception where he'd assume he was thinking straight, even though he wasn't, like a pilot flying too high without oxygen, slipping into a nether zone of absolutely believable delusion. This was his fate since his face had been sloughed away—to endure by balance, to linger at the edge of delusion but not to step over, to be constantly tempted by relief but never able to taste deliverance.

Mondragón turned the front of his head to the window again. Just a slight shift in focus made the city rush away at warp speed, and then his own reflection was staring back at him: eyeballs and lips . . . a fucking horror show.

Then he picked up a wafer-thin translucent mask. Molded into the shape of a face, it was made of special materials that would fend off the infectious grit-laden smog of the city's night air. He carefully placed it over his face, attaching it to the back of his head with two Velcro straps. He took a moment to adjust the gel and membrane inner surface of the mask to the front of his head, making it as comfortable as possible. He could wear it only a couple of hours before he would have to remove it. But it would give him a little time to maneuver outside his car.

He looked out the window of the car and thought of the people inside the buildings he was going by. He thought of the millions of people in the city. In the whole universe, only one life meant anything to him at all. The others were nothing. They were mere bits of debris, blown and whipped about in the eddies of history, spinning out their stupid and irrelevant hours and days in meaningless in-significance.

But not Ghazi Baida. Not his old friend. Not that one certain soul. He deserved a special place in the scheme of things.

He poured a bit of scotch into a glass and carefully sipped it through the mask. He had to keep the buzz going, especially while he was in the killing house. The buzz would help him focus his thoughts on the events of the coming hours.

He thought of the faces of the people who were about to die, and he thought of all the people who died every day—how many? tens of millions?—who no longer needed their face. God threw away a city of faces every day, so many faces assigned to fire and decay every day, wasted every day, that if you had them all in one place, you could shove them around with a bulldozer. You could push them into piles; you could build mountains with them. Every beggar and pustule on the globe had a face, and it was as nothing to him, no more important to him than his own ass, which he never saw. But he saw his face every day, and no one, *no one,* appreciated the significance of what he saw staring back at him from a mirror, or a bucket of water, or a puddle, or a window along the street.

Mondragón thought of the ubiquity of the human face, billions of them throughout the earth. A vast sea of faces. Mountains of faces pushed into the sea of faces, and every day they kept coming, gargantuan piles of faces, a face for every birth, a face for every death. Mondragón was haunted by the idea of dying without a face.

Chapter 35

They both heard a faint tickling at the door handle, but neither of them had a chance to react before the door was pushed open and two men stepped inside, automatic weapons ready, although not pointing at them. As Susana gathered the front of her dress and started buttoning it, one of the men raised his hand for them to be calm.

Mazen Sabella came through the door between the two men.

"My apologies for coming in this way. Sorry."

He was holding a paper bag.

One of Sabella's guards went into the bathroom and then came out again.

"I have some coffee," Sabella said, holding the bag up to them. "And a few pastries." He was wearing the same clothes he had worn when Bern met with him. They were a little more wrinkled now.

The same guard went to the armoire and opened it. Then he got down on his knees and checked under the bed.

"What's going on?" Bern asked.

"You and I have to talk," Sabella said. "You've done a very good job of cleaning yourselves. The street is clean." He addressed Susana. "Your cell phone, please."

She reached for her purse, retrieved the phone, and gave it to Sabella, who gave it to the second guard. The man left the room with it.

"You'll get it back," Sabella said. "We just don't want to be overheard." He looked around the room. "So we'll talk here." Then he spoke to Susana again. "But I'm afraid we'll have to talk alone. My men will take you across the street for a bite to eat. We'll be able to see you from the window."

Silence.

"Now?" Susana asked.

"Yes, please."

Giving Bern a level look that told him nothing, she stepped into her shoes as she picked up her purse, then left the room with the two men. Bern and Sabella were alone now.

Sabella walked around the bed and sat in the chair where Susana's bag had been. He opened the sack and put one of the paper cups of coffee on the nightstand, then placed a hard *pan dulce* beside it. He took the other coffee for himself.

Bern came around the end of the bed, too, and glanced down at the street, where Susana was crossing Calle Pasado to the *pastelería*. The lights inside the *pastelería* gave it a cheerful glow. Susana went to the glass display cases to order while one man sat at a table and the other one waited outside, where a light fog moved along the street.

Bern went over and sat down on the bed, picked up the

pan dulce and the coffee, and bit into the bread, which was sweet and crumbly. His stomach was churning. What in God's name was going to happen now?

Sabella sipped his coffee and looked at Bern with large dark eyes that sagged at the outside corners. They were bloodshot, the irises deep brown, melting into the pupils. Bern tried to swallow the bite of *pan dulce,* but it was too dry and hung in his throat. He sipped the coffee. This was Sabella's show. He would have to handle the opening scene himself.

"We are completely alone," Sabella said. "No one listening. Only the two of us. My people aren't listening. Your people aren't listening." He gestured at Bern with his coffee. "You and I are alone."

Bern stared at him, still trying to make the bread go down. Sabella stared back.

What did a man like Sabella think about in such a moment? Was he thinking strategically, trying to foresee how Jude would react to what he was about to say, and then trying to decide what his own reaction should be in response to that? This moment of hesitation, was it a moment of doubt? What could he be thinking as he sipped his coffee and watched Bern trying to hide the fact that he was nearly choking on a chunk of sugared bread, trying to hide the fact that he was petrified that his outrageous lie had been discovered by these violent people who had seen and used every imaginable trick to kill and to survive.

"Jude the smuggler," Sabella said pensively. He sat in the straight-backed chair as if it were a throne, occupying it with confidence and shrewdness. His legs parted in a posture of stolid resolution. His back was straight, and wiry black hair showed through the open front of his shirt, while on his wrist, as on Baida's, a black military watch counted down the diminishing hours.

"We talked about so many things, didn't we, Judas, in Ciudad del Este?"

Bern nodded. He wanted to appear . . . Jude-ish. Wiser than Bern. With more guts than Bern. With a view of the world that made him unflappable, and with a cynicism that Bern would never be able to understand.

"Do you know what I think, Judas?" Sabella's eyes were alert, but his face was benumbed by the gravity of his game, by the high stakes involved. "I think you know . . . precisely . . . who Ghazi Baida is." He paused, letting the surprise do its work in silence. Then: "He's not just some guy who wants to move twenty kilos of something in a box. And you're not just a smuggler who doesn't care what it is, who will move anything but dope. You're not just some guy who's trying to save his ass, who wants a bundle of money."

Sabella raised his coffee and blew on it softly, his eyes remaining on Bern all the while. But he didn't take a sip of the coffee.

"I think you know Ghazi Baida . . . intimately, Judas," Sabella said, "the smell of his breath, the way he understands the color of light, the way he tastes something . . . the way he hates. I think you know . . . every tiny thing about him. You have memorized him from dossiers. You know his shoe size. You know the women he's slept with. You know the brand of cigarettes he smokes, and you know how many he smokes a day."

Bern sipped his coffee. He felt sweat popping out along his hairline. He saw faint shadows behind Sabella, clumps of fog prowling along the street. He felt not entirely within himself, as if he were pulling loose from his own personality, the discombobulated Dr. Jekyll.

Sabella lifted his chin in a kind of acknowledgment and went on.

"You know, too, that we have not been able to find out a damn thing about you, my friend. Nada. You appear, in fact, to be Judas Teller. An artist. A smuggler. A fucker of many women. A loner. A nobody much. Perhaps a bitter man."

Now Sabella sipped his own coffee. He swallowed, nodded to himself.

"But . . . Baida smells you, Judas. He smells the shit on you. He doesn't care what he can't prove; he knows what he knows. Ghazi is not an idiot."

His face didn't change. He didn't blink. His voice was curiously pensive, with no edge to it, no urgency.

"What is it?" Sabella asked. "They want to kill him? Is it you? Are you supposed to do it yourself? It's not the right time yet? Not the right place? And Mexico makes it more difficult for you, doesn't it? Maybe it has to look like something else. It wouldn't do for the CIA to be involved in an assassination scandal in a country so close. So there has to be some elaborate planning. That takes time. Not easy, huh?"

Bern watched Sabella's face, and he knew what was happening. Sabella was giving him a polygraph test, his own version of that dubious examination. He had seen this kind of penetrating scrutiny too many times on Alice's face, the impaling gaze that saw the unseen, that read the unreadable, the gaze that crawled inside the head, and even inside the heart, and sniffed out the lie. After more than twenty years of running and hiding with Baida, Sabella's whole being had become a trembling sensor for the lie. It had kept them alive, this tremulous humming within him, attuned to deceit. Bern remembered reading the incisive interviews that Jude had had with Sabella before Baida even showed his face. Extraordinary.

"I don't know," Bern said. "But I think there's a big misunderstanding here."

Something changed in Sabella's face, subtle, hardly there at all, Bern couldn't even describe it, but he knew that Sabella had just gotten the answer that he knew was there all along.

Sabella leaned forward, lowered his voice.

"Ghazi Baida wants to make a deal," Sabella said.

Bern swallowed. He couldn't help it. He didn't even have the presence of mind to take a sip of coffee to cover it.

"A deal," Bern said. What did he do with this? He was numb. He couldn't make his mind put together a response.

"He wants you to kill him," Sabella said. "He wants you to put him out of his misery. And in return, he will spare ten thousand American lives."

Chapter 36

Jude would listen. Bern had no doubt of that. But he knew, as surely as Jude would have known, that there was a downside. If he listened, he would practically be admitting that he was who Sabella suspected him of being. If he wasn't, he wouldn't listen, because he would know damn well that in this business, knowing too much would get you killed.

Bern cursed himself for not being able to read Sabella's face. Though he had made his living studying faces, his recent experiences with Alice had taught him that despite his experience, he had never really penetrated the face's deeper dimensions. He knew bones. He knew tissue and muscle. He knew the mechanics of tension and structure and elasticity. But he had never gone beyond that; he had never seen the unseen like Alice, like Sabella himself. At this moment, he could see only that Sabella's face had softened, that it had changed, but that was all. He couldn't explain the inner landscape, or decipher the hidden story.

Whatever this man was about to say on Ghazi Baida's

behalf, it would have been a surprise to Jude. No one—not Kevern, not Mondragón, not anyone in Washington— would have expected Ghazi Baida to turn around and face his enemy—and appeal to him for help.

"Ghazi and I have worked together for a long time, Judas," Sabella began. "Almost from the beginning. I met him shortly after Rima Hani was killed, and he was like a man on fire. Hatred emanated from him like a molten aura."

Sabella's assumption that Bern would know who Rima Hani was demonstrated how sure he was of Jude's real role.

"We were young warriors together. Of course, I recognized immediately that I had none of Ghazi's brilliance. Ghazi was exceptional—his ability to innovate, to see things that others couldn't see, to imagine things others could not imagine. Those are Ghazi's gifts, and he has used them well and selflessly in the service of Allah for these twenty years."

He had lowered his voice yet again. They might be alone, but for Sabella, alone was never alone enough.

"My talents were more humble," he continued, "but they were necessary to Ghazi's success. Hundreds of us have happily served his vision, working in our own small ways to make it a living reality.

"But everyone has enemies, and men like Ghazi have more than most. Not only do leaders of Western governments want to see him dead but so do some in rival factions of Islam's armies. Life has become very difficult, almost impossible. Like an old lion, Ghazi is having to devote more and more of his energy to just staying alive."

Sabella paused to sip his coffee, but his eyes never left Bern; their intensity never subsided.

"But from great trials come great opportunities," Sabella said. "Let me explain. There are plans," he said tentatively, carefully testing the water, "that your government should know about. There are developments going on even now that it would be fatal for your country to overlook. Ghazi has a sensitivity to such things, having lived as both American and Arab; he sees many sides to both worlds. He knows how both sides think.

"In the months following the events of September eleventh, he saw a country that most Arabs didn't see. He told me that it was like watching someone and being able to see his skeleton. Ghazi has always said that in revolution, as in life, success depends upon one's ability to see beyond the obvious. The obvious is reality's whore. Anybody can have her, but only fools believe it's love."

The two men had been watching each other closely, but it was just beginning to dawn on Bern that Sabella was under a lot of pressure. His controlled demeanor was only a disguise. Being Ghazi Baida's lieutenant and intermediary was a punishing role.

"I can give you an example," Sabella went on. "By the end of the first year following the crashing towers, while many jihadis were still rejoicing, Baida told me that he saw something quite different happening. It didn't even take a year, he said, not even a year, for most of your country to return to its old rhythms of living, to its old preoccupations, to its old business of being busy.

"In New York and Washington, D.C., of course, that was not the case perhaps. And maybe even in other large cities the population was skittish, if not vigilant. But everywhere else—for example, in that beloved 'heartland' that American politicians love to speak of—life returned to normal almost immediately. After all, they had little to fear themselves. There were no buildings in the heartland that were considered symbols of American power and domination, targets to the symbol-loving terrorists. There were no subways to trap people in, no density of population to gas or blast or spray with germs. The patterns of life didn't change in the heartland because there was nothing there that offered itself to the imaginations of the terrorists, who love the idea of spectacle."

Sabella glanced at his military watch. The gesture was fleeting—if Bern had blinked at that instant, he would have missed it.

"So, what do I fear if I live in a small town in Kansas? What do I need to be afraid of in Maryville, Ohio? Or in San Angelo, Texas? Or Tempe, Arizona? Terrorists? No, they want the Sears Tower. They want the White House. They want the Golden Gate Bridge. They want symbols. If it happens again, hell, they know they can watch it on television.

"What Baida saw, just one year later, was that America hadn't really been terrorized at all," Sabella continued. "Even the people in New York and Washington, D.C.,were afraid only occasionally—when they saw something that reminded them of what had happened, when they recalled a sound, a smell, tasted a particular thing that brought it back again. But that was only an occasional thing. It didn't preoccupy them anymore."

Sabella paused and shook his head. "That's not terror, Ghazi says. That is shock, a temporary thing. Terror is something altogether different. You do not have to recall terror, nor be reminded of it, because it never leaves you. It creates a perpetual foreboding, a constant dread, which suffocates your peace of mind."

Sabella's soft manner of speaking combined with his now-visible difficulty in containing his agitation presented an eerie, frightening context. It was discordant, like laughter at a funeral.

He reached out and put his coffee on the edge of the nightstand.

"Listen to me," he said, his voice so soft that Bern found himself leaning forward on the bed and concentrating on Sabella's mouth in order to decipher the words; "America will be in a hell of a lot of trouble when terrorists finally realize that the heartland is the ideal target. The captains of counterterrorism are watching the great American symbols that reside in the nation's metropolitan centers. That's where your government has put its funding. But security in the heartland? Nonexistent. Office buildings in Des Moines? No security. The crowded stadium at a regional football playoff in Oklahoma City? No security. A statewide basketball tournament in Indianapolis? Nothing. A school, a restaurant, a movie theater . . . in any heartland town?"

Suddenly, the small room seemed claustrophobically intimate to Bern. The fog outside was so heavy now that it even dampened the sounds of the city. Calle Pasado seemed isolated, a foreign country all its own, a place far away, on the borders of the imagination.

Sabella stared stoically at Bern. "Who could be more deluded about their safety than heartlanders? When you really get down to it, their belief that they don't have anything to fear, that something like that really can't happen to them, is pathetic. And that makes them the perfect targets."

Bern was horrified at the implications of Sabella's monologue, and he was horrified that he had been placed in this position, with so little understanding of what he should do. It didn't do him any good to imagine what Jude would do. This was way beyond that kind of simple role-playing. And it was far too important to be left to the inexplicable currents of intuition.

Bern put his own coffee beside Sabella's on the night-stand and stood. He stepped to the windows and looked down at the *pastelería*. Susana was sitting at a table with the bodyguard. They weren't talking. She was staring out into the gray morning light through the plate-glass window of the shop.

He turned to Sabella.

"Explain it to me very simply," he said. "Exactly. Precisely. No innuendo. No implications. I have to know exactly what you want and what you are offering in return."

Sabella looked down at his hands. His fingers were interlocked, the thumb of his right hand kneading the base of the thumb of his left hand. It wasn't much of a gesture, but Bern was stunned to see it. This was forbidden body language, a small but profound blunder, one that gave away Sabella's state of mind. He was under some kind of crushing pressure.

He lifted his head and looked at Bern.

"You can get this to the right people?"

Bern's heart pummeled away at his chest. This was wild. He had no authority to answer this. He had no way of knowing even if he should answer it. It was a wild, out-of-control feeling, a mad, plunging ride, where absolutely everything was at stake.

"Yes."

Sabella nodded, regarding him. "I thought so."

Without warning, rain started falling, a sudden deluge. Bern looked across the street. He could still see Susana's dress through the smear of rain.

As he watched her, wishing desperately that he could see her face, he realized that he had just given away everything. Without any effort at all, Sabella had learned that Jude was connected to American intelligence. A warm, damp fear washed over him. He was suddenly nauseated, and he could almost feel the barrel against his temple. Slowly, he turned to Sabella.

But Sabella wasn't holding a gun. With sagging shoulders, he sat gazing at Bern, his deeply wrinkled white shirt profusely stained with sweat. The sound of the rain almost drowned out his soft voice.

"Ghazi wants you to stage his assassination," he said. "Then he wants you to prove to Mossad that he is dead. And prove it to all the others, too. Then he wants you to hide him somewhere and protect him."

Bern saw him swallow.

"In exchange, he will give you everything: names, dates, relationships, strategies . . . a thousand reasons never to sleep again. He will take you into the wilderness of killing where we have lived together for so many years."

Chapter 37

The case of a dozen items that left the burning warehouse in the industrial zone in the northern *colonias* of Mexico City was driven to Benito Juarez International Airport on the city's east side. Within an hour the case was airborne, traveling on a mixed cargo commercial jet headed for Chihuahua City, the capital of one of Mexico's northernmost states.

In Chihuahua City, it was off-loaded, along with several crates of brass, fiberglass, and plastic stamp plates used in the manufacture of thermostat components for refrigeration units in one of the scores of *maquiladoras* on the edge of the city. At the *maquiladora*, everything was loaded onto a warehouse dock. The raw materials used for the thermostat components were eventually taken into the warehouse to be distributed, while the box of counterfeit product waited alone at one end of the dock.

Within fifteen minutes, a panel truck pulled up to the dock. A man got out of the passenger side of the truck and loaded the box through the rear door, stacking it alongside twenty-three other boxes with identical markings. The truck drove away, and in another ten minutes its headlights picked up the highway sign the driver was looking for: Chihuahua State Highway 16. The truck turned and headed for the Mexican border town of Ojinaga, across the Rio Grande from Presidio, Texas.

The foreman on the loading dock at the Chihuahua City *maquiladora* pocketed five hundred U.S. dollars for ignoring the cardboard box on the side of his dock for fifteen minutes.

It was a three-hour drive through the dark Mexican desert to the Ojinaga border-crossing station, and the van arrived at the tollbooth at 6:30 A.M. The guards on the Mexican side were used to seeing the Rivera Materiales Refrigeración van that came through the border station twice a week from the *maquiladora* in Chihuahua City, and they waved the van through.

On the U.S. side, it was another matter. One guard, a sour gringo who had the reputation of being one of the strictest inspectors at the station, was, in fact, on the smugglers' payroll. He could be bought off on any particular shipment so long as the contraband wasn't drugs. He wouldn't do drugs because he never knew when a drug-sniffing dog would be brought to the station on a deliberately unscheduled visit.

Now, in fact, there was a drug-sniffing dog on duty in these early-morning hours, and the guard expertly covered his anxiety as the animal and its trainer did their business, going over the twenty-four cases of sixteen-ounce cans of V-belt aerosol lubricant for commercial refrigeration compressors. The Rivera truck brought through a variety of products twice a week. When the dog lost interest, his trainer called him off, and the guard waved the van on. Then he poured another cup of coffee from his thermos and looked across the empty bridge to Mexico, satisfied that the serious sweat that he had expended during the last ten minutes had been worth the thousand dollars a minute that he had been paid.

Chapter 38

Mazen Sabella left Hotel Palomari as abruptly as he had arrived, and in the midst of a downpour. The knock on the door didn't seem to surprise him, and when the door swung open and his men stood there soaking wet, it was time to leave.

"Wait a second," Bern said. "What . . . what . . ."

Sabella said something in Arabic, and his men stepped back out into the narrow, dreary hallway and closed the door. He turned to Bern.

"Just find out if they will do it," Sabella said. "We can work out the details later. And the sooner the better. There are . . . pressures on Baida that make this window of opportunity very small. When it closes, it cannot be opened again."

"And to get back with you?"

"The hospital. Same instructions."

"Yeah, okay."

"Stay here five minutes. Susana will stay in the *pastelería*." Sabella took a step toward Bern, put his left hand on

Bern's right shoulder, and gripped it. He was going to say something else, then changed his mind and turned and walked out of the room.

Bern turned to the window and looked down to the front door, over which hung the Palomari's anemic blue neon sign. Nothing. After a couple of minutes, they still hadn't stepped out into the thundering rain. But he knew they were gone.

He looked across the street through the screen of driving rain and saw Susana standing close to the plate-glass window, looking up at him. He motioned to her that he was coming over. He saw her nod, and then he turned and headed for the door. Screw the five minutes—he wanted out of that hotel room.

He banged against the wall in the narrow stairwell, making the turn without even seeing his own feet. Suddenly in the foyer, he hardly registered that there was more to the astonished expression on the old man's face than merely being surprised by Bern. In a breath, he was across the white tile floor and out the Palomari's doorway. The rain was sweeping across the street at an angle, and he was completely soaked before he hit the sidewalk on the other side.

When he burst into the *pastelería,* it took him only an instant to realize that the astonished faces and frozen postures of the two women behind the pastry counter had nothing to do with his arrival. He looked in stunned disbelief at the overturned table and chairs next to the plate-glass window, the splattered coffee running down the glass. The two women were still frozen, eyes wide, expectant.

Then he bolted out into the middle of the street, frantically scanning the rain-blurred sidewalks, looking everywhere at once. The downpour was deafening. But there were no cars. No people. Nothing. Just the rain.

He stood in the middle of the street in the driving rain as if he had been clubbed. He just couldn't think. And then when he could, all he could think of was Susana—what was happening to her right now, how she must feel, the fear, the panic, the wild confusion.

And he thought of what might happen to her if he wasn't ready when he needed to be ready, ready for whatever was going to come later, because he knew in his gut that something sure as hell was going to come later. They weren't through with him. Nobody was through with him. Everybody wanted something more, and he had a feeling that Susana was going to be used somehow, and he was going to have to be ready . . . for something.

All of this flashed through his mind in milliseconds, and then he started running toward Insurgentes.

He grabbed the first taxi on Insurgentes and told the driver to get to the Glorieta Insurgentes at Avenida Chapultepec as fast as he could. Maybe hoping for a big tip for his efforts, the driver pushed his way through the dense traffic as if his life depended on it. But Bern was oblivious of the driver's frantic efforts, his mind replaying what the two pastry shop clerks had described to him of Susana's abduction. As soon as the two men who were with her bolted from the shop and crossed the street, Susana went to the window and looked up. She stayed there until she seemed to catch someone's attention in the window of the hotel across the street, and then immediately two other men burst into the shop and went after her. There was a struggle during which she was slapped to the floor, and then the two men took her out into the rain and led her to a waiting car.

That was all they saw, all they knew, and after telling him about it two times, they wouldn't say any more. Bern played this scene over and over in his mind during the trip up Insurgentes. Just after the taxi driver crossed Alvaro Obregón, Bern told him to turn right on Durango, and suddenly the cab was at Plaza Rio de Janeiro. Bern grabbed everything he had in his pocket, flung it into the front seat, and jumped out of the taxi.

He ran across the dark, empty plaza, past the statue of Michelangelo's *David,* and bolted across the street and into the building on the corner. He was met at the foot of the stairwell by the man who had been smoking a cigarette outside the door when he and Susana had come here.

"Hey-hey-hey!" the guy shouted at him as he crouched, his gun drawn and pointing at Bern, the other hand up, palm out.

"I need to talk to Kevern," Bern wheezed, sucking air. "Okay? I need to see him."

The guy produced his cell phone, pushed a button. "Bern's here . . . in a hurry." He slapped the phone closed and frisked Bern, then said, "Come on," and they ran up the stairs together.

Kevern and the two women were waiting as they pushed through the door, faces registering controlled alarm.

"What's the deal?" Kevern growled, his face hard, anticipating bad news. The two women's eyes were devouring him.

The rooms reeked of the leftovers of old take-out meals and lack of circulation. They got him a chair, but he wouldn't sit down, couldn't stop pacing.

Suddenly, he was light-headed, too much running for an elevation stingy on oxygen, and he had burned more than was available. Dizzy, he must have swayed a little, because the guy behind him helped him into the chair, where he sat, heaving like an asthmatic. The Mexican woman stepped into the other room and came back with a plastic bottle of water. Twisting off the cap, she handed it to him. He nodded to her and then gulped a few mouthfuls from the bottle, staring at the floor. His thoughts were bouncing all over the place. He decided to go to the heart of it.

"I've just finished a meeting with Mazen Sabella. Baida wants to defect . . . for protection." He was looking at Kevern, whose mouth actually dropped open.

"Jeee-susss," Kevern said.

"After the meeting, I crossed the street to a . . . uh, pastry shop, where Susana was waiting with two of Sabella's men. The place had been wrecked. Two women there said that two men ran into the place, grabbed Susana, who put up a struggle, and left with her."

The strawberry blonde wheeled around and looked at the monitor.

"Her GPS is dead," she said to the others without looking at them.

"Sabella said Baida wanted to de*fect*?" Kevern rasped.

Bern gulped another couple of mouthfuls of water and nodded.

"How long's it been?" Kevern snapped.

Bern shook his head. "Ten, fifteen minutes."

Without taking his eyes off Bern, Kevern reached out, dragged over a chair, and sat down.

"Let's hear the story."

Chapter 39

"The hospital" was how they referred to this dirty building on a dark street in a forgotten *colonia* near the Benito Juarez Airport. It was a favorite interrogation location for Quito's men, because at night everyone went inside and locked their doors against the things that happened in the dark. In the deep hours of the night, the featureless street, which always smelled of smoke from God knew where and constantly rumbled with low-flying jets that sprayed their spent lubricants over the *colonia*'s flat rooftops, became a wasteland.

Making a tight turn at a narrow intersection of three streets, Mondragón's driver pulled to the curb under a dying *pirul* tree and left the engine running. Mondragón stared through his mask at the grim warren of hovels that stretched into the darkness in every direction. He gazed at the dull jaundiced light in the windows of the building across the street while a jet lumbered low overhead, a prolonged whistling, throbbing explosion that made the raw flesh on the front of his head tingle with vibrations.

When it was gone, Mondragón opened the door, got out of the car, and crossed the street to a murky doorway. One of Quito's guards met him and silently led the way through a junky corridor littered with empty butane tanks, electrical parts, crumpled plastic bottles, and a pile of discarded car batteries that were leaking puddles of acid onto the gritty floor.

They entered a bare room, where Quito and several men were standing around smoking and drinking beer. They were sweaty, taking a break. The only light was a bare bulb hanging from the ceiling, a newspaper shade taped around the cord just above it. The yellow paper threw a stale light through the layers of cigarette smoke that hung in the stuffy air.

Quito stepped aside with Mondragón and led him out another door. Quito's men were well trained, and they ignored Mondragón as if he were the Invisible Man. They stepped into a kind of breezeway that led into another hallway. On either side of the hallway were two rooms, doors slightly ajar. The light in the rooms, though dim, was lighter than in the breezeway, and Mondragón could see people moving around.

"We found the girl at Domingo Huerta's," Quito said. His tie was undone, and his expression was sober with the business of the evening.

"What the hell was he doing?"

"Jude had given Huerta's girls copies of the pictures of Baida that he had drawn, and he had them asking if anyone had seen this man. These girls were doing this through their family connections, circling several particular families—"

"The de Leóns, the Carballidos, the Marmols, the Zubietos . . . all the people we were in school with."

Quito nodded.

"And then he gave this piece of paper to Bern."

Quito nodded again. "And it said, 'Estele de León Pheres.'"

They both paused while another jet lunged off the tarmac, the sound so deafening that it made their hair vibrate. It seemed to go on forever. Quito dragged on the last of his cigarette and flicked it against a wall. Mondragón stepped over and peered past one of the slightly opened doors. In this room, they had been questioning the girl found at Mingo's. He saw the naked legs and bare shoulders of the young woman tied to a straight-back wooden chair. Her head was thrown back, and she appeared to be unconscious, her long dark hair hanging down over the back of the chair. A guy with an ice pick was walking around, head down, talking to himself.

As the roar began to subside, Quito lighted another cigarette, and Mondragón came back, glancing at the men in the room he had come through a moment ago. They were talking again, one of them tapping his leg with a beer bottle, his middle finger jammed into its long neck to hold it.

Mondragón knew what the girl had been through. With these men, some things were inevitable during the questioning of a woman.

"Estele?" Mondragón asked.

Quito gestured with his cigarette to the other door.

Mondragón stepped over and peered through the slight opening. He hadn't seen Estele in six or seven years, hadn't spoken to her in maybe ten. She was handsome, as she had always been. Being older hadn't changed that.

She was sitting on a wooden bench in the middle of the bare room. Above and just to one side of her dangled another single dingy lightbulb covered with another yellowing newspaper shade. She wore a dark cotton jersey-knit dress, belted at the waist, the tight sleeves pushed back slightly from her wrists. Her dark hair was not long, as if she thought that a woman of her age should not pretend to sexy locks cascading over her shoulders, but the manner in which she wore it was stylish, the sides swept back to accent the graying at her temples. She sat with her legs together and angled to one side, ankles crossed, hands folded in her lap.

Mondragón put his hand on the doorknob, opened the door, and went in, his emotions well cauterized in anticipation of her reaction. She turned around while Mondragón was still in the dark shadows at the edge of the room, and as he approached, she watched, her face changing from curiosity, to consternation, to shock, to repulsion, and then to fear, a sequence of changes that Mondragón had seen over and over during the past two years.

He grabbed the only other chair in the room, a rusty chrome kitchen chair with a cherry red vinyl seat and back. He put it in front of her, but at the edge of the pool of jaundiced light. Then he sat down.

She stared at him in horrified amazement, which even her rigid social correctness could not conceal.

Crossing his legs and then crossing his arms in his lap, he looked at her and modulated his voice in the unlikely event that she might recognize it.

"Do you know why you are here?" he asked.

"Apparently, I've been kidnapped," she said, her voice a mixture of uncertainty and defiance.

Mondragón could almost see her gather her resolve to look directly at him, willfully resisting the natural repulsion she felt. But he saw, too, that her curiosity compelled her to try to figure out what exactly it was that she was seeing in the shadows at the edge of the pool of light.

"Do you remember last week, or the week before, that a young woman visited you and showed you a picture, a drawing, of a man that she was trying to locate?"

There was no hesitation. "Yes, I do."

"You recognized him."

"Yes."

"Who is he?"

She hesitated. "Why?"

"You may not ask me questions," he said. He knew precisely the right tone to use, and saw its effect in her rigid reaction, as if he had slapped her. Mexico City's culture of violence made intimidation easy for men like him. People were quick to believe that their luck had finally run out and that they had at last been caught up in the city's notorious grotesquerie of crime.

"Who is he?" Mondragón repeated.

"Daniel Spota."

"And . . ."

"He is the man seeing my sister Carleta."

"How long has she been seeing him?"

"Off and on for maybe a year."

"He lives here?"

"He lives in Bogotá."

"You've met him? Talked to him?"

"Three or four times."

Mondragón regarded her a moment. Had she actually been around Ghazi Baida with his new face and not recognized something familiar about him? Had she really been duped? Or was she covering for him? Would she not recognize Mondragón, then? She would have no reason to. After all, Baida thought Mondragón was dead, so if she was indeed collaborating with him, she would have no reason to think of Mondragón. The old days were just that, old and gone, never to return. Ever.

"I need to talk to this Spota," Mondragón said. "How can I get in touch with him?"

"I don't know." She paused. "He dates my sister when he is in the city. That's all I know." Another pause. "Really, I don't know," she protested.

"What is your sister's address?"

Estele was looking at him, eyes wide. She swallowed. Mondragón could see her thinking, running through her options. If Estele was completely innocent, she would give this Spota over immediately if she could. If not, she would try to play this out in some elaborate way.

"I need to see Spota as soon as possible," Mondragón said.

For once, the haughty Estele de León Pheres was bewildered, incapable of uttering a sentence.

"Ah, the Lebanese stick together, don't they, Estele?"

Suddenly, even through her fear, her eyes narrowed.

"Yes," Mondragón said. "I know all about the Lebanese. Are you going to help me?"

She gaped at him, unable to decide on her best course of action.

"I'm going to have my men come in here, take off your clothes, and take turns with you," he said. "And then I'll have them bring Carleta in here and take turns with her. And then I'll have your little sister, Juana, brought in here.

Ah! Yes, of course," he said, noting her surprised reaction, "I know about her, too. And so many other things. Anyway, sooner or later one of you is going to tell me how I can find Señor . . . Spota."

He stood up and started toward the door, skirting the edge of the light as she followed him with her eyes. Suddenly, she stood, too.

"Wait." She was kneading her hands. "What—how do I know you will protect us?"

"Protect you?"

"You have to promise this can't be traced back to me."

He turned to her and took a step toward her. "I'm here to get information, Estele, not to offer protection, not to make promises. You have to give me what I want. Beyond that, I don't give a shit what happens to you."

She stared at him, appalled at his crude response and at the stark hopelessness of her situation.

He walked out of the room, leaving her standing under the bleak light, alone.

Chapter 40

Kevern didn't waste any time moving on the information Bern had given him. First, he introduced Bern to the other three people in his unit. The whole tenor of the operation had changed on a dime, and now Bern needed to start feeling as if he could depend on these people, that he was tied to them, that he was no longer out there working alone.

Then Kevern immediately called Mondragón and told him to stand down. "Just hold off doing anything until I get in touch with you again," Kevern said. "I'll explain everything later."

Kevern was pumped way past any operational high that he had ever experienced, except in a life-threatening situation. But he had his enthusiasm well under control. It wasn't hard to do. Things weren't rosy by any means. Bern's account of the events of the last twelve hours revealed the best and the worst thing that could have happened. A defection by someone of Ghazi Baida's stature would be the crowning achievement of a career. A huge, huge coup, one that would wash over a lot of past sins.

On the other hand, Susana's disappearance was a potential disaster. If she was killed, the blowback could create a shit storm in any number of different directions. Baida's defection would have to be judged in light of the loss of a highly trained clandestine operative. Somebody would have to pay for a loss like that.

In Kevern's mind, however, Baida's defection, if Kevern could pull it off, would wash away the other disasters, if they didn't develop into anything monstrous. But if he couldn't make it work, this was the end of his life. So, in for the bet, in for the pot: He decided not to call Richard Gordon about any of this. He would play it out a little way first, see where it was going, see what his chances were for redemption.

A lot would depend on the continuing success of the long-shot role of Paul Bern. Kevern had passed along to Gordon that Bern had successfully encountered Mazen Sabella and Ghazi Baida and was now waiting for a confirmation for a second meeting. Like Kevern, Gordon was stunned by Bern's ballsy drive. Mondragón's harebrained long shot had succeeded—so far.

But now Bern was going to have to keep it up, and it would be Kevern's responsibility to keep him focused. Right now, he could tell that Bern was distracted, and he knew why.

He grabbed a soft drink from a Styrofoam cooler sitting on the floor by his desk, pulled a chair over in front of Bern, and sat down. Bern was still sitting in the chair they had given him when he rushed into the room. He had just about emptied his water bottle after almost an hour's debriefing. Kevern knew that the stress of Bern's situation had to be weighing heavily on him.

Jack Petersen had gone back down to his post in the building's foyer, while Mattie and Lupe were busy with chores that Kevern had barked out to them earlier. Mattie was sitting at a makeshift table, poring over a computer screen, while Lupe was on the other side of the room, her back turned to them, talking into her cell phone, her voice a discreet murmur.

Kevern popped the top on the soft-drink can, tugged at the thighs of his pants, and took a sip, keeping his eyes on Bern. A soft groan that seemed to be squeezed out of him preceded his words.

"Look," he said trying to sound like he was on top of this thing, "we may not know who's got Susana, but we know she's okay, because whoever's got her wants something from us, and her continued good health is their ticket. There's not a damn thing we can do about it until they contact us and tell us who they are and what it is they want. Then we can start working on a strategy."

Kevern saw something shift in Bern's face, an expression that reminded him of Jude when Jude thought he was about to get screwed, or slighted, or not be taken as seriously as he thought he should be. It was a look Kevern had always hated to see because it had meant that Jude was digging in. That he was circling his wagons around his team . . . his team of one. Jude had always thought that if he had to, he could fight—and win—every war by himself. When he hit that resolve, anything could happen. Kevern did not like seeing that look in the face of his twin brother.

"Go ahead," Kevern said, "spit it out."

"This will be over, sooner or later," Bern said. "Don't lie to me now, because I won't forget it. And I don't have anything to lose in this game."

"Fair enough," Kevern said. He understood. You didn't spend a few days and nights with a woman like Susana, in circumstances like these, especially if you were inexperienced in this stuff, especially if you were Jude Lerner's twin brother, and not start feeling something for her.

"But I'm not screwing with you," Kevern said. "This's the way it is. We've got to play *this* hand. If we see an opening, we'll take it. All of us have worked with Susana before. We give a shit. That's something you'd learn if you did this long enough. Okay?"

Bern nodded, skeptical, Kevern could tell, but that was expected. In a way, Kevern liked seeing that. Bern didn't seem to be intimidated by what he was about to do. This guy's balls were the real thing, and Kevern still found it a little creepy looking at him and talking to him and knowing that he wasn't Jude. Jude'd had the biggest balls—had been the most buffalo—of any guy Kevern had ever met. And here he was, sitting in front of him again, come back from the dead. Only it wasn't him, and this guy had come into this thing under the most bizarre circumstances Kevern himself had ever seen in his life, and still he was hanging in there like a pro. Shit, he admired that. He respected that it was in Bern's blood.

"Right now," Kevern said, "getting our hands on Ghazi Baida is what we're focused on. The thing with Susana is tied in with it somehow, and it'll resolve itself. We've got to play this out, and that's the hard truth of it."

Kevern upended the soda and drained it in three or four big gulps, then tossed the can into a paper sack on the floor near the window. He looked at his watch.

"We've got fifteen minutes till we can call the hospital on the schedule Sabella gave you. Any questions?"

"What if they tell me to go somewhere right now?" Bern asked.

"Do it. We're going to put a tag on you, and you're going to tell him about it. If this defection thing is for real, he's not going to be bothered by that. He'll know it's necessary, and he'll know why."

"Okay, tech's up and running," Lupe said, coming over to them and handing her phone to Bern. "Mattie's ready anytime."

Kevern checked his watch.

"We've got a few minutes," he said, examining Bern for signs of stress. He didn't see them, but he knew they were there. Operational butterflies were a hell of a thing. It was tough. But again, he admired the way Bern was dealing with it.

The room fell silent. Everybody had stopped. The guy they had been trying to kill for the past year was about to get on a cell phone with a dead man, and he was about to do something that would've seemed outrageous if anybody—*anybody*—had ever mentioned it as a possibility.

This was the goose that Lexington Kevern lived for. This was it. In this business, it *always* came out of nowhere, came suddenly, came with head-spinning, disorienting surprise. And it was the sweetest feeling in the world, better than any number of things that got you high, that got you limp with bliss. Having an operation turn sweet on you was like no other accomplishment in the fucking world, and Kevern was going to relish this one more than any other sweet deal that he had ever experienced. Because the stake here was . . . everything.

Without getting the nod, Bern started dialing. It caught

Kevern by surprise, but it didn't matter. He was in the slip-stream of an operation turned sweet.

When the phone was answered, he asked for the pharmacy. When the pharmacy answered, he asked for Flor. Silence. Prolonged silence. He looked at Kevern, who was listening on another phone, as was Mattie on yet a third phone. Kevern showed nothing, just sat there as if he were waiting for the information operator.

"Flor," she said in English.

"This is Luis," Bern said, expecting the woman to draw a blank and ask, "Luis who?"

Pause. "Oh, yes. *Momentito, por favor.*" Her voice was flat.

Silence. Then suddenly she was reciting a telephone number. Slowly. Deliberately. At the end, she paused, then repeated it in the same disinterested tone of voice.

"You have that?" she asked.

"Yes, I have it."

"Tomorrow morning, go to Colonia Santa Luisa," she said, again speaking very deliberately. "Go to Jardin Morena. It is a small park, and it is market day there to-morrow. There is a man there who sells old issues of comic books on the sidewalk on the north side of the park, in front of Farmacia Pedras. There is a telephone on the side-walk by the pharmacy door. There will be a red dot by the number six on the keypad. At precisely ten o'clock, use that telephone to call the number I just gave you."

Bern was watching Mattie, who stood behind Kevern, writing furiously. She looked at Bern and nodded.

"Repeat that to me, please," Flor said.

Bern did.

"Do you want me to repeat anything?" Flor asked.

"No," Bern said. "I have it."

The line went dead.

Bern lay on one of the cots in a third room in Kevern's safe house on Plaza Rio de Janeiro. The lights were out, but as always in this city, the ambient illumination came in through the windows like an eerie twilight. He could see a couple of overnight bags on the floor, some clothes hanging here and there. He could smell perfume on the bedcovers beneath him. And looking toward the windows, he could see and hear the rising and falling language of the rain.

Sleep was out of the question, but he hoped he would slip in and out of consciousness. The others were still working in the adjacent rooms. He didn't know how they kept it up. He was exhausted, and scared. And he couldn't get Susana off his mind. He wanted to believe that Kevern was being honest with him, and he wanted to believe what he read in Kevern's body language—that it wasn't time to be alarmed yet. These things had a degree of predictability, a range of expectations. And these people were not totally without an understanding of what was happening to them.

He thought of Susana. He just wanted her to be safe, and to be with her again in a place as far away from this insanity as they could get.

He closed his eyes and listened to the rain.

Chapter 41

When Bern finally roused himself the next morning, he felt stiff and hungover from a dearth of sleep. He looked at the window and saw that the morning was still overcast and rainy. He found everyone already back at their posts, getting ready for Bern's meeting with Baida. He poured a cup of coffee for himself from the pot on a hot plate in the corner of the room where they were working, then walked down the hall to the bathroom, where he washed his face, scrubbed his teeth with his index finger, and washed out his mouth. He did the best he could with his hair. He looked like hell.

When he got back to the offices, Kevern motioned him over to where he was sitting on the edge of one of the folding tables, which were laden with computers, radio receivers, and other kinds of electronics whose usefulness was lost on Bern.

"Give me your belt," he said.

Bern handed it over and Kevern gave it to Lupe, who began gluing a tracer bug on the underside.

"It ain't sophisticated," Kevern said, "but it'll get the job done. Now listen. Sabella and Baida have set up this meeting the way they want it to go, to give themselves maximum protection. I'm guessing Sabella's going to jump with him."

Kevern sipped his coffee. His eyes were pinched from only a couple of hours' sleep, but Bern noticed that he was closely shaven. Military discipline. He was running on caffeine.

"The thing is," Kevern said, groaning softly as he paused, "as soon as these two guys jump ship, their lives won't be worth a nun's fart. They'll instantly become traitors, and their own men will kill them in a heartbeat. So you can bet they've gone to a lot of trouble to isolate this meeting from their guys. It's just Baida and Sabella. Which means they aren't going to have their usual protection. But they'll have something going, and they'll be as touchy as hell. They could call it off in an instant. If that happens, don't sweat it. They'll reconnect."

Lupe Nervo came over to him, pushing buttons on a cell phone.

"They might take this away from you immediately," she said, handing the phone to him, "but until they do, you can connect to Lex instantly by punching four, seven, star. Just slide your finger down the last three buttons on the left side. Don't even have to look at it."

After a few more words of caution and instruction, Kevern stopped and studied Bern carefully.

"Now listen," he said, speaking more slowly and in a less operational tone, "when defectors decide to come over, they always have aces in their pockets, something juicy to sweeten their arrival. Sometimes these guys have time-critical information, some imminent action that they can tell us about that'll make them heroes.

"I'm guessing Baida's in this category. When Sabella came to you at the Palomari Hotel, he mentioned that he could spare us ten thousand lives. He was getting at something. And all that talk about the American heartland . . ." He nodded at Bern. "Okay? See where I'm going here?"

Kevern shifted his weight on the edge of the table, causing it to creak.

"As soon as you can," he went on, "you get to that. You ask him if he's bringing us time-critical information."

Bern walked out of the building on the corner of Plaza Rio de Janeiro. The rain had stopped, leaving wet sidewalks and fresh air, the usual smoggy shroud having been washed away by the night rains.

Bern half-believed that none of this was going to work. But he didn't say so. He just went along with everything as if he bought into it, just as if he believed. An atheist among the faithful, keeping his doubts to himself.

He walked up Calle Orizaba, and at Avenida Alvaro Obregón, he picked up the first taxi he saw and directed the driver to head south on Insurgentes. Colonia Santa Luisa was just off of Insurgentes, nearly to the artsy *colonia* of San Angel.

Insurgentes itself was a busy thoroughfare. Though not a wide street, it was densely packed with buildings and pedestrians and bumper-to-bumper traffic. Progress was slow and halting, but Bern was oblivious. Block after block, he watched the traffic and the teeming sidewalks without seeing them, his mind's eye obliterating his physical vision.

He didn't give a damn what Kevern said; Susana was in a hell of a spot. Kevern's reassurances meant nothing to him. In fact, he was furious that Kevern had even tried to downplay the serious risk in Susana's situation.

At the major intersections, newspaper vendors threaded their way through the lanes of stalled vehicles to sell the latest edition of *Reforma* or *El Universal* or the left-leaning *La Jornada*. Lottery vendors did the same, as did an occasional seller of bright plastic toys that dangled from sticks and fluttered in the wind.

Suddenly, a little boy was at Bern's window, holding up a newspaper with screaming headlines, his urgent pleas growing faster as the traffic in front of them began to move. The boy rested the newspaper on the window frame so that the paper filled the whole space, and he moved with the taxi as it started up.

The driver yelled at him to get away, and then suddenly something shot out from the newspaper, hit Bern in the side, and fell into the seat beside him. And then the boy disappeared as the taxi sped up with the traffic.

In the next few seconds, Bern's mind worked in jerky still frames: It was small and black. It was a bomb. Some kind of bomb. He was practically sitting on it. In his mind, the explosion lifted the taxi off the street in a ball of fire. He was grabbing at it. Throw it out.

And then it began to ring, and he slapped at it, and it rang again. He looked down at a cell phone. His heart stopped. Started. Stopped. Started. The cell phone ringing. Ringing. Stunned, he picked it up. He looked at it in his hand as it rang a fourth time. He opened it, lifted it to his ear, and said hello.

"Paul . . ." It was Susana. "Paul, listen, I'm okay. I'll be—"

Her voice broke off. He couldn't believe it. . . . What had happened? Silence, and then: "This is Vicente Mondragón. We are four cars behind you. Tell me what is happening."

Susana was with Mondragón?

"What the hell's going on?" Bern asked. "Those were *your* people who took Susana?"

"Yes. Tell me quickly what is happening," Mondragón insisted.

Bern's thoughts swarmed. Kevern said that there would be demands. Whoever kidnapped Susana would contact them and tell them what they wanted in return for her safety.

"For Christ's sake," Bern said, "what are you doing? What's this all about?"

"I want to know where Ghazi Baida is. That's what we've all been doing for over a year."

"You're still trying to find Baida?" Bern asked.

"Of course."

"I was with Kevern when he called you, told you to hold off. I heard him tell you to wait until he got in touch with you again. What're you doing?"

"Oh, yes, he did tell me that," Mondragón said, sounding amused that Bern knew this. "And just why did he do that, Paul?"

Bern was tired, confused. He didn't trust anyone anymore except Susana, and he really believed that there was a good chance that this freak he was talking to was going to kill her.

"What I want to know," Bern said, growing heated,

pissed at Mondragón, pissed at Kevern, pissed at all of it, "is what in the hell is going on here with Susana? What are you up to?"

"It's not important," Mondragón said. "It's a little matter of insurance."

"Insurance? Insurance against what?"

"I need to be sure you will cooperate with me in whatever way I need," Mondragón said.

"Well, what do you need?"

"Right now, Paul," Mondragón said slowly, trying to get past Bern's confusion and panic, "I need to know what is happening. I need to know where you are going and why. Do you understand that I need to know that? Susana's life depends on it."

There was a pause while Bern locked onto this last remark and processed it. For all the gravity of his mission regarding Ghazi Baida's defection, the foremost concern in his mind was getting Susana away from Mondragón. It happened in an instant.

"Baida wants to defect," Bern said.

This time, the hesitation came from Mondragón's end of the line.

"To defect?"

"Yeah, that's right."

"He doesn't suspect that you are not Jude?"

"No, he doesn't suspect anything," Bern said.

"How do you know he doesn't suspect you?"

"Goddamn it! He doesn't. I'd sense it. I'd know. He doesn't!"

"Where are you going now?"

"Colonia Santa Luisa. There's a little park there, Jardin Morena. I make a phone call from there."

"And then what?"

"Somebody tells me what to do."

"To make the arrangements for his defection?"

"That's my guess. Just make the call, he said, so that's where I'm going, and that's what I'm going to do."

"Will he be at Jardin Morena?"

"I don't know."

"Why is he doing it like this?" Mondragón asked, talking to himself as much as to Bern. He sounded suspicious, either of Bern or of Baida. Then he said, "Listen to me carefully, Paul. I will say this only once. I know you must have a way of communicating with Kevern. Do not tell him that we have spoken. Do not tell him that I am still looking for Ghazi. Now that I have found you, I will not let you out of my sight. I have people in front of you, and now I'm going to send others to Jardin Morena. They will be everywhere around you now, all the time.

"Three things you have to remember to stay alive: Do not tell Kevern what I am doing. Do not even mention my name to Ghazi Baida."

He stopped, waiting for Bern to ask the question.

Bern obliged. "And the third thing?"

"If you are lying to me," Mondragón said, his voice reflecting a chilling lack of passion, "Susana is fucked."

Chapter 42

When they heard the phone ring, the three of them exchanged puzzled glances. They were gathered around a receiver and a digital recorder, watching the lime green display numbers flying by as if they were comprehensible words.

"Cabbie's phone," Mattie conjectured.

"No, he's not answering it," Lupe said.

"Well, it's not Bern's cell," Mattie countered.

She and Kevern were sipping soft drinks. Lupe was still nursing a cup of coffee. All three of them were sitting on chairs, leaning over notepads on the table in front of them. Lupe was doodling, drawing *caracoles,* three elaborately spiraled snails.

The phone stopped ringing.

"Nobody's talking," Kevern said. They could hear traffic in the background.

"He's listening," Lupe said. "Bern is."

"Not on our phone, he isn't," Mattie insisted again. "Where'd he get another cell?"

They exchanged looks.

"Those were your *people who took Susana?"* Bern asked incredulously.

Kevern was leaning his beefy forearms on the table, making it sag a little, staring hard at the receiver. Bern continued, asking the person on the other end what he was doing, what he wanted. Silence while Bern listened, and then he asked, *"You're still trying to find Baida?"*

"Oh shit," Kevern said in dismay. "He's talking to Vicente. It's Mondragón."

"I was with Kevern when he called you, told you to hold off. . . . What're you doing?"

They listened to more expressions of Bern's incredulity. And then: *"Insurance? Insurance against what?"* Bern asked.

Silence ensued while Bern listened to Mondragón. And then Bern said, *"Baida wants to defect."* Silence. *"Yeah, that's right."* Silence. *"No, he doesn't suspect anything."*

"Well, there it is," Mattie said. "Now Mondragón knows why you pulled him off the hunt."

Heated words from Bern followed as he insisted that Baida didn't suspect anything, that he would know if Baida did, that he would sense it.

Then Bern told Mondragón where he was going and what he was supposed to do when he got there.

"We should've told him the phone was live," Lupe said, shaking her head, looking at Kevern. "He could've worded all of this differently. He could've been more informative, passed a lot more to us."

Kevern shook his head resolutely. "It would've been a mistake. He would've tried to tell us too much, repeated things Mondragón was saying to let us know what was going on. Vicente would've been all over that. No, we're fucking lucky we didn't tell him."

"The paperboy," Mattie said, still bothered by the sudden appearance of another cell phone. "He threw the phone in there. That's what happened."

"Listen, listen." Kevern leaned into the recorder. Nothing but traffic, horns, someone yelling, hawking something. The screech of brakes.

"He's giving him instructions," Lupe conjectured. "Wants him to do something?"

"And the third thing?" Bern asked.

Silence. More traffic. A snippet of music. No more conversation.

"He's giving him a list of things to do," Mattie said.

Lupe had left off wth the snails. "Or not to do," she said. "Vicente's threatening him."

"That's what picking up Susana was all about," Mattie said. "Mondragón wants Bern to do something. And Susana's screwed if he doesn't do it."

Kevern began his subdued groan, seeming to hold it back. The two women looked at him.

"What the hell is Mondragón planning?" Kevern asked no one in particular. "He wants to get to Baida anyway?"

He stood up and looked at his watch. Grunting softly, he moved around the room, rubbing the back of his neck, his head down.

"He's not calling us," Mattie said. "You'd think he'd call after he got off the phone with Mondragón."

Kevern shook his head. "Vicente threatened him, like Lupe said. Vicente didn't want him to call us."

"So Bern's holding on to our phone," Mattie said, "and

he's sure as hell hanging on to Mondragón's phone, too."
She listened to the transmissions. Again street sounds, but
they were fading. "They've turned off Insurgentes," she
said. "He's going to be at Jardin Morena pretty soon, Lex.
What're you going to do? Do we call Bern?"

"No," Kevern snapped, stopping his pacing and turning to them.

"Call Mondragón," Lupe said. "Tell him he's about to
screw up in a fucking big way."

"Then he'll know Bern's wired," Kevern said. "He'll
work around it. This way, if he thinks the threat to Susana
is going to buy Bern's cooperation—and it looks like it
will—he'll think he can communicate with him. We'll have
a shot at it at least."

Kevern's situation looked bad. Though he directed the
operation and controlled the purse strings, he had to use
Mondragón's tech people, Mondragón's intelligence, Mondragón's muscle. Now it seemed that Mondragón suddenly
had his own agenda, leaving Kevern toothless.

Normally in an emergency situation, he would automatically turn to the CIA station's technical services. But of
course this wasn't a normal situation. If he did that, he
would be blowing Heavy Rain, which was running off the
books right under the Mexico City station's nose. Not only
would it cause a shit storm inside the Agency, but the resulting brawl within the Agency could very well boil over
into the intelligence community's gossip mills. Within
hours, it would be in the press, and that would automatically trigger an international incident.

But if his hunch was right, he just might have to take
that risk anyway in order to save Baida from being assas-
sinated by Mondragón. Jesus, talk about irony.

Why Mondragón was hell-bent to do this, Kevern couldn't imagine, and he didn't have time to try to figure it out. But he was sure of it. He felt it in his gut—shit, he felt in his nuts, right down inside the core of him, so solid, so right, he had no doubt about it at all. No proof, but it was a fucking certainty.

Lexington Kevern was scared.

He looked up, unaware that he had had his head ducked, staring at the floor, until he saw the two women staring at him. Then suddenly, they heard another transmission. Bern was paying the taxi driver.

Kevern had to decide. In for the bet, in for the pot.

"Lupe, get the GPS monitor," he snapped, going to his desk, taking his handgun out of the drawer, and clipping it onto his belt. He pulled his cell phone out of his pocket and hit a number. "Jack, get the car."

Chapter 43

El Paso, Texas

By eight o'clock the next morning, the Rivera van was pulling into another warehouse district, this one on the outer edges of El Paso. At a regional distribution center for refrigeration products and supplies, the twenty-four cases of aerosol V-belt lubricant were off-loaded in their usual section of the warehouse. The inventory foreman checked them in, and the van headed to the Cordova Bridge on the Rio Grande and back to Mexico.

The floor foreman directed his three employees to move various stacks of inventory to new locations, a temporary reshuffling, he said. The jobs took them to the far side of the warehouse. When they were gone, he went to the waiting cases of Dempsey's Best lubricant and found the one with a red dot on the lower right corner of each side.

Opening the case, he removed four cans with red dots on their concave bottoms and substituted them for four regular cans in a second case. He resealed the second case, added red dots to each of its lower right sides, and labeled the case for pickup by the Rocky Mountain Refrigeration Supply van.

He followed the same procedure with another four cans of the red dot lubricants, again opening an unmarked case of lubricant and substituting four red dot cans for regular cans and resealing the case, adding red dots to the lower right corner of its four sides, and labeling it for pickup by the Ames Midwest Air Conditioning Supplies van. He resealed the original red dot case, which now contained only four cans with red dots on their bottoms and eight cans without red dots, and relabeled the case for pickup by the American Industrial Refrigeration Supplies van.

Within an hour, all three vans had picked up their cases of Dempsey's Best aerosol V-belt lubricant. Hidden among these cases in each van was one containing four cans with red dots. These red dot cans were headed for a dozen different destinations in a dozen different states. Within forty-eight hours, every red dot aerosol can would be in the hands of the men who would use them.

The El Paso warehouse foreman who enabled the distribution knew nothing about what he was doing except that he had agreed to shuffle cans with red dots and to keep his mouth shut about it. In exchange, he would receive twenty thousand dollars for his troubles.

At three o'clock in the afternoon, he received a telephone call from Juárez confirming that all the red dots were safely on their way. Mission completed. The money was his. He told his boss that he was coming down with a stomach virus, then took the rest of the afternoon off. He drove across the Cordova Bridge, headed to a motel in Juárez to collect his money.

But he never returned.

On the Mexican side of the border, murder went for 3,500 American dollars a pop. It was a bargain. Money well spent, from a security point of view.

Chapter 44

Jardin Morena in Colonia Santa Luisa was not on the tourist maps of Mexico City. It was just a neighborhood plaza, a small park shaded by laurels and jacarandas and a few palms. A fountain with a traditional stone basin anchored the center of the park. Broad sidewalks radiated out from the fountain to all sides of the plaza, with flower beds and patches of lawn in between.

Girdling the park on all four sides was a wide *paseo* where old men haunted the wrought-iron benches in silent fear of the noonday demons and where couples and families strolled in the cool of the evenings. But on market days, sidewalk vendors laid out displays of their wares on the *paseo* and the whole place turned into a bazaar.

Bern didn't have the presence of mind to tell the cabdriver to drop him on the north side of the plaza, and he had never been quite straight about where any of the compass directions were in this Babylon of oblique streets. So when he stepped onto the *paseo* and confronted the phalanx of vendors, who seemed undaunted by the threatening rain, he didn't have the slightest idea where the seller of comic books might be.

Without any plan whatsoever, he started walking, eager to get on with it, driven by a sense of urgency inspired by the multiplicity of disastrous possibilities before him. He imagined Mondragón's men spreading out, hiding in plain sight among the casual shoppers drifting by the vendors who surrounded the plaza.

An organ-grinder's faint piping drifted to him through the crowd and the trees of the plaza as he walked past an old woman wearing two straw hats, one on top of the other, and selling brilliant magenta flowers. A man with a potpourri of socks spread out in a creative sunburst design on a piece of blue plastic offered them with an elegant sweep of his arm. A middle-aged Indian woman with pigtails crouched on her knees on a rush mat, perfecting her pyramid of chili red *chapulines,* tiny fried grasshoppers stacked as high as her waist. On the other side of her, a man sat glumly on a bright yellow blanket, his wild assortment of offerings scattered out in front of him: old crazed fountain pens, a stack of 78-rpm records in their original brown paper covers, a fanned display of rusty bottle openers, three small identical plaster statues of a laughing white-aproned waiter, and a pink plastic Buddha wedged in between two human skulls.

The array of weird wares only added to Bern's sense of being caught up in a time warp, an alien strata of someone else's imagination. As he wondered where Mondragón's men were, he couldn't help remembering what they had done to Khalil's cell in Tepito the night after Jude's death. Was something like that even possible in buildings surrounding this pleasant plaza?

He turned a corner in the plaza and started up another side, when he spotted the pharmacy. But when he got parallel with it, there was no seller of comic books. He searched for the phone box. There it was. He crossed the street and walked slowly by, pausing, pretending to look into the window of the pharmacy. There was no red dot beside the number six.

Wait. Wait. He looked up at the name of the pharmacy: Farmacia Morena. Shit. Why the hell hadn't the woman warned him that there were two pharmacies? She could've said that. He moved on, this time staying on the street side, watching the plaza from there.

Had he imagined it, or had there been men moving along with him in the midst of the crowd in the park? What did it matter? He knew Mondragón's men were there.

He crossed the street and turned along the third side of the plaza. The music from the organ-grinder was still remote. Children laughed, and a man selling balloons on the *paseo* hawked them in a sing-song litany, which one of the children began to mimic.

He almost stumbled on the comic book vendor. There, spread out in front of him on an old blanket on the front of the sidewalk, was a gaudy collection of horror comics. All of them were battered old copies of *Fantomas, La Amenaza Elegante,* the covers portraying a handsome dark villain with a cape menacing a variety of heroines with scant clothing, large breasts, and long thighs provocatively spread in vulnerable poses of distress.

And to his left: Farmacia Pedras.

He turned and approached the telephone, saw the red

dot, put the required coins into the slot, and punched in the number. Two rings.

"Judas, you're being followed," Sabella said.

"Shit." It was a stupid response. Stupid.

Sabella asked, "Do you know who it is?"

Bern thought of Alice. He thought of Susana. "No," he said. "Don't have a clue. I thought I was okay."

"You need to face the plaza, Judas. Careful, don't be obvious. I'm going to describe things to you."

Bern shifted his weight, rested an arm on the phone box, shifted again as he turned.

"The guy coming down the sidewalk from the same direction you came," Sabella said, "he's following you. He's probably going to go right by you into the pharmacy. They're going to try to wrap you up."

"Okay," Bern said, and the man walked past him, nearly brushing his shoulder, and went into the pharmacy.

"I've got him," Sabella said.

Bern wasn't sure what that meant.

"Was he wearing an ear mike?" Sabella asked.

"Yes."

"Shit. Okay, now across the *paseo,* buying the balloon."

Bern wiped his forehead on the arm of his coat and spotted the guy.

"Okay."

"To your left," Sabella went on. "The guy who just sat down at the sidewalk café."

"Mustache?" Bern asked.

"Yeah. And just now crossing the *paseo* by the woman selling lottery tickets."

"Dark suit," Bern confirmed. "Sideburns. Smoking."

"Yes," Sabella said.

Across on the *paseo,* the guy who had bought the balloon was giving it to a little girl, who was glancing at her mother to see if this was okay. Then the guy strolled over to a fruit vendor and bought a couple of slices of mango wrapped in a piece of paper and stood by a trash container to eat them.

Sabella had fallen silent.

Bern checked the others. They were staying in place. He made a mental note: So Sabella was there, somewhere on the plaza, running interference for the reclusive Baida, as always. Probably they were in one of the buildings on the north side, since that's where all the action was right now and they were seeing all of it.

Still nothing else from Sabella. Bern waited.

Somewhere lurking on the perimeter of the plaza, Vicente Mondragón was waiting, too, peering out through the smoky windows of his Mercedes. With Susana.

There was no use in pretending what was going on here. Bern knew, somehow, that Mondragón, for whatever abominable reasons, was going to kill Ghazi Baida despite Kevern's order to stand down. That meant that as far as Lex Kevern was concerned, Mondragón had turned rogue. And that meant that Bern had become the pivotal player right smack in the middle of a dilemma.

"What's the word from your people?" Sabella asked suddenly. His voice was hushed, as if he had to speak softly to keep from being discovered. Where the hell was he?

"It's a deal," Bern said. He had been so preoccupied trying to figure out all the angles of what was happening to him that he was unaware of the physical effects of the stress he was under. When he spoke, there was hardly enough air to push out the words. "They need to know . . . have you got a plan—"

"Yes. There's a plan." Sabella was curt; an edgy impatience had slipped into his voice now. "But first, Judas, I have to know what's going on here. Who the hell are these people?"

Bern was sweating, his hand massaging the telephone as he tried to keep a grip on it. Something was changing. What was Sabella seeing? Bern saw nothing. None of the men had moved. They were waiting. Everyone was waiting.

A ray of sun pierced the clouds, sending a thin bar of laser-bright light transiting the plaza.

God, thought Bern. All of his options were risky, and he was taking too long to make up his mind. Each person involved here was dangling by his own slender strand; each was betting on Bern to do the thing he wanted him to do.

Mondragón was waiting for him to lead him to Baida, and Mondragón was betting that he would do this because of Susana. Sabella was betting that he would deliver Baida and him from twenty-two years of killing and fear and hiding and sleeplessness. Kevern was betting that Bern could live his lie just a few more hours and bring about the richest intelligence coup of the terrorism wars.

And Susana. Bern guessed that for all her training and professionalism, for all her personal bravery, she was, at this moment, simply thinking like a terrified woman. She knew what Mondragón was capable of, and deep within her she must be weak with fear, knowing that the only thing standing between her and Mondragón's violence was the judgment of an equally petrified Paul Bern.

But ultimately, Bern's decision came down to the husk of a memory that might well have blown away in the gale of intervening events. But it, too, had waited on Bern, suspended and latent in his subconscious.

The last thing Sabella had said to him before leaving the room in Hotel Palomari was that there were pressures on Baida that made this window of opportunity very small. "When it closes, it cannot be opened again," he'd said.

"Judas," Sabella said, speaking slowly, as if his suspicion had reached critical mass, "what have you done?"

Chapter 45

"Listen, Mazen," Bern said, turning his back to the plaza again. He hunched over the phone box as if protecting a private conversation, then carefully pulled Kevern's phone out of his inside coat pocket.

"I've got a secure cell phone to my people, and I'm opening it right now," he said, running his thumb down the three digits as Lupe had showed him. "Okay?"

"Yes, okay," Sabella said.

Bern waited, listening to the hum, the click, the connection.

"I'm here," Kevern said.

"Now . . . I'm talking to both of you," Bern said into both phones. "You're both hearing what I'm saying at this moment. Okay, Mazen?"

"Yes, okay."

"Lex?"

"Yeah, go ahead." Kevern's voice had slipped into the smooth monotone of operational dispassion. Be cool, it said to Bern. Be careful. Don't let the juice confuse your thinking.

"Lex, let me bring you up to—"

"We know," Kevern said quickly. "Your phone's been live all this time. We're up to speed."

Bern was stunned and pissed, but there was no time for that.

"Well, shit, then," he snapped, "are you sending someone?"

"We're on the way," Kevern said.

Move on, move on, Bern kept telling himself.

"Mazen, I know you're at a vantage point where you can see this side of the plaza. Are you in rooms above Farmacia Pedras?"

"Hurry," Mazen said.

Flustered, Bern went on. "Okay, these men in the plaza are Vicente Mondragón's. He's got Susana, and he said he'd kill her if I told you, or contacted my people. He's expecting me to lead him to you. I don't know what he's doing, what he's planning, but we've tried to stop him. Now he's broken communication with us."

Bern was talking fast, cramming everything in.

"Mazen, listen, you said that we had only a small window of opportunity here and after that it would be too late. Were you referring to information that you have that's time-critical? Do you need to tell us something now? Do we need to do something?"

The ensuing lack of response was the most unnerving silence Bern had ever experienced. Weirdly, he began to experience an alteration in perception, not of sight or sound or touch, but of the flow of time. Sabella's silence extended through the afternoon and into dusk.

"Mondragón," Sabella said. His voice, too, was accommodating the numbing stress of their situation. "Yes, that was a good choice, Judas. A good choice, because we didn't even know that he was still alive." His voice had lost its tension, and he seemed composed. Or was it the serenity of resignation?

"Where's Vicente now?" Sabella asked.

Bern told him about Mondragón catching up to him on his way to Jardin Morena, about the phone, the conversation they'd had, the threats.

"So I don't know where he is," he added. "I guess he's in the area somewhere."

"Yes, hanging back," Sabella agreed.

"But Kevern is on the way with people."

"Four of us," Kevern interjected.

"Four," Bern said to Sabella.

"We don't have any people here," Sabella said, and this time Bern could clearly hear the resignation in his voice. And yet it wasn't quite resignation, either, it was more like an intimacy with fate, as if he held no rancor for the inevitable. It was a philosophical acceptance of the inevitable.

"We come to Plaza Morena twice a week, if we can. We've done it for over a year now. But we come alone. We have a very elaborate process that we go through that allows us to come here—safely, alone. When we enter Plaza Morena, we're just two more anonymous *capitalinos*, nothing more."

"Twice a week?"

"Ghazi has a woman here," Sabella explained.

Oh shit. "He's with her now?"

"Yes."

"And *no* bodyguards?" Bern couldn't believe it. Despite what Kevern had told him, he thought Sabella and Baida would have *someone* to help them.

This explained why Sabella seemed to know the plaza so well. He must have spent hours sitting by the window, wherever the window was, gazing down at the plaza. When you are familiar with the daily rhythms of life on a street or in a neighborhood, you acquire a sense of what normal is in that place. A new face or a change in routine is like an alarm going off.

Bern related Baida's situation to Kevern and then asked, "Where the hell are you?"

"We're about halfway there."

"Look, when you get to the Jardin Morena," Bern said, "I'm—"

"There's GPS on your cell, Paul. We know exactly where you are."

"He's taking too long," Quito said, referring to Bern talking on the pay phone. He was sitting in Mondragón's Mercedes, around the block from Jardin Morena. Susana was in the backseat with Mondragón, and Quito was sitting beside the driver, working the radio equipment that was keeping him in touch with his men on the plaza. "He's talking to Kevern or Baida, telling them what's happened."

"I don't know," Mondragón said. "Baida's plan will be very elaborate, complex. He will want to give himself plenty of room to check and cross-check."

"He's not writing anything down," Quito said.

"Baida wouldn't let him do that," Mondragón replied. "Bern could be memorizing the route, the time sequence. Maybe repeating it back to Baida, rehearsing it."

"Or he could be spilling his guts," Quito insisted.

"You know," Mondragón said, "Jude might have done that. He was just crazy enough to take the risk that we wouldn't shoot her. But Bern's not that tough, doesn't have that kind of discipline."

"But he's taking too long," Quito warned.

In truth, Mondragón was uneasy about the amount of time Bern was spending on the phone, too. Quito was probably right, damn it.

"Where's Kevern now?" Mondragón asked, spritzing the front of his head.

"They've just passed Parque Hundido."

"*Perfecto*," Mondragón said. "Wait until they are approaching the on-ramp to the *circuito* and do it there."

"Judas," Sabella said, breaking the silence. "Stay where you are. I'm going to be off the phone for a few minutes, but I'll be back."

"What? Wait!"

"Just stay where you are. Stay on the phone. Talk to your man. I'll be back. Do it."

Bern couldn't believe it. "He just left the phone," Bern said to Kevern.

"Left the phone? Whatta you mean?"

"He left the goddamned phone. Said for me to stay on the phone. Not to leave the phone."

"Shit, he's running," Kevern said. "He's running, goddamn it!"

Mondragón's man inside the pharmacy could see Bern through the front window. He kept one eye on him as he milled around the rows of shelves in the small shop. There was no one there at first, and then a young woman came in with a child, one of those children who simply stared at you in sober silence and could not be charmed into any kind of reaction at all. And yet she wouldn't stop looking at him. Gave him the creeps.

The store was L-shaped, so he went around the corner into another row of shelves to get away from the kid, although still keeping Bern in sight. Good, magazines. He looked for some sexy covers and picked up one of them just as another woman entered from the back door of the shop, which opened into a typical courtyard.

The woman was nice-looking, late thirties, her dark hair done up quickly. She wore a blue shirtwaist dress that buttoned up the front. The top button was undone, exposing a very nice set of *chichis*. He glanced at Bern.

The woman came right at him, apparently interested in the magazines, too. But she seemed to want to see the ones on the other side of him. Gathering her skirt delicately, she begged his pardon, and he stepped back to let her by. For one sweet moment, they were face-to-face as she slipped past him, her eyes modestly averted as her bosom wafted by right under his nose. On the other side now, she turned her back to the front of the store, Bern behind her, and bent down to search through the magazines on the bottom shelf.

Her position couldn't have been better for him. His eyes only had to move a slight flick to switch from Bern to her bosom, where gravity swelled her breasts to the spilling point.

Then suddenly, the little girl was in the picture again, appearing squarely in the center of the aisle behind the woman, her moronic stare fixed on him once more, her head poking up just above the woman's hips, as if it were balanced on top of them.

Tits, child, Bern. Tits, child, Bern. The kid was irritating the shit out of him. The woman moved a few magazines, looking under them, her movements causing her breasts to shift and roll. The kid stared at him. Bern talked. With all the bending, the woman had to adjust herself, slipping a pretty hand inside—

The kid's moronic eyes shifted slightly to a position over the man's right shoulder, her expression still as dumb as a rock.

The hand coming over his shoulder and covering his mouth hardly registered on him before the knife did its work on his throat. He knew he was dying. The woman straightened up and walked past him as if he weren't there. Then he felt himself being dragged backward.

The last thing his eyes registered was the mute, imbecilic stare of the little girl, who did not run or blink or react to what she was seeing. She seemed to think that watching a murder in the back aisle of a pharmacy was no extraordinary thing.

Chapter 46

Bern gripped the phone and kept his head ducked next to the phone box as if listening intently. In fact, nothing was happening. Silence on both ends. What all of this was leading to was beyond him, beyond his imagining, almost beyond belief. But it kept going on and on.

Suddenly, Kevern was screaming, "Jack! Jack! Look out! Lookout! Lookout!" And then a woman screamed and there was a thunderous crash.

The old junker car slammed into them out of nowhere, flying at highway speed from a side street and ramming into the driver's side like a torpedo. The two cars, twisted together, left the main street in a cloud of burned rubber and sparks, then careened off of two other cars before coming to rest just a few yards outside the window of a restaurant on the cross street.

Jack Petersen was killed instantly. Lupe was in the backseat on the same side, dying, a piece of chrome the length of a yardstick driven through her rib cage, pinning her to the rear seat. Mattie was dying, too, a fist-size lump of something lodged in her left temple.

Kevern had all the luck in the world.

He was dazed, his collarbone broken, a cut on his forehead bleeding freely, but he was conscious and fighting his seat belt even before the noise stopped. He knew what had happened, and he knew what was going to happen next. His door had been ripped off, and while the car filled with thick acrid smoke, he got free of his seat belt and simply rolled to the side and fell out of the car, hitting the ground in the narrow space between the twisted cars and the restaurant wall.

While the entire restaurant clientele stood back from the windows and watched the smoldering cars in stunned silence, Kevern crawled unobserved against the building's wall, pulling himself along as fast as he could to the corner and then around to the other side. Just out of sight, he stopped to get his breath. He thought he was all right, but his guts felt as if they were swollen all out of proportion. His head was still throbbing from the impact, his hearing almost gone.

Within seconds, two helmeted motorcyclists roared up to the smoking cars. The driver of the junker, also helmeted, staggered out of his car on wobbly legs and crawled onto the back of one of the motorcycles, while the other cyclist goosed his machine right up to Kevern's smoke-engulfed car. Instantly, he opened fire with a stubby automatic weapon, sending the horrified diners onto the floor of the restaurant. He emptied a full magazine into the car, and then he reloaded and did it again.

Then the shooter reached into his leather jacket and pulled out a hand grenade and lobbed it into the backseat of the junker. Both cyclists roared away, and by the time the grenade exploded, setting off a second and third explosion as the gas tanks blew, the two cyclists had hit the on-ramp onto the *circuito,* and they were gone.

The whole incident lasted less than a minute.

"Judas." Sabella was back on the line. "Put down the phone and walk into the pharmacy. When you get inside, hurry straight to the back of the shop and go out the door into the courtyard."

"Wait—"

"Mondragón's man inside is gone."

"But I just heard—"

"Do it!"

Bern slammed the phone down in its cradle, pocketed the cell phone, and went through the pharmacy door, a few steps away. Inside, he quickly oriented himself, then headed around a corner into an aisle, suddenly confronting four people gathered around something on the floor.

They all looked up in puzzled disbelief as he approached. At a glance, Bern sized them up as the white-jacketed pharmacist, his wife perhaps, also wearing a white jacket, a child, and a woman who appeared to be her mother. He didn't stop to figure it out, just pushed through them, nearly slipping on the stuff that they were looking at.

By the time that he realized that he had walked through a pool of blood and then realized how it had gotten there, he was opening the door to the courtyard. A woman grabbed him.

"*¡Andale!*" she said, already turning to lead the way, her blue dress swirling around her legs as she took him around the courtyard, through a door on the far side and into another courtyard, and then immediately up a flight of stone stairs that led to the second floor. They turned into a corridor and came face-to-face with Mazen Sabella.

"I dragged the guy under a stairwell down there," he said to the woman. He looked at Bern, and there was an awkward moment in which Bern felt as if something was happening but he was missing it. He saw blood on Sabella's clothes. He was sweating and out of breath.

Sabella broke eye contact with him and looked at the woman.

"I'm going down to get the car ready. I'll be waiting for you across the street. You know where."

Suddenly, he was gone, and the woman pushed Bern through a doorway and out into an open-air patio. They crossed the patio and then burst into an apartment.

Baida turned to them. He was standing by a pair of open windows that overlooked the plaza. They were above the Farmacia Pedras. He had an automatic pistol in one hand and with his other hand he held a tiny headset to his ear.

"Your man's not coming," Baida said. "They're dead. All of them."

Bern gaped at him, stupefied.

Baida held up the headset and the automatic.

"Sabella got these from the guy downstairs in the pharmacy. I heard the report to Mondragón that it was done."

Bern knew it was true. There was no doubt at all.

"Mondragón's boys saw you go into the pharmacy," Baida said. "They tried to contact this guy, and when he didn't answer, they switched frequencies. It's no good now," he said, flinging the tiny headset across the room.

"And down there," he added, jerking his head toward the plaza, "they've all disappeared."

Baida was talking fast, his celebrated composure showing signs of fraying.

"I've called my people," he said, lunging across the room to an armchair where a gray nylon bag lay open. He jammed the gun inside. "I have to go."

The woman, who still hadn't said a word, was pulling things out of an open drawer in a chest near the entrance to another room. She brought a packet of something wrapped in clear plastic—it looked like documents—to Baida, who jammed it into the bag. He was sweating profusely.

"I'm going to give you a number," Baida said. "You won't remember it . . . with all this. . . . I'll show you where to hide it. Pull down your pants. *Carleta, un bolígrafo!*"

The woman grabbed a ballpoint pen from the top of the chest and gave it to Bern, who unbuckled his pants.

"Write it high on the inside of your thigh. If they strip you, they won't see it there."

"Who—"

"Anybody! Hurry!"

Bern bent over and with a trembling hand wrote on the inside of his thigh the number Baida recited to him. Baida repeated it, and Bern nervously traced over the numbers. Hell, someone would figure it out later.

"When you get to our people, use the number," Baida said. "Time is running out."

Time was running out. Bern pulled up his pants and buckled his belt. In fact, he was damned convinced that it was gone entirely, and that the numbers he had just written on his skin were useless.

Baida started to zip the bag, then stopped suddenly. He looked up at Bern. Then he pulled the gun out of the bag and handed it to him.

"My advice," Baida said. "If you get a chance to kill Vicente, do it."

The pistol was lighter than Bern expected. He didn't even know the caliber. He found the safety above his thumb on the grip. He checked the magazine and was surprised to see that it was loaded. Jesus. He shoved it back into the grip.

Baida quickly zipped the bag, and all Bern could think about was Baida walking out of there with his terrible secret. Without thinking, he reached out and grabbed Baida's shirt.

"Wait! Listen—"

In a move that Bern didn't even see, Baida ripped Bern's hand off his shirt and was holding another pistol to Bern's forehead before Bern could even recoil.

"Listen to me, my friend." Baida's voice was tight. The barrel of Baida's automatic was cutting Bern's forehead. His face was inches away from Bern's, and every pore was moist, every nerve taut.

"The deal for my cooperation was my guaranteed safety," Baida panted. "That isn't happening, is it? And it doesn't look like it's going to. In fact, it looks like Vicente is in the process of wiping out your whole operation. I think you need protection as much as I do." He was trembling. "But . . . if there is a miracle anytime soon, you know how to reach me—the numbers are warming your balls."

In the silence of the moment, an incredible sound seeped into the room through the windows overlooking the plaza: the gentle, serene whisper of a slow rain. Bern concentrated on it. In fact, he clung to it as if that sound alone could redeem him to reality, to sanity, offer him deliverance from this nightmare.

Baida lowered his pistol.

"You'd better get the hell out of here," he said.

Chapter 47

Kevern lay in a hedge of some kind at the far side of the restaurant and watched pedestrians craning their heads toward the sound of the collision on the other side of the building. He heard the unmistakable rivet-driving sound of an Ingram MAC-10 machine pistol. He heard screams, saw the pedestrians retreating, heard the pause to reload. He heard the ripping of the second magazine. He saw people running away now, heard the screaming of the motorcycles as the riders full-throttled them onto the expressway. Then the grenade blast and the immediate explosion of the first gas tank, and then the second one.

People yelling. The pedestrian flow stopping now, reversing itself, and surging in the other direction as people headed toward the explosions and the billowing smoke.

That was the anatomy of a killing. People reacted the way people always did, terrified, then horrified, then, as the assassins fled, curious as hell.

He had checked all of them as he was fighting his seat belt. He had seen a lot of people die. He had seen a lot of people dying. It was creepy how you knew instantly. You didn't have to check the vital signs; you just threw them a look, and you either saw death looking back at you or you saw death crawling onto them like a little monkey, impatient to get inside at the first chance. When you saw that, you didn't wait around.

He looked at the street again. He was on the back side of the restaurant, looking around the next corner, where *sitios* sometimes waited for customers. There were a couple of them, the drivers out of their cars, craning their heads toward the direction of the disaster.

When a small group of people fled the restaurant and took the first *sitio,* Kevern knew he couldn't wait. Grimacing with pain, the pressure in his stomach intensifying, he crawled out of the hedge and staggered toward the second *sitio.* The driver, seeing a second group of people fleeing the restaurant, was getting ready to take them, when Kevern ran up to him and showed his automatic. The deal was done.

They got into the black Lincoln and drove away.

Mazen Sabella left through the courtyard of the building and made his way to the street. At every corner, he waited, scanning the cars parked along the street, scanning the windows in the buildings opposite, taking a moment longer to consider every darkened doorway.

In some ways, it was more difficult to escape surveillance in the rain. People running surveillance were taking cover from the rain, hiding from the weather as well as from their targets, and therefore doing a better job of concealing themselves. And for the target, the rain itself was a distraction from detecting surveillance.

But in other ways, the rain offered possible advantages. In hiding from the rain, the surveillers often sacrificed a wider field of vision to stay dry, sometimes opting to squint through a narrow space or peer through a foggy window.

Either way, Sabella took it all into consideration without even thinking about it, these small adjustments having become second nature to him. Every compensation made to adjust to the environment was only a reflex now, embedded long ago into his unconscious.

The car was only a few doorways away, but it wasn't parked on the street. It was behind a closed garage door that opened right onto the street.

The rain had been coming in waves, a hard, driving downpour, followed by a momentary letup, and then another hard, driving deluge. Sabella waited in the corridor doorway for the downpour, waiting the way a dancer waits for his body to get into the stride of the music before he moves into the stream of dancers.

And then it came, a roaring, thunderous downpour. He stepped out into it and ran, ignoring the rain and the swollen gutters. He was concentrating on timing and on what his eyes picked up along the street. Did a parked car suddenly turn on its wipers? Did he see a hand wiping the fog from the inside of a window?

He punched the button on the garage-door opener and darted into the garage without even breaking stride. The keys were in his hand as he opened the car door, and he was already turning the ignition by the time the garage door hit its stopping position above the car. He backed out into the street and drove away in the rain.

With one hand on the wheel, his eyes darting to pick up any movement outside the windows, his right hand flipped on a radio receiver sitting on the passenger seat. The reception was strong.

"My advice," Baida said. *"If you get a chance to kill Vicente, do it."*

"Wait! Listen—" Bern's voice was frantic.

"Listen to me, my friend," Baida said, his voice taut, urgent, impatient. *"The deal for my cooperation was my guaranteed safety. That isn't happening, is it? And it doesn't look like it's going . . ."*

Sabella continued listening to the tense situation in the apartment above the pharmacy overlooking the plaza at Jardin Morena. It was a riveting exchange, and the farther he got away from it, the better he felt.

But he wouldn't be able to relax just yet. Learning that Mondragón was alive and in pursuit had been a stunning surprise. It had almost panicked him. But then, through the fog of sudden dread, Sabella had had a revelation: This new development was actually a hell of a piece of luck, an opportunity to turn the fast-moving and unstable events to his advantage.

Now, as he leaned toward the windshield to peer through the sweeping rain, he listened closely to the transmission from Jardin Morena. If he knew anything about human psychology, about hatred and revenge, then he knew that he would soon be hearing a familiar voice. When he did, then he would know that all of his meticulous planning was about to pay off. It would soon be over. Finally.

Chapter 48

Again, Bern had the sensation of the moment stretching out into the long, rainy afternoon. Killing Baida was possible now. He was right there in front of him, stuffing one last thing into his bag, and all Bern had to do was flick the safety off, raise the gun, and fire. The terrorist whom a secret U.S. operation had been trying to hunt down and kill for over a year would be dead.

But the game had changed. Even if Bern could actually muster the guts to kill a man up close like that, to murder him, he couldn't be sure that he was doing the right thing. Ghazi Baida had put his defection on the table, and suddenly there was a hell of a lot of incentive not to kill him, but to keep him alive at just about any cost. And Baida had even increased the stakes—and the tension—by implying that there was an imminent terrorist action in progress that would kill thousands of people . . . and he was the only one who could stop it.

And now Mondragón's betrayal had changed the game

yet again. The options had shifted. The odds had shifted. Bern was no longer sure of anything.

When the door burst open, all three of them spun around at the same time. The woman was between Bern and the door. There was a loud smack, and her head flew apart in a liquidy red spray, drenching him in the living warmth of her last moment.

Baida shot the man, flinging him back, as Bern fired wildly into the empty doorway.

Then Baida went down for no reason at all, falling awkwardly on his own arm.

A soundless bolt of fire blew through the outside of Bern's left thigh, spinning him around as two men barreled through the door.

The gentle rain of a few minutes earlier had become a drumming downpour now, hammering on the roof of the Mercedes like the roar of a train. When Quito's phone rang, it was almost drowned out by the noise. He answered it and listened. Glancing over the backseat at Mondragón, he nodded.

"There was a woman with Baida, and they killed her. Cochi is dead. Baida was shot in one leg and one arm. Bern was shot in the leg."

"I want to go up there," Mondragón said.

"The boys used silencers," Quito said, "but Baida got off two shots and Bern three. So there has been gunfire. People may have heard that, even in this flood."

"I want to see him right where he was knocked down," Mondragón said. "I want him to see me with the body of Carleta."

He picked up his mask and gently began putting it in place while Quito told his men that they were coming up, then closed the phone. He looked at the driver and told him to stay with Susana, and then he got out of the car with the umbrella and went round to open the door for Mondragón.

When Mondragón had his mask in place, he glanced at Susana. He hadn't spoken a word to her, acting as if she didn't exist. He glanced at her hands, which were bound with a plastic security band, and then his door opened.

The two men made their way across the street in the downpour and entered a doorway that took them into a corridor that opened out into a courtyard. The gutters in the courtyard were throwing water out onto the flagstones in loud waterfalls as the two men continued around the covered walkway to the stone stairs that led up to the second floor.

Quito went through the door first. They had dragged the woman and Cochi out of the way, off to one side of the room, behind a sofa. Bern and Baida were both sitting in armchairs that roughly framed the windows that overlooked the plaza. They were gagged, their hands bound with plastic bands. The men's wounds had been wrapped in pieces of a bedsheet that had been ripped up for the purpose.

On the dining room table, behind Baida's armchair, were Bern's and Baida's pistols and the gray bag with all of its contents dumped out, the passports and documents displayed in neat order.

The lights were out in the apartment, and the room was washed in the gray light of the noonday rain. The windows were open, and a little spray was glistening on the windowsills.

Chapter 49

When Mondragón came into the room, he glanced at Bern, but immediately his masked head turned to Baida and stayed there. He approached Baida and stood in front of him, saying nothing, his tall, lean frame immaculately clad, as always. Even with his trousers rain-soaked up to his knees, he was elegant.

Bern's leg was killing him, but his only fear was bleeding to death. He didn't know what kind of ammunition they were using, but he still had the woman's blood and brain tissue all over him to prove what it must have done to his leg. But even that worry took a backseat to watching Vicente Mondragón.

The room was silent, save for the sound of the rain. Everyone waited.

Mondragón reached up and carefully removed his mask and stood before Baida, looking down at him, the mask dangling from his hand. Baida's eyes showed nothing, not fear, not defiance, not shock. Nothing.

Mondragón turned to Quito. "Drag the woman over here."

Quito raised his chin at the other two men, and they went over behind the sofa and pulled Cochi off the woman. Then they grabbed her feet and pulled her around, dragging her through her own blood. Her dress came up as they dragged her, and her bare flesh squeaked on the polished wood floor. They left her between Bern and Baida, off to the side a little, nearer the doorway.

"Get out," Mondragón said to the men. They glanced at Quito, who nodded at them, and they headed for a bedroom. "No, outside," Mondragón said. Again they got a nod from Quito. "You, too," Mondragón said to Quito.

Quito turned and followed them out and closed the door.

Mondragón stepped over to the woman and looked at her. Her dress was bunched up around her waist now. Mondragón turned back to Baida. "No underwear? You know, I spoke with her sister Estele just a few hours ago. She would be surprised by this." He looked at her again. "Carleta. It would be difficult to tell, with not much of a face to speak of." He hissed. "Not much of a head, even." He extended an elegant bespoke shoe and nudged the woman's bare hip. "But I recognize her *panocha*." He nudged her again, as if to confirm her lifeless condition.

"Well, at least you were screwing the middle one," he said. "Estele was getting a little long in the tooth for a really good screw. Besides, we'd already worn her out in the old days, hadn't we?"

He turned and went to the dining room table, glanced at the passports, and got a chair, which he took over and set down in front of Baida, a little to one side. He sat in the chair, his back to the windows and the rain. He crossed his legs and then crossed his forearms over his lap, his long hands dangling open on either side.

He took a small spritzer out of his coat pocket and misted the front of his head.

"This is my constant companion now," he said, holding up the spritzer. He held it up for a long time before he lowered it again.

Mondragón looked at Baida in silence. Deliberate silence. He was relishing whatever was happening between the two men now. He owned the moment and, finally, he owned Ghazi Baida, too.

"I know you appreciate irony, Ghazi," Mondragón said. Even if he didn't have a face to read, Mondragón's body language—the angle of his head, the tilt of his shoulders, the occasional flip of a relaxed hand—clearly conveyed his satisfaction at being in control of the situation.

"There's a hell of a lot of irony in this moment right now," he said, "that we meet here, to settle an old score after nearly three years, and neither of us has the face now that we had back then. I'm not looking at the face I've hated all that time since London. And you, Ghazi, well, you aren't looking at a face at all, are you?"

Mondragón shook his head slowly in feigned amusement, and his lips, even without the rest of a face, managed to communicate a disdainful sneer.

"It was a good thing that it happened in London," Mondragón said. "They have good doctors there. They saved my life." He looked at Carleta de León, his lidless eyes darting over her. "I have plans for her," he said. "But I want to wait awhile for that. I want to make sure you can't shut your eyes when I do it.

"You should have sent someone other than Colombians to do the job in London," he said. "They have passion for their work, but sometimes they are so slapdash about it. Apart from being crazy, of course. They told me who had sent them, and they told me not to be afraid, because they had strict instructions not to kill me." He paused. "Not . . . to kill me." Another pause as he let the emphasis sink in.

"Then they forced me to take drugs, all kinds of drugs, everything. They loaded me up on them because, they said, that would anesthetize my system, keep me from going into shock. They said they wanted me to have . . . a vivid experience. And then they tied me to my bed. They were taking drugs also. All kinds of stuff, I think. And then they just went to work on me.

"It took hours," he continued. "They drank my liquor and smoked *bazuco* and played music. They would cut awhile, look at me, play around with pieces of me. I remember that they had special fun with my nose, flicking it at one another on the ends of their knives, laughing like idiots when they managed to hit one another with it. Then they would smoke some more *bazuco*. Drink some more. Visit awhile. They talked about women, about sex. Then they would cut some more."

Mondragón spritzed his face. He looked at Carleta de León. The rain had slackened again, and now a fine mizzle was drifting across the plaza.

"It was a miracle that they didn't blind me," Mondragón said. "And why they avoided my mouth, why they didn't cut off my lips, that will always be a mystery. Then sometime during the early-morning hours, they just lost interest in what they were doing. Too much *bazuco*. Too much liquor. Not enough brains. They passed out.

"Sometime around dawn, they left. I didn't know it. I had passed out again, too. I think what happened was that when they finally came around the next morning and saw what they had done to me, saw how much blood there was—I almost bled to death—when they saw the pieces of me scattered around all over the place, I think they just assumed that they had gone too far with it and that I was dead. That's understandable."

Mondragón looked at Carleta. "Just like her. I'll bet those boys out there didn't even check her heart. They just assumed that she was dead. I assume she's dead, too."

He spritzed his face and looked at Baida for a long time.

"Four million dollars, Ghazi. That's all I stole from you. And you sent those fucking Colombians to do this to me. And you wanted me to live . . . with this."

He shook his head and took a deep breath. "Again, you know, I was lucky it was London. The British understand the importance of being discreet. My business manager found me later that day. It was she who managed to pass out enough bribes—yes, even the British—to keep my situation quiet. At least out of the press.

"I had heard that you thought those idiots had killed me. So I went along with that as best I could. I sold my place here and bought another one under a different name. I did my best—spent a fortune, really—to disappear. To be forgotten. Of course, I began to make plans for you from the beginning. This moment, right now, I've thought about it every single day for nearly three years.

"I began to offer the same services that I had offered before, only under another name. I always worked through Quito and a whole line of intermediaries he provided. I became a nobody. A recluse. A night dweller. Through intermediaries and our old connections, I was able to follow you pretty well, but I could never get close. Then you turned up in Iguaçú Falls, in Ciudad del Este. Then, God bless you, Ghazi, you came back to Mexico City."

Chapter 50

Kevern hung his handkerchief out the window of the *sitio* to get it wet, then cleaned his face with a trembling hand while his terrified driver headed for Colonia Santa Luisa. The driving rain gnarled traffic and slowed them down. Kevern had a huge lump on his forehead, and sometimes he felt nauseated and dizzy. His stomach felt gorged. Still, he was lucky. He had gotten out of the damned thing alive.

His cell phone had been knocked out of his hand in the crash, so he was completely cut off from Bern. The only damn thing he had going for him in this whole sorry enterprise was that Mondragón thought he was dead.

He knew from the GPS where Bern had been when he made his phone call. He knew the vantage point Sabella was speaking from. And he agreed with Bern that Sabella was probably in an upper-story room on the north end of the plaza.

But he needed to have some idea where Mondragón was. He knew how the son of a bitch worked, and Quito, too. They were hanging back off the plaza, waiting for their boys on the street to shuffle the cards and stack the deck. And Quito's boys were good at that, so it wouldn't take too long. Vicente would be sitting in his beloved Mercedes, probably a block away from Jardin Morena. Kevern only hoped he wasn't too late and that they hadn't all moved on somewhere else.

When they arrived in Santa Luisa, Kevern told the driver to keep a two-block distance from the plaza, approaching each perimeter block from one end so he could look the length of it for the Mercedes. He spotted it on the second turn. Holy shit.

Taking no chances, he had the driver pull to the curb a block away.

"Give me your keys," he told the driver. He did. "Give me your cell phone," he added. He did. "I'm not gonna hurt you," he explained. "I'm one of the good guys, but I've just got to have a car at my disposal in case I fuck this up."

He got out of the car in the driving rain and started back toward the Mercedes, hugging the walls of the buildings to try to ward off a drop or two. It didn't work. The poor man's architecture in Mexico City wasn't big on overhangs. Every drop that fell went out of its way to land on him.

But God loved him anyway. When he spotted the Mercedes again and saw where it was sitting, everything was perfect. It was in the middle of the block on the opposite side. On his side, cars lined the curb. He would have cover all the way, until he got even with the Mercedes. Then it would be just a sprint across the narrow *calle* and he'd be at the driver's window.

Or he could take his chances and shoot from cover. He

thought about it. The only person he could be sure about was the driver. For whatever reason, Vicente always sat directly behind the driver. Susana would be on the other side. Vicente didn't carry a gun, but there was one behind the driver for him. Big question: Was Quito on the passenger side? Or was he off helping the boys?

Kevern decided that a long shot was too risky. If he missed the driver, and if Quito was there, he'd have three people shooting at him. If he got up close and fired fast shots point-blank through the driver's window, he'd have a good chance of getting Quito, too, if he was there. No good going after Mondragón, as he might hit Susana in the process.

Shit. Enough planning. Suddenly, his stomach rebelled. He didn't vomit, but he spit up a ropy dark bile that burned his throat. He was sweating furiously.

Wiping his mouth on his jacket sleeve, he crouched and ran through the rain, staying behind the cars along the curb until he was even with the Mercedes. And then there was more proof that God loved him. Two—not one, but two—cars came along the street from his left, slow cruisers, as if they were wading through the surf. Beautiful.

He waited, soaked through and through, until the first one was even with him and then he started across the street. When the second one slipped past, he was two steps from the driver's window. All he did was reach out and pull the trigger twice. He saw the splatter at the same time he jerked open the back door, all set to jam the barrel of his automatic into Mondragón's chest.

"Lex!! Oh! . . . Oh God . . . Lex! OhGodohGodohGod."

He crawled in beside Susana and slammed the door.

"Where the hell are they?" he asked, digging for his

pocketknife. He cut the plastic on her wrists, then reached down and swiped the blade through the one around her ankles.

"Baida's place."

"How many?"

"Two. Quito. Mondragón."

"Four altogether, then?"

"Yeah, yeah. One was killed . . . in the pharmacy, and then the other when they stormed into the apartment. They killed a woman with Baida. Bern's shot in the leg, Baida, too."

"Then Quito and Mondragón went up?"

"Yeah, yeah, they went up."

"That's it?"

"Yeah, yeah, but they're going to kill Baida. He wants to defect? Is that right . . . is that what Bern was saying?"

"Right," Kevern grunted, nodding.

"Incredible. Incredible. Then we've got to hurry. We've got to stop it. . . . Where . . . are the others?"

"Dead. It's a flute. It's a fluke I'm here, just a damn fluke."

Susana stared at him taking it in. "Then . . . they think you're dead."

"Yeah."

"Good good good," she said. She had rammed the fingers of one hand into her thick hair, holding them there, thinking.

Kevern grabbed Mondragón's gun from its cradle in back of the driver's seat, then reached over into the front seat with a strained groan and wrestled the driver's pistol out of the holster at his waist.

"Which one you want?"

She took the driver's big Sig Sauer because the magazine capacity was thirteen.

"Okay, let's think," Kevern said, beginning to feel woozy again, worried that he had busted something inside. He was a little chilled, although sweating like a fool, which you couldn't tell because he was soaked from the rain.

"You okay?" She had checked the Sig and was looking at him now, frowning.

"Yeah . . . you know, shit, it was a hell of a wreck. I'm just rattled. Listen, let's just take it easy goin' in. If they're tending to business inside, somebody's going to be looking out. . . ."

"Let's go," she said. "They're going to check in with this guy sooner or later, and then we're screwed."

"Yeah, listen. I've got a *sitio* stranded over there, okay? A block away." He pointed with his gun. "Just so you know . . ."

Then they opened the doors and stepped out into the rain.

Chapter 51

Mondragón sat in silence for a few moments, his goggle eyes resting on the woman. Bern looked at Baida, whose eyes were fixed on Mondragón. Bern could hear him breathing. He knew Baida had been shot somewhere in the shoulder. He didn't know how bad it was, but the piece of sheet they had wrapped around the wound was completely soaked in blood.

Without speaking, Mondragón stood and walked out of the room, in the opposite direction from the bedroom. Bern could hear him opening drawers, hear things rattling. He was in the kitchen. When he returned, he was carrying a butcher knife and a small paring knife. He sat down in the chair again and put the knives on the floor between his shoes.

"You know, Ghazi, you were more a human being when you were a Mexican," Mondragón said. "When you got mixed up in that Middle East shit, the real Ghazi died. Hezbollah. Muslim Brothers. That fundamentalist Great Satan shit. That wasn't you anymore. So it didn't bother me to steal the damn money from a radical Islamist. Stupid fuckers." Mondragón shook his head. "But the Latin American game, the Colombian game, the Mexican game, you forgot what that was like. You forgot that it's a different kind of chaos here.

"You came back with this big badass reputation. Mr. Terrorism. The demonic genius. Yeah. And right away I fucked you out of four million dollars. Then Mr. Terrorism sends two little maggots from Bogotá to London. Now here we are, and I'm about to fuck you again. Only this time, it's going to cost you everything."

Mondragón swiveled his eyeballs at Carleta de León's body. Bern guessed that he was doing that only to taunt Baida, to ratchet up the anticipation of what he was going to do to her.

Then Mondragón smiled and looked at Baida. It was the first time Bern had seen a smile on those lips, and it was shocking. Mondragón jerked his head toward Bern.

"This guy here," he said to Baida, "Judas. This isn't Judas. Judas really was killed in Tepito. This is his twin. No shit. *Identical* twin. Those dummies Khalil and Ahmad, somehow they learned that Judas was U.S. intelligence—I still don't know how that happened—but they killed Judas before you could find out that they had brought a spy into your operation, and then they blamed it on a drug deal gone bad. And then a few nights later, my boys killed them. All of them. Then we put the word out on the street that it was drugs again and that Judas hadn't been killed after all. Big, elaborate, complex operation, Ghazi. All dreamed up just to get you."

Mondragón shook his head, the lips sneering again.

"The point is, Ghazi, I have been circling you for a long

time, getting closer. If you pissed on a bush, I'd piss on top of that. If you left your scent on a tree, I would rub mine over it. Your life has been getting shorter and shorter all the time because I had grabbed your future in both my hands, and I was tearing pieces off of it as fast as I could. When I couldn't take a lot, I'd take a little, whatever I could get."

For the first time since Mondragón had come through the door, something began to stir in Baida's eyes. Bern was fascinated by the animation that he saw awakening there. It was fear, yes, but it was something more than fear, too. Baida wanted to say something; Bern could see that. Baida even began to make noises, wordless sounds uttered from behind his gag. An outpouring of inflections and modulations issued from him, a desperate effort to communicate.

Mondragón was oblivious. He turned around in his chair and leaned close to Baida, his goggle eyes and fleshy lips looking more eerie than ever as he jutted his head forward in a menacing posture.

"You see this, Ghazi?" Mondragón asked, his words coming slowly now, his voice strained by a scarcely contained rage. "You wanted to do the worst that you could do to me, to obliterate my face, the heart and center of my self, my visible soul. Killing me would have been merciful. But you wanted me to die not once, but every day. And so I have."

Mondragón paused, and Baida ceased his furious effort to convey an urgent plea or explanation. Now Bern could hear them both breathing, as if the breath that left one of them was sucked in by the other, the hatred passing back and forth between them.

"But your desecraton has given birth to a paradox, Ghazi. By taking away my face, you have created another one in its place. Look well at this," Mondragón said, leaning in even closer and slowly turning his head slightly this way and that so Baida could see into his flesh. "This is the face of your own death."

God loved Lex Kevern. His luck held out.

As soon as he and Susana entered the corridor that opened off the street, they huddled together to catch their breath and settle their nerves. But they didn't take long. With Kevern going first, they eased forward to the lighter end of the corridor to check the courtyard. Luckily, it took Kevern only a few seconds to locate the guy who had been sent down to ground level to keep an eye on the courtyard entrances.

Smoking a cigarette, he was leaning against the wall under the arch of the corridor that led out to the street around the corner from the plaza. He was hardly visible, just an elbow, and now and then a puff of smoke.

Kevern stepped back and leaned toward Susana, his lips close to her ear for a few moments. Then they both returned the way they had come, and at the corridor's entrance, they turned in opposite directions, walking out into the rain again.

Susana made her way around the block to the entrance on the opposite side of the courtyard from the guard smoking in the doorway. The moment she entered, she began searching for a prop, something to give her a reason to be going out into the courtyard. She found it halfway down the corridor. Two wash buckets sat in the empty hallway, a mop leaning against the wall between them.

She hid the Sig Sauer under her dress, wedging it beneath the waistband. The rest of it she would do out in the open. Picking up the two buckets, she walked to the entrance of the corridor and eased up to look across the courtyard. The guard was still there.

On the other side of the building, Kevern eased up to the corridor entrance and looked around the corner. The guard was still leaning on the wall at the far end; nothing had gotten his attention yet. Kevern jabbed Mondragón's pistol into the small of his back, pushed off his shoes, dug the pocketknife out of his pants, and opened it.

On the other side of the courtyard, Susana stepped out into the portico and walked over to one of the cascading gutters, which was spewing a stream of rainwater out onto the flagstones. Setting down the buckets, she kicked off her shoes and began gathering the hem of her skirt, pulling it up high, exposing as much of her legs as she could as she tucked it into the waist of her dress. Then she picked up one of the buckets and placed it under the gutter, her back to the guard. Pretending to adjust the bucket, she bent over, giving him a chance to have a good long look at her butt through her rain-soaked panties.

When Kevern looked around the corner the second time, he could see that the guard's body language had changed. He was standing up straight now, his attention fully engaged by something across the way. Kevern eased around the corner, grateful for the roaring rain, which drowned out the little sounds that could spell disaster.

He had to slash the short blade across the guard's throat twice to do the job and then he held him while he lost consciousness. As Kevern eased him down on the floor, he looked across at Susana, who had just gone back under the portico and was turning around. Kevern waved her toward the plaza side of the courtyard.

Before they even started up the stairs, they discussed what they might find. When they had played out the most probable variables, Kevern handed Susana the silenced pistol he had taken from the guard. She had the most experience with sound-suppressed weapons, and accuracy was going to be critical.

They were surprised to find that Quito and the other guard weren't directly outside the apartment door. There was a small open-air courtyard with plants and a few pieces of patio furniture outside the door. It was maybe fifty feet across the courtyard to the short hallway where Quito and the guard were biding their time. The landing where the stairwell surfaced on the second floor was another fifty feet away from them.

Another brief whispered discussion. Then Kevern backtracked, going all the way around to the other side of the courtyard to an identical stairwell. He removed his shoes and started up the stairs, hurrying as best he could, headed for the second floor, where he would circle around and be within a few feet of Quito and the other guard.

But then it all began to catch up with him. The nausea hit him again like a slug to the stomach. He didn't even have time to bend over before he started vomiting, repeated waves that shot burning liquid out of his mouth and knocked his legs out from under him. And then he saw the granular black vomitus, and he knew that he wasn't going to get to the top of the stairs . . . ever. He felt as if he were sinking into warm liquid that was rapidly turning cold. He looked across the courtyard, but he couldn't see her . . . and he couldn't call her. The stairs began to fold back on him, rippling like a ribbon in the wind. He couldn't believe it. Well, shit . . .

Susana waited, counting out the seconds. At two minutes, she crept up the stairs until her head was even with
the floor; then she eased up until her eyes cleared the landing. Looking through the wrought-iron railing, which
helped conceal her, she looked for Kevern's feet. Nothing.
He should have been there by now, just an arm's reach
away.

Carefully, she turned and looked around the landing,
her eyes sweeping slowly at floor level. Kevern was
nowhere in sight, and suddenly she had a bad feeling. She
remembered his sweating, his nausea, his bent posture.

Jesus. Her first impulse was to go back and find him,
but then she checked herself. There was more risk to the
operation in doing that, a chance that she would blow the
slim margin she had now. Kevern had miraculously sal-
vaged what had become a hopeless situation, but he had
taken it as far as he could. Now she had to take it as far as
she could.

Turning slowly back to the men, she raised the pistol,
its barrel extended by the addition of the silencer, and
rested it on the floor, angling it up toward the two men. She
would take the other guard. Quito was the more important
one. She would need Quito.

She eased back on the step where she was sitting, held
the pistol in both hands at arm's length, and steadied the
barrel on the floor.

She concentrated or modulating her breathing.

She mellowed out.

She pulled the trigger.

Chapter 52

Having someone's head explode all over you while you are talking to them provides a jolt of astonishment that even a seasoned killer can't instantly overcome. The few beats of disorientation can give the shooter the edge she needs, even if she has to spring up a couple of steps.

Susana was within twenty feet of Quito, and already dropped down in a shooter's crouch before he could even pull his pistol. He raised his hands shoulder-high. Her accuracy had already been proven.

She waggled the long muzzle of the pistol at him.

Quito could not believe what he was seeing, but he knew the drill. He was careful. This woman knew all the tricks of handing over a weapon, and he didn't want to die. Buying time, no matter what that time might hold, was every man's first thought when faced with the prospect of instant death.

He carefully put his pistol on the floor and shoved it out of his reach without Susana even having to tell him.

"What's the story inside?" she asked.

He didn't bother about being clever. He had instantly calculated what it had taken for Susana to be crouching there, and he had a great deal of respect for a woman who could overcome those kinds of odds after he had just left her in the backseat of Mondragón's Mercedes with her hands and feet tied. By his calculations, there was no one left but him and Mondragón. His other people were too far off, and not nearly as experienced at close work as the men who had already been killed.

"Baida and Bern have their hands tied," he said.

"Where are they?"

"As you go in the door, there's the body of the dead woman on the floor in front of you. Behind her, across the room, Bern is tied in an armchair on the left. Baida is tied in another chair on the right."

"And Vicente?"

"I don't know." Quito swallowed. "But he's not armed."

"What's happening in there?"

Quito swallowed again. "I don't know, but it's not good."

Susana stood and, being careful not to slip on the blood and brains on the floor, moved to the doorway that opened out into the patio outside Baida's apartment. It was still raining, but not driving like before. It had slackened a little.

She stepped on the other side of Quito to get away from the guard's body.

"We're going to walk across the patio to— Are there any windows on this side?"

"No."

"Okay, then we're going to walk across the patio to the

front door. Are the lock and latch broken from your guys going in?"

Quito nodded.

"Then we can just push it open?"

Quito nodded.

"Okay. Then we're going to stop just outside the door. No talking. You in front of me. When I tap you on the shoulder with this"—she waggled the silenced pistol again—"I want you to hit that door and charge into the room. I want you to charge Mondragón and take him to the floor. If you don't do that the second we clear the door, I'll kill you."

Quito nodded. "And then what?"

"Get your hands into the air so I don't have to think about them. Let's go."

Quito stepped over the body of the guard, and Susana followed him out into the rain. They crossed the patio in the drizzle. By now, Susana had been soaked through and through several times, but she didn't even know it. She was concentrating on the precise movements she would make as she entered the room.

At the front door, Quito paused as instructed. Susana looked over his shoulders at the door latch. It was splintered apart, as he had said, and she could tell the door was slightly ajar. Good.

She tapped Quito on the shoulder.

His arms went up, and he burst though the door, slamming it back against the wall as Susana followed him in, as close behind him as she could get.

After what seemed an eternity of muted and pitiful squealing, Baida had finally passed out, and for the last quarter hour Bern had alternately watched and turned away from Mondragón cutting away at Baida's face. About half of it was gone. And Mondragón hadn't spared the lips.

At the moment Quito burst in, Mondragón was beginning a new flay line under the left side of Baida's jaw. He spun around just in time to catch the full impact of Quito's body, which took both of them off their feet and sent them crashing into the dining table behind Baida's armchair.

Susana snatched the butcher knife off the floor and swung around and swiped the blade through the plastic ties around Bern's feet and hands. She thrust the Sig Sauer into his hands, then swung around again as she leveled her pistol at Quito and Mondragón, who were scrambling to their feet near the overturned table.

Bern quickly ripped off his gag and blurted, "Guns on the table!"

Susana knew instantly what the calculating Quito had done, and she yelled at him: "Don't do it! No! No!"

But Quito stepped out from behind Mondragón, swinging up the pistol that Baida had given Bern.

Again, Bern heard the same smacking sound that he had heard when Quito's men shot Carleta de León, and Quito slammed back against the dining room wall with only half his head.

Susana then turned her pistol on Mondragón, who froze.

It was only then that Bern looked again at Baida. He was aghast to see blood spurting out of the side of Baida's throat. Quito had burst in at exactly the wrong moment, and Mondragón's knife hand had flinched . . . or had he had the presence of mind to be deliberate about it?

Bern lunged over to Baida and slapped his hand over the wound and held it there, reminding himself not to choke him to death trying to stanch the hemorrhage. By now, both pieces of the sheet that had been wrapped around Baida's shoulder and leg were thoroughly saturated and were seeping blood. And, of course, his face was gored with blood from Mondragón's hacking lacerations.

Bern couldn't believe it. He was frantic, glancing around the room, not even knowing what he was looking for, just some answer . . . some answer.

"Jude," Susana snapped, unaware of what she was calling him in the adrenaline rush of the moment, "has he talked?"

"No!"

"Nothing? You don't know anything?"

"No!" Bern released the pressure and the blood swelled through his fingers like a fresh spring. Baida seemed to be in shock, or in a coma. Shit, thought Bern. He couldn't tell which, didn't know how to tell. Ghazi hadn't had the benefit of the anesthetizing drugs that Mondragón had mentioned having had during his ordeal. His right eye was closed, but the lidless one was motionless and gazed outward to infinity. If it saw anything at all, it saw an apocalyptic vision; Bern was sure of it.

Again, irrationally, Bern eased up on his hand and was surprised to see that the flow of blood was subsiding.

"Oh!" he said. "God." Hopeful, he lifted his hand some more. The blood still came, but it was seeping, and even that was subsiding. "Shit! Good, good!"

"Jude," Susana said again, trying to get his attention, and then she caught herself, but before she spoke again, she saw that Bern already had begun to realize that Baida was dead.

Remaining on his knees, Bern knelt there awhile—he didn't know how long—and stared at Ghazi Baida. He looked at the half-flayed face of a terrorist and a drug trafficker, the face of hatred and fear. The face of hopelessness. The face of a man.

Bern slowly got off his knees, turned around, and looked at Susana. She hadn't moved an inch. She hadn't—not even for a second—taken her eyes off Vicente Mondragón.

"Stay right there," Bern said to her.

He walked out of the living room and into the kitchen, the way he had seen Mondragón go to get the knife. He went to the sink and washed his hands under the faucet and then bent down and washed the blood and brains of Carleta de León off his face and neck. Methodically, he soaped his hands, lathered them, and then soaped his face. Then he rinsed off his face and hands, and washed the woman and Ghazi Baida down the drain.

He dried his hands and his face with a towel that he got off a hook on the side of the cabinet, and then he hung the towel back on the hook. He returned to the living room and picked up the Sig Sauer that was on the floor beside Baida's chair.

He gave the gun to Susana, who seemed to intuit everything perfectly, as if they were sharing the same mind. She held both pistols on Mondragón until Bern took the one with the sound suppressor from her. He walked over to Mondragón.

The two men looked at each other. Bern remembered the first time he saw Mondragón, the sad, hideous spectacle of his disfigurement. He remembered how Mondragón had challenged him to look his fill, to get his morbid curiosity out of his system so that they could move on to more important things. More important things. God, if Bern had only known then.

"Did you know what we were trying to do?" Bern asked. "Did you know what Ghazi Baida was going to give us?"

Mondragón seemed to hesitate. It was strange, but even without a face, he seemed to convey a sense of defiance, an imperious attitude of self-absorption that swept aside everything that got in its way. Nothing was more important to Vicente Mondragón than his own outrageous suffering, suffering that he knew would not end until he drew his last breath, suffering that could never be revenged enough, not even at the price of ten thousand lives. His grief for himself was insatiable.

"Ghazi Baida was a fucking liar," Mondragón said.

Bern raised the pistol and shot him in the front of his head.

Chapter 53

The plan had been in the works for nearly a year, before Ghazi Baida was even brought into the mix. It had been an obsession for Ziad Khalife ever since he had accidentally come across a mother lode of death in Islamabad: two kilos of plutonium 240 that had been smuggled out of an Obninsk nuclear research laboratory in Russia.

He scraped together the money and then began shipping the lode to India, where he knew a disgruntled nuclear research scientist in Madras who had, until a year earlier, worked at the Bhabha Atomic Research Center. But the scientist was skeptical. Big risk. The aerosolizing of plutonium was a delicate process. It made the element more unstable than in its solid state. Not out of the question, but delicate. And it was costly. The equipment. It would take a small team of scientists. That was costly also.

Khalife flew to Riyadh and took his case to the Muslim Brotherhood. It was then that Ghazi Baida was first mentioned, and that sealed the deal. If Baida would agree to do the American end of it, then Khalife would get his financing.

Khalife flew back to Madras with enough money to put the scientist in business, and then he put the word out to the kind of people who would know such things, saying that he would like to talk with Ghazi Baida.

Three months later he walked into a café in Doha, Qatar, and sat down with Baida to talk business. Khalife explained everything. The necessary ingredients would be smuggled into Mexico City in six months' time. Also, following the scientist's specifications, Khalife was arranging for the purchase of Benning Technologies AeroTight propellant-filling equipment to be purchased by a dummy company in Mexico City. The equipment would be set up in a warehouse, and the scientist from Madras would provide the personnel to process and package the aerosolized plutonium. Khalife was personally arranging all of that. The logistics were complex, so it would be several months before the equipment would sail for Veracruz. From there, it would be trucked to Mexico City.

Baida agreed to take the job of building a cell to distribute the plutonium.

It took Baida several months to select his men. He wanted English and Spanish speakers, not an easy combination to come by in the Middle East. But then, he wasn't going to look for them in the Middle East. As soon as he could make the arrangements, he flew to the Triple Border region. There was a huge Muslim population there and, among them, a significant Lebanese presence. He had been there before, and he knew plenty of sympathetic Latin American Muslims who could speak Spanish and could easily pass for Mexicans.

Within a month, Baida was set up in Ciudad del Este and began recruiting his men. At the same time, he began planning the best way to distribute the aerosolized plutonium. He had already developed his theory about the vulnerability of the American heartland. All he had to do was to decide the best way to exploit it.

And, always the entrepreneur, Ghazi began building a drug-smuggling operation. The profits he made from drugs would be used to help finance other operations that he had in the works but which he had temporarily set aside when he agreed to contract with Khalife. If he was going to be in and out of Mexico City, he figured he might as well take advantage of a booming market. It wouldn't be difficult. He had contacts both there and in the Colombian territories that were controlled by that country's largest rebel group, the Revolutionary Armed Forces of Colombia.

Within two months, Ghazi Baida had fine-tuned his plan and had his men. It hadn't been difficult. If their Muslim zeal wasn't enough to carry the day for them, it didn't matter. Baida was paying them well and promising them even more. And, he told them, there was no personal risk. Baida hired an out-of-work Brazilian chemical engineer to pose as a scientist and give the men a "safety" lecture. Just wear a simple hospital mask and everything would be okay, he told them.

Soon, Baida moved his operation to Mexico City and stepped up the level of training. The men received a full six-week course in refrigeration servicing and even received certificates—from a bogus refrigeration-training school in Houston, Texas.

To make sure the men followed through with their task and didn't just take advantage of a free ride to the United

States, the lion's share of what they were to be paid was payable only after they had dispensed the aerosol plutonium at their targets. This, they were told, would be confirmed by instrumentation that had been installed by a team that had preceded them. As soon as they dispensed the aerosol, they were to go to a certain address, where the confirmation would have already been made, and they would be paid.

Bueno. That seemed fair enough. Everyone was happy. Baida was always amazed that the more convoluted the lie, the more likely people were to believe it.

In another sixty days, Baida had each man's documentation in order and began sending them into the United States in pairs. Twelve good men. Seven fewer than Al Qaeda had used on September 11.

Chapter 54

Austin, Texas

Susana sat on the sofa, and Bern and Richard Gordon sat in the two armchairs that were gathered around the big mesquite coffee table in Bern's studio. Bern's bandaged leg was propped on an ottoman, and beyond the glass wall to his left the sun glittered off the rippling surface of the lake in laser shatters. And, as always in the long Texas summers, the lake was scattered with sailboats tacking in the southern breezes.

Gordon had arrived shortly after lunch, accompanied by two athletic-looking young men wearing dress pants and polo shirts and carrying side arms. The two men stayed away from the studio, and occasionally Bern would see one them on the terrace outside the dining room, looking out across the lake.

This was Bern and Susana's second debriefing since their return from Mexico City a week earlier. A team from Tyson's Corner had come down the day after they arrived in Austin and stayed three days. It was a thorough and intense debriefing, which included Bern and Susana being questioned separately and then together. There was hardly a minute of Bern's four days in Mexico City that the team didn't know about when they flew back to Tyson's Corner.

Now, two days later, Gordon had come for a conversation. It seemed that mostly he just wanted to hear the story from them in their own words, but he also had a lot of questions that Bern assumed had been provoked by digesting the debriefing transcripts. As the afternoon progressed, the questions moved from the specific to the general. He wanted to know about impressions, about their "sense" of things. He asked about suspicions and hunches, and he started a lot of questions with "Did you have the feeling that . . ."

Bern was already trying to wean himself off the painkillers, so his leg was a constant irritant, although not exactly a distraction. The pistol shot to the outside of his upper left leg had plowed right through the tissue, blowing out a good chunk of his leg but missing the bone. He had lain awake a portion of every night since their return wondering how in the hell he had gotten through it all with only this much damage. The whole ordeal had been unbelievable, right up to this very moment.

Gordon took off his reading glasses and laid them on the fat arm of his chair. He studied the grain of the mesquite table for a bit, then looked at Susana. He had seemed particularly careful with her all day, respectful. He picked up his reading glasses and fiddled with them.

"I had some luck in Mexico City," he said. "We had a guy in El Salvador who flew in the same night and quickly pulled together a team of his own people, a totally different crowd from the one Kevern usually worked with. Luckily, the bodies in the car were charred too badly to tell that they were even gringos. That gave our man time to pull the strings to get them out of the morgue."

Gordon cleared his throat. "There was a hell of a lot of cleaning up. A couple of the members in the group wanted to call in people from the Mexico City station to help, but we argued them down. The guy from El Salvador worked his ass off, cleaned up the safe house in Plaza Rio de Janeiro, Jude's apartment, Mondragón's penthouse in Residencial del Bosque, Mingo's place. Good disinformation leaked to the media.

"This guy was something, did it all without the station knowing anything at all. I don't know how he did it. Even got the bodies back into the States. Anyway, miracle of miracles, we didn't lose it. The whole thing stayed black. The whole thing. A damned miracle."

He shook his head, sighed, and slumped back into his chair.

"But everyone's discussing what you two came out of there with. They're going over your debriefing transcripts. They're combing through other intel out of the Triple Border region and Mexico. They're overlaying matrices. Shit, they're looking at everything. They're taking it seriously, I have to say."

"But . . ." Susana said, wanting him to get to the point.

"But we're afraid it's too little, too fragmented, too vague, too subjective . . ." His voice trailed off.

"We knew that," Susana said quickly.

Bern guessed she wanted to cut off any kind of commiserating. The failure to salvage Baida's defection haunted both of them, but in addition to that, Susana was still trying to cope with having invested more than two years in an operation that had completely reversed its mission in its final hours, only to have the original mission accomplished by an accident of great misfortune. Despite elaborate preparations by some of the very best people in the intelligence business, operation Heavy Rain had failed because they had been blindsided by reversals, the unforeseeable twists of fate that every intelligence officer lives in fear of.

And to add to the surprises, the wild flier they took with Bern had been successful. And no one but the psychotic Mondragón had had any faith in it at all.

Suddenly, a huge sailboat emerged from behind the point, coming from the direction of the marina. They all turned to look at it as it came close in, clearly visible from the right side of the glass wall. It glided serenely by the little inlet below Bern's walls, and for a few brief moments its massive white sails caught the sun's brilliance, igniting the canvas like billowing sheets of phosphorus against the cobalt sky. And then it was gone.

No one said anything, as if the vision's departure had carried their thoughts away with it. Then Gordon sat up in his chair.

"They could've been lying," he said.

"What would've been his reasons for that?" Bern asked.

Gordon shook his head. "I don't know," he said. "I don't know."

"I keep thinking about it," Bern said, shifting his leg to relieve a sharp spike of pain. He had replayed his conversations with Baida and Sabella over and over, had seen their faces in his mind's eye and even in his dreams. He had gone over every crease and wrinkle, every perspiring pore, and had to see the whole of the message in the assembly of their features.

He winced and put both hands around his thigh and massaged it.

"I think they were telling the truth," he said simply.

Susana suddenly got up from the sofa as if she couldn't get enough air to breathe and walked over to the windows. She put one hand on her hip, wrist in, and thrust the other into the front of her thick hair and held it there. Both men looked at her, waiting. She was easy to look at.

Gordon folded his reading glasses and put them in his shirt pocket. He picked up his notebook and stood, punching a single button on his cell phone before putting it away.

He walked over to Bern and handed him a piece of paper.

"Here's the address you wanted," he said. "She knows pretty much everything. Not classified stuff, of course, but in general."

He reached down and shook Bern's hand.

"Thank you both," he said. He glanced at Susana, who remained with her back to him, looking out at the lake.

One of the security guards came in off the terrace, and the other came in the front door of the studio. Richard Gordon walked out of the studio with them.

Bern looked at Susana. Beyond her, far out on the lake, he could see the visionary sailboat, its shimmering sails gleaming like a daystar against the wooded cliffs.

Chapter 55

In the United States, money continued to grease the wheels for Ghazi Baida's heartland operation. Because these men were not zealous in their fundamentalism, they were not compelled to separate themselves from society; these were not the tight, isolated little cells that intelligence officials quickly recognized as typical of the September 11 terrorists. That profile of the terrorist agent simply melted away in Baida's heartland operation. Instead, it was the open and gregarious nature of the huge Latino communities in the United States that provided great cover for Ghazi Baida's new kind of sleeper agents. It was easy for them to disappear in plain sight.

Each of the twelve men had a single contact to get in touch with when they reached their designated cities. The wisdom of reducing the terrorist cells to two was obvious. These single contacts, known as mentors, were a little higher up on the evolutionary scale of Islamic fundamentalism. They all had been instructed in the Wahhabi strain of Islam, and they knew who Ibn Taimiyah was and what he meant to their faith. Their devotion to jihad was absolute.

After the red dot cans of Dempsey's Best aerosol V-belt lubricant departed El Paso in three separate vans, they were soon scattered across the American heartland, each group of cans ultimately dividing two more times at ever more distant locations. When each can finally arrived at one of twelve different destinations, it was the mentors who retrieved them and made sure, one way or the other, that the men from Mexico City had a means of accessing their targets.

The objective was to gain access to the heating, ventilation, and cooling systems of a variety of buildings in twelve different cities scattered throughout the country. The buildings had been picked because of their particular types of self-contained air systems and because of their high population density within a specific time frame. The specific window of opportunity was no greater than fifteen hours, beginning on Saturday night and extending into midmorning Sunday—a difficult time for headline news to spread very fast if something should go wrong.

By the time the men from Mexico City arrived in the United States, the mentors had already been in place a year or more. Time enough to make the necessary access possible. There was no single way that this could be done, or should be done. After all, twelve targeted buildings, the locations of which spanned the distance from North Carolina to Nevada, allowed for some flexibility.

Each mentor was left to his own devices. Some made friends with the engineers in charge of the Heating, Ventilating, and Air-Conditioning systems in a given building, thereby gaining access to those systems without arousing suspicion. Some cased the HVAC systems of their target buildings as if they were casing a bank. A break-in was a piece of cake in most instances, and this became the pre-ferred method of access. Two mentors had actually gotten jobs as HVAC engineers in their target buildings.

By the end of the second week following Richard Gor-don's return to Tyson's Corner from Paul Bern's house on Lake Austin, everything in Ghazi Baida's heartland opera-tion was in place and ready to go. The mentors patiently awaited the go-ahead sign from Ghazi Baida.

Each target facility awaited a very simple application of aerosol spray, delivered from a common aerosol can found in every HVAC equipment room and on every HVAC re-pair truck. When the time came, a full can of Dempsey's Best V-belt lubricant would be sprayed into the air-handler vents of the HVAC systems. Each can contained five ounces of finely aerosolized plutonium 240 with an aver-age micron size of three. In less than two minutes, every-one in the target buildings would receive a lethal dose of plutonium radiation.

No one in any of the buildings would even be aware of what had happened to them. Within a few days, people would begin dying, and it would take a few days more for epidemiologists to see the pattern.

The targets had been well chosen. The Starlight Grand Music City on the famous 76 Strip in Branson, Missouri, held an average Friday-night crowd of about 850 country music fans. The Marion Seely Hospital in Montgomery, Al-abama, usually had a weekend-night occupancy of around 650. Other locations included a convention center in Den-ver; a country-and-western dance club in Lubbock, Texas;

a retirement center in Phoenix; a music venue in Nashville; and a midsize casino in Las Vegas.

But the easiest targets didn't come available until Sunday morning. By eleven o'clock on a Sunday morning, the HVAC systems of five large midtown and suburban churches and synagogues in Oklahoma City, New Orleans, Little Rock, Charleston, and Raleigh would be sprayed with Dempsey's V-belt radiation.

By noon on the designated Sunday, over seven thousand people would have received lethal doses of aerosolized plutonium. All of them would die.

It would take just one phone call. But the sleeper mentor who was responsible for disseminating the signal once he had received it waited in vain for the message.

Still, he waited. Like all the other mentors, he had been selected for this operation because of particular attributes he possessed. Patience was among them.

Chapter 56

Determined that no one would see any change in his life, Bern immediately accepted several jobs that had been waiting for him when he returned. To the few people who asked where he had been for a couple of days, he mentioned something about a spur-of-the-moment minivacation, a break from a hectic schedule. His leg injury he explained away as a fall on the rocks while working on his quay. Susana was introduced as an old friend from Cuernavaca. Eventually, of course, a better explanation would be made to Dana and Philip Lau, but time and friendship would take care of that.

Bern began working on the quay again as soon as he was able to support himself on his leg. It was tricky business, negotiating the lakeside rocks on a muscle-ripped leg, and at first he did little more than piddle. He and Susana would get up around sunrise, have coffee on the terrace, then put on their swimsuits and go down to the water's edge and begin hauling rocks to the pile that he would eventually cover with concrete. After the sun cleared the point, they would quit and go for a late-morning swim in the cove.

Alice resumed her visits to the studio as well and, much to Bern's surprise and relief, she accepted Susana's presence with equanimity. He had feared, at the very least, an awkward period of adjustment, but, in fact, Alice treated her as if she were a very interesting object that had turned up at Bern's studio—an exotic seashell or a wonderfully smooth river stone that Bern had brought home. Alice liked looking at her, and she liked being around her.

For her part, Susana was comfortable with Alice's quirky, lively behavior from the beginning. She seemed to intuit even better than he the jumbled meanings in Alice's symbolist gabbling. She was completely at ease responding to Alice's verbal nonsense in a kind of pigeon palaver of her own, sometimes peppering it with Spanish, which delighted Alice, often making her laugh uproariously for no apparent reason.

On the mornings when Alice came, they all went to the studio, where Bern worked while Alice and Susana read and listened to music. In the afternoon, Alice and Susana would swim in the cove while Bern continued to work. Sometimes when Dana arrived to pick up Alice, she would bring her suit and join them for a swim and then stay for a glass of wine.

But the late afternoons belonged to Bern and Susana. Often he cooked on the terrace around sunset, and then they would swim in the cove once again as night fell across the lake. Afterward, they would sit in lounge chairs with drinks and watch the night boats move across the water against a backdrop of scattered lights on the far shoreline.

It was during these hours that they talked about what they had been through. Gradually, they disclosed their lives to each other by an intricate progression of small revelations, as if they were providing each other with a mosaic of themselves that could only be assembled slowly, over time, piece by piece with the mortar of insight and understanding. It was an unconscious process, which in its unfolding brought them closer together than either of them had anticipated.

But for Bern, the nights were troublesome. He never slept for more than a couple of hours at a time before waking up with nightmares, sweating. Over and over, he jolted awake at the very instant that Mondragón's blood exploded across his face. Time and time again, Carleta de León's brains splattered into his eyes, and Jude's face—his own face—appeared on Kevern's body, or on Mondragón's, or on Baida's. Over and over, Mondragón's flayed head stared back at him when he looked into dream mirrors. This happened so often and with such vivid effect that Bern began to dread looking into mirrors even when he was awake.

But with time, the nightmares began to subside. As the heat of late summer slowly retreated and the harsh light of August softened into September, Bern began to assemble a perspective of what had happened in Mexico City that allowed him a rough peace with those events. He couldn't have done that without Susana. She had become the Angel of Solace for his restless discontent.

At the end of the second week in September, Dana Lau's mother underwent heart surgery in Chicago, and Phil and Dana flew up to be with her for a few days. Alice stayed with Bern and Susana for the weekend. The weather had been sultry and heavy as a seasonal tropical storm roiled westward along Louisiana's Gulf Coast, pushing wet, heavy clouds inland. It had drizzled for several days, and then a little cool front came down across the plains and pushed the low-pressure system back out into the Gulf. The temperatures dropped to the high eighties, and the sky cleared to a clean, brilliant azure. It was the first real break in the oppressive weather of the season, and it gave everyone hope that the withering summer heat was not, after all, interminable.

Bern spent all of Friday morning interviewing the sole survivor and witness of an armed robbery that had ended in a triple homicide. He had promised the homicide detectives who had flown from Dallas with the woman that he would work up a series of drawings of each of the two assailants over the weekend and have them ready by Monday. He planned to work all weekend.

Around seven o'clock, when the shadows covered the terrace and the water's edge, Bern grilled fresh vegetables and, following Susana's directions, prepared *camarones al ajillo,* shrimp grilled with garlic and chilies. They ate while watching the sun set on the far shore. After clearing the dishes, they returned to the studio, where Bern continued working while the girls played a card game that Alice loved, and they listened to a CD of serene Duke Ellington selections.

Around 9:40, Susana brought their attention to the nearly full moon rising above the hills across the lake. Using the remote he kept in his pocket, Bern turned off the lights in the studio, and they moved to the sofa to watch one of the lake's loveliest spectacles. After a little while,

Bern noticed that Alice was nodding off in her corner of the sofa.

Susana got up and poured a Glenfiddich for herself and one for Bern, and then she wandered over to the glass wall, leaned on the window frame, and stared out at the palely luminous landscape. Bern lost track of time, but Charlie Haden's sax was only a few bars into "Passion Flower" when he sensed the mood in the room change, and he looked at Susana, who had turned her head to look at him, the right side of her face illuminated by the moonlight.

Instantly, a warm flush of alarm washed over him.

"There's a boat in the cove," she said. There was almost a hint of the incredulous in her voice.

Alice, so sensitive to voice tone, stirred awake, and in the moon glow flooding the room, Bern could see her face as she looked at Susana.

"*In* the cove?" he asked. "Not on the point?"

"In the cove," she answered, and the incredulity was gone and something harder had taken its place.

Alice, sensing their concern, sat up. Bern reached for the remote control and snapped off the music as he stood. Alice got up from the sofa, too.

"You don't see anybody?" he asked as Susana reflexively moved back along the wall.

"No, just the boat. A powerboat."

Bern and Alice joined her at the window, where the moonlight created the illusion that the boat was floating in the air about a foot above the water.

"You recognize it?" Susana asked.

"No."

"If ever there was a blue tree, I wouldn't know myself, either," Alice whispered, taking Susana's arm.

"What about the doors?" Susana asked.

But Bern was already heading toward the front. He heard a noise behind him: A drawer was opened and closed in the cabinet that stood a few feet from the studio door that led out to the terrace.

"We shouldn't . . . we shouldn't open our eyes for the singers to be scared," he heard Alice say in a dramatic stage whisper.

He had cleared the steps and was crossing to the front door that opened into the courtyard corridor at the same moment that Susana was approaching the door that led to the terrace. Just as Bern reached out to put his hand on the dead bolt, Susana hissed, "Paul—"

Suddenly, both doors flew open, knocking them back into the room. Bern staggered backward, falling on the steps and tumbling down to the floor in front of his drawing tables. Alice screamed as Susana was hurled into her, sending both women reeling, overturning chairs and a side table and smashing a lamp.

A man yelled something in Spanish. Alice screamed back something unintelligible, which was followed by a second sharp bark of Spanish.

Silence.

Chapter 57

Bern's head hit the concrete floor at the bottom of the steps, making him dizzy momentarily, but he was already recovering as someone roughly pulled him to his feet. By the time he was dragged across the room and shoved into one of the armchairs, Susana and Alice were already sitting on the sofa. In the pale light coming through the glass wall, he could see that Susana had been cut on the forehead. Alice was helping her stanch the bleeding with bunches of tissues from the box sitting on the coffee table.

"I'm okay," Susana said, her voice a little shaky. "The edge of the door—"

"*¡Las luces!*" someone commanded.

"They want the lights," Susana said.

"The remote's on my drawing table," Bern said.

"Shit," another voice said. "Get it, then."

Suddenly, Bern was alert, his mind scrambling to place the familiar tone and inflection.

As Bern stood, a man came up to him and followed him

around to the drawing table. Bern knew where he had left the cell phone, and as he pretended to feel around for the remote, he hoped he would be able to feel the right buttons fast enough in the dark. Nine-one-one-send. Nine-one-one—

But the instant he touched the keypad, it lighted up, and the guy beside him swung his arm down like a sledgehammer, smashing the phone and sending shattered pieces pinging all over the dark room.

"That was brilliant, Judas," the familiar voice said from across the room. "Just turn on the damn lights."

Bern felt the remote in his pocket and punched on the lights, pretending to leave the remote on the drawing table. As the lights came up, he was stunned to see two Mexicans with MAC-10s and . . . Mazen Sabella.

"Jesus," Bern said, glancing at Susana, who merely looked at Sabella in silence. Alice's eyes were huge, but she was controlled, helping Susana but throwing nervous glances at the two men with the MAC-10s.

Bern returned to his chair by the sofa, hiding the small remote in his hand as he walked past Sabella, who was wearing jeans, a pair of scruffy loafers, and a dress shirt with the sleeves rolled to the elbows as before. Bern noticed that the black military watch was still there, and that his shirt was just as wrinkled as the one he'd been wearing in Mexico City.

"This isn't going to take long," Sabella said to Bern, "but I just had to know if what Vicente had said to Ghazi was true."

He picked up the overturned end table, put it down near Bern's chair, and sat down on it. He studied Bern.

Bern didn't say anything. A two-day stubble covered

Sabella's face, and he had begun growing a Vandyke, which looked to be a couple of weeks old.

Sabella leaned toward him. "Twins," he said, lowering his voice to hoarse whisper, "he said you were Judas's identical twin."

Bern saw no reason to deny it now. "That's right," he said.

Sabella continued looking at him. Was he angry? What did that expression in his eyes reflect? And why in God's name would it matter at this point?

"This is very creative," Sabella said, nodding as his eyes made their way over Bern's features "even for the CIA. Sending twins through all of that training, waiting years for just the right time, just the right operation when they could use them somehow. Hell, I'm flattered."

Flattered?

Sabella looked around the studio. "So this is your cover, then? You're a artist, too? Shit. A forensic artist? Amazing coincidence!"

The tone was insolent as he pretended to be gulled by the outrageous concoction of the twin scenario.

"It's not a cover," Bern said.

Sabella nodded, waiting for the explanation.

"I'm not CIA."

Bern could see that Sabella didn't believe him, but he thought he saw a flicker of doubt creep in at the edges of Sabella's eyes, even a slight change in his mouth.

Bern shook his head. "I'm a forensic artist." He gestured at the room. "This is my life. Mondragón came to me, said they needed me to stand in for Jude for a few days, that's all. He said I wouldn't have to do anything, just pretend to be Jude for a few days."

Sabella continued looking at him, skeptical, yet tempted perhaps. He knew better than Bern that the truth could be even more complex than this, so convoluted, in fact, that sometimes it could never be unraveled. Or it could be just as Bern said. As simple as that.

Sabella looked at Susana. "What about you, then? Just switched brothers? Just like that? Didn't matter to you which one you were screwing, huh?"

Bern felt the sudden heat in his face. What the hell was Sabella doing? What did he hope to accomplish by humiliating her? Jesus Christ.

Susana still said nothing, looking at Sabella without emotion as she held the bloody tissue to her head.

Sabella turned his eyes on Alice.

"Who are you?"

Alice glowered at him. The drama of the last few minutes had clearly cast him as the villain in her mind.

"She's a friend's daughter," Bern explained. "How did you find out about this?" He wanted to get the attention off Alice as fast as he could. "You had the room bugged, didn't you, the room at the Jardin Morena?"

Sabella pulled his eyes away from Alice. "I listened to the whole damn thing. Vicente bragging to Ghazi about how smart he had been, crowing and strutting around." He looked at Susana and then back to Bern. "But he didn't get to enjoy it very long, did he?" He pondered a moment. "How was that for you, anyway? You being just an artist, just an average guy, shooting a man like that. Point-blank. Murdering him."

He smirked. "Of course, you knew that he'd killed Kevern and the others. And he'd killed Ghazi. And he'd snatched Susana because he had already planned to screw

Kevern's operation even before Kevern had called him off. And, of course, he would have killed you, too, both of you, if time hadn't run out on him. Vicente was burning his bridges. He'd done it before."

Yes, Bern had indeed realized all of this, but it hadn't made it any easier to pull the trigger.

He glanced at Susana to see if she was following the drift of Sabella's performance. She met his look, and then she slowly looked down at her side, shifting her hip against the arm of the sofa. Jesus, he couldn't tell anything from that, except that she seemed to be uncomfortable.

Bern didn't want to talk about what he'd done to Mondragón. "How did you find me?"

"You find a loose thread, you pull it, things unravel," Sabella said. He shrugged, dismissed it, studied Bern a little bit longer, then glanced around.

"So they just came to you with this idea, then?"

"Yeah, that's right."

"And you just did it."

"After some persuasion."

Sabella nodded. "Vicente's persuasion."

"Yeah, I think he wanted Baida more than the Agency wanted him."

"That son of a bitch," Sabella said. "He and Ghazi went to school together. *¡Pinche cabrón!* Ghazi looked out for him. When Ghazi got involved in the Middle East, in Lebanon, he stayed in touch with Vicente, and threw a lot of business to him. Vicente had his great intelligence connections through CISEN. Shit, we practically had escorts through Mexico for our stuff. And we ran guns through Latin America, explosives, drugs. They did a lot together, running stuff through Cuba, Spain, Algeria.

"But the son of a bitch wasn't getting rich fast enough, so he stole four million dollars from us."

Alice had begun to squirm on the sofa. Bern had noticed that she had started to watch Sabella after a few minutes, her attention no longer focused on tending to Susana's bleeding forehead. Something about him was irritating her. Bern glanced at her. Jesus, this just wasn't a good time for any of her crazy stuff.

She caught him looking at her.

"He's *not* doing the thing that is," she snapped, looking at Bern and shaking her head indignantly, her attitude making it clear that Sabella wasn't fooling her. "He's not doing the real place, not in his mouth he isn't."

"It's okay," Bern said to her, already anticipating Sabella's reaction to her nonsense. "It's okay."

"What the hell's she saying?" Sabella was frowning, suspicious. "What's the matter?"

"It's . . . she has a disability," Bern said. "A brain dysfunction."

Sabella looked at her, and Alice glared back, her disapproval of him very clear to everyone.

"What's the matter?" Sabella asked again.

"Look," Bern said, "what do you want? I don't have anything to do with this anymore."

Sabella dragged his suspicious eyes away from Alice.

"Oh, you just want to be left alone, I guess," he said, giving it some thought.

Bern didn't like any of this. Sabella, of course, was lying about something and Alice was picking up on it. But Sabella's world wasn't a place that her subtle talents could comprehend. Lying wasn't an anomaly in his Wonderland, where every utterance was a chess move, never complete in itself, but always calculated against an anticipated response that hadn't yet entered the other person's mind. Alice couldn't know that Sabella's lying was a given. For Bern and Sabella, it wasn't a deception, but an assumed behavior.

But something else about her reaction bothered him. Sabella hadn't really said anything that Bern didn't already know to be generally true. He hadn't really lied about anything. What was she picking up on, then? His sarcasm? His hateful words to Susana? Maybe, but she had never reacted like this to anything but lying. But then, he had never seen her afraid before, either. Who knew how that would affect her.

"I can't help you," Bern said, wanting it to be over. But he knew damn well that Sabella hadn't come just to satisfy his curiosity.

Chapter 58

"Your brother," Sabella said to Bern, leveling his eyes at him, "was good, but he wasn't as good as Ghazi Baida. And he never would be. When they met in Ciudad del Este, it was a contest of masters from the start. Judas was trying to lure Ghazi into Mexico, and he had decided to play a very risky game to achieve that, a game of . . . insouciance. Do you know that word . . . Paul?"

"Yes, I know the word." But Bern had taken note of the way Sabella had hesitated before saying his first name. And he also noticed something that he hadn't seen in the previous few minutes. As he had done that night in the Hotel Palomari, Sabella seemed to be covering up the fact that he was under a lot of pressure. Perspiration was beginning to glisten on his temples, and an underlying note of tension had begun to show through his relaxed manner.

"Unworried," Sabella said. "Unconcerned. Take it or leave it. That was Judas. When that game is played well, and Judas played it very well indeed, it can be most enticing. If the target—in this case, Ghazi—senses that this insouciance is an act—then it's all over. But Judas was a master of the fuck-off attitude. He offers you a deal, but it is slightly in his favor. He pretends not to notice this, but he knows that you do. And then he tells you to take it or leave it. He bets the whole table on his attitude, and on this moment when his target might say, Okay then, I'll leave it. If he says that, it's over. Taking that kind of risk, all or nothing, that takes very big balls."

Sabella looked a the two women, then back to Bern.

"But you know what?" he went on. "Insouciance, genuine insouciance, can be seductive. Why? For the same reason that gold is seductive, or certain kinds of pearls, or love. Because it is rare."

Sabella leaned a little more toward Bern, his body language suggesting he was about to share a secret.

"Ghazi Baida saw himself in Judas," Sabella said softly. "He saw the same kind of man that he was looking back at him from Judas's eyes. And he accepted Judas's challenge. Why? Because it was the ultimate challenge, to bet your life—everything—against a man who is exactly like yourself. Ghazi accepted Judas's challenge, and he came to Mexico City, stepping willingly into Judas's advantage."

Sabella paused and smiled, despite his barely subdued agitation.

"And he won," Sabella said.

Suddenly, Alice burst into a tantrum.

"No! No! Nonononono! *He's* the who man! Just really . . . really the shitty no man," she blurted at Bern, flinging a look at Sabella, her Asian features hardened into an indictment. "*He's* the who of the whole thing about him."

Sabella flinched and locked his eyes on Alice, anger, alarm, and suspicion mingled in his expression.

Before Bern could speak, Susana intervened.

"Alice, Alice, listen to me . . . listen . . . the lights . . . the lights . . . don't worry about it . . . anytime. Just the lights. It's okay. Understand? Understand?"

Bern was caught off guard, and it seemed for a moment that Alice was, too. She looked at Susana, her eyebrows raised in puzzled fascination, and then she began to rock her head from side to side.

"You need to *listen* to me, Alice," Susana went on. "The lights . . . okay. Now! The lights now!"

"Okay," Sabella snapped. "That's enough of this shit. You think you can do this? You think I'm an idiot, Judas? You don't have any idea what's happened to you."

Bern was dumbfounded. Sabella really thought he was Jude!

"Wait a second," Bern said, his head growing lighter, his disbelief at what was happening almost scrambling his thinking. "This is . . . insane. Look, I'm not Jude. I can prove it."

"No!" Sabella said, stretching out an arm as one of his guards handed him a small tape recorder. "Let me prove something to *you*."

He clicked a button the recorder, and they listened to Mondragón's final moments in Carleta de León's apartment overlooking the plaza Jardin Morena.

There was a loud smashing noise as Quito and Susana burst into the room, sending Mondragón and Quito crashing into the dining room table and chairs.

"*Guns on the table!*" Bern yelled.

"*Don't do it!*" Susana screamed as she swung her gun around to Quito, who was scrambling to his feet. "*No! No!*" But Quito brought up his gun anyway.

They heard the *punt* and smack of her silenced bullet blowing out the back of Quito's head. There was the sound of Bern rushing to Baida's side as he tried to stanch the hemorrhaging wound in his neck.

Silence. Then: "*Jude,*" Susana snapped, "*has he talked?*"

"*No!*"

"*Nothing? You don't know anything?*"

"*No!*"

Another prolonged silence while Bern continued to stanch the bleeding in Baida's neck, and Susana had her gun on Mondragón.

"*Oh! God. Shit! Good, good!*" Bern said, momentarily deluded into thinking that Baida's bleeding was stopping. In fact, he was dying.

Silence.

"*Jude,*" Susana said again, trying to get his attention.

Sabella punched off the recorder.

Shocked, Bern and Susana looked at each other, realizing what her slip of the tongue had done to them.

Silence.

Alice, picking up on the building tension in the room, was growing increasingly flustered. Then suddenly her arm flew up and she pointed a finger at Sabella and began yelling.

"*He's* the who man! . . . The who man! . . . The who man! . . ." she chanted, her eyes flashing at Sabella. "*He's* the who man! . . . The who—"

385

Sabella's two bodyguards threw nervous glances at everyone, shifting their weight from foot to foot as if to be ready for anything, as if Alice's wailing could unleash some hidden threat.

"The lights!" Susana yelled at Alice. "Goddamn it, the *lights*!"

The last word hit Bern with a flash of understanding, and his thumb hit the bottom button on the remote.

Instant darkness.

Alice screamed, a prolonged high-pitched shriek.

Everything was crowded into the short burst of the next few seconds.

Sabella yelled, "Shoot! Shoot! Shoot!"

But the bodyguards' hesitation was fatal.

From Susana's corner of the sofa, one, two, three shots blasted through the darkness, and one of the guards flew backward as the other guard lunged away, ripping off a wild burst from his weapon an instant before Susana's fourth and fifth shots blew into him, driving him into a worktable and knocking over glass jars of Bern's old paintbrushes, everything crashing into the darkness.

"He's Ghazi!" Susana screamed. "He's Ghazi!"

Unconsciously, a stunned Bern was keeping track of the sounds of the choreography: one down, two down, the third man bolting across the paths of the other two.

Bern threw himself at Baida just as the Lebanese reached the glass wall, their momentum and combined weight exploding the glass and hurling them through the railing on the deck and over the side.

The two men embraced.

The fall lasted for days.

Bern's face was buried in Baida's sweaty shirt, and he could smell the other man's fear and his violence, and he could feel his taut muscles and energy and even the painfully slow boom . . . boom . . . boom of his heartbeat as it demanded life, even in the airy fall through the moonlight above the lake.

Chapter 59

She lived in Tarrytown, one of the older genteel parts of Austin, its quiet streets canopied by trees as old as the neighborhood itself. Her yard and two-story brick home were shaded by an almost unbroken shelter of oaks. The only sunny spots were at either end of the half-circle drive, where two pair of magenta crepe myrtles formed brilliant arches to arrive and leave by.

Susana parked Bern's old black Triumph in front of the house, and together they walked slowly along the short sidewalk. Bern was still stiff and wanting to favor every wound, though he was determined to hide it for the next hour or so. Luckily, the scores of stitches scattered all over his upper body, except the dozen crossing the bridge of his nose and sliding under his left eye, were all hidden by his long-sleeved shirt.

They went up a few steps to the front porch as blue jays and mockingbirds punctuated the rhythmic background sound of an old sprinkler in one corner of the yard. Bern had hardly made it up the last step when the front door opened and a woman who appeared to be in her late sixties came out to meet them. Her dark hair, generously streaked with silver, was pulled back in a proper chignon. Without hesitating, she approached Bern, smiling.

"Paul," she said gently, and embraced him. It didn't hurt; he didn't let it hurt. She held him close, her arms wrapped tightly around him, and he could feel her breathing, feel her wanting to absorb him, feel her reluctance to release him. But then she did, looking at him closely for just a moment. She noted the stitches, but her eyes were seeing something else. Then she turned to Susana.

"Susana, I'm sorry, you'll have to forgive me." She embraced her, too, and kissed her lightly on the cheek.

She turned to Bern again, suddenly caught up once more by the presence of her son. For a few moments, she was lost in his face, and Bern knew and understood the emotions churning in her, sweeping away the logic of the moment. Then she caught herself.

"Oh, please," she said, reaching out and touching his arm, jogged from her fascination. "Come on, let's get in out of the heat."

She led them into the coolness of the house, an old and spacious home with a living room, a staircase, a dining room, and a large kitchen, where she led them unpretentiously to a table that overlooked a back lawn, a brick-walled garden.

"Would you like some iced tea?"

"That would be great," Bern said, and while Susana helped Jude Lerner's mother, Bern stood at the windows and looked outside. There was a large birdbath, a sundial that would never tell the time in the deeply shaded yard, a patio with furniture. Jude had grown up here, in this yard, in this kitchen, with this gentle woman as his mother. The kitchen smelled of family and of memories.

For a while, they spoke in generalities. Bern told her a bit about his life, where he lived, what he did. She rambled a little, sometimes flustered, it seemed, by her situation, telling of Jude growing up, saying that she had not seen as much of him in his last years as she would have liked.

Bern was impatient, but he struggled not to show it. Still, he rather quickly steered the conversation around to how he had come to be in this situation, being careful to follow the parameters that Susana and Gordon had made clear to him. He told her what he knew of his past, the little that his aunt had revealed to him just before he went to Mexico City.

As he talked, Regina Lerner devoured him with her eyes; he could almost feel her gaze. It would've been disconcerting if he hadn't experienced something like this himself while living Jude's life.

After a while, Bern couldn't put off the question any longer.

"Mrs. Lerner," he said, "did you . . . do you have any idea who our biological parents were?"

She smiled, the same melancholy, understanding smile that his aunt had smiled when he visited her in Houston and asked the same question.

"Well, you should call me Regina," she said. "All right?" And then she hesitated a moment before she added, "Not for many years, I didn't know." She looked away and then down at her hands on the table. "Jude was just out of university," she said, lifting her eyes to Bern. "He knew he was adopted, but he never particularly showed any interest in his biological parents. I don't know why. So many people do. But he didn't. And he knew that we would've happily helped him find them if he had wanted. We'd always made that clear to him. But he never asked to pursue it."

She studied her hands again, smiled, and shook her head.

"And then one day—this is still so strange to me, even now—I answered the doorbell. A woman was standing there . . . and very abruptly she said that she was Jude's mother and that she would like to talk to me.

"It was a cold, drippy day, early December, and I had a fire going in the living room in there. She was chilled, and I made coffee. We sat in there and talked, a couple of hours, I guess it was. She never told me her name. I begged her . . . but she was resolute."

Regina sipped her iced tea, and it seemed to Bern that she wanted to get the words right. He glanced at Susana, who had her eyes fixed on the woman.

"She told me," Regina said, "that she had terminal cancer and that while she was still well enough to talk about it, she wanted me to understand Jude's beginnings. If I wanted to tell Jude about her and what she had to say, fine. If not, that was up to me. She just didn't want the truth of it all to die with her."

Regina sighed and began her story.

"She was from a small town in the South, wouldn't say exactly where. She said that when she was seventeen, she discovered that she was pregnant, and that the father was the son of a prominent judge in the county. The boy's family wanted her to have an abortion to prevent a scandal. But her parents—her father was a grocer—disagreed, saying they wanted the child and that they weren't ashamed of anything . . . except that the boy wasn't standing by their daughter.

"The judge then began to bring certain pressures to bear against the girl's family: Bank loans were suddenly called in; insurance policies were canceled for esoteric reasons. . . ." Regina shook her head. "A small town like that, uncommon deference to powerful men is not out of the ordinary. You can imagine. Anyway, the upshot of it was that the girl ran away, to spare her parents even more of the judge's wrath. Her parents were heartbroken, but she wouldn't reveal where she'd gone. The judge hired private detectives to try to find her."

Regina sighed again. "It was a sad and sorry story. During this time alone, running, the girl discovered that she was expecting twins.

"It seemed like too much for her to bear," Regina said, "working at menial jobs, unwed, pregnant, visiting charity Hospitals. When the boys were born—she wouldn't tell me where—she got on a bus and traveled to St. Jude's Charity Hospital in Memphis. She abandoned one boy there. Jude. That was the name they gave him there. We kept it. The other baby she took elsewhere. She didn't say where. I guess it was Atlanta, the old Lanier Memorial, as you said."

"Why in the world did she go to so much trouble to separate the babies?" Bern asked.

Regina nodded. "Well, the story of what was happening slipped out, as things like that have a way of doing, and the judge's family was shamed into changing their own story, putting a different spin on it. Now they claimed that the girl had kidnapped the children and that their son wanted desperately to have custody of what was rightfully his. The girl was obviously irresponsible. The judge hired private investigators to find her. When . . . your mother learned of this, she vowed that the judge would never have her children."

Regina looked at Bern. When she spoke, her voice was compassionate, softened by years of seeing the unfairness of life, the dangers of rushing to judgment. "You have to understand. She was young and not terribly sophisticated. She thought the judge could pull strings everywhere, not just in their small town. As she saw it, the only thing to do was to separate you. Twins would be so much easier for the judge's investigators to track down. So, different hospitals, different cities."

Bern was amazed, but he could imagine the rest of it.

"And St. Jude's' records were intact," he said. "That's how she was able to go back there and find you."

Regina nodded.

"And the old Lanier Memorial's records were fouled up somehow."

"That seems to be the way it happened." She nodded. "Yes."

"And then years later," Susana said, "when the CIA came to you for their standard interview when Jude applied, you told them about Jude having a twin."

"Yes, I did."

"Did you tell Jude about it, after our mother came here?" Bern asked.

"Yes, I did. I told him just what I've told you."

"Then he knew he had a twin."

She nodded.

"And how did he feel about that?"

"He was pretty sobered by it. As I said, the woman

wouldn't leave her name, gave no information about herself. She said it wouldn't do any good. She said that I was Jude's mother and that's the way it ought to stay."

"And then she . . . just left?"

"Yes, but first, sitting there in the living room before the fire, she opened her purse and took out a small envelope. Then she took out a little pair of scissors. She cut a lock of her hair and put it in the envelope, then sealed and put it next to her cup on the coffee table. 'For DNA,' she said. 'And maybe a memory.'

"A taxi came for her. I remember standing on the front porch and watching the smoke coming from the taxi's exhaust in the cold gray air as it disappeared down the street. For some reason"—she shrugged, tilting her head to one side with a sympathetic smile—"that struck me as a particularly lonely sight."

Bern stared into his glass. He was glad to know that much at least. Regina Lerner's story was both satisfying and dissatisfying, and he decided that that's the way it would have been regardless of what the story had been. That's the way the beginning of his life was, a conundrum woven of *whys* and *if onlys,* a sort of logic worked out in the frightened mind of a lonely young girl who was trying to be wise for her parents, and for herself, and for the two little boys she didn't want to grow up in the old judge's cruel world. You couldn't blame her for being young.

But he couldn't help but wonder if she really was terminally ill, or if that had just been a story to give them all a reason to put an end to it, to put it all to rest. Of course, if he was going to doubt that, he might as well go ahead and doubt all of it. How could he pick and choose his truths?

Regina reached out and placed her hand on his. She held it there a moment as they looked at each other, and then she removed it.

"Mr. Gordon," she said, "Richard Gordon, told me about some of what happened to Jude . . . and to you. And he told me that since Jude was nonofficial cover, or even something more . . . I don't know, more secret than that, we couldn't talk much about it."

"I guess not," Bern said.

"And you're an artist, too," she said.

"Yes."

"That's . . . amazing." She smiled, marveling, taking a moment to look at him again, as if his face revealed wondrous things to her. And Bern imagined that it did.

"Well, anyway," she went on, "I'm going to Mexico City next week. To clean out his apartment. Mr. Gordon said the embassy would have someone stay with me. I can ship it all back, he said. Everything."

She looked at Bern, and he said that was good. She glanced at Susana and then back at Bern.

"I'd like to do that alone," she said. "But when I have everything back here, would you like to come over? We'll divide his things. I . . . want you to have whatever you'd like to have."

"Yes," he said. "I'd like that very much."

She looked down at her own hands, which she was clutching together on the table now. "Mr. Gordon said that there's no body. I'm . . . I'm so sorry about that, but I know . . . I know how Jude loved what he did. And I've known all along that there would always be secrets, maybe even painful ones.

"But I'm going to have a memorial service. My husband is dead—Jude's father was a doctor, a very wise man, and a wise father—but I have close friends who knew Jude all through his years of growing up. I want to do that . . . for all of us."

Bern nodded.

"You'll come, won't you? Both of you?"

"Of course," Bern said, and he was surprised to see Susana reach out and put her hands on Regina's.

In the quiet that followed, Bern said nothing about the skull wrapped in velvet scraps and stored in the old ebony paint box that he had used in Paris. And yet something told him that if she had known about it, Regina Lerner would have forgiven him for his secret.

Chapter 60

The ingenuous ruse that Ghazi Baida had managed to design and execute—in which he, in the guise of Mazen Sabella, was able to micromanage his terrorist operation while hiding in plain sight—died with him. His death remained known to only a handful of men and women in the intelligence community.

In the final analysis, Susana and most intelligence analysts believed that Baida (Sabella) had never intended to defect. It was all a ruse to have the Americans witness "Baida's" death. Whoever the poor devil was who had been playing the role of Baida with a new face was being set up. The real Baida was going to kill him, or have him killed, in the apartment above the plaza Jardin Morena, with U.S. intelligence operatives acting as the official witnesses.

And then capricious fate stepped in. Baida learned from Bern that Vicente Mondragón was still alive and was in close pursuit, hell-bent on killing Baida for what he had done to him. So the real Baida fled in the rainstorm and let it happen. Mondragón did the job for him.

The fact that the real Ghazi Baida had died in the shallow waters of Lake Austin in Central Texas, six weeks after he was thought to have died in Mexico City, convinced U.S. intelligence that Baida had most likely had time to put together the final details of some kind of a terrorist operation somewhere inside the United States. His appearance at Bern's house seemed to suggest that his work was finished. His last visit to Jude Teller was the icing on the cake, a triumphant swagger before the man who thought he had outsmarted Ghazi Baida, a last victorious strut before the endgame, when Baida would kill Jude and bring it all to a close.

Again, it was the grim consensus of most analysts that the launching of the operation that Baida had put in place during the last six weeks was only awaiting the final signal from Baida himself. If his ego hadn't demanded one more face-to-face encounter with Jude Teller to prove to Jude that Baida had finally "won" after all, his operation would most likely have been executed within a few days.

Now nearly everyone agreed that the operation probably remained cocked, awaiting the final signal—one that only Baida would know—that would trigger the event. Therefore, the secrecy surrounding Baida's death was of paramount importance. If his death were known, someone, somewhere, sometime, would retool the operation and set it into motion again. The longer his death could be kept secret, the more time counterterrorist agencies had to try to uncover some thread of the operation.

As it stood, there was an uneasy peace. How long did sleeper agents sleep? How long would it take before the terrorists on the edges of the operation realized that Baida must surely have met his death somewhere, and then how long before they would begin trying to reconstruct Baida's design? And how long would it take them to locate the twelve sleeping mentors and their agents and reassemble an operation that had been so carefully scattered and compartmentalized? It was a design that did not anticipate the present circumstances, and it would be as difficult to rebuild from within as from without.

The U.S. intelligence community could only hope that the famous discipline of Baida's mentors would remain intact and, God willing, that they would sleep forever.

Paul Bern's life eventually returned to an altered version of what it had been before. He resumed his work as a forensic artist, and played a central role in identifying Mazen Sabella. Sabella's skull was x-rayed. The plastic surgeon in Zurich who had given Ghazi Baida a new face was finally located and an X ray of Baida's skull was obtained from him. The two X rays were overlaid and then were matched point for point by computer enhancement in order to confirm that the two men were the same.

But Paul Bern never again looked at a face in the same way that he had before the tragic events that began when a stranger walked into his studio with a box containing the skull of his twin brother. He compared himself to a blind man who had suddenly been given the gift of sight, but he knew deep within himself that what he had really gained was the gift of insight.

Bern had acquired a modern glimpse into an ancient belief; that a man's face is much more than its physical features. It is, rather, a physical representation of his personality, of his soul even. But modern man has easily deceived himself about the landscape of the face and has often trivialized its value, reducing it to the simple elements of attractive or unattractive.

There are some people, however, who look at a face and see the world of the inner man. Bern had seen evidence of this kind of insight in the acute intuitions of Alice Lau, whose own gifts were unknown to her. He had seen it in the clever perceptions of Ghazi Baida, and in the cruel grief of Vicente Mondragón, who revenged himself on the wrong man and died without a face, fulfilling his worst fear.

But most often now, Bern saw evidence of this when he looked into the mirror. He no longer saw merely his physical features there. He saw the complex and mysterious mind of his brother. He saw a self that he had never known before, a whole other man, someone capable of thoughts and deeds that until now had remained hidden from him.

And he saw the face of the assassin.

By good fortune, or God's grace, or the laws of physics, he and Ghazi Baida had hit the shallow water in the very same position in which they had left the edge of the deck. Baida hit the shallows first, with Bern on top of him, clinging to him in a viselike embrace triggered by an adrenaline-driven animal instinct for survival. Both men were stunned, but Baida bore the brunt of the weight and the shock.

Bern recovered his senses first, and he fought furiously to gain his footing in the shallows. He grabbed Baida by the throat and shoved him under the water. As Baida began to recover and found himself struggling for his life, he fought desperately. Suddenly he had a knife, and he slashed and jabbed viciously, finding his target again and again with wild and random stabs. But Bern let them come; his hands never left Baida's throat.

In the end, Paul Bern had completed the job that his identical twin, whom he had never known, had spent nearly three years planning. And Ghazi Baida died at the hands of a man whose face he knew but who was, in fact, a stranger.